DEEPER
THAN THE
OCEAN

THE DEEP SIX • Book 4

JULIE ANN WALKER

To Aryn, for having the courage to be your true self.
You are an inspiration to me.

*"Dream higher than the sky
and love deeper than the ocean.
~Unknown*

PROLOGUE

June 27th, 1624…

The end of the mangrove branch was as hard and as sharp as the devil's thumbnail when it tore into Captain Bartolome Vargas's cheek.

Searing pain was followed by the feel of hot blood sliding down his sweaty face. He leapt over a knobby-knuckled tree root. 'Twas no easy task given his legs burned with fatigue.

Not so long ago, he could have sprinted from the Bridge of Segovia to King Philip's Court without losing his breath. Now? He was lucky to skirt a fat sea grape bush without falling flat on his arse.

His lungs were afire when he raked in a gasping breath of hot subtropical air. Thirst and starvation wreak havoc on the body, he thought desperately. And if his own sorry state was not enough to convince him, all he need do was look to Rosario, his stalwart midshipman.

Rosario kept pace beside him, but a harsh wheeze issued from the depths of the young sailor's chest. The sunken, bruised flesh around Rosario's eyes spoke of restless nights made worse by the continuous grumblings of a hungry belly. And Rosario's lips were so dry and cracked, Bartolome's own mouth smarted in sympathy.

Of the 224 brave souls who had set sail aboard the Santa Cristina on her doomed voyage, only thirty-six had survived the storm and subsequent wreck. In the weeks that had followed the early season hurricane and the sinking of the galleon, three more of Bartolome's crew had succumbed to illness and the elements.

Now, if the French sailors from the small ketch that had dropped anchor beyond the reef, the ones who had rowed to shore and who were at that moment traipsing up the beach, happened upon them? Bartolome knew he would lose still more of his loyal men.

"What do we do, Capitán?" Rosario held a grubby hand to the stitch in his side as they darted and weaved through the sand and trees toward the slapdash camp set up in the center of the tiny island they now called home.

"We hide." Bartolome swiped at the hot, sticky blood dripping from his chin. "And if they find us…we fight."

Rosario's Adam's apple lurched in the wind-burned column of his throat. Doubt flashed in his black eyes.

Bartolome had counted fifteen sailors aboard the newly arrived French vessel. Which meant if it came to a battle, the crew of the Santa Cristina outnumbered the intruders more than two-to-one. Even so, it was obvious the midshipman held little faith they would come out the victors in any conflict with the newcomers.

Bartolome shared Rosario's fear. The rest of his crew were in no better shape than he or Rosario. What we gain in numbers, we give up in strength.

He considered commanding his men to surrender to the scurvy French bastards. To save themselves.

The wreck had already taken so many souls and that loss of life weighed heavy upon Bartolome's spirit. The thought of delivering more members of his courageous crew into the hands of the Reaper? 'Twas almost too much to bear.

And yet, if they turned themselves over, surely they would be keelhauled—or worse—until they gave up the location of the Santa Cristina's enormous bounty.

Bartolome and his men had not spent the last few weeks liberating the tons of gold and silver coins, the barrels of jewelry and uncut gemstones from the Santa Cristina's sunken carcass simply to have it land in the hands of the French king.

Louis XIII was el hijo de puta of high renowned. Doubtless the vile monarch would use the Santa Cristina's riches to further the conflict already brewing between France and Bartolome's homeland of Spain.

That could not happen. Not if Bartolome had breath left in his body.

His midshipman was the first to burst into the dirty clearing where the Santa Cristina's surviving crew gathered around a small campfire, smoking the small batch of fish they had pulled from the sea earlier that morning. By the time Bartolome wrestled past the last bush, most of his men were on their feet, looking at him in alarm.

"Francés," he gasped, flinging more blood from his face and sparing it but a glance as it landed on the sand in a shower of shining crimson. After two deep breaths, he added, "Grab your weapons."

To a man, the sailors scrambled to arm themselves with the rudimentary spears and clubs they had fashioned from downed limbs and the few pieces of sturdy driftwood harvested from the beach. A handful of them wielded the blades and daggers they had clung to during the perilous swim to shore after the big ship went down.

Bartolome had prepared his men for the day they would be discovered by their enemies. For the day they would have to battle for their lives and the safety of the spoils meant to fund the might and continued glory of Spain.

It seemed that day may have come.

He took comfort in knowing the treasure was secure in its new home. And he held out a small spark of hope the Frenchmen would leave the island without venturing too far inland. That spark was doused, however, when raised voices sounded through the trees.

As a child, he had found the French tongue beautiful— almost musical in tone and cadence. Now, it sounded to him as harsh and unforgiving as a clanging death knell.

'Tis time, he thought gravely. Time to dance with the darkness once again.

As King Philip's most decorated sea captain, he had seen his fair share of fighting and recognized the hot, oily anticipation of battle when it slicked through his veins.

Habit had him reaching for his trusty cutlass, but his fingers landed only on the cracked leather of his belt. He had lost his prized blade in the storm.

"Here, Capitán." A gunner by the name of Juan José handed Bartolome a bone-handled dagger. "May the good Madré Maria be with you, sir."

"May she be with each of us," Bartolome agreed with a firm dip of his chin.

He had barely spoken the last word when the group of Frenchmen stumbled into the clearing. Once the newcomers saw the haggard faces of the Santa Cristina's crew staring back at them, their expressions registered varying degrees of confusion and surprise. Then, understanding dawned in the eyes of the leader of the group. That understanding was quickly replaced by a prurient gleam.

"So here you are," the man said in badly accented

Spanish, rubbing a hand over his stubbled chin so his rough palm rasped against his whiskers. It reminded Bartolome of a snake in the grass, and he could not shake the feeling this newcomer might prove as deadly.

"Every ship that sails these waters has been looking for you since the storm. But fortune favors us, it would seem." The French leader cocked his head, a slow, greasy grin slipping over his tanned-leather face. "Tell us where to find the treasure."

Bartolome brandished the dagger in his hand, squinting when a ray of sunshine cut through the trees overhead, making the blade sparkle with menace. "We will die before we tell you," he growled through gritted teeth.

The newcomer's gaze alighted on each of Bartolome's crewmen. No doubt taking their pitiful measure.

For one long moment, no one moved. No one dared breathe. The tension vibrating through the air was thick enough to cut with a rapier.

Finally, the French leader shrugged. "So be it." Lifting his blunderbuss, he aimed at Juan José's chest and pulled the trigger.

The blast from the weapon was obscenely loud in the silence of the clearing. But it was nothing compared to the pain-soaked cry that peeled from the back of Juan José's throat when the young sailor was flung backward by the force of the large bore shot. He hit the sandy ground, his hands scrabbling ineffectually at the bloody, bony mess that had once been his sternum.

For a few heartbeats, Juan Jose's brain refused to believe his body was already dead. But then reality set in, and the young gunner breathed his last. As his spirit left his body, his bladder emptied itself.

The smell of rancid urine perfumed the air, making Bartolome's nostrils flare.

Death is such an indignity, he thought as rage rolled through him. His voice was a crack of thunder when he bellowed, "Attack!"

Bless his crew, they did not hesitate. Hurling themselves toward the newcomers, they fought with what little strength remained in their enfeebled bodies.

Battle cries, the boom of weapons, and the clash of steel echoed through the trees. But Bartolome heard none of it. He was deaf to all but one man. The bastardo who had so callously killed Juan José.

Bartolome's deadly intent must have registered on his face. When he charged the newcomer, he was met with a sneer and the zinging of a cutlass pulling free from its scabbard. He did not do as his instincts prompted and viciously attack the man in a bid to slice him bloody.

A dagger had no hope of defeating a cutlass in hand-to-hand combat. But what the small blade lacked in reach, it more than made up for in maneuverability. When he was but a few paces from his target, Bartolome flung the knife with all his might.

The force of his throw caused two buttons on his tattered vest to pop off and fall into the sand. And the dagger spiraled through the dense air, silver and ivory mixing together in a pinwheel of color.

The flight was silent.

The end of the flight was not.

The blade buried itself in the Frenchman's chest with a solid thunk.

When the intruder saw the dagger had planted itself deep, his eyes flew wide. Bartolome could see the delicate web of veins cutting through the whites. The Frenchman wrapped a hand around the bone handle, but that was the last move he made before his eyes rolled back and he toppled sideways. Dark blood oozed from the corner of his open mouth to pool in the sand beneath his head.

Bartolome might have taken a moment to bask in the precision of his throw, but a familiar voice cut through the cacophony of battle with a desperate cry for help. A quick glance to his left showed Rosario wrestled with a man twice his size.

Without hesitation, Bartolome pulled the dagger from the lifeless body of the Frenchman. Letting loose with a banshee cry, he launched himself onto the back of the puto cabrón pinning Rosario to the ground...

CHAPTER 1

Present Day
4:45 PM...

Even *a small mouse has anger.*

Ray "Wolf" Roanhorse's grandmother had used the saying to teach him that rancor was never a bad thing, but rather an emotion that everything from the tallest man to the tiniest rodent felt. It was how one *dealt* with it that mattered.

Wolf stood still as a stone outside the weathered beach house on Wayfarer Island, dealing by keeping his damned mouth shut.

What was the cause of his foul temper you ask?

It was twofold.

First, after months of fruitless searching, he and his salvage partners had *finally* located the sunken remains of the legendary *Santa Cristina, Praise the Lord and pass the ammunition*. They'd pulled up a few religious artifacts— some ceremonial cups and crosses and rosaries. They'd stumbled upon a handful of weapons—a sword, two daggers, and one coral-encrusted musket. But the mother lode? The millions of dollars in coins and gold bars? The silver ingots and uncut emeralds clearly reported on the ghost galleon's manifest?

Nothing. Nada. Zippo. Zilch.

Which meant it was looking highly unlikely they'd recoup their life savings—which they'd invested in starting their Deep Six Salvage business—much less strike it rich.

Should've stayed in the Navy, he mused bitterly.

Then again, he and his former SEAL team members had all been getting long in the tooth. And every spec ops guy worth his salt knew what that meant.

Doesn't matter how good we were—and they'd been better than most—*if we'd kept spinnin' that chamber, all of us would've eventually checked into the Horizontal Hilton.*

In fact, it was already too late for one of them.

Rusty Lawrence had been a tough, stubborn sonofabitch. His body had been riddled with bullets the day they dragged him out of a dusty compound in Aleppo after an op that'd gone tits up. But he hadn't succumbed to the horror of his wounds before making all of them promise to wave goodbye to the lives of Frogmen.

Rusty had known he would be the first to go, and the bastard had done the one thing he could to make certain he was the last.

Which meant when their contracts expired, none of the remaining seven members of The Great Eight had re-upped. Instead, Michael "Mad Dog" Wainwright had returned to his hometown of Atlantic City to make babies with a saucy redhead. And the other six SEALs from their unit had traded sorties for scuba tanks, firefights for swim fins, and joined their lieutenant, a man by the name of Leo "the Lion" Anderson, in the search for the storied *Santa Cristina*—a prize treasure hunters had been after for centuries.

Wolf and his SEAL brothers all had big plans for the cabbage they hoped to pick up from the salvage.

Leo, or LT as they called him in a nod to his rank, wanted to buy Wayfarer Island, the small spit of land rising out of the Caribbean that his family had leased from the U.S. government way back when Ulysses S. Grant sat pretty at 1600 Pennsylvania Avenue. The same lump of sand and mangrove forest they all called home.

Then there was Spiro "Romeo" Delgado, who leaned against the palm tree next to Wolf. Romeo planned to use his slice of the pie to start a charity in L.A. for kids like himself. Kids who had grown up on streets so mean that a run-in with drug addiction, gun violence, and rival gangs just meant it was a Tuesday.

Mason "Monet" McCarthy hoped to buy a row house in Beantown and season tickets to the Red Sox. Brando "Bran" Pallidino made noises about opening an Italian restaurant in his fiancée's hometown of Houston. And Dalton "Doc" Simmons had his eye on a ranch back in Montana.

Then there was Wolf himself. His aims, though not so grandiose as buying an island or funding a charity, were of no less personal significance.

You see, he had himself a trio of sisters, and each of them had worse taste in men than the one before.

Wolf had read a quote somewhere once. *"I view each and every one of your glaring red flags as a personal challenge,"* and he reckoned that summed up how his sisters went about choosing partners. Which wouldn't have been a bad thing, except Rebecca, Roxanne, and Robbin were also fertile as turtles.

Between the three of them, they'd gifted Wolf with ten nieces and nephews. A whole brood of Roanhorses, and not a single baby-daddy offering up child support among them.

Which meant the cheddar needed for braces, baseball cleats, and college funds was nearly impossible to come by.

Wolf had *hoped* to be the one to make it rain. Had hoped to provide his sisters' little crotch goblins with all the creature comforts he had done without while growing up on a scrubby piece of property outside Tahlequah, Oklahoma. But with every passing day, that hope dimmed. In fact, at this point it was little more than a glimmer.

Thinking of the women in his life who confounded him brought his thoughts around to the *second* thing giving him fits.

Her name was Christina Szarek. Chrissy for short. And she was as long limbed and blond as her Polish surname implied.

He'd had a thing for blondes ever since he was five years old and found himself in Miss Featherstone's kindergarten class. Miss Featherstone had reminded him of a sunflower, sweet and radiant. Then there'd been Dana Teague in the sixth grade, a bubbly soccer player with a pleasant smile and long, thick braids. She'd been followed by Keely Potter in high school. Keely had turned out to be a bottle-blonde—a fact Wolf learned only after she let him get to third base under the bleachers at the football stadium. But none of those flaxen-haired sirens had ever made him *want* quite like Chrissy did.

Want *what*, though?

That was the million-dollar question.

Want her kisses? Certainly. *I mean, have you seen her mouth?* Want her long, curvy body stretched out beside him in bed? Undoubtedly. *I mean, have you seen those legs?* Want her cool, slim fingers running over his skin until he shivered and moaned and begged her to let him take her? You betcha. *I mean, have you seen those hands?*

Still, there was something more he wanted from her. Something nebulous and shadowy he couldn't quite put a name to.

All he could say for sure was she was a pressure in his chest. A void in his stomach. *And a pain in my ass, because she breaks out the Heisman move every time I get close,* he thought as he let his eyes travel over to her.

Chrissy stood in the sand at the base of the beach house's front porch steps, her hands shoved deep in the pockets of her cutoff shorts as she listened to the gathered group discuss the *Santa Cristina's* missing mother lode. From the top of her messy ponytail to the tips of her unpainted toenails, everything about her screamed islander.

Thanks to hours spent on the water, her skin was tanned a light cognac. Her blue eyes glittered in the rays of hard subtropical sun slanting down through the fronds of the palm tree overhead. And she'd paired her red bikini with a tank top that read: *Key West... Nearly perfect. Far from normal.* A simple silver bracelet with abalone charms in the shapes of sea life was her only jewelry.

The charms tinkled quietly when she lifted a hand to tuck a stray lock of hair behind her ear. For the billionth time, he noted the simple grace and purity of her movements. They reminded him of the weeping willow that grew next to the cattle pond on his family's land, how it would sway when the wind preceding a summer shower swept over the plains.

Sensing his scrutiny, she darted a look his way. The instant their eyes clashed, heat stole across his skin. The devil in him had him winking at her, but he wasn't sure she saw. She'd quickly returned her attention to the group.

Oh, she saw, he thought a moment later when a wash of pink that had nothing to do with the cloudless morning they'd spent diving down on the wreck stained her cheeks.

She tried to act as if she was immune to his charms, as if keeping him in the Friend Zone didn't cost her a moment's work. But he'd spent the better part of his thirty-four years studying women, and he recognized the subtle signs they gave when they were attracted to him.

Chrissy? She wasn't a subtle sign. She was blinking neon.

So why the hell weren't they upstairs in his bedroom knocking boots...er...flip-flops, as the case may be?

Simply put, because he'd screwed the pooch. Royally. And it didn't matter she'd since forgiven him for The Night That Shall Not Be Named, or that it'd been an honest mistake to begin with, she still—

"Damn, man." Romeo pushed away from his languid lean against the palm tree to clap a hand on Wolf's shoulder. Hitching his chin toward Chrissy, the flyboy added, "You went and caught *all* the feels. Admit it."

Wolf hated being obvious.

Then again, he'd read somewhere that, *"Honesty and transparency make you vulnerable. Be honest and transparent anyway."*

So, fine. He was being obvious. *At least I ain't the only one.*

"I'll admit I caught feels for Chrissy," he muttered from the corner of his mouth, "when *you* admit you're catchin' feels for Mia."

He shot a finger gun toward the woman gesturing excitedly and saying, "I know you're all disappointed not to have found the *Santa Cristina's* cargo. But stop for a moment to appreciate what you *have* found. This site is a time capsule. We're getting a firsthand look at what life was like 400 years ago aboard a sizable sea-faring vessel."

According to state and federal law, when a salvage crew stumbled upon a wreck, they were required to bring in a marine archeologist to catalog the site and oversee the excavation.

Enter Mia Ennis. A strawberry blonde with a penchant for avocados and expensive skincare products.

Two hours after they'd hauled up the first of the *Santa Cristina's* bronze deck cannons, they'd contacted the state of Florida to report their find. Thirty-six hours later, Mia had landed on their doorstep with bags in hand. In the nearly four weeks since, she'd not only become part of their crew, she'd become part of their family.

Wolf supposed that was inevitable given they were military men, honor-bound to protect those softer than themselves. And Mia Ennis? She was the gentlest, most soft-spoken woman he'd ever met. Not to mention…there was a broken quality about her.

He wasn't sure what tragedies marred her past, or if her quiet disposition was simply a part of her nature. He just knew the only time she raised her voice much above a whisper was when she talked about the excavation site. And the only time her eyes lit with an inner fire was when she was inspecting the artifacts they hauled up from the sea bed.

Or when she looked at Romeo.

There was no mistaking the way her cheeks heated and her pupils dilated whenever the sailor-cum-pilot-cum-salvor entered the room.

Speaking of the sailor-cum-pilot-cum-salvor…

"Maybe I *am* catching feels for the marvelous Mia Ennis," Romeo admitted with a laconic half-smile. "You think she'd be interested in a former fighting man like me?"

Wolf considered the marine archeologist for a few seconds more before whispering to Romeo, "Actually, I think she probably only dates men with IQs in the double digits."

Navy SEALs never passed up an opportunity to feed

each other heaping helpings of shit. And it didn't matter that neither he nor Romeo wore the gold Trident pin of the brotherhood anymore. Once a SEAL, always a SEAL.

"Guess that counts us both out then, eh?" Romeo winked, not one to be outdone. "It's just as well," he added with a dramatic sigh. "She's too good for me anyway."

"You'll hear no argument from me on that score," Wolf agreed gamely.

"Would y'all shut the fuck up?"

LT Anderson was no longer their superior, yet they snapped to attention at the sound of his snarl. Old habits were hard to break. Old training? That was even harder.

"He started it." Wolf hooked a thumb in Romeo's direction.

Romeo gasped in mock outrage. "You know what, Wolf? Today we're making *Fuck You* pie. You take a cup of *piss off*, add a dash of *get bent*, and throw in some *go take a flying leap*. You'll want to give that a good stir, then take a big ol' spoonful and shove it straight up your ass."

Wolf pulled in his lips, but couldn't stop the laughter that bubbled inside his chest. That ridiculous recipe was enough to dull the edges of his bad mood. He thanked Romeo by offering him a pseudo salute.

Romeo, clearly tickled by his own sophomoric wit, smiled so wide his black goatee became little more than a frame around a mouthful of white teeth.

"I'll never understand how you guys spent years running missions and maintaining covers when you have the emotional maturity of fourteen-year-olds," LT's wife, Olivia, said with a roll of her eyes.

"It's a talent to be sure," Romeo conceded at the same time LT complained, "Hey! You're not lumpin' *me* in with these jackasses, are ya?"

"Never." Olivia pulled off LT's aviator sunglasses and

planted a loud, smacking kiss on his lips. When she leaned back, there was so much love in her eyes, Wolf's own heart ached something fierce.

Will a woman ever look at me the way Olivia looks at LT?

Of their own accord, his eyes tracked back to Chrissy.

He knew the instant she felt his gaze. The skin over her jaw tightened. Instead of looking back at him, however, she made a face of disgust at the newlyweds. "Ugh. Get a room you two."

"We have one." Olivia grinned. "It's right upstairs."

Chrissy pretended to pout. "Are you *trying* to make me jealous? I haven't had a date in…" She shook her head. "I can't remember when."

"Weren't you supposed to go on a date with this one?" Olivia hooked a thumb Wolf's way.

"Yeah. But it didn't work out."

"That much we all know." Olivia narrowed her eyes. "What we *don't* know is why?"

"Wasn't meant to be, I guess." Chrissy shrugged, unwilling to expand on the subject.

Wolf supposed he should thank her for that. And maybe he *would* thank her if she'd ever let him talk about it. But every time he brought it up, she lifted a hand and said, *"No. It's water under the bridge."*

"Curiouser and curiouser." LT tapped his chin.

"Not really." Chrissy crossed her arms a little defensively, which made her cleavage deepen. Wolf guessed if he dragged his tongue up that valley, it would be as soft as satin and taste like sunscreen.

The thought had his blood rising so quickly, he had to adjust his stance.

Romeo noticed and snorted loudly. Then he leaned in close to whisper in Wolf's ear, "Bruh, I bet your palms are as chafed as a teenage boy who's been left home alone with unlimited access to the internet, huh?"

Wolf held back from punching Romeo in the bean bags. "You're a dickhead, Romeo."

Romeo countered with, "Profanity is the product of a lazy mind."

"You stole that from Spencer W. Kimball. And what he said was, 'Profanity is the effort of a feeble brain to express itself forcibly.' If you're goin' to quote someone, at least get it right."

"I'd tell you to go fuck yourself, but I get the feeling you'd be disappointed."

Wolf burst out laughing, but his humor was short-lived when Chrissy glared at them. "Do you two come with mute buttons?" She had one of those faces that always held a hint of mischief. Right now, however, she only looked exasperated. "We're trying to talk business here."

If Mia Ennis was shy and reserved, then Christina Szarek was her polar opposite. Despite her unwillingness to discuss That Night, she was about as plainspoken as a person could get. Combine that with a rapier wit and a penchant for razor-sharp remarks, and Wolf thought perhaps he'd finally met his match.

Too bad she doesn't feel the same.

Although, on second thought, it was probably more accurate to say too bad she doesn't feel the same *anymore*. Because once upon a time, they'd *both* been impatient to see where their shared chemistry would lead them.

Or…at least he'd *thought* they'd both been impatient. Then he'd seen her draped all over some guy at Schooner Wharf Bar in Key West, and that little green-eyed monster had sunk his teeth into him.

Wolf should've taken the blond dude's presence like a man. After all, he and Chrissy had made no vows of exclusivity—hell, they hadn't even gone on that first date. He should've gone over and introduced himself to the Chris Hemsworth-looking bastard instead of ignoring Chrissy's wave and turning his attention to the busty redhead who'd sidled up beside him, thinking to himself *two can play this game*.

If that had been the extent of his blunder, Chrissy probably would've forgiven him and they might have found themselves competing in a two-person bedroom rodeo even now. Just like the busty redhead, the flaxen-haired Adonis hadn't made another appearance after that fateful night. Which meant Mr. Tall, Blond, and Handsome had been no one important and certainly not worth Wolf's jealousy. Unfortunately, that had *not* been the extent of Wolf's error in judgment.

Oh, no. He'd gone and made things a hundred times worse in that dark storage closet.

For weeks after That Night, Chrissy had treated him like a cow patty, avoiding him like he'd ruin her shoes if she got too close. Then, a hair-raising encounter with a group of Iranians had precipitated her forgiving him.

Near-death experiences tended to put things in perspective, and Chrissy hadn't been immune. She'd agreed to wipe their slate clean.

Sadly, her definition of a "clean slate" and his were two different things. He'd thought it would be a return to all the flirting and teasing touches from before. But *she* had insisted all she wanted from him was friendship.

Friendship...

Never in his life had that word sounded more wretched than the day it come out of her pretty mouth.

"It's still possible the cargo might be found among the ballast." Mia returned them to the subject. "We have a lot of rubble left to pick through."

Seventeenth century galleons carried huge loads of stones stored deep in their hulls to keep their centers of gravity low in the water. The *Santa Cristina's* ballast pile was twenty feet wide, one-hundred feet long, and stood almost as tall as Wolf.

"You know good and well the treasure won't be found there," LT muttered and Mia blushed at the perceived rebuke. Seeing her stained cheeks, LT was quick to add, "I appreciate you tryin' to sprinkle sugar on this bowl of shit and call it candy, but there's no denyin' we're screwed six ways from Sunday. The *Santa Cristina's* mother lode is missin'."

For a long moment, silence reigned. They'd all begun to suspect what LT said was true, but that was the first time the words had been spoken aloud. The syllables hung in the air like a dank, foul-smelling fog.

"Let's think this through for a minute." Alexandra Merriweather was the diminutive historian and ancient language aficionado they'd hired to help them read the old documents relating to the wreck. "We assumed Captain Bartolome Vargas skuttled the ship where he did to make free-diving salvage possible. And we assumed the entire crew was lost in the storm since there's no mention in the records that any of the *Santa Cristina's* sailors were found or rescued. But what if there *were* survivors? Would they have salvaged the wreck themselves?"

LT shot her a thoughtful look. "It's possible. But then what? They haul up the treasure and do what with it?"

"Bury it." Alex adjusted her tortoiseshell glasses higher on the bridge of her zinc oxide-covered nose. "The old texts talk about how the seas were swarming with pirates and privateers hell-bent on claiming the *Santa Cristina's* riches for themselves. Any of the ship's survivors would've known this. Since they were loyal to their king and country, and since they would've been unwilling to see the bounty fall into enemy hands, no doubt they'd have done everything they could to ensure it stayed hidden."

"And then what?" LT asked. "They lived out the rest of their lives on the island?"

"Who knows?" Alex shrugged. "Maybe they died of disease. Maybe once the treasure was secure, they made a suicide pact and ran into the sea. Anything is possible."

"So what's that mean for us? We stop diving down on the *Santa Cristina* and start combing the island with metal detectors? That could take days." This from Doc. He sat on the porch steps and, as usual, his face was hard and craggy, cut by the cold Montana wind. But it was his eyes that held Wolf's attention. They looked weary. Bone-tired, actually.

Come to think of it, *all* of the Deep Six Salvage crew looked exhausted.

Treasure hunting sounded like a grand adventure in theory. In reality it was hard, backbreaking work done under the relentless Caribbean sun.

"Buck up, Sad Sack," Bran Pallidino winked at Doc. "You're sounding like a glass half empty kind of guy."

"Right now, I'm a glass *fully* empty kind of guy," Doc admitted. "And the only reason you're wearing that shit-eating grin is because you're marrying into one of the richest families east of the Continental Divide. You don't need this score like the rest of us do."

"That's not fair." Bran frowned. "Just because Maddy's family's got money doesn't mean I—"

"Gentlemen," LT cut in with his languid Louisiana drawl. "This is no time to turn on each other. If Alex is right, we'll need to work together to get this entire island searched."

"At least if we're stuck on land, we won't be burning fuel on Wayfarer II." Doc referred to their salvage vessel.

It guzzled MDO quicker than the tourists on Key West could down boat drinks.

"Look at you," Bran winked at Doc. "Suddenly silver-lining this situation."

Doc acted like the itch beside his nose could only be scratched with his middle finger.

"Is that an invitation?" Bran wiggled his eyebrows.

"You wish," Doc snorted. "Just count your blessings and keep on stepping."

The men of Deep Six Salvage were brothers in every way except blood. Which meant they were quick to take swipes at each other, but just as quick to forgive those swipes.

"So…" LT ran a hand through his hair. "We need metal detectors. More than the three underwater ones we keep on Wayfarer II. Who's up for a trip to Key West?"

"I'll go!" The words were out of Wolf's mouth quicker than a bull at a gate. In an instant, his brain had managed to run through the following facts.

One: Chrissy lived and worked on Key West—she was a dive shop owner.

Two: She'd made a deal with Deep Six Salvage to bring clients out to the wreck site. This agreement benefitted Chrissy, seeing as how folks were willing to pay top dollar for a chance to dive down on a bona fide seventeenth century Spanish galleon. It benefitted the Deep Six crew since they got more eyeballs helping them hunt for their treasure.

Three: This arrangement meant Chrissy and Wolf never got a chance to be alone. During the day she was busy directing her diving clients, and in the evenings she flew back home.

Four: Maybe if he went to Key West tonight, she'd agree to have dinner with him.

Five: Dinner might turn into drinks. Drinks might turn into a long walk along the beach. A long walk along the beach might end in a kiss.

Six: Umm…he didn't dare hope for a number six. He didn't want to jinx himself.

"Me too." Romeo lifted a finger. "We'll take the Otter." With a hitch of his chin, he indicated the single-engine, propeller-driven amphibious aircraft that rested on the beach, its two pontoons firmly parked atop the golden sand.

"Can I go?" Mia asked. When the group turned to her en masse, her next words were barely above a whisper. "I need to file some paperwork with the state. And I'd like to see if I can find someone to cut my hair." She held up a wavy lock and grimaced. "I'm starting to look homeless."

"You couldn't look homeless if you tried, honey pie," Doc drawled.

His words made Mia blush. Which made Romeo grind his teeth.

Yeah, Wolf thought. *Dude's got it bad.*

"Done and done." LT clapped his hands together. It was his standard signal that a plan was set.

Meat, the fat English bulldog who was their mascot and self-proclaimed garbage disposal, had been sprawled on his back at the top of the steps, napping with his twig and berries out to catch the passing breeze. But LT's sudden gesture had him springing to his feet with a confused bark.

Li'l Bastard—a Welsummer rooster who took it as his personal duty to whittle down the island's bug population— had been contentedly roosting next to Meat. Now he flapped his wings and answered Meat's bark with a loud *cock-a-doodle-do!*

Everyone living on the island was so used to the exchange, they ignored the animals.

"You three go have some fun on Key West tonight," LT continued. "And tomorrow come back here armed with as many metal detectors as you can scrounge up."

As the group broke apart, Chrissy turned toward the half-moon-shaped strip of sand that partially encircled the island's lagoon. The eight divers she'd brought with her for the day were near the water's edge, drinking wine and snacking on fruit salad, cured meats, and expensive cheeses.

Chrissy made sure to treat her clients right. No one could ever accuse her of being a lackadaisical businesswoman.

It took Wolf a bit to catch up with her since her legs were a country mile long. When he did, she glanced at him curiously. Up close, he could see the different striations of blue in her irises, from cobalt to cornflower, and he felt a sudden breathlessness.

He tried blaming it on the heat of the sand beneath his bare feet. But he knew the real reason O_2 had trouble reaching his brain.

It was her.

It happened every damn time he came within two feet of her.

Swallowing past the constriction in his throat, he managed, "Have dinner with me tonight."

He'd meant for it to be a question. But the part of him that was hungry for her didn't want to leave any room for rejection.

CHAPTER 2

5:01 PM...

Chrissy Szarek was no dummy.

Thanks to her mother's example—*rest her soul*—Chrissy recognized the galaxy of warning signs that flashed around Ray "Wolf" Roanhorse.

Not that she hadn't initially been fooled by him. Wolf quoted religious leaders, famous folks, and philosophers as easily as most people breathed. He practiced Tai-Chi in the mornings. And he liked to walk along the beach collecting seashells.

Seashells for Pete's sake, like a granny from up North who'd come down on vacation.

Given all that, who could blame her for thinking that, despite his flashing black eyes, razor-sharp cheekbones, and carpenter's square of a jaw, Wolf might actually be woke. As in, more than a pretty face. As in, so much deeper and more complex than those broad shoulders and six-pack abs implied.

Joke's on me, she thought, looking at him now and trying not to let his nearness steal her breath away. That night at Schooner Wharf Bar had proved Wolf was no better than her mother's four husbands and copious boyfriends. A man who was nice to look at, nicer to kiss, and probably even *nicer* to bounce around on for a few weeks. But not a candidate for anything else. Anything *permanent*.

And thanks to her recent thirtieth birthday, she was officially on the hunt for something permanent. Gone were the days of fun-for-now-but-not-forever. It was time to get serious about her ultimate goal.

As an only child, she'd spent her youth dreaming of a big, boisterous family that would fight and love and play cards around the kitchen table after Thanksgiving dinner. As a grown woman, that image remained.

Trouble was, she'd been having a hell of a time finding a man who would make that dream a reality.

There were the dating sites, of course. Some folks thought Tinder was like Amazon. You go online and pick what you want. But in her experience, it was less like Amazon and more like eBay. Meaning she'd sorted through her fair share of other peoples' leftover junk and—

"Didn't reckon the thought of havin' dinner with me would require you to do so much ponderin'," Wolf said in that Oklahoma accent that split the difference between a Southern drawl and a Texas twang. He crossed tattooed arms that were roped with muscle and frowned so hard it made the scar at his temple pull tight and pucker.

The combination made him look incredibly forbidding. Which, for some reason, made her want him all the more.

Seriously, the urge to tackle him onto the sand and forcibly sit on his face was damn near overwhelming.

Tick tock! her eggs screamed up at her.

I hear you! she silently yelled back. *But he's not the one!*

"Sorry." She made a face. "My mind wandered." She didn't add that it had wandered to images of her squeezing his ears between her thighs. "Ummm, dinner? No can do. I have plans."

Something flickered across his face. "Hot date?"

"I wish." She twisted her lips. "But no. Winston and I have a standing Friday night business dinner to tally up the week's receipts, go over inventory, and figure out what equipment needs to be serviced or replaced."

Winston Turner was a childhood friend who'd grown up to become her high school boyfriend. They'd ended their youthful romance, however, when Winston moved to the mainland to get his degree. He'd returned to Key West after graduation, but by that time, they'd decided they were far better as friends and business partners than life partners, and so he'd joined her in opening the dive shop.

"How about meeting me for a drink after?" Wolf's expression was casual. Yet there was something in his voice that sounded hard-edged.

"What is this?" She cocked her head. "I thought we agreed to be friends?"

"Friends can't share a drink on a Friday night?"

"Sure. But this feels suspiciously date-ish."

"Woman, if I was askin' you out, I'd do it right. I'd get reservations at a nice restaurant with an amazin' water view and come pick you up with flowers in hand."

"Boy oh boy. Aren't you the traditionalist? And would you pull out my chair? Pour my wine? Try to seduce me with your best line?" She fluttered her lashes theatrically.

"I'm thinkin' the best lines are less about seduction and more about statin' your offer straight out."

"Really?" She was intrigued despite herself. "So come on." She wiggled her fingers in a come-hither motion. "Lay it on me."

"You sure you can handle it?"

She rolled her eyes. "I think I've proved I'm immune to your masculine wiles."

Liar! her eggs shouted. The little buggers were becoming more annoying by the day.

"If you say so." He shrugged. Then he...*smoldered* at her. That was the only word for it. "This face leaves in ten minutes." He pointed to his intriguing aquiline nose. "I'd like for you to be on it."

Where is that wheezing sound coming from?

Oh, right. From the depths of her chest because... Hot damn!

When she realized her mouth had slung open, she snapped it shut. "That's good." She ignored the blood that had left her brain to race to parts decidedly south. "But it's not the best I've heard."

"Oh yeah?" One slashing black eyebrow slanted up his forehead. "You think you can do better."

"I know I can." She tossed her ponytail over her shoulder and leered at him. "You have a kind face, sir. The kind I'd like to sit on."

His startled expression was better than she could have hoped for.

Licking a finger, she made an invisible hash mark in the air. "Score one for Chrissy."

Was it her imagination or was his voice raspy when he said, "Do you *ever* let anyone get one over on you?"

She looked at him as if a colony of oysters had grown from his ears. "It that a real question?"

"I thought there was a pretty obvious question mark on the end."

"Why in the world would I let someone get one over on me?" She loved their banter. Too bad that was all they could share. "Where would be the fun in that?"

"Oh…" He shrugged and she was momentarily mesmerized by the way his shoulder muscles bunched. She remembered how unforgiving they felt beneath the tight grip of her fingers. "I don't know. Sometimes it's nice to let your opponent take the lead. There's so much satisfaction in stealin' it back from them."

"Is that what we are, Wolf? Opponents?"

"Never," he swore. "You and me? We're Lance Bass and Justin Timberlake." When she tilted her head in confusion, he finished with, "In sync."

She made a gagging noise. "I think I like you better when you're walking around sounding like a fortune cookie." When he opened his mouth, she lifted a finger. "But *don't* take that as an invitation to start throwing quotes my way again."

He faked a pout. "First you tell me I can't quote folks, and now you're sayin' you don't like my cheesy metaphors either? What's left to me, woman? Dad jokes?"

"Don't you technically have to be a *dad* to tell dad jokes?"

"Not accordin' to my nieces and nephews."

The thought of him surrounded by a bunch of kids all clamoring for his attention made her heart ache so much she couldn't think of a good comeback.

He took pity on her and filled the silence. "So? What do you say?"

"About dad jokes?"

"Drinks."

"Oh…" She tried to think of a good excuse, but her mind kept seizing on the truth. Which was that she was scared to have drinks with him. Once she got some rum in her blood, she might not be able to resist the urge to strip him naked and pounce on him. And if she stripped him naked and pounced on him, she'd undoubtedly lose a bit of her heart to him.

Because as much as she hated to admit it, she'd inherited more than her mother's wide smile. Josephine had also passed down a penchant for forming emotional attachments to the exact *wrong* sort of man.

Chrissy realized she'd been quiet for too long when he tilted his head and regarded her thoughtfully. "It isn't a marriage proposal, Chrissy."

"Ha!" She shouted too loudly. To cover up her gaffe, she chucked him on the arm. "Okay, buddy. Sure. How about we meet at Schooner Wharf Bar at nine o'clock?"

"You mean the scene of the crime?" Both of his sleek, dark eyebrows reached for the sky.

"Aha!" She pointed to his nose. "So you admit your behavior was criminal."

His mouth flattened. "It was a figure of speech. And anyway, you said I'm off the hook."

"You are," she assured him. "But even if you weren't, I'd choose Schooner. The Salty Cod Band is playing tonight."

"They're the ones who turn hip-hop into lounge tunes?"

"Yes. And it's hilarious." She lifted her hand to shield her eyes against the sun at the sound of an approaching aircraft. "My ride's nearly here." She hitched her chin toward the seaplane that seemed suspended like a marionette against the blue of the sky. "Better go help my clients get packed up."

She was half a dozen steps down the beach when he called, "Chrissy?"

She hoped she was far enough away that he didn't notice how his deep, resonant voice caused goose bumps to erupt over the back of her neck.

"Yeah?" she asked over her shoulder.

"I'm lookin' forward to tonight. I hope you are too." His smile was soft and lazy.

Now the chills weren't only across her neck. They'd migrated to her arms, legs, and belly. The latter of which flopped around like a fish on dry land.

"I always enjoy a night filled with good music and good drinks," she told him airily. Or at least she *hoped* she sounded airy.

His response was a wink and a two-finger salute before he turned and ambled toward the beach house.

She noted the bulge of his calf muscles and the economical way he moved along the sand all while thinking, *Oh, god. Why do I feel like I'm about to step off the edge of the Marianas Trench with a fifty-pound rock tied to each foot?*

CHAPTER 3

8:38 PM...

I'm having an existential crisis."

Chrissy looked at Winston seated on the barstool next to her and smirked. "Well, that's self-indulgent of you."

His mouth thinned into a straight line. "I'm *serious*, Chrissy. I'm thirty-one years old and I have no romantic prospects on the horizon."

She let her gaze take a circuit around Pepe's Cafe. The rickety-legged tables were filled with sunburned tourists. Most of the folks lounged around the bar were locals. "Don't tell me your biological clock is ticking too."

Winston frowned around his cocktail straw as he sipped morosely at his Rum Runner. "I don't think it's so much my biological clock as it is my lonely heart. Don't you want to fall in love?"

"Now you sound like my mother," she said distastefully.

Winston sighed. "I miss Josephine every day."

A steel spear of pain stabbed into Chrissy's heart. For all of her mother's terrible taste in men and even worse taste in drinks—*Who puts ice in their rosé, I ask you?*—Josephine had been a good mom. Quick to laugh. Quick to play. Quick to kiss a hurt away.

"I miss her too," Chrissy admitted freely before adding, "And to answer your question, *no*. I don't want to fall in love. Saying you want to fall in love is basically announcing to the universe there's something missing inside you. A hole only another person can fill. You remember how Mom was constantly hunting for 'the one'?" Chrissy made air-quotes. "Then when she couldn't find him, she settled for bastards unworthy of her big, squishy heart?"

"Nuh-uh." She shook her head. "I swore from a young age I wouldn't fall in love. That I wouldn't *need* to fall in love. That instead I'd focus my energy on the world around me. Appreciate each sunrise. Be thankful for a cold beer at the end of the day. Enjoy the genuine smile of a stranger. And when it came time to choose a partner, I'd do it with my head, not my heart. *That's* the mother effin' key to true happiness. Not *falling in love*."

Winston narrowed his eyes. "You really believe that?"

She squared her chin. "Did I stutter?"

"Oh, no. Your monologue was clear, and peppered with just the right amount of pseudo-obscenities to make you sound certain."

"*But?*" she prompted, sure she'd heard that unspoken word tacked onto the end of his sentence.

"But how do you square that with your burning desire to have kids? Isn't *that* a hole you're trying to fill?"

"Are you being intentionally obtuse? The urge to have children is biological. It's what we were born to do. To procreate. To proliferate. Romantic love? Pfft." She waved a hand. "That's a human construct."

"If you say so," he demurred. She could tell he was humoring her.

"I *do* say so."

"Or…" He lifted a finger. "And hear me out. What if the urge to have children and the urge to fall in love are the same thing?"

"What do you mean?"

"They're both part of our desire to know the full gamut of life's experiences."

"I could buy that"—she nodded—"if I wasn't convinced that *some* of life's experiences are vastly overrated."

"Maybe that's true. Or maybe you're simply in denial."

She sniffed. The couple at the table behind them had ordered a dozen raw Gulf oysters, and their briny scent tunneled up her nose. "Denial is underrated. Besides, it's only denial if you end up being wrong."

"Good god." Winston groaned. "Now I remember why we broke up. You're as stubborn as a mule."

"That's not why we broke up. We broke up because you went to school in Miami and got all googly-eyed over some girl named Rosa."

He had the grace to wince. And if she wasn't mistaken, maybe blush a little. It was hard to tell given the depth of his tan. "Rosa was a symptom of our breakup. Not the disease."

"Oh? And what was the disease?"

"You didn't want me," he said simply. "Not like *that* anyway." Now it was Chrissy's turn to wince and blush. To which Winston added, "Don't feel bad. The chemistry wasn't there."

She leaned back on the barstool and wiggled her eyebrows. "But it was there with Rosa?"

"Oh yeah." His expression went dreamy. "I buttered that biscuit so many times I'm surprised Rosa—"

She lifted her hand. "Please spare me another trip down memory lane where you rhapsodize about you and Rosa's sex life. I get it. You two were crazy hot for each other." When Winston gifted her with a half smile that was wholly amused, she cocked her head. "Whatever happened there anyway? You never said."

"What happens to so many college sweethearts." He hitched a shoulder. "She got a job in Tallahassee, and the Keys are in my blood."

"Why'd you come back home?" Chrissy remembered asking him over beers while helping him move into a one-bedroom apartment above a souvenir shop on Duval Street. *"Won't you miss the bright lights of the big city?"*

"Miami was a ton of fun, but it was too noisy," he'd told her. *"There are too many cars. Everyone seems pissed and in a hurry and lays on their horns. I missed the quiet here. The slower pace."*

She certainly understood that. Conchs—the nickname given to people native to Key West—only ever honked to warn other motorists of the chicken, scooter, or drunk guy crossing the road. There was no road rage on the island. In fact, the concept was inconceivable.

In her estimation, Key West was paradise. And not only because of the sand and the sun and the palm trees swaying in the wind. It was because the locals didn't look up or down on anyone because of what they had or wore or drove. The idea of "whatever makes you happy" was pretty much the philosophy folks lived by. And most Conchs accomplished less by Friday than mainlanders did by six PM on a Monday.

"You should look her up," Chrissy told Winston now. "Maybe she's through with north Florida. Maybe she's still single and ready to mingle and—"

Her phone screen lit up with the reminder that it was

time to meet Wolf for drinks. For some reason, the whitefish she'd had for dinner reanimated inside her stomach and started swimming around.

"Speaking of someone who's single and ready to mingle." Winston glanced pointedly at her phone.

"I told you this isn't a date." She wagged a finger. "Wolf and I are friends."

He laughed. "If by friends you mean horny as hell for each other, then sure."

"I might want his hot bod, but come on. Give me some credit. The last thing that man is is relationship material."

"Oh, I don't know. You can't judge the guy by that one night."

She frowned. "Sure I can. He's a tomcat, a player. But even if he wasn't, can you see him settling down here with me in the Keys when his whole life has been one grand adventure? No." She shook her head vehemently. "Wolf isn't the one."

Funny. She wasn't certain who she was trying to convince more. Winston? Or herself?

He stood from the barstool and offered her a hand. "Come on, then. I'll walk you over to meet your...*friend*."

She decided not call him on his total misread of the situation. He'd simply accuse her of being in denial again. Instead, she looped her arm through his and breathed deeply of the island breeze after they exited the restaurant and strolled down the street toward the marina.

Cloud cover made the night inky black. The air felt close, like invisible hands were pressing against her skin. It gave her an uneasy feeling.

"Storm's moving in," Winston observed as the wind picked up and tousled his curly brown hair. He had one of those classic profiles that shouted *boy-next-door*—which he'd quite literally been when they were young.

Too bad he was right about their lack of chemistry. He was *exactly* the kind of guy who'd settle down with the house and the wife and the kids. The kind of guy to coach soccer and drive to dance lessons. To be blissfully middle-class and live the American dream and—

He interrupted her thoughts with, "Want to cut through the old warehouse?"

Obliterating the view to the water was a large metal building that had once been the spot where shipping vessels stored their wares after offloading them onto the island. It had been abandoned years earlier when the big docking stations for the cruise ships—along with their high-tech, machine-operated warehouses—had been built. Tourists avoided the place now because of its menacing air. But the locals knew it was a shortcut to the bars and restaurants along the waterfront.

"That place gives me the creeps after dark." She shuddered.

"Oh, come on," Winston cajoled. "Some of the best times we ever had were in that building after sunset. Remember the rave Eddie Johnson hosted there our senior year?"

She flattened her mouth. "I remember you took Molly and spent half the night staring at the glitter on your arms and the other half asking to braid my hair because, quote, 'It feels like corn silk, Chrissy!'"

He laughed. "Whatever happened to Eddie anyway? He was the only guy I ever knew who could pull off wearing a conch shell necklace un-ironically."

"Last I heard he was doing a dime after getting caught trying to sell the grouper he found on the beach outside his folks' house."

Drifting microwave-size packages of cocaine were known locally as "groupers." After being jettisoned by smugglers fleeing the authorities, the packages sometimes washed up on the beaches or else were found floating out at sea by fishermen. No one knew exactly how *many* drugs were recovered. The mishmash of agencies, from the DEA to the Coast Guard to the local cops, didn't tend to share information with each other. Also, a good number of the found drugs never made it into the hands of the authorities.

A lot of locals sold their "catch" on the streets. Despite the risk of prison time, one grouper could net an islander more money in a week than they could make in a year from their fishing boats or T-shirt shops.

"That's too bad," Winston frowned as he pulled her toward the slightly ajar door on the side of the warehouse. The chain that had kept it locked had been cut years ago. Now the busted links lay on the ground in a rusty pile. "I always liked Eddie."

He slid through the door, dragging Chrissy in after him. The air inside the warehouse was dank and foul-smelling. At night, the place was pitch black, the only light coming from the moon shining through the holes in the roof or from the flashlight feature on a cell phone.

Chrissy reached into her hip pocket to pull out her phone, but stopped when she realized one of the old cargo doors facing the water's edge was open. The ambient glow from the lights along the wharf drifted into the warehouse, casting everything in shades of deep gray.

She blinked until her eyes adjusted. Once they did, she saw the dark shape of a pickup truck parked next to the open cargo door.

"What in the world?" Winston whispered as a diver climbed up the ladder leading down into the water. Sitting on the edge of the loading bay, the diver pulled off his fins and shrugged out of his tanks. Then he stood and dripped water onto the stained concrete floor as he walked to the back of the truck. The sound of him throwing his fins and tanks into the metal bed echoed around the empty space like a cannon shot.

Chrissy's heart beat a fast rhythm. The hairs along the back of her neck stood up. Something wasn't right.

"Let's go." She tugged on Winston's arm.

"Way ahead of you," he whispered, having already turned to herd her back through the cracked-open door.

"Who are they? Do you recognize them?" she hissed over her shoulder.

Winston didn't have a chance to respond before a loud *bang* blasted through the warehouse. Instinct made Chrissy duck. When she turned back, it was to see a dark stain blooming like a fiendish flower across the front of Winston's T-shirt. His eyes flew so wide the whites glowed in the gloom, beacons of disbelief and terror.

"Winston!" she cried and grabbed his outstretched hands. But his fingers slipped through her grip as he fell backward.

He wasn't a small man, so he timbered like a redwood, hitting the floor and bouncing sickeningly.

Horror made her blood run thick and hot, and she instantly dropped to her knees. Which meant she saw Winston's eyes roll back in his head and heard the long, rattling breath that exited his big chest right before he fell ominously still.

A noise like an animal caught in a steel trap pealed from the back of her throat. Abject terror had a sound, and she was making it.

Winston, no!

Another loud report reverberated around the warehouse and a neat hole opened up in the metal wall over her shoulder. The streetlight outside lasered its golden glow through the breach.

Her heart was the surf during a storm, crashing violently against her ribs. Her breaths were fast and shallow and seemed to bring no oxygen. But her brain was still functioning.

It screamed, *Get out, get out, get out!*

Grabbing Winston's ankles, she heaved with all her might. Her heels scrabbled against the slick floor, and from the corner of her eye, she saw a man round the hood of the truck. Not the slightly built diver. No, this guy was *big*.

The end of the gun in his hand blinked bright orange a split second before another bullet whizzed by her, slamming into the door behind her and pushing it open another inch.

Fear was fuel for the adrenaline that scorched her veins. For a split second she was caught between the need to save her friend and the need to save herself. Instinct made the decision for her when she saw the huge pool of blood spreading from beneath Winston's body. It was black and sparkled evilly in the dim light of the warehouse.

Winston needed help. *Fast.* There was too much blood.

With a sob that nearly choked her, she plunged through the door into the dark night. Her legs tried to buckle beneath her as she ran the length of the warehouse, heading toward the party lights strung along the back of Schooner Wharf Bar even as she fumbled in her pocket for her phone, needing to call 9-1-1. The street gave way to the worn boards of the dock built along the waterfront, but every stumbling step made her feel as if she was stuck in a nightmare. It seemed the faster she ran, the farther away her destination moved.

Bam!

This time she felt the air displace by the bullet as it blasted past her. Glancing over her shoulder, she saw the gunman racing along the dock at the back of the warehouse. He was nothing but a dark silhouette. The pistol in his hands was darker still.

There was something about the way the man moved that she—

Bam!

This time the flash of fire from the end of the weapon preceded an odd *clinking* sound. Searing pain ripped through the top of her shoulder and sent her stumbling off the dock, her phone smacking into the weathered boards on her way down.

Time stood still.

Or, at least it slowed. Because she was falling forever. Falling, falling, *falling*.

And then…water.

It smelled of anti-fouling paint and fish. But it was cool and dark and welcoming. As it closed over her head, she thought, *My heart is full of longing for the secrets of the sea.*

She'd heard Wolf quote that once. He'd said it was from a poem, but she couldn't remember which.

Strange that the words should come back to her now.

CHAPTER 4

9:07 PM...

Chrissy was late.

Which meant Wolf's mood was quickly approaching the depths to which it'd sunk earlier. And the jackhole sitting on the barstool on the other side of Romeo certainly wasn't helping matters.

The guy was drunk and getting drunker by the minute. He'd been rude to the bartender, wiggling his beer bottle and snapping his fingers when he ran low on brew. And he'd made comments about every woman who walked by in a voice loud enough to be heard over the crooning lead singer of The Salty Cod Band.

In short, the man was the human equivalent of gas station sushi. A guy garan-damn-teed to give everyone around him a bad case of the shits.

Wolf leveled a stony stare at the drunk's nose and wondered how good it would feel to plant his fist there.

Good, he decided. Awful good. *A little somethin' to take the edge off.*

Unfortunately, he had to satisfy himself with a grumble under his breath as he turned back to his own beer. If he'd formed actual words, they would not have been polite. Which would inevitably have started a fight. Which would have led to him putting the douchebag in a chokehold until the bastard went limp. And even though that entire exercise would have been *soooo* satisfying, with so many witnesses, no doubt he'd have ended up spending the night in an eight by ten, looking at assault charges.

As his grandmother told him many times, *"The way of the troublemaker is thorny."*

He already had enough things giving him fits—*cough, Chrissy Szarek, cough, cough*—without adding Mr. Drunkovich to the mix.

Apparently, Romeo wasn't of a similar mind. When a young woman in a green halter top walked by—she couldn't have been much older than twenty-one—and the drunk said, "I bet she sucks dick like there's a prize inside," Romeo turned and growled lowly, "Hey fuckwit, how about you shut your face-hole before I stick my fist in it, eh?"

One of the drunk's eyelids hung lower than the other, but his voice was surprisingly clear when he said, "Fuckwit, huh? In my experience with humans, the ones who cast the first stones are usually the most guilty."

"Oh, yeah?" Romeo's smile was patently false. "Well in my experience with fuckwits, you are one."

A storm cloud that would put a supercell to shame fell over the drunk's face.

Wolf sighed heavily and carefully set aside his beer. He might've let the better angels of his nature win out when it came to starting a fight, but the devil in him wasn't going to let him walk away from a brawl once it was in the making.

Especially one that involved one of his closest friends.

To his surprise however, the drunk didn't take a swing at Romeo. Instead, the dude grabbed his beer and slid off the stool, muttering something about guys who couldn't take a joke as he stumbled into the crowd.

Guess Mr. Drunkovich wasn't so wasted he hadn't seen the two-on-one odds were stacked solidly against him.

"Don't let the door hit you where the good Lord split you, *pendejo*," Romeo snarled at the dude's back before taking a long slug of beer.

The heavy vein beating in the side of Romeo's throat told Wolf that Romeo's blood was up. Well, that and Romeo only slipped into Spanglish when he was super excited or super pissed.

Spiro "Romeo" Delgado had been given his nom de guerre not only because he was known to woo more than his share of the fairer sex, but also because he took chivalry to the next level. Romeo revered woman. Treated them like queens. The quickest way to get on his bad side was to disrespect a lady.

Wolf decided to take Romeo's mind off the drunk. And if he happened to take his own mind off Chrissy being—he looked at the large black diver's watch on his wrist—ten minutes late? Well…win/win.

She wouldn't stand me up, would she?

Chrissy was many things, but flaky wasn't one of them. Maybe she and Winston were nose-deep in business discussions and she'd lost track of time.

Yeah, he assured himself. *That's got to be it.*

"What do you reckon the odds are of us findin' the treasure buried somewhere on the island?" He picked at the label on his beer with the edge of his thumb. The cold bottle sweated in the humidity of the night, and the drops of condensation had softened the glue beneath the paper.

Romeo shrugged. "Alex's instincts have proved infallible so far. So I'd say better than fifty-fifty."

"Lord, I hope so." Wolf took a swig, enjoying the taste of hops on his tongue. "Caleb needs new basketball shoes. He made the JV team."

Romeo frowned. "Which one is Caleb again?"

"Roxanne's oldest. The one who broke his arm last year on the rope swing."

"The same one who pulled the whoopee cushion prank on his biology teacher?"

"No. That was Eli, Rebecca's middle boy." Wolf smiled, remembering how pissed his sister had been while relating that particular tale.

"I can't keep all your nieces and nephews straight."

"Tell me about it. And brother, I swear, when someone decides to have kids, they might as well go light a pile of money on fire."

Romeo lifted a considering brow. "Meaning you plan to remain childless?"

Wolf sighed, but the sound was lost in the noise as The Salty Cod Band started in on their snappy version of "Baby Got Back" and the crowd in Schooner Wharf Bar went wild.

"That would seem like the smart move, wouldn't it?" he asked when the cheers died down. "But I got the urge to be a father same as the next guy."

For the last few months, ever since he'd started staring down the barrel of his thirty-fifth birthday, that urge had been growing stronger. And, yeah, okay. His recent brush with death via an Iranian bullet that barely missed his brainpan and netted him a two-week stay in the hospital probably had something to do with it as well.

"Nuh-uh." Romeo shook his head. "Not the same as this guy." He hooked a finger toward his chest. "The world is overpopulated enough as it is. I'm not adding to it."

Wolf studied him. "But what if you meet a woman who wants kids?"

"Settle down and get myself an old lady? Pfft." Romeo shook his head. "Have you met me?"

Wolf shrugged. "I spent more than a decade watchin' you work your way through the female population, but I can't help noticin' the time you spend on the prowl has gone way, *way* down in recent weeks. You reckon that's got somethin' to do with our resident marine archeologist?"

"Coincidence." Romeo waved him off while taking another long draw on his beer.

"Right." Wolf nodded. "But before you get that on a tattoo, you might want to consider what Albert Einstein said."

"E equals MC squared?"

"Sure. That and, 'Coincidence is God's way of remainin' anonymous.'"

"Why do you keep busting my balls on this?"

Wolf chuckled. "Because they're such low hangin' fruit?"

Romeo glared at him. After a few moments he said, "Please don't take my silence as agreement. No one plans a murder out loud."

Wolf's chuckle turned into a full-on belly laugh. The way Romeo's mouth curled up made him think the guy might join him. But then Romeo stiffened and turned to look over his shoulder.

When Wolf leaned forward, he saw Mia Ennis had wandered up to place her hand on the barstool Mr. Drunkovich had vacated.

"This seat taken?" Wolf couldn't hear her words, but he read her lips.

"It's all yours," Romeo told her, at the same time waving to the get the bartender's attention. "What are you drinking?"

Wolf didn't catch Mia's response, but apparently Romeo did. He ordered a gin and tonic. After the bartender turned away to make Mia's drink, Romeo inspected Mia's new haircut—which in Wolf's estimation didn't look much different than her old one.

"I like it," Romeo told her. "It looks pretty under these neon lights."

Mia's expression turned sheepish and Wolf had to strain to hear her response. "Everyone looks better under neon and—" She stopped mid-sentence, her eyes going pie-plate round as she stared at something over Wolf's shoulder.

He turned to see what had caught her attention and nearly shit his own heart.

Like so many establishments on the island, Schooner Wharf Bar was open air. It backed up to the marina. Which meant he had an unencumbered view of Chrissy stumbling up the wooden dock.

She was soaked clean through, splashing huge pools of water onto the weathered boards. Even from a distance, he could see her face was contorted with pain. No doubt caused by the long rivers of blood that slid down her arm to drip from her trembling fingertips.

He didn't remember jumping from the barstool. He didn't remember pushing his way through the crowd. In fact, if you'd asked how he got to Chrissy, he would've said he flew.

"Wolf." She reached for him when he was still a few feet away.

"Christina!" He caught her before she crumpled onto the dock, cradling her like a baby as she fisted the front of his shirt in a desperate grip. His lungs lodged firmly in the center of his throat, making it impossible to breathe. Still, he managed, "What happened? Who did this?"

"Dunno," she wheezed, her blue eyes frantic as she pushed her cell phone into his hand. "The old warehouse. Winston. He's shot. I think—" Her eyes squinted shut and a loud, choking sob hit his ears like an atom bomb. "I think he's dead!"

He cradled her to his chest as he thumbed on her phone to make an emergency call. No go. Her phone's case was cracked and water had seeped into the device, rendering it useless. Yelling over his shoulder for someone to call 9-1-1, he didn't recognize his panicked voice as his own.

He'd been scared plenty of times in his life—contrary to popular belief, Navy SEALs did *not* have ice water running through their veins. But he'd never experienced the kind of heartrending terror that gripped him when he glanced down at Chrissy and found her chalky pale and leaking blood over his forearm.

"It's okay, darlin'." He brushed a strand of wet hair away from her forehead. "Don't you worry about a thing. I've got you now."

CHAPTER 5

9:24 PM...

We didn't have any other choice. They saw us."

JayJay looked over her reading glasses at Mateo Hernandez. He'd been her right-hand man for the last ten years, but never once had she seen him take out the pistol he kept tucked into the waistband at the small of his back.

She'd known he was a killer, however—a gal didn't hire a pantywaist to do her dirty work. And she'd bet her left tit his dick had gotten hard when he smoked the woman and the man in the warehouse.

Poor souls, she thought briefly. Then she turned her attention to the million questions crowding her head, because, really, what was done was done.

Besides, she'd lost her softer sensibilities years ago.

Once you've stared into the abyss for as long as I have, she thought philosophically, *you stop flinching at the harsher realities of life...and death.*

"Who were they?" she asked. "If they were cutting through the warehouse, they were locals."

"Yeah, yeah. Which is why Mateo had to off 'em." Ricky, who was standing on the other side of her office desk next to Mateo, nodded his head enthusiastically. The tip of the cigarette held between his thin lips showered ash onto her tile floor.

She wrinkled her nose, but said nothing of his nasty habit. Like Mateo, Ricky had his uses. And in her line of work, a gal had to take the good with the bad.

"Not sure." Mateo shrugged. "It was too dark to identify them."

"You're certain they're dead though?" she asked.

"Don't miss what I aim for, JayJay." Mateo had a big, barrel chest that puffed with pride.

Everyone else on the island referred to JayJay by her given name, but not Mateo. He used the nickname her mother had given her, the name she'd gone by until she opened her business. And it felt…intimate in a way that made her skin crawl.

"Well, that ain't exactly right." Ricky scratched his patchy chin. As far as JayJay could figure, Ricky only shaved about once a week. Around the same time he took a shower. "Took you a couple shots to get the woman."

"Like I said, it was dark," Mateo insisted. "Took the dude down with one bullet, didn't I?"

"True, true." Ricky had an annoying habit of doubling down his words, making him sound like a parrot. But he had a nose for finding fish, which kept JayJay's customers happy, so…again…*have to take the good with the bad.*

Standing side-by-side, Ricky and Mateo looked like Mutt and Jeff. Mateo was so big you'd be hard pressed to knock him down with a hammer, and he liked to keep his jet-black hair high and tight. By contrast, Ricky was tall and scrawny.

He nearly disappeared when he turned sideways and his stringy hair looked like the last time it'd seen scissors was back when Barack Obama was a senator.

JayJay didn't care for either man. But what they lacked in likeability, they more than made up for with loyalty and the ability to follow orders without question.

Of course, those things might have less to do with their fealty to her and more to do with the fat paychecks she cut them after each shipment. A fistful of greenbacks tended to buy the devotion of guys like them—men whose moral compasses didn't exactly point due north.

"And you didn't leave any evidence behind?" She looked pointedly at the cigarette hanging drunkenly from Ricky's bottom lip. "No cigarette butts? You wiped down the cargo door and the hard surfaces to get rid of any fingerprints?"

She'd been born and raised in the Florida Keys. She knew that while there were plenty of bar fights, some opportunistic thievery, and the occasional domestic dispute, the string of islands boasted very little gun violence. Which meant the local cops were going to be all over this like sunscreen on a tourist from Minnesota.

"Just like you said." Mateo nodded.

"No one saw you leaving the scene? Your gunshots didn't bring rubberneckers?"

"Ya know how it is down by the marina after dark." Ricky made a dismissive gesture. "Can't hear nothin' over the music from the bars. And even if ya could on a normal night, ya can't tonight. Wind's up 'cause of the storm blowin' in. The riggings on all the ships are makin' an awful clatter."

"And the cargo?" She lifted an eyebrow, her heart picking up its pace as she awaited their answer.

She flinched a little at the idea of a couple of locals being sent to meet their maker, but the thought of explaining a missing bale of snow-white Colombian gold to the cartel?

That was enough to have her breaking out in a cold sweat.

The seas between her and her Colombian contact hadn't exactly been smooth sailing recently. A month earlier, the Coast Guard had intercepted a narco-sub near the Marquesas Keys. It'd been carrying 180 million dollars worth of nose candy, and the cartel was looking to make up for that loss by putting pressure on JayJay to accept additional deliveries.

Muling drugs was always a risky business, but it'd gotten more dangerous since the big bust had brought heightened Coast Guard and DEA scrutiny to the area. JayJay wanted *fewer* shipments while the heat was on, not more. But her contact wouldn't hear of it.

Because of that, JayJay had come as close as she ever had to getting busted.

Earlier in the day, Mateo and Ricky had been forced to jettison their latest load near the old warehouse when they realized the Coasties had been checking the ships coming into the marina. No easy task given the two men had been sailing with a boat full of customers.

Thankfully, the group of Kansas Realtors who'd come down looking to hook some mahi mahi had gotten so drunk on the way back from the fishing grounds, they'd been passed out on deck and hadn't seen Ricky affixing weights to the bales of coke before chucking them overboard.

"We hauled up every ounce," Mateo assured her. "Luckily, the tide was on our side and kept all the bales pushed up against the warehouse's piers."

She heaved a sigh of relief.

"Yeah, yeah." Ricky nodded eagerly. "Everything's copacetic."

Big word for a guy who couldn't read without moving his lips. Probably saw it on his word of the day calendar and had been itching to use it.

"Good." JayJay dipped her chin. "That's good." Her

heart rate returned to its normal rhythm, but picked up the pace once again when the high squeal of sirens sounded outside. Even muted by her office walls, she could tell the direction the emergency vehicles were headed.

The marina.

"That was quick," she muttered, staring hard at Mateo and Ricky.

Mateo shrugged unconcernedly. He barely had a neck to begin with, and the gesture made it disappear altogether. "Some local probably tried to take a shortcut through the warehouse and found the guy. Or maybe the woman's body floated up next to a boat in the marina. Like I said, we're fine."

"Go find out for sure." She hitched her chin toward the front door. "But stand by and watch. Don't go putting your dick in it; this situation is already fucked enough as it is."

Mateo looked like he was about to roll his eyes but thought better of it at the last moment. He turned toward the door instead.

"Call me when you know anything," she said to his broad back.

Ricky rubbed his hands together. "Lookin' forward to watchin' the pigs work. It'll be good entertainment." And with that, her two lackey's—there was no better word to describe them—sauntered into the night.

After the door slammed behind the men, she leaned back in her desk chair. The worn leather made a familiar sound against the fabric of her shirt, and the springs in the seat let loose with a comforting squeak.

She'd bought the chair not long after starting her business…how many years ago had that been? Twenty-eight? No, next month would mark the twenty-ninth year since she opened her front doors.

How times flies, she thought wearily.

Back then, if someone had told her there'd come a day when she'd find herself in bed with the Colombians, working to get drugs from South America to the US mainland, she would've laughed her ass off.

She'd been so young and naive. She sure as shit hadn't fathomed the hard times ahead of her. Hard times that'd forced her to make hard decisions. Hard decisions that'd finally culminated in two people losing their lives.

Funny how a person breaks bad, she reflected. It didn't happen all at once. Like the sea battering rocks on the shore, it was a slow process.

She hadn't noticed how much she'd changed until tonight, when Mateo told her he'd murdered two people and she'd only experienced a fleeting moment of regret before her mind turned toward her responsibilities.

She had three grown children who all operated subsidiary business on other islands in the Keys. If she went down, she'd take them with her. But not just them, the eight grandchildren—with one on the way—they'd gifted her, as well. There were cars and mortgages and college educations to contend with.

There were *always* cars and mortgages and college educations to contend with. In fact, it'd been those exact things that'd led her to fall into bed with the Colombians all those years ago.

Now look at me...

There was no more denying her emotional coastline had been altered by the constant pummeling of the compromises she'd made day after day, month after month, and year after year.

So many compromises she barely recognized herself.

And she could never turn back.

CHAPTER 6

11:02 PM...

Mia hated hospitals.

The bright lights, the smell of bleach, the sense of urgency and fear that hung over everything like an ominous black cloud. It was horrible. A stark contrast to the sweet scents of suntan lotion and fresh-falling rain that permeated the warm air outside.

She had the overwhelming urge to flee. To leap out of the hard plastic chair and run through the emergency room doors into the wet night.

But that would be crazy, right? Not to mention selfish.

She didn't know Christina Szarek well. But in the month since she'd been working with Deep Six Salvage, she'd grown to appreciate the blonde's dauntless nerve and acerbic way with words. She'd come to think of Chrissy as...well, maybe not a friend, but at least a friendly acquaintance. And to leave now? Before she knew if Chrissy was okay?

She couldn't. She *wouldn't*.

Which meant there was no more outrunning the old memory that lived rent-free inside her head. The one that'd been scratching at the back of her brain ever since she sat down.

Time to give in and let it replay itself. Get the whole horrid experience over and done with so she could—

She was seven.

Her nanny had taken her to see A Bug's Life, *and that was the last thing she remembered before blinking open her eyes to find a stark white ceiling staring back at her. Her head felt like it was stuffed with rocks when she turned it to the side, only to discover the walls were the same unforgiving color as the ceiling.*

This wasn't her room.

Her room was painted a soft purple, and it didn't smell like harsh chemicals and sickness. It smelled like crayons and the flowery powder the housekeeper sprinkled on her rug before running the vacuum over it.

Mia's heart hammered against her ribs until her bones ached. She tried to call out, but choked on the effort. Something was shoved down her throat. Something that made her feel like she was drowning.

"Nurse!"

Her father's voice! Where was he? Why wasn't he helping her?

She clawed at the thing taped over her mouth. Her stomach rolled, and she felt the urge to retch like the time she'd eaten too much Halloween candy.

"Nurse! She's trying to rip out her breathing tube!"

There. There was her father, leaning over her, his hair sticking up in every direction like he'd been running his fingers through it. He grabbed her hands, forcing them away from her face.

"Daddy!" she tried to say, but only managed a strangled gag.

A woman in an outfit similar to the one worn by the doctor who had treated Mia for strep throat stood beside the bed. She whispered something in a soothing voice, but Mia couldn't make herself stop struggling long enough to listen to the words.

She couldn't breathe. She was dying. Hot tears spilled from the corners of her eyes to burn trails down her temples into her hair.

The woman pulled on the plastic thing in Mia's mouth, and Mia felt movement deep inside her throat. Whatever was in there burned like fire on the way out. Once it was gone, she dissolved into a spasm of coughing that made her curl into a miserable ball on her side.

Everything hurt. Her chest. Her head. Her throat.

"Pumpkin?" Daddy brushed her hair back from her brow. His voice sounded funny. When she blinked at him, she saw his eyes swimming with tears.

Her father never cried. If he was crying now, it meant something was very wrong. She must be really, really sick.

This room looked like the one her grandmother had stayed in after she broke her hip. Which meant Mia was in a hospital. Only sick people went to hospitals, right?

"I'm so sorry." Daddy's words broke over a hard sob as he bent to kiss her temple. His breath was hot and smelled bitter, like old coffee.

Mia tried to wrap an arm around his neck, but a loud beeping came from the hallway. Daddy stood up before she could pull him close.

"Code blue!" shouted a disembodied voice from somewhere outside the room. "Room thirty-six!"

"Thirty-six?" Daddy stared wild-eyed at the woman who gently patted Mia's shoulder. "That's Andy's room!"

Before Mia could blink, Daddy ran around the end of the bed and disappeared through the open door.

Andy? Was her baby brother sick too?

Mia desperately wanted to follow her father. But when she tried to get up, the pretty woman held her firmly against the mattress.

"Shhh, sweetheart," the lady crooned. "You rest and relax. Everything is going to be okay."

Mia didn't believe her and she fought with everything she had against the hands restraining her until her head began to throb like she'd hung upside down on the jungle gym for too long. Bright lights, like fireflies, blinked in front of her eyes. And then...darkness.

Blessed, cool, painless darkness.

"Breathe."

Mia came out of her uncomfortable reverie with a start, only to discover Romeo had planted himself in the plastic chair next to hers.

"I thought I was," she whispered.

"Mmm-mmm." He shook his head, and she dragged in a rattling breath that blew the last of the cobwebs from her brain. "That's good," he praised. Then he added, "She's going to be okay, you know."

For a second Mia wasn't sure which "she" he was referring to. Then she remembered. *Chrissy!* And berated herself for having fallen into the dark depths of her past when there was a real crisis in her *present.*

Chrissy had been shot. *Shot!* That wasn't supposed to happen in real life.

"How can you be sure?" she asked.

Romeo lifted a shoulder and let it fall. The move drew her eye to the tattoo on the inside of his forearm. Those black, stylized words all the owners of Deep Six Salvage sported. *For RL.*

One night after a hard day diving down on the wreck, she and the rest of the crew had been relaxing around a beach bonfire. When Alex noticed Mia staring at Romeo's tattoo, the diminutive historian had explained about the ink. About how the Deep Six guys had lost a SEAL brother, and about how that loss had precipitated all of them leaving the Navy and starting the salvage company.

Strange to think the men Mia had come to know, the ones who donned scuba tanks and swim fins, who ran around in sunglasses and flip-flops, had once been counted among the best of the best, the very tip of Uncle Sam's spear. They seemed so...normal.

Then again, what did she know about normal?

"I've witnessed my fair share of gunshot wounds, and hers isn't bad," Romeo explained. "It's not much more than a flesh wound, eh?"

"Okay, Monty Python." As soon as the words left Mia's mouth, she wanted to suck them back in.

Peeking over at Romeo, she expected to find him insulted. Quite the contrary, his head was cocked at an angle. "Did you just make a joke?"

"Sorry." Shame stained her cheeks. "Now's not the time, I know. Blame it on my hatred of hospitals. Is it hot in here, or is it just me?"

She fanned her face, unsure if she was sweating due to anxiety or because she could feel Romeo's immense body heat wrapping around her. The man was literally and figuratively H.O.T.

"I wasn't sure you knew how to make a joke," he said and she frowned. "Shit," he added quickly. "That didn't come out right."

"It's fine." She waved a hand. "You're not the first person to assume I lack a sense of humor."

People often confused her saturninity for an absence of whimsy, but she enjoyed sarcasm and the occasional bout of witty banter as much as the next person.

"Does that bother you?" he asked.

"No." She shook her head. "I stopped caring what people think of me a long time ago."

His glittering, black eyes tracked to her new haircut, and she automatically touched her freshly highlighted roots.

"I can see how you'd be skeptical," she murmured. "But I don't do this for anyone but me. I like to keep myself put together. I always have."

It was a coping mechanism left over from her childhood. Back then, her mother had been drunk as much as she'd been sober. Her father had been absent as much as he'd been present. Every nanny or housekeeper Mia ever loved had eventually left, unable to stomach the poisonous atmosphere of the Ennis household. And Mia had lacked control over all of it. The one thing she'd had agency over was herself. Her skin, her hair, her clothes.

"I guess it's true what they say," Romeo murmured. "Still waters run deep."

"You think I'm still?" She hadn't stopped squirming since she sat down. Even now, her knee bounced.

"Maybe *still* is the wrong word. *Quiet* is probably more apt."

"You know, when people comment on how quiet I am, it always catches me unawares."

"Really?" He looked shocked.

"My brain makes so much noise inside my head, I forget other people can't hear it."

"And what are you thinking about right now?"

When he stared at her like that, gazing so deeply into her eyes, she got the unsettling impression he could see into the very heart of her.

Heaven help her, she hoped not. Then he'd know she had a crush on him. Like, a silly, schoolgirl, write-his-name-on-the-cover-of-her-binder crush.

How pathetic am I?

Romeo was way, *way* out of her league.

On a good day, she was a six out of ten. Romeo? He was a straight-up twelve.

In fact, when he first came into the emergency room, there'd been a lady in a wide-brim panama hat walking out. One look at Romeo and she'd turned to whisper to her friend, "Ooh-la-la. Now *that* tall drink of water wasn't made in Key West."

"Glad we're at the hospital," had been the friend's reply. "Because he's stealing my breath away. I might need CPR."

Romeo had been oblivious to the exchange. Or maybe he was so used to that type of attention, their conversation hadn't registered. But Mia had heard. And she'd agreed with every word.

Romeo was a bona fide lady-killer, with deep dimples, a loose-hipped swagger, and a face so perfectly symmetrical it belonged on the silver screen.

"I was wondering how you can sit so still for so long," she told him since she couldn't very well admit what she'd been thinking about was what it would feel like to have his wide, firm lips pressed tight against her own. "We've been here almost two hours and I don't think I've seen you move except when you got up to go get a coffee."

He'd offered to grab her a cup, but she'd waved him off, not wanting to add caffeine to her already jittery nervous system.

"You learn patience as a Navy SEAL." His tone was calm, casual. It was a minor balm to her nerves. "Contrary to what people are led to believe, spec ops involves a whole lot of sitting around waiting for stuff to happen. Being part of the Teams is like hanging out at the DMV twenty-four hours a day, seven days week. Except occasionally you get to blow shit up or someone tries to kill you."

She glanced at the far wall where Wolf was doing his level best to carve a rut into the tile floor with his pacing. "Apparently that lesson didn't sink in for him." She hitched her chin toward Wolf.

Romeo tracked his friend's path from one end of the room to the other. "I think pretty much every life lesson you learn gets thrown out the window when the woman you…" He hesitated and finally finished with, "care about gets shot."

Mia thought about the times she'd caught Chrissy gazing longingly at Wolf, and the times she'd seen Wolf watching Chrissy with a hot, hungry look in his eyes.

"No one knows what happened between them?" She squeezed her knee in an effort to stop its agitation.

Romeo shook his head. "As my *abuela* used to say, 'stubborn as stone.' The both of them."

Talk of grandmothers made Mia think of her own. Her hand automatically lifted to fiddle with the diamond stud in her ear.

The move drew Romeo's eyes to the glint of the hard gem. He gently pinched her earlobe to get a better look, and a soft whistle sounded through his teeth. "These would get you snatched off the streets in East L.A."

Other than an introductory handshake, and the times they'd inadvertently brushed by each other in the beach house, they'd never actually *touched*.

Mia supposed now she should be grateful for that. Because the moment his callused fingertips kissed her bare skin, a jolt of awareness shot through her system. In its wake, an eruption of goose bumps that covered her entire body.

She wasn't aware her jaw had unhinged until Romeo said in a deep, dark voice, "Careful. You'll get flies in there." He hooked a finger under her chin to close her mouth. There was a knowing look in his eye.

Well, of *course* there was. Could she *be* any more obvious?

Jeez, Mia. Get a grip.

Firming her shoulders, she managed to stutter, "Th-the earrings were a g-gift from my grandmother."

His grin revealed a set of straight, white teeth that contrasted starkly with the black hair of his goatee. "And here I thought grandmothers only gave gifts of *chile rellenos* and *tres leches*." He pronounced the dishes with a Spanish accent and the sounds swirled inside her ears like a tongue.

She heaved a sigh of relief when his attention was snagged by a guy wearing jeans and a sport coat who walked into the waiting room. Upon closer inspection, she saw what'd caught Romeo's eye. It was the police badge clipped to the newcomer's belt.

Before she had time to speculate about the officer's arrival, the doctor who'd initially come out to tell them Chrissy would need to be put under general anesthesia to flush out the wound and clean it properly pushed through a set of swinging doors. Dressed in scrubs, and with the quick, hurried movement everyone in her field adopted, the doctor ripped off her surgical mask as she glanced around the room.

Mia and Romeo jumped from their seats at the same time Wolf spotted the woman and raced over to her.

"Chrissy?" There was so much anguish in Wolf's voice, Mia felt it in her own heart.

"The bullet missed Miss Szarek's collarbone and most of the muscle," the doctor said. Her intelligent eyes matched the blue of her scrubs. "Which is good. Soft tissue damage is easier to fix than a shattered bone. In fact, when it comes to a GSW, she's incredibly lucky. We probably could've stitched her up using a local. But I wanted to make sure none of her shirt got stuck inside the trauma site since that can lead to infection. Anyway, once we put her under, we were able to get everything cleaned up. And I'm a perfectionist, so that's what took so long back there." She hooked a thumb over her shoulder, indicating the bowels of the hospital. "She's coming around from the sedation now, and I'd say—"

"Does that mean she's ready to answer some questions?" The police officer had joined the group.

"And you are?" the doctor asked with an arch look.

"Bill Dixon." The man shot out a wide-palmed hand. "*Detective* Dixon."

"Ah." The doctor nodded, shaking his hand. "You should give her an hour or so before you start with the questions. She's going to be groggy for a while yet."

"We've got two gunshot victims." The detective's mustache and loosened tie, not to mention the world-weary look in his eyes, epitomized every crime drama dick Mia had ever seen on TV. It was like he'd come straight from central casting. "And only one of them is in any condition to provide us with information on what the hell happened out there tonight. I want answers."

Wolf slowly turned to the detective. The look in his eyes was enough to make Mia shrink back. She thought he might punch the cop in the mouth. She definitely saw his right hand curl into a fist.

Romeo casually stepped in front of Wolf before pasting on a charming smile that didn't quite reach his eyes. "And I'd like a house in the Bahamas filled with women in bikinis, Detective," he said. "But wanting it isn't going to make it so."

When Dixon bristled, Romeo softened his tone. "Look, man, our friend has had one hell of a night. I don't think you giving her an hour to recover is too much to ask. How about I take your number and call you the minute she's lucid enough to answer questions, eh?"

To anyone looking on, Romeo appeared the picture of friendly poise. But Mia could feel the ominous current running beneath his words. He wasn't really asking.

The detective proved he was no fool when, with a deep sigh, he passed Romeo a business card. "When a person suffers a trauma, they start forgetting important details quickly. You call me sooner rather than later."

"You have my word." Romeo tucked the detective's card into his hip pocket.

Dixon turned to leave, but stopped in his tracks and swung back. "Did she say anything before they took her back to stitch her up? Anything about the shooter?"

Mia's gaze was drawn to the two men who'd come into the emergency room not long after she'd arrived with Wolf and Romeo. Originally, they'd snagged her attention because the tall, skinny one reminded her of the Walmart version of Liam Neeson. You know, if she squinted and held her mouth just right—it was the man's prominent nose and high cheekbones. Now her eyes landed on them because they shifted uncomfortably, sitting forward and eyeing the detective.

Probably carrying weed without the requisite medical marijuana card, she thought, remembering how her own mother got fidgety and restless around law enforcement.

Wolf spoke to the detective for the first time. The impatience in his voice made it obvious all he wanted was to get to Chrissy, and Dixon's interference was fraying his last nerve. "When I asked her who did this, all she said was, 'I don't know.' Now, if you don't mind."

Wolf didn't have to make a shooing motion with his hand. His tone, not to mention the hard look on his face, made the gesture for him.

Dixon touched a finger to his brow before heading toward the exit.

"Will you be releasing her tonight?" Wolf asked the doctor.

"It's late." The surgeon shook her head. "And Miss Szarek's had quite a shock. I'd like to monitor her overnight."

"Can we see her?"

"Follow me." The doctor pushed through the swinging doors and the smell of iodine and blood tunneled up Mia's nose.

She didn't realize she'd become living granite until Romeo leaned close and whispered in her ear, "In through your nose. Out through your mouth." His breath was warm against her earlobe. The comforting hand he placed at the small of her back was warmer still.

Blowing out a deep breath, she fisted her hands and prepared to venture deeper into the belly of the beast.

CHAPTER 7

11:17 PM...

With hot tears standing in her eyes, Chrissy watched her stepfather pack his suitcase. Her mother sat quietly on the edge of the bed, not making a sound.

Chrissy desperately wanted to scream, "Make him stop, Momma! Make him stay!" But the words lodged in her throat like they were weighted down by anchor chains.

Didn't Momma love Doug anymore? Or had Josephine gotten tired of eating the lasagna he cooked on Wednesday nights? Or maybe she was finally fed up with the way he never managed to get both dirty socks into the bathroom hamper? Or could it be she was over how he yelled at the TV when the Miami Dolphins were playing?

Even if all of that were true, Chrissy *still loved Doug. She still liked his lasagna, although sometimes he added too much salt. She didn't mind stepping over his one dirty sock. And even though he was too loud during Monday night football, she thought it was funny when he called the refs bad names.*

Didn't any of that count? Didn't she *count?*

Doug zipped his suitcase and dropped it on the carpeted floor. With one last, longing look at Momma, he said, "For whatever it's worth, Josephine, I am sorry."

Chrissy's mother sat stony-eyed. "If I'm being honest"— her voice was as hard as her expression—"it's not worth a thing."

A sad look came over Doug's face, but it was swiftly replaced by resignation. Taking a deep breath, he turned to Chrissy and knelt in front of her. "You're a natural fisherwoman Chrissy, my girl. Don't give up on it."

Her throat clogged with tears, making her voice hoarse. "But who'll take the fish off the hooks for me when you're gone?"

Doug had been the one to teach her to tie on a lure. To cast a line. To untangle a backlash. They'd spent hours fishing the surf around the island, or watching their corks bob in the water at the end of the pier. Chrissy cherished each and every one of those quiet adventures. But maybe she would've cherished them more if she'd known they'd come to an end.

"You're big enough to do that yourself." Doug chucked her under the chin.

She'd never known her biological father, so even though Doug had only been married to her mother for a little over two years, he'd quickly become the dad she never had.

And now he was leaving.

The pressure in her chest was too much to bear.

Is this what a broken heart feels like, *she wondered? But if it was her heart that was shattered, what was wrong with her lungs? Why was it impossible to breathe?*

"Just because I don't want to wake up to your cheating

*face every day, that doesn't mean you can't visit Chrissy,"
Momma said quietly. "She'd love to see you."*

*Doug scratched his head. "Sure. Of course. But here's
the thing. I kinda promised Marla I'd move to the mainland.
I'm not sure how often I'll be coming back to the Keys
and—"*

*"Then say your goodbyes, Doug," Momma interrupted.
Her tone was back to being rock hard and cold as ice. "And
make them good."*

Doug's throat made a funny clicking *sound when he
swallowed. He returned his attention to Chrissy, and his
expression reminded her of the time Momma had caught
him pulling money out of the "Rainy Day Fund" cookie jar.*

*"Come here, baby girl." He dragged Chrissy in for a
hug.*

*She hiccupped on a sob when he patted her back. Even
her eight-year-old brain was mature enough to realize this
was the last time she'd smell his comforting sunscreen and
aftershave scent. The last time she'd hear his deep, melodic
voice that hinted at the mainland. The last time she'd feel
safe inside the circle of his strong embrace.*

*Before she could wrap her arms around his neck and
cling to him like a barnacle on the underside of a boat, he
stood and grabbed his suitcase. She was helpless to do
anything but watch him push through the bedroom door, his
wide shoulders nearly touching the jamb on either side.*

*"Guess it was too much to expect a man that pretty to
stay true to one woman," her mother muttered as he made
his way down the hall with its peach-colored walls and
photos of the three of them as a family. Photos Momma
would surely take down now that he was leaving. "Too
many women willing to offer up too much temptation," she
added.*

Doug paused at the front door, turning to stare back at

them. Chrissy lifted her hand to wave a final, tearful farewell when his face began to change. At first his features simply faded, leaving nothing familiar. Then his flesh morphed and molded until another man stood in his place.

Doug had become Wolf.

Which meant he was even more handsome than before. His mouth was fuller, his square jaw more defined, his gaze more direct and piercing. Even the harsh scar near his temple didn't detract from his striking beauty and—

"Chrissy?" A smooth, deep voice echoed through her head. But she was looking right at Wolf and his lips weren't moving.

"Chrissy? Wake up, darlin'."

That sure sounded like Wolf. All slow and twangy and sensual without trying to be.

"Atta girl. Come on now."

Chrissy emerged from the dream slowly, inch by inch, breath by breath. But even as her mind registered it *had* been a dream—or at least part memory, part dream—her body still felt weightless. As if she'd been caught up in a high tide and set adrift.

"Mmm," she heard herself murmur. Her eyelids weighed ten pounds each, and it took all her concentration to lift them.

Then it was like she was back inside her memory/dream. Wolf's ridiculously appealing face filled her vision as he leaned over her. All high cheekbones and slashing eyebrows and skin that reminded her of the old bronze penny she kept for good luck.

His hard, beautiful features matched his name. He looked like a wolf, sleek and fierce and dangerous. But then he smiled, and the expression was so sweet and pure it slipped past her drugged-up haze and sank deep inside her heart.

Tough and tender don't have to be mutually exclusive.

He'd taught her that.

Too bad he'd also taught her that her mother had been right when it came to pretty men.

They never stayed true.

"There are those baby blues that torture my dreams." He offered her a teasing wink.

Ever since she'd told him she only wanted to be friends, he'd cranked up the charm. *We're talking a magnitude 9.0 on the Richter scale.* The kind of charm that shook the ground beneath her feet until her knees felt as sturdy as jellyfish tentacles.

She acted like it annoyed her, but the truth was she secretly loved it. *What hetero woman* wouldn't *want that kind of laser-focused attention?*

Although loving it felt masochistic since she couldn't take him up on what his flirtation offered.

Once bitten, twice shy, baby.

"The part of hovercraft doesn't suit you, Wolf." Whoa. Was that her voice? It sounded like she'd been eating beach towels for dinner.

Dinner...

The warehouse.

Winston!

It all came back to her in a blinding flash. The truck. The men. The shooting. The blood. "Winston!" She bolted upright.

The sudden move brought a sharp pain to her shoulder that made her vision crackle around the edges and coated her tongue with a metallic taste.

She hadn't realized she'd cried out until Wolf gently pressed her back into the mattress. Dragging in a shuddering breath, she nearly gagged at the combined scents of marina water, iodine, and blood. She realized she was smelling herself.

"I've reached the highest levels of krav maga," Wolf said quietly. "I'm rated in every weapon that holds an edge or shoots a projectile. And I've done combat tours on just about every continent on the planet. But I've never found a way to handle a woman's tears. So, darlin', I'm askin' you to do me a favor and stay still so you don't hurt yourself."

Slowly, without opening her eyes, she took a mental inventory of her body. Her left shoulder had a thick bandage taped across it, and her arm was secured in a sling.

Her memory came in fits and starts. There were vague images of a paramedic with a red ponytail bending over her. The harsh sound of a siren as she rode in the back of an ambulance. The bright lights of the emergency room.

The prick of a needle.

The hot rush of anesthesia.

The welcome embrace of darkness.

"The bullet missed anything vital," Wolf's assured her. "But you'll be mighty sore for a week or so, I reckon."

Her mind's eye once more returned to the carnage inside the old warehouse. To Winston lying in a pool of his own blood.

Sore for a couple of weeks was nothing compared to being dead forever. He *was* dead, wasn't he? He *had* to be dead.

A low, keening sounded inside her head.

No. Not inside her head. That terrible noise came from the back of her throat.

She covered her eyes with her good hand as scalding hot tears soaked her palm. She thought she heard Wolf curse long and low, but couldn't be sure since her own sobs drowned out the world around her.

She had experienced grief plenty of times in her life. When her dog Charlie got hit by a speeding scooter.

When Doug left. The year her mother got sick, and those first terrible, lost, lonely months after Josephine died.

She recognized this physical ache, the painful pounding at her breastbone.

Hello heartache, my old friend.

"Winston." His name was barely a whisper, and she wasn't sure if she said it as a prayer or in penitence.

Winston never would have gone into that stupid warehouse if it weren't for her. If he hadn't felt obliged to walk her to the bar because, no matter how many times she'd tried to tell him she didn't need an escort, he hated for her to be out on her own after dark.

Oh, god! Winston's dead! The little boy who'd taught her to ride a bike, the teenager who'd given her a bouquet of flowers on her twelfth birthday, the man who'd held her hand as she stood over her mother's grave.

"He's alive," a soft voice whispered.

She sucked back her sobs, sure she'd misheard or else was having a morphine-induced hallucination. But upon opening her eyes, she saw Mia and Romeo standing at the foot of her hospital bed. Mia grabbed her toes beneath the blanket, giving them a soft squeeze. "He's alive, Chrissy," she repeated in that whisper-soft voice of hers.

Chrissy turned to Wolf. A desperate question in her eyes.

He took her hand and held it between both of his. She realized her fingers were freezing when his big, callused palms nearly burned her.

She might not trust him with her heart, but she definitely trusted him to tell her the truth. If there were two things Ray "Wolf" Roanhorse wasn't, it was a liar and a bullshitter.

The man didn't know how to do anything but shoot a person straight.

"It's true." He nodded, and she choked on a hard sob of relief that made the pain in her shoulder throb anew. She didn't care. She could withstand *two* bullet wounds right now because…

Winston's alive!

"You gettin' to me and tellin' me where to find him, where to send the paramedics, is the only reason he's still breathin'. You *saved* him, Chrissy." Wolf brushed a strand of hair behind her ear. "I've seen trained soldiers who didn't have the wherewithal to do what needed doin' when push came to shove. But you nailed it."

She didn't know about *that*. All she knew was she hadn't felt the pain of her wound. She hadn't felt the cool wetness of the water. When she pulled herself out of the marina, she'd been laser-focused on getting to Wolf. She'd known if she could get to him, he'd know what to do. He'd make everything better.

And no. That didn't mean she'd changed her mind about him. Wolf might be the first person she ran to when bullets started flying—duh, the man was a Navy SEAL—but he was still *him*.

She wasn't a big believer in there being deep, dark meanings behind dreams. *Sometimes a pickle is simply a pickle, Sigmund Freud.* But there was no mistaking the significance of the one she'd had as the anesthesia loosened its grip on her mind.

That old saying *monkey see, monkey do*? Well, in her case it was more like, *monkey see, monkey learn hard life lessons, monkey do everything in her power not to make her mother's mistakes.*

"Can I see him?" she asked.

Silence met her question.

Romeo and Wolf had pretty good poker faces, but remind her never to pick Mia as a card partner.

Chrissy pinned Wolf with a look. "Tell me." The words were cold and clipped, which was the exact opposite of the hot blood rushing through her veins until it pounded like surf in her ears.

"Winston was shot in the chest," he said carefully.

That much she knew. The memory of Winston's shirt blooming like a red flower had her gorge rising.

"The bullet split in two as it tore through one of his lungs. A piece of it exited near his breastbone, but the other fragment is still inside him. He's lost a lot of blood. Too much. The doctors gave him transfusions, but they've had to put him in a medically induced coma until he's stable enough for surgery."

She didn't want to ask this next question, but her mother had taught her never to shy away from a cold, hard truth. "What are his chances?"

Wolf dropped his chin and stared at the thin blue blanket that covered her lower half and kept her modesty intact despite the flimsy hospital gown that was printed with...*are those snowflakes?*

The irony of the pattern given nary a flake nor flurry had ever graced the island wasn't lost on her.

After a deep breath, he glanced back at her and admitted, "Not good. They're tellin' us it's less than fifty-fifty."

Her heart sank so fast she was surprised it didn't bust through the skimpy mattress and fall onto the tile floor beneath the hospital bed. Wetness once again welled in her eyes and slipped unencumbered over her lids.

"Hey now." Wolf used his thumbs to wipe away her tears. "A wise man once said we should laugh at the odds and live so Death would tremble to take us."

She knew he was trying to reassure her. In his Wolf way. And so she pasted on a wobbly scowl since that's what he expected. "What have I told you about the fortune cookie thing?"

Just as she'd known it would, one corner of his mouth

hitched up. That beautiful mouth she knew tasted like damnation and salvation all at once. "Your brass is comin' back." He dipped his chin. "That's good."

Was it? She couldn't say for sure. All she knew was succumbing to the breakdown she so richly deserved wouldn't help Winston or anyone else.

She had learned what *not* to do from her mother when it came to men. But Josephine had also been a role model on what *to* do when the world went pear-shaped. Namely, take a deep breath, square your shoulders, and keep on keeping on.

"Speaking of brass." Romeo spoke for the first time. "A detective named Dixon would like to ask you some questions about what happened tonight."

Chrissy frowned. "I don't know how much I can tell him."

"Every little bit counts," Romeo assured her, taking a business card out of his hip pocket. "I'll call and let him know you're ready, eh?"

When she nodded her agreement—she'd do anything to catch the bastards who did this to Winston—he headed toward the door to find a phone. Wayfarer Island was hell and gone from the nearest cell tower, so those who lived there had given up using the devices.

"Here." Mia pulled an iPhone from her hip pocket. Obviously she hadn't been on Wayfarer long enough to cancel her cellular plan. "You can call on mine."

No sooner had the words exited her mouth than her phone chimed. Mia glanced at the screen, shook her head, and then handed the device to Romeo as the two of them ducked into the hallway to make the call.

Speaking of cell phones… Where was Chrissy's? Someone needed to call Winston's parents. "Has anyone told Maryanne and Curtis Turner what happened?"

"The hospital called them when Winston came in," Wolf

assured her. "They poked their head in here for a bit, but you were still out. They're with Winston now."

"That's good." She nodded, comforted by the thought. "I'm glad they're with him."

"And I'm glad you're okay. When I saw you walkin' up the dock, wet as a drowned rat and bleedin' a river down your arm, it's a wonder I didn't go tits up then and there. I can't imagine a world without you in it, darlin'. It'd be a darker place. That's for certain."

His expression was so raw and open. It slid past the hard shell she wore like a hermit crab and hit her smack dab in the middle of her vulnerable heart.

The truth was, despite him being a playboy, he was still a good guy. The *best* guy in many ways. Strong but sweetly sensitive. Smart without being too much of a smart-ass. Capable of acting equal parts serious and silly.

"T-takes a lot more than a little bullet to put me down." She'd tried to sound brave, but her stammer gave her away. Heaven help her, she *liked* him. As a person. As a man. As a friend. Which made it that much harder not to want him for more.

Again, he tucked a lock of hair behind her ear. This time, a chill followed the path of his fingertips. Even when he pulled back, she would swear she could feel his flesh against hers. A seductive warmth lingered.

"How are you *really* feelin'?" His ink-black eyes were penetrating.

"Fine as a fiddle." She mimicked his accent.

He wasn't fooled. "You're a terrible liar. It's one of my favorite things about you."

"Yeah, well, talking about how I can feel my heartbeat in my shoulder doesn't help distract me from it, sooo..." She made a rolling motion with her hand.

Immediately, a teasing gleam entered his eyes.

Uh oh. She knew that look.

"If it's distraction you're after." He reached for the hem of his T-shirt. "I've been known to do a pretty good striptease."

She wouldn't have thought it was possible to laugh on a night like this, but that did it. Or, at the very least it brought a wobbly smile to her face.

"I need you getting naked in the middle of my hospital room about as much as I need a third nipple." The instant she said the word "nipple," his gaze dropped to her breasts.

"Nope." She lifted the blue blanket higher and held up her hand when he opened his mouth. "Not a word. I knew it was a mistake as soon as it left my lips."

A deep chuckle rumbled up from the depths of his chest. It was a sound so sweet and sexy, it made a gal want to slap her momma.

Her momma...

Something Josephine had said came to Chrissy's mind.

"That man is a downed power line. He looks *harmless. But get too close and he's capable of causing you pain like you wouldn't believe. The kind of pain that cracks you wide open. You can heal from it, but you'll always carry the scar."*

Her mother had been talking about her third husband. But the truth in those words applied to Wolf too.

Chrissy would do well to remember that.

CHAPTER 8

11:45 PM...

What color was the truck?"

While Detective Dixon awaited Chrissy's answer, Wolf watched him use a blunt-tipped finger on his cell phone's screen to zoom in on her face.

Gone were the days of pocket notebooks, ink pens, and Sony voice recorders. Now all a cop had to do to take a witness statement was grab his cell phone and record a quick video. Wolf couldn't help thinking this new protocol lacked a certain...*je ne sais quoi.*

Of course, what Detective Dixon gave up when it came to old-timey interrogation equipment, he more than made up for with his messy hair, mustard-stained tie, and rumpled sport coat. The man was a Columbo lookalike—sans the glass eye and plus one mustache.

And, yes. Wolf was too young to have watched Peter Falk take down the bad guys in primetime. But his grandmother loved tuning in to the reruns, and he loved his grandmother. Anytime he was back home in Oklahoma, they made a game of seeing who could guess when Columbo would mutter his "just one more thing" catch-phrase.

Chrissy shook her head now. "I think it was, like, black or blue. But you know how colors change in the dark. For all I know, it could've been maroon."

"Make?" Modern Columbo asked. "Model?"

"No clue. It wasn't big like a Dodge Ram or Chevy Silverado. It was smaller than that." She looked pained that she couldn't give Dixon more.

Pained and exhausted.

Deep circles bruised the skin beneath her eyes, but she was chalky white everywhere else. Her five feet, nine inches of pure man-eater, built-like-a-brick-shithouse body seemed small and frail inside the hospital bed.

Seeing her so reduced was a total gut punch. Wolf wanted to run Dixon out of the room so he could take her in his arms and stroke her hair while telling her everything would be okay.

Not that she'd thank him if he tried. In fact, she'd probably kick his testicles clean off his body.

A secret grin curved his lips. He'd never met a more stubborn, more independent, more *fierce* woman than Chrissy. Well, except for maybe his grandmother. His *elisi* had never batted a lash at charging hell with nothing but a squirt gun.

Perhaps *she* was the reason he'd always been drawn to strong, bullheaded women.

"And the two men?" Dixon pressed. "You're *sure* you didn't recognize them?"

Chrissy closed her eyes like she was trying to picture the men in the warehouse. To the casual onlooker, she appeared completely poised beneath her pallor. But Wolf noticed the way her shoulder stiffened, saw the little beads of sweat that popped out on her upper lip.

He'd seen his share of bloodshed and butchering. Which meant he knew exactly what was playing out on the backs of her eyelids.

The doctors had said it was a piece of .45 caliber that exited Winston's chest, and that kind of ammo could do some serious damage at close range. Despite what it was costing her peace of mind, Chrissy was forcing herself to relive that horror.

Brave, he thought. *Add brave to the list of her attributes.*

A list that was already longer than a south Texas summer.

"Everything's hazy," she finally muttered, a deep frown wrinkling her brow. "I don't know if it's the pain meds or what, but my brain feels like a smoking wreckage and I'm sitting here trying to sift through it for the black box and—"

When she stopped suddenly, Detective Dixon's posture changed. He reminded Wolf of Wolf's uncle's old bird dog when it was on point.

"What?" Dixon's voice rose an octave. "Are you remembering something?"

"The big guy..." Chrissy said. She always spoke with the laid-back cadence of the islands, but those three words came out even more slowly than usual. "Something about the way he moved sends an odd feeling sliding across the back of my brain. It's not quite recognition, but..." She opened her eyes and shook her head. "No. I'm sorry. I have the mind of a goldfish tonight."

"It's fine." Dixon stopped recording and pocketed his phone. "You've given me a place to start." He reached into his breast pocket and pulled out a business card. "I'm going to leave this with you. If you remember anything else, please don't hesitate to call." After depositing his card on the small table next to Chrissy's hospital bed, he turned to leave.

She stopped him with, "Detective Dixon? Why did those men try to kill us?" Her voice sounded small, nothing like the confident, strident tenor Wolf was used to hearing from her.

His feet instinctively inched closer to her hospital bed.

"The forensic unit hasn't finished their job at the warehouse, so I can't say for sure." The detective had a bushy set of dark eyebrows that formed a near perfect V when he scowled. "But if I had to lay down odds, I'd bet ten to one this is about cocaine."

Wolf frowned. "You think Chrissy and Winston stumbled in on a drug deal?"

Heaven knew men had killed for lesser perceived offenses, but he thought it highly unlikely the two guys in the warehouse would've resorted to homicide over a dime sack of blow.

"No." Dixon shook his head. "I think Miss Szarek and Mr. Turner happened upon a couple of bastards retrieving a shipment. The Coast Guard did searches of all the boats entering the marina this afternoon, so the perps probably dropped their haul near the old dockside warehouse, figuring they could pick it up in the dark without anyone the wiser. Used to be, the traffickers flew their wares northward on non-commercial aircraft. But nowadays most of the powder makes its way to the mainland in pleasure boats and fishing boats."

Chrissy grimaced. "They figured they could pick it up without anyone being the wiser and then Winston and I barged in like a couple of bumbling idiots."

Dixon made a face. "Can't tell you how many times I've taken a statement from someone who happened to be in the wrong place at the wrong time."

"That's cold comfort," she muttered.

Dixon shrugged and nodded before once again heading for the door.

A thought occurred to Wolf, and it was icy enough to chill him to the bone. "Hold up, Detective. Whatever those guys were up to made them feel like they needed to off any witnesses. What's to stop 'em from tryin' again once they find out they didn't succeed the first time?"

"Way ahead of you." Dixon hitched a chin toward the closed door. "I have one officer stationed outside here and another right next to Mr. Turner's room. I'll keep both witnesses covered until we catch the sonsofbitches who did this." He winced and glanced at the two women in the room. "Excuse my language, ladies. My wife tells me I'm not fit for mixed company."

Once Dixon had arrived, Mia and Romeo had taken up positions on the uncomfortable love seat pushed against the far wall, doing their best to stay out of the way while Chrissy answered the detective's questions. To Wolf's surprise, it was Mia who spoke up now.

"Don't worry, Detective. These two—" she pointed to Romeo and Wolf "—were both in the Navy and have the mouths to match. You sound like a preacher by comparison."

"Hey!" Romeo faked affront. "Neither of us are as bad as Mason."

"True." Mia grimaced. "Mason is from Boston and uses the F-word like it's a comma."

Wolf lifted an eyebrow. Did Mia make a joke?

"Thanks for your help," Dixon told Chrissy. "Try to get some sleep. You've had one helluva night."

When he opened the door, the room was immediately filled with a chorus of voices from outside.

"Whoa," Dixon said as a crowd of people pushed into

Chrissy's room despite a uniformed police officer trying to block their path and a shift nurse hissing stridently, "It's nearly midnight! I told y'all visiting hours are over!"

A middle-aged lady with spiky gray hair shook her finger at the officer's nose. She was tanned like leather, and reminded Wolf of the kind of woman who should be holding a martini glass in one hand and a lit cigarette in the other.

"Denny Parsons," she scolded, "you know damned good and well you don't have to protect the patient from us." Then she turned to the shift nurse. "And don't you sass me, Megan Foster. I'll bend your ear like I did when you were seven and I caught you stealing Snickers bars in Judy's store."

The nurse, er Megan apparently, had the grace to look chagrined. "I didn't understand how money worked, Miss Jill! I thought we could take whatever we wanted!"

Jill harrumphed and Dixon took that as the cue to make his escape. He muttered something to the uniformed officer and then disappeared into the hall.

With a put-upon sigh, Nurse Foster told the gathered group, "Fifteen minutes. That's all you get," before she stepped out of the room and closed the door behind her.

Jill rolled her eyes, muttering something about young people getting too big for their britches as she made her way over to Chrissy's bed. The mishmash of islanders who'd barged in with her trailed along in her wake like a gaggle of goslings following a mother goose.

Wolf had the distinct urge to toss each and every one of them back into the hall. Chrissy looked more peaked by the minute. And if not for the soft smile that curled her lips when Jill grabbed her hand, he probably *would* have pulled the big, bad Wolf card and growled and bared his teeth until the newcomers ran like scared jackrabbits.

"Chrissy." Jill patted Chrissy's hand. "The phone tree was activated and we all stumbled out of bed and came running as soon as we heard."

As if to prove her point, she gestured to an elderly gentleman who wore a robe over a set of striped pajamas. Wolf glanced at the man's feet, expecting to find slippers, but instead discovered a pair of hot pink Crocs.

Gotta love the islands.

And the islanders, he supposed. Although he would love them *more* if they were somewhere, *anywhere* besides here in Chrissy's hospital room.

Chrissy introduced the locals. Striped Pajamas turned out to be Fred Moore, the editor of the *Key West Citizen*. Then there was Janice of the purple shorts, and Judy with the impossible red hair and the oversized Buddy Holly glasses. A T-shirt shop proprietor, and the head honcho of convenience mart respectively. Along with Jill, who ran a parasailing outfit, they had storefronts on the same block as Chrissy and Winston's dive shop.

Once the pleasantries were finished, Jill demanded, "What the hell happened tonight?"

Chrissy shook her head dolefully and relayed what little she remembered. When she got to the part about Winston, she choked up.

Jill pulled a flowered handkerchief from the depths of her impressive cleavage and dabbed at Chrissy's cheeks. "And you didn't recognize them?" she asked. "I mean, if they were using the warehouse, they were locals, don't you think? Who else would dare go in there?"

"It was so dark," Chrissy whispered. "The big guy looked familiar somehow, but I can't put my finger on where I've seen him."

"Gotta be something to do with drugs," Janice posited.

"Not necessarily." Jill frowned. "Maybe it was mob

related. Maybe the diver had fitted a rat with some cement galoshes, and Chrissy and Winston caught him after he came up from stuffing the body under the pier."

"Jesus, that's dark." Judy grimaced.

Newspaper Man Fred shook his head. "No way. The mob moved out of Florida years ago. And any organized crime that's left is in Miami, not Key West."

Jill hitched a shoulder. "I'm just saying it doesn't *have* to be about drugs. Why do we always jump straight to drugs?"

"Because the simplest answer is usually the right one," Fred insisted.

"Is that what you're going to print in tomorrow's paper?"

Fred scoffed. "You know me better than that. I won't print anything I don't get from the horse's mouth." He turned to Chrissy. "You're lucky it's Detective Dixon working the case."

Chrissy's brow furrowed. "Why?"

"Most of the local yokels wouldn't know their butts from a pan of buttered biscuits much less how to work an attempted murder investigation."

When Jill opened her mouth to argue, Fred lifted a staying hand. "Now, I'm not saying that to besmirch my fellow Conchs, Jilly Bean. Don't get your back up. My point is, the local boys don't have experience with this kind of thing."

"And this Dixon fellow does?" Judy lifted an eyebrow that was fire-engine red and plucked into a death-defying arch.

"He worked narcotics in Miami for twenty years before moving here to get away from it all." Fred made a face. "Looks like trouble followed him, though."

Funny how that happens, Wolf mused, remembering

how many scrapes and skirmishes he and the rest of the Deep Six crew had fought since bugging out of the Navy.

He'd thought the Navy SEAL motto, *the only easy day was yesterday*, would stop being true once they became bona fide civilians. But like Detective Dixon, their past kept catching up with them whether they wanted it to or not.

And they most definitely did *not* want it to.

Of their own accord, his fingers moved to the scar he'd received courtesy of one pissed off Iranian admiral bent on revenge. The Navy didn't tell guys before signing them up for BUD/S training, but being a SEAL meant getting up close and *real* personal with some of the world's ugliest operators. Sometimes those operators didn't forget about you simply because you quit the biz.

"What can we do for you, Chrissy, my dear?" Judy pulled Wolf from his dark musings.

"I'm fine. It's Winston we need to worry about." Chrissy forgot about her wounded shoulder and shrugged. The resulting pain completely blanched her already pale face of whatever color had remained.

Wolf suddenly felt as if a whole herd of buffalo stampeded across his chest. "Okay." He clapped his hands. "Out."

Jill scowled at him. "Are you asking us or telling us?"

"How about we agree you can tell folks I asked?"

Jill puffed up like a disgruntled game hen, eyeing Wolf as if she meant to give him a piece of her mind. Something in his face must've made her reconsider. She deflated and turned to Chrissy. There was a small grin playing around her mouth when she said, "Your man has an economical way with words."

"He's not my man."

Damned if Wolf didn't feel a knife slice of disappointment that Chrissy was so quick with her correction.

Jill gave him the once-over and leaned in to stage whisper to Chrissy, "Well, why not? Have you seen him?"

Afraid Chrissy might actually mention The Night That Shall Not Be Named—she *was* still a little stoned on drugs, after all—he rounded the hospital bed, herding the locals along as he went. "I'm sure Chrissy would love to see y'all again tomorrow. During *visitin' hours*," he stressed this last part.

"Get some rest, sweetie," Jill called over her shoulder before Wolf could shove her out the door. "We'll check in on you tomorrow."

"Oh, wait!" Chrissy called, and every head turned back to her. "Judy, there *is* something you can do for me. I don't know where my phone is, so would you mind calling your nephew and asking him if he'll take out the diving group I have scheduled to go to Sambos Reef tomorrow morning at eight?"

Wolf remembered a one-time meeting with a blond-headed kid by the name of Tommy who'd filled in for Winston on a dive. He'd bet dollars to donuts that's who Chrissy was talking about.

"He should have keys to the shop and the boat," Chrissy continued, ever the kick-ass businesswoman even when she was lying in a hospital bed, recovering from a bullet wound. "And all the equipment is ready to go."

"He'll be there." Judy winked. "I'll make sure of it."

"Thank you. I'd hate to have seen what would've happened to my Yelp rating had no one showed up for tomorrow's dive. Keyboard warriors are absolutely brutal." Chrissy blew out a breath as if she'd discharged the last of her responsibilities and a giant weight had lifted from her shoulders.

"Okie, dokie." Wolf clapped his hands again. "Now that that's taken care of, good night, everyone."

Jill eyed him askance, like she wanted to say something. But then she thought better of it and shooed the group out of the room.

The second they were in the hall, Wolf shut the door behind them, barely refraining from dusting off his hands and letting loose with a "Good riddance."

Turning back to Chrissy, he found her tentatively trying to find a more comfortable position for her wounded shoulder. Her hair was a mess. Mascara smudged her lower lids. And there was scrape on her cheek from who knew what.

She'd never looked more beautiful.

She was beaten but not broken, had been brave without a hint of bravado.

In short, she was everything he'd never known he wanted. Everything he should have been a whole hell of a lot more careful with. And everything he'd give his left arm and two inches of his dick to get another shot at.

"We should let you get some rest." Romeo stood from the love seat, offering Mia a hand up. The strawberry blonde seemed to hesitate, but eventually let him pull her to her feet.

Was it Wolf's imagination or did Romeo hold on to Mia's fingers a second or two longer than was strictly necessary? If the blush staining Mia's cheeks was anything to go by, the answer to that question was a resounding *yes*.

He loved Romeo like a brother, but the man had never made any bones about his goal of Hugh Hefnering his way through life, romancing as many members of the XX persuasion as humanly possible before dying in a smoking jacket at the ripe old age of ninety-one.

Not that Romeo was a hound dog or anything. The guy was one-hundred-percent honest with every woman he met. He told them straight up what he was and wasn't after, and when they walked away? Well, they always did it with a smile.

But Mia was different.

She was softer. Gentler. She struck Wolf as the kind of woman Romeo could hurt even if he tried his best not to.

Then again, maybe Romeo was exactly the kind of man Mia needed. Maybe some time spent with the High King of Having a Good Time would help her poke her head out of her introverted shell.

"Y'all go on," he told them. "I'm stayin' here tonight."

"Wolf." Chrissy frowned. "You don't have to do that. The police officer outside will—"

"I'm stayin'." They were only two words. Two *small* words at that. But they held a whole lot of meaning.

"Suit yourself." She waved a hand, but he thought he saw a flicker of relief in her eyes.

He'd spent his fair share of time in hospital rooms. He knew exactly how isolating they could be. How cold and lonely.

Following Mia and Romeo to the door, he waved goodbye and then flicked off the light switch as soon as the door closed behind them. Not to be too autocratic and domineering, but Chrissy needed sleep. Then, stepping to the love seat, he girded himself to spend a sleepless night on the piss poor excuse for furniture.

Back when he'd been a SEAL, he could pass out on anything. The hard, rocky ground of a cave in the Hindu Kush? *No problem.* The cold, steel floor in the back of a thundering transport plane? *Hello, Sandman.* But he'd gotten soft since becoming a civilian. He was used to his comfy featherbed back at the beach house and—

"Wolf?" Chrissy's voice was husky as it searched him out in the darkness. He would swear it came equipped with gentle fingers that brushed against his ears.

"Yeah, darlin?"

"You don't have to fold yourself onto that love seat. You can sleep up here with me. You know…" Her voice sounded hesitant. "If you don't think it'd be too weird."

The little head housed behind his zipper sent up a rousing chorus of *hoorahs* as if it truly believed it might get lucky. Fortunately for Wolf, he'd stopped listening to that idiot and started paying attention to the *big* head on his shoulders around age thirty.

Okay, maybe he'd been closer to thirty-one.

Fine. Thirty-two at the latest.

"I'd hate to bump your shoulder," he told her.

"I'm not worried about that. I'm more worried you won't get any rest on that thing."

"I'll be fine."

"You're going to make me say it, aren't you?" There was exasperation in her voice. "I don't usually need much from anyone. But I could really use some comfort and connection tonight. Some human warmth to remind me I'm alive. So would you please sleep up here with me?"

He remembered a night not too long ago when she'd asked him that same question. It'd been after the terrible firefight with the Iranians. There'd been blood and carnage then too, and she'd needed someone to lie beside her to keep the demons away. To keep the darkness at bay.

"Should I grab the cushions off the love seat to make a pillow fort like I did last time?"

"There's not enough room for that." Her jaw cracked when she yawned. The adrenaline and drugs were taking their toll.

He was glad it was dark so she couldn't see the smile that curved his mouth. "Okay, then."

He hurried to her uninjured side. After kicking off his shoes, he carefully lifted the thin, blue hospital blanket and crawled onto the narrow mattress beside her, doing his level best not to jostle her around too much.

She'd scooted to the other side of the bed, but he still had to lay on his side. If not for the guardrail plastered along his back, he'd have spent the night with his ass hanging over the edge of the mattress.

"This okay?" He gingerly placed his head on the pillow next to hers, loving the feel of her body heat reaching out to him. Loving the sound of each soft breath as it exited her lungs.

"It's good," she assured him, scooting to give him more room he didn't want. "Thank you, Wolf."

How many times had he dreamed of her calling him into bed? How many times had he imagined having her laid out next to him exactly like this?

Of course, none of those fantasies had included a hospital room. And they'd certainly never included her suffering from a bullet wound.

She'd come so close to—

He couldn't finish the thought. Anytime he touched on it, he felt an ache so deep inside his stomach he wondered if he might be developing an ulcer.

He hadn't been lying when he told her he couldn't imagine a world without her in it. A world without her sunny smile or her blue eyes or that laugh that burst out of her like fireworks on the Fourth of July.

So many people simply existed, neither adding to nor subtracting from the world. But not Christina Szarek. She brought sass and fun and banter wherever she went. And although she'd never admit it, she also brought generosity and grace.

Put simply, people liked Chrissy because she was likeable. *He* certainly liked her. Had from the moment he met her and—

He stilled, feeling himself edging toward an epiphany he wasn't ready to have.

"Sorry I smell so bad," she whispered into the darkness.

It took everything he had to hold himself away from her, to lie beside her without touching her, but he contented himself with leaning forward to take a covert sniff of her hair. Sure, it smelled of marina water tinged with antiseptic, but it also smelled of her. Of salt spray and sunshine and coconut oil.

An island girl from top to tail.

"I've smelled worse," he assured her and grinned when she snorted.

"Damned by faint praise." She relaxed beside him, her uninjured shoulder nestling against his chest.

He wished he was shirtless. Wished he could feel her skin touching his.

Slowly, so as to give her plenty of time to stop him, he slid his arm across her waist. Her stomach radiated heat through the thin hospital gown, and he loved the feel of her hip bone and how it perfectly fit the curve of his hand. "This okay?" he asked.

She gave his forearm a squeeze, and relief rushed through him. "Thank you for staying." Her voice was barely above a whisper. "You're a good friend, Wolf."

Friend.

There it was again. That wretched word.

He didn't want to be her friend. He wanted—

Suddenly, he wasn't edging toward that epiphany; he was tumbling over it. Head over heels. Ass over tits. One long somersault that left him dizzy and yet somehow completely clear-eyed.

What he wanted was…*her.*

And not only for some naked, sweaty times—although he certainly wanted *that.* But no. He wanted all of her. All the time. For all the things from sunrise to sunset. For lazy Sunday mornings and sensual Saturday nights. For dancing in the dark and laughing in the sun. From now until eternity because…

I'm in love with her.

The words went off inside his head like a mortar round, leaving him stunned. Leaving him breathless. Leaving him more than a little dismayed.

Letting go of his forearm, she entwined her fingers with his. Her palm was cool and her fingertips were callused from hours spent servicing diving equipment. It was her turn to ask, "This okay?"

"Mmm," was all he could manage given his mind was spinning in ever-tightening circles.

I love her, but I won't have anything to offer her if we can't find the Santa Cristina.

I love her, but I fucked up and now she only wants to be friends.

I love her, but she doesn't love me.

I love her, but…

But nothing, he decided.

He loved her. Full stop. End of sentence.

"Sing me a song, Wolf." Her voice was garbled with sleepiness. "Sing me a song so I can't hear the heart monitor beeping in the next room."

She could hear the heart monitor in the next room over the thunder of *his* heart inside his chest? How could that be? The damned organ was drumming to beat the band.

"Any particular song you have in mind?" Could she hear the hoarseness in his voice?

"Didn't you tell me your grandmother loved to hear you sing?"

He remembered that morning on Wayfarer Island. She'd been standing in the sunlight, fishing pole in hand, the lithe muscles in her tanned arms moving rhythmically as she reeled her lure through the surf.

Christina of the Sea he'd called her. She'd looked so at home with the ocean breeze in her hair and her bare toes buried in the sand.

It was the day she informed him she only wanted to be friends. This was right after *he'd* informed *her* he very much wanted to shake the sheets with her. They'd met in the middle by agreeing to be pals if Chrissy conceded to granting him one favor at some point in the future. No questions asked.

At the time, he hadn't known what the favor would be. Hell, he *still* didn't know. But he was now certain it would need to be good. Something tender and romantic and guaranteed to make her reconsider their current relationship status because…he was determined to make her love him too.

"Yes. My *elisi* loves it when I sing," he admitted quietly.

"What's one of her favorite songs?"

He grimaced. "She's an indigenous woman who was born and raised in Oklahoma. In her mind there are only two forms of music worth a damn. The first is traditional, and I wouldn't shame my ancestors by attemptin' one of those songs. And the second is country and western."

"So sing me a country and western song then."

He thought of the one his grandmother hummed whenever fall rolled around and she gathered up the hickory nuts that fell from trees. She let them dry in the sun for two weeks before using them to make *kanuchi*.

Unable to deny Chrissy anything, he cleared his throat and softly began singing Garth Brooks's "I've Got Friends in Low Places." He expected her to chuckle at his song choice, but instead she snuggled closer, her breaths growing slower and deeper as he made it through the first verse and partway through the chorus.

"Wait," she cut in, sounding suddenly wide awake. "Did you just sing, 'I'm not big on sausage gravy'?"

He'd been known to get song lyrics wrong before. She herself had given him hell for thinking Bob Marley's "Stir It Up" was about breakfast cereal.

"Y-yeah." He frowned as her laughter filled the hospital room.

"Ow." She gasped. "Don't make me laugh. It hurts when I laugh."

"What did I get wrong this time?"

"It's, 'I'm not big on *social graces*.'" She continued to chuckle. "There you go again thinking all these musicians are singing about food."

He felt his lips quirk. "I guess not bein' big on social graces makes more sense. I mean, who doesn't love sausage gravy?"

"Heathens," she declared vehemently. "Otherwise known as health nuts."

"Exactly." He tightened his fingers around hers. She was now fully pressed against his length. His nose touched her cheek and he very much wanted to replace it with his lips.

Up until that moment, the biggest threats he'd ever come up against had been measured in calibers. But now he had Chrissy. More than anything or anyone, she had the power to end him. To shatter his heart into a million pieces.

Some guys would turn tail and run at the thought.

Not him.

When the devil offers you something you can't live without, he thought, gently rubbing his nose across her temple and loving the way she let loose with sigh, *you dance with the devil.*

CHAPTER 9

12:58 AM...

JayJay paced behind her desk, waving her hand through a cloud of cigarette smoke when she ran face-first into it.

"Put that damned thing out." She scowled at Ricky, coughing when the foul smoke invaded her lungs. "I need to think and I can't do it if I can't breathe. Your brain might not need oxygen to function, but mine does."

Ricky sat in one of the two armchairs facing her desk. He obligingly snuffed out his smoke on the sole of his flip-flop before tossing the crushed butt into her wastepaper basket. She waited for the used tissues inside to ignite, and then breathed a sigh of relief when they didn't.

An office fire would be exactly what she needed to make this clusterfuck of a night complete.

Mateo shot Christina Szarek and Winston Turner. Chrissy and Winston!

The news was all over the island.

"Not sure what there is to think about," Mateo muttered. Between his overpowering aftershave and Ricky's cigarette smoke, her office smelled like a dive bar. "She doesn't know who we are. I told you that big, black-haired dude said as much to the detective at the hospital. And didn't you just say—"

"*Tonight*," JayJay stressed. "She doesn't know who you are *tonight*. But that doesn't mean she won't recognize you from the warehouse if she sees you out and about tomorrow or next week. This isn't New York City. You're bound to run into each other eventually."

If that happened, if Chrissy fingered Ricky or Mateo, the next stop for the cops would be JayJay. Even though the fishing boat Ricky and Mateo ran wasn't in her name—she operated it under a limited liability corporation—the cover was flimsy at best. A little digging was all it would take to discover *Catch of the Day* was owned by none other than JayJay herself.

"No way, no way. I'm not movin', if that's what you're suggestin'." Ricky crossed his arms and set his jaw at a sullen angle. "I like it in Key West."

She pushed her reading glasses down to the tip of her nose and stared at him over the tops of the frames. "Are you allergic to logic?" Her jaw was so tight she could barely form words. "*Of course* you can't move. I need you here, running the business, taking the deliveries."

"So what's the solution?" This from Mateo. He had on a baseball cap now, but it was flipped around backward, making him look like he had thug-life written all over him, and jackass written all over that. When JayJay hesitated, he continued, his voice drilling a hole into her already aching head. "Never mind. You *know* what the solution is. I'm just waiting for you to say it."

She had absolutely *zero* interest in going where this

boatload of shit wanted to take her. But she didn't have a choice. She was being carried along on a tide that wasn't of her making.

Damn the Colombians and their eagerness to recoup their losses!

Although the cocaine business was criminal, JayJay had initially agree to get into it because she figured it was largely victimless. It wasn't like she was muling laced meth to the projects and watching the poor and pathetic overdose on it. No. It was the richy-riches in Miami who bought the blow she trafficked. They liked their nose candy about as much as they liked their Brazilian butt lifts and fake boobs.

But now there was no more fooling herself.

Painful circumstances call for painful solutions.

"Do it," she said forcefully thinking of her family, of her children and grandchildren. "Wait until she's released from the hospital and then do it. But make it look like an accident if you can."

"No problem." Mateo's grin was positively evil. He was being subtle about how much he was looking forward to the task. You know, if "subtle" was hitting someone in the teeth with a tire iron.

There was enough of the old JayJay alive and kicking that she felt compelled to add, "And try to make it quick, okay? I don't want her suffering if there's a way around it."

Mateo's expression was pitiless. "Death is always dirty."

Death.

She hated that word. Preferred more euphemistic terms like *kicked the bucket* or *gave up the ghost*. They were far more palatable. Less...*final*.

Chrissy Szarek. What a shame.

"Fine," she spat. "However you want to accomplish the deed is completely up to you. But once you're finished with..." It was hard to say Chrissy's name aloud given she was standing there openly discussing the young woman's demise. "Once you're finished with Chrissy, we still have another problem." She lifted a finger in the smoke-tinged air.

"Winston." Ricky proved he wasn't completely lacking in functioning synapses.

"Exactly."

Again, Mateo hitched one massive shoulder. "Word on the street is he probably won't wake up."

"And if he does?" JayJay lifted an eyebrow.

"Then we take him out too."

Mateo was right. They needed to make sure two *attempted* murders became two *successful* ones.

This whole thing started spinning out of control the moment the Coast Guard ran into that narco-sub. And it's swirling faster and faster with each passing day.

JayJay was caught in a whirlpool. The only thing to do now was to ride it down and see where it took her.

CHAPTER 10

1:04 AM...

Romeo watched Mia attempt to slide her key card into the slot on her hotel room door. She missed and dropped the plastic rectangle on the floor when her cell phone buzzed.

The damned thing had been going off at regular intervals all night. While they waited in the emergency room. While they hung out with Chrissy at the hospital. On the short cab ride to the hotel.

Each time it did, Mia glanced at the screen, read whatever was there, and then put the device away again.

He'd initially thought she was receiving desperately adoring messages from a boyfriend or a lover—*and never mind that twinge of jealousy; we're just going to ignore that*—except she never responded. Which meant whoever was texting her was having a monologue, not a dialogue.

That's not how a woman acts with a lover. At least not in his experience. Women, the wonderful creatures, were only too happy when they were chitchatting.

And never mind that rush of relief; we're just going to ignore that too.

"You getting stock price updates or what?" He bent to retrieve her key card. When he handed it to her, their fingertips brushed—hers were cool and soft compared to his hard calluses—and a current of awareness shot up his arm.

Douchebagistan, he thought to himself. *Population: you.*

He had no business being attracted to the likes of Mia Ennis.

For one thing, she screamed *relationship material*. Which he did his best to steer clear of. When it came to the ladies, he liked them easy like Sunday morning.

Mia was a Monday morning for sure.

For another thing, she was a girly-girl, all sweet and shy and soft-spoken. Too refined, too wholesome, and far too good for a reformed gangbanger like himself.

Not that she'd give him a chance even if he were inclined to ask for it. Which he wasn't—*No, really. I'm not*—because while he might've worked his way around to ignoring that she was too damn good for him, or rationalizing a way to get her naked despite her striking him as the kind of woman who wouldn't know the first thing about a one-night stand, he couldn't discount she was scared of him.

Like, straight up panic-stricken. She shuddered every time he touched her. And nearly jumped out of her shoes when he opened his mouth to speak.

He wasn't sure what he'd done to deserve her fear. They'd only had a handful of interactions. In fact, barring their short conversation in the emergency room and the two times they'd been paired as dive partners on the wreck and had been forced to do equipment checks together, they were looking at a big, fat goose egg.

Although, on second thought, *a lot* of things seemed to agitate Mia. Hospitals. Having a hair out of place. So maybe he shouldn't take her reactions to him too personally.

"No." She shook her head. Speaking of having a hair out of place, her new haircut was shorter in the back than the front, styled in loose, beachy waves. Even in the dimness of the hotel hallway it caught the light and shimmered with health. "It's my cousin," she explained. "When I come here and get cell service, he takes it upon himself to fill me in on the family drama I missed while I was out of range."

Romeo lifted an eyebrow. "Must be a lot of drama."

"You have no idea." She rolled her eyes.

This time she succeeded in unlocking her door. He waited until she opened it and turned on the interior light before telling her, "I'm right next door if you need anything."

It'd been one hell of a day, and he was beat. In fact, the last time he remembered being this tired, he'd still been with the Teams. The minute his head hit the pillow, he knew he'd be lights out.

He was halfway to his hotel room when Mia's voice reached out to him. "Do you want to come in for a drink?"

He stopped in his tracks and considered the possibility he'd misheard her. Was exhaustion making him hallucinate?

Do you want to come in for a drink? He turned the words over in his head, replacing them, rearranging them, trying to come up with something that *sounded* like them but wasn't really them.

Nope. He was at a loss.

Okay, so she *had* asked if he wanted to come in for a drink. And usually *do you want to come in for a drink* was a euphemism for *I want you to come tear off my clothes and bounce me around on the mattress until the sun comes up, big boy.*

But this was Mia Ennis. So...

He turned slowly and found her watching him with big, worried eyes. If she wrung her hands any harder, she might pull off a finger.

She certainly didn't look like a woman who was itching for a little sumpin' sumpin'. In fact, she looked like a woman who was two seconds away from losing her shit.

"I—" Her mouth opened and closed. She tried to shutter her expression, but he could read the message in her amber-colored eyes—those cat eyes that'd mesmerized him since the moment he caught sight of them.

She *was* agitated. But this time it wasn't because of him.

"Breathe," he instructed instinctively. The woman had a terrible habit of holding her breath. It made her anxiety worse.

Once she released a shuddery breath, he asked, "Is everything okay?" as he moved closer and closer to her, ignoring the urge to turn around and dart into his hotel room when it grew stronger and stronger.

Damsels in distress were his weakness. They called to the part of him that wanted to defend and protect.

"I, um." She kept twisting those thin finger of hers and it took herculean effort not to reach out and grab her hands to stop her fidgeting. He had to shove his fists deep into the pockets of his jeans. "I'm keyed up after everything. I think some gin or vodka would help calm my nerves, but I make it a point never to drink alone."

He watched her eyes cloud over. "My mom is an alcoholic," she explained. "Like, the blackout drunk, smash things, hurt herself and those around her kind of alcoholic. According to Carter..." She lifted her phone. "That's my cousin. The one who's been texting? Anyway"—she shook her head—"according to him, she's fresh out of rehab. *Again*."

Her face contorted around a look of…he wasn't exactly sure. Pessimism, maybe? Mixed in with a smidge of grief? Before he could respond, she continued.

"I've read enough books on the subject and been to enough Al-Anon meetings to take seriously the science that says it runs in families. Hence my hard and fast rule never to drink alone. Which is why I'm trying to convince you to come in and share one with me. What?" She cocked her head. "What's that look for?"

"I've never heard you string that many sentences together at one time." He shook his head in wonder. She had a nice voice when she wasn't keeping it to barely above a whisper. It was low and raspy. The voice of one of those old film noir actresses.

"Which goes to show I wasn't lying when I said I was keyed up. So? How about that drink?" Now there was a beseeching look in her tired eyes.

He recognized it well. He'd worn that same look plenty of times when he'd been young and trying like hell to stay out of 'the life,' and then again at the end of just about every mission he'd ever run for the SEALs where he'd been forced to mete out death and destruction. It was the look someone wore when they weren't physically tired, but instead suffering from a mental exhaustion that made them want to crawl into a hole and never come out.

Against every single ounce of his better judgment, he pressed open her hotel room door and gestured for her to precede him. "By all means then, lead the way."

I will not look at her ass. I will not look at her ass. I will not…

He looked at her ass as he followed her into the room because he couldn't *not* look.

Mia was a slight woman, with thin arms and legs, a narrow waist and small breasts. But when it came to her posterior?

Sisquo said it best. The woman had dumps like a truck. One of those perfect peach-shaped butts made for twerking or for smacking gently when a man was doing her from be—

Head out of the gutter, pendejo!

He gave himself a mental slap and forced his gaze away from her juicy behind. Since the only other thing to look at was her hotel room, he gave it a once-over.

Queen bed, wood veneer desk, and mini-fridge. It wasn't the Ritz-Carlton, by any means. Certainly not the luxury she'd grown up with in Chicago. But exactly as she had done while settling into the Wayfarer Island beach house, she seemed to have made herself at home.

Her expensive skincare products were neatly arranged on the bathroom vanity, perfuming the air with their scent. It was an aroma he liked to call "money." Her overnight bag was open and some of its contents were laid out on the bed. A pink T-shirt. Pink sleep shorts. Pink panties.

When she saw the ensemble, she blushed and hastily shoved everything back into her bag. Her cheeks were the exact color as the garments she'd hidden away.

What other parts of her are cotton candy pink? he wondered. Then, *No, goddamnit! You're here as a friend, a compadre, a drinking buddy. Get that through your thick skull!*

Moving to the mini-fridge, she squatted and scanned the little bottles of liquor. "What's your poison?"

When he was quiet for too long because he'd forced his gaze to the ceiling, she turned to frown at him over her shoulder.

"Would I be a total cliché if I admitted it's tequila?" He tried to insert levity into the awkwardness of the situation.

He'd never been in a woman's hotel room without taking her in his arms and kissing her lips until she begged him to kiss other parts of her that were decidedly *lower* than that.

What the fuck am I supposed to do now? Sit on the bed? Grab the desk chair? Keep standing here like a complete and total assclown?

"Why would that be cliché?" She blinked at him.

"Uh." He drew his eyebrows together. "Because I'm second-generation Mexican-American?" He pointed to his face. "If this doesn't give it away, then surely my name does. Spiro Delgado?"

"Oh." She looked embarrassed. "Right." She shook her head. "I'm usually quicker on the uptake than that. Blame it on the letdown of adrenaline."

Grabbing a plastic cup, she upended the mini bottle of Jose Cuervo into it. "Ice?" she asked.

His grandmother had always taught him good tequila was for sipping, straight up, or with a sangrita chaser. But Cuervo wasn't made with one-hundred-percent blue agave, so he told Mia, "Couple of cubes," as he shifted his weight from foot to foot, feeling like the walls were closing in on him.

One drink, he told himself. *You can endure this for one drink.*

After handing him the tequila, she chose the bottle of Bombay Sapphire for herself and emptied it into a cup she'd filled to the brim with ice. Taking a quick sip, she motioned with her hand toward the desk chair. "Sorry. I'm being a terrible hostess. Please, make yourself comfortable."

He settled into the faux leather seat, feeling each one of the hours since he'd risen with the sun that morning. She arranged herself cross-legged on the end of the bed.

He thought they might sit and sip in awkward silence, so

he was relieved when she said, "Your name is Spiro, but everyone calls you Romeo. Why is that?"

"Well…" he began, absently scratching his chin and then smoothing the goatee hairs he'd ruffled. "I tell my mother it's because I'm like the character in the play, handsome"—he wiggled his eyebrows—"intelligent and sensitive."

She smiled slightly over the rim of her drink. "And what's the *real* story behind the nickname?"

He was a little chagrined to admit, "In my younger years, when I was a fresh-faced squid, I was known to be a bit of a…" He searched for the right phrase. *Horn dog?* Nah. Too middle school. *Man whore?* Nope. Too disrespectful. "Ladies' man," he finally finished.

"Why do I get the feeling that's an understatement?" She looked like she was biting the inside of her cheek, and he relaxed back into the chair.

Some light, flirty banter with a woman? Even one he had no intention of bedding? *This* was familiar territory. He could do this with his eyes closed.

"I don't know." He batted his lashes innocently. "I can't imagine."

She chuckled while she took another sip. Then she screwed up her lips. "Spiro. Hmm. I like it. Does anyone still call you that?"

"Sure." He nodded after a quick drink, loving the harsh bite of the tequila on his tongue and longing for a hit of salt and a squirt of lime. "My mother." He knew his face darkened when he added, "And my brother."

She cocked her head, having picked up on the change in him. Talking about Alejandro always made a pit form in his stomach, so he was glad when, instead of asking about his brother, she said, "But no one else?"

He shook his head. "I joined the Navy when I was seventeen years old. I celebrated my thirty-fourth birthday this spring. So I've officially been Romeo as long as I was Spiro."

She held her drink in her lap and regarded him for so long he was hard pressed not to shift beneath her searching gaze.

What does she see when she looks at me?

A delinquent from the bad side of L.A. who'd been forced to leave or else wind up like his older sibling? A foul-mouthed military man? A scruffy salvor with engine grease stuck under his nails?

He was all of those things. And he couldn't imagine any of them were anything she'd be interested in.

"Do you mind if I call you Spiro?"

He wasn't sure what he'd expected her to say, but it certainly wasn't *that*.

He'd left "Spiro" Delgado, that world-class fuckup, behind years ago—*good riddance to bad rubbish*—and he was only reminded of that snot-nosed punk when he called home to talk to his mother. Or phoned up his brother in Pelican Bay.

Yet…his given name on Mia's tongue sounded sweet. Almost like a benediction.

"If you want to," he agreed, and then felt as if someone punched him in the nuts when she smiled at him.

Mia wasn't only careful with her words, choosing them wisely when she chose to use them at all. She was also careful with her expressions. In fact, he'd never met a woman more inscrutable.

He'd seen her lips twitch in amusement. He'd even witnessed a grin or two. But he'd never seen her smile. Not a full blown, ear-to-ear smile.

Now he was glad of that. Her smile was so blindingly radiant he was struck dumb. All he could do was sit and stare.

"So, Spiro,"—this time when she said his name, chills rippled up his spine—"what's the plan for tomorrow?"

"Fuck," he swore. "With all that's happened, I forgot everyone on Wayfarer will be expecting us to fly in with a plane full of metal detectors."

She ran a finger over the rim of her glass, her expression contemplative. "We can still make that happen. I mean, if the way Wolf is hovering over Chrissy is any indication, I suspect he's going to be spending the foreseeable future glued to her side. But I can help you get what's needed."

More time alone with Mia. Exactly what Romeo *didn't* need.

Especially now that I've seen that smile.

That thing was going to haunt his dreams. And undoubtedly make more than a few appearances in his fantasies.

Okay, time to adios yourself.

"Sounds like a plan," he told her. "I'll knock on your door around oh-eight-thirty. That'll give us time to grab breakfast before heading out to finish errands, eh?"

Her face fell when he pushed up from the desk chair, tossing his empty cup into the wastepaper basket. She wasn't ready to be alone, but damned if he trusted himself to stay in this room with her for one more minute.

The urge to sit beside her, to run his finger down her cheek to see if it felt as satiny as it looked, had become overwhelming.

He was nearly to the door when the book on her nightstand caught his attention. "You read P.J. Warren's Night Angels series?"

She glanced at the book, then blinked at him in surprise. "Yes. Don't tell me *you* do?"

He nodded. "My brother got me hooked on them." Prison afforded a guy a lot of time to read, apparently.

"But…" She shook her head. "They're *romance* novels."

"And?"

"They're…well… I thought they were for women."

"That's sexist, don't you think?"

She blushed. "I—I—"

"I'm just giving you shit." He waved off whatever stuttering response she would've made. "I know romance novels are marketed to women, but the truth is, every guy on the planet could benefit from reading them. Some real insider information in there, if you know what I mean." Again, he wiggled his eyebrows.

Her blush deepened when she realized he was talking about the sex scenes. P.J. Warren wrote top-notch, set-your-eyeballs-and-sheets-on-fire sex scenes. Romeo wasn't ashamed to admit he'd been known to reenact a few of them.

"There's so much more to these books than *that*." Her voice had gone back to its quiet timbre. And she seemed to have found something of incredible interest in the bottom of her cup.

"You're right." He took pity on her. "There are angst-ridden vampires, warring werewolf clans, mayhem and mystery and suspense and even some comedic relief thanks to Winifred the Legless Ghost."

"Oh my *god!*" Mia's gaze jumped to his face. "I *love* Winnie! She's my favorite character. In the third book, when she—"

"Stuffed napkins into the toes of everyone's shoes!" he said with her and they dissolved into laughter.

"Everyone in Wisteria Manor thought their feet had grown or their shoes had shrunk!" There it was again, that beaming smile that lit her entire face until it shined like a beacon in the night. "You have no idea how I would *love* to pull that trick at the beach house. Unfortunately, everyone there wears flip-flops or goes barefoot."

"Mia Ennis." He tsked. "You've had us all fooled for a full month. Here we thought you were this shy, retiring sort when secretly you're a prankster."

What had caused her to hide her light under a bushel? To shutter herself away behind a demure demeanor and a silent mouth?

Up until tonight, he'd simply assumed her properness was a result of her upper crust upbringing. Had thought she held herself separate from the rest of the Deep Six crew because they were too proletarian, too loud and foul-mouthed and unrefined.

Maybe he'd been wrong. Maybe there was more to it.

Maybe there was more to *her*.

"Have you read this one?" She held up the hardback with its embossed cover. The title was *In Darkness and Dreams*. The Night Angels books were always titled *In Darkness and*...fill in the blank.

"No." He shook his head. "What number is it?"

"Seven in the series. It might be my favorite yet."

"I stopped at book six. I didn't even know seven was out."

"Oh my god." She scooted over and patted the mattress beside her. "Come lay down. I have to read the first chapter to you. It's *amazing!*"

When he hesitated, her smile faded. "No. I'm sorry. You're right. It's late. We've had a big day and we have another one ahead of us tomorrow."

She actually assumed his hesitation stemmed from him wanting to go to bed? Alone? In the other room?

Fuck, no. His hesitation stemmed from wanting with every fiber of his being to crawl into bed beside her, to feel the mattress move when she did, and to listen to her read in that film noir voice of hers.

But then what? What happened when she *stopped* reading?

He knew what he'd *want* to happen. He'd want to turn to her. To touch all that soft, warm skin and—

"I'd love for you to read to me," he assured her, and then lowered himself to the bed. Reclining back against the pillow, he was careful to keep as much space between them as he could. In fact, if he moved any more toward the edge, he'd fall onto the floor.

"Oooh, goodie!" She clapped her hands and settled her back against the upholstered headboard. "You're in for *such* a treat," she added, opening the book.

He closed his eyes against the sight of her next to him. Tried closing his nose to the smell of the expensive lotion that wafted from her skin. But he refused to close his ears to the sound of her soft voice as she began to read.

It wrapped around him. Wound through him. Filled him up until it seemed as if she inhabited him.

Never had he thought he'd like being possessed. Then again, never had he thought his possessor would be the wildly intoxicating Mia Ennis.

"Lazarus Luxido"—her tone infused the vampire's name with dramatic significance—"had just murdered a man…"

CHAPTER 11

8:48 AM...

Wolf was being charming.
Too charming.
Again.
The jerk.

He had remained in bed with her all night, lending comfort when the pain meds the nurse administered in the wee hours brought on a drug-induced night terror where she was back in the warehouse, hearing that terrible shot, seeing that look of fatalism contort Winston's handsome face right before his eyes rolled back in his head.

Wolf had shaken her awake by crooning, "Shh, darlin'. It's okay. I gotcha. You're okay."

And she *had* been. Because she'd done something she never did. She'd abdicated all her control, and placed all her fear and worry onto his broad shoulder with the thought, *Wolf's here. I'm safe. I don't have to worry.*

And then she'd slept. Slept like the dead. Slept like she hadn't slept since she was a little girl and knew nothing of the weight of the world.

When she finally opened her eyes hours later, it'd been to see him standing at the window, the rising sun silhouetting his manly form.

The rays of light had made love to his tall, lean body. Streaming past his bold profile. Emphasizing his trim waist. Curling around the plump, hard rise of his ass in those jeans that should definitely come with a warning label.

She'd felt her heart skip a beat—the organ was nothing if not totally cliché. And then he'd gone and made everything so much worse by turning to smile at her. That sweet, hot smile that transformed his normally fierce-looking visage into something almost boyish.

"You're up early," she'd complained, picking at a piece of lint on the blue hospital blanket and castigating herself for having been so fragile the night before. For *needing* him so much.

"I don't sleep much," had been his reply as he walked to her bedside. His onyx eyes had swept her from head to toe, examining, scrutinizing every inch until she thought she could *feel* them moving over her like a gentle, searching touch.

She'd loved it and hated it at the same time.

She blamed that for her acerbic reply, "They say sharks never do."

One sleek brow had winged up his forehead, making the scar near his temple pucker. "Oh, so now I'm a shark?"

"If the teeth fit."

Instead of getting offended, he'd playfully snarled at her, displaying his straight, white teeth to full effect.

See? Charming. *The jerk.*

Then, when the morning shift nurse had come in to

check Chrissy's vitals, Chrissy had asked the woman when she would be released. All she'd wanted then and now was her own bed and a bath—but in reverse order.

The nurse had hemmed and hawed, and Chrissy had been glad the blood pressure cuff had been taken off. She was sure her levels had spiked through the roof.

Wolf had clearly read the situation and stepped in. "Have a heart," he'd cajoled the nurse. Was it Chrissy's imagination or had he thickened his aw-shucks accent? "There's nothin' more to be done for her here. Send her on home so she can eat ice cream and watch Netflix. Isn't that what *you'd* want after gettin' shot?"

The nurse had preened at Wolf—and it *hadn't* been Chrissy's imagination when she saw the woman squeeze her arms together to deepen her cleavage. "Well, since you asked so nicely, I'll see what I can do."

Once the nurse had left, Wolf had swung back to Chrissy with a self-satisfied grin. "We'll have you out of here in no time."

And he had. Thirty minutes later, she'd been signing her release papers and changing into the scrubs the nurse had procured for her since the ER docs who'd helped her out of her wet, bloody clothes the night before had simply stuffed the items into a plastic bag, rendering them still wet and still bloody this morning.

Also, she'd finally located her phone! Wolf had placed it in the bag with her clothes. Alas, it hadn't survived the night completely intact. The fall from the dock had broken her Otter case and allowed water to seep in.

After she'd emerged from the bathroom in her new outfit, her arm supported by the sling, Wolf had thanked the nurse and smiled that schoolboy smile until the poor woman blushed so hard Chrissy thought it was a wonder her cheeks didn't ignite.

See? Charming! *The jerk!*

And *now* he'd gone and said all the right things to Curtis and Maryanne Turner. Talking about how brave Winston had been and assuring them he'd seen softer men than Winston suffer harder wounds and still pull through.

He'd been *so* charming, in fact, Maryanne pulled Chrissy aside and whispered into her ear, "You know I always hoped you and Winston would get together, but now I understand why that'll never happen."

"Maryanne," Chrissy hissed, "you know as well as I do Winston and I are way better at being friends than we are anything else. *That's* why we'll never get together. It doesn't have anything to do with Wolf."

Maryanne was one of those women who got better looking with age. Her large nose and high cheekbones— features that'd made her look harsh in her younger years— now made her look chic and sophisticated. Which is why she could pull off the imperious, slightly haughty look she gave Chrissy when she shrugged. "If you insist."

Chrissy opened her mouth to do exactly that, but Maryanne moved away from her to return to Winston's bedside.

Winston.

Chrissy hated seeing him like this.

He was so pale he nearly matched the hospital sheets. His eye sockets were bruised and sunken into his head. A respirator kept him breathing, and a heart monitor beeped. Its steady rhythm was a small comfort in the sudden silence of the room.

"I'll come back this evening to check on him." Chrissy moved next to Maryanne. She placed her hand on top of Winston's, glad to find it warm with life.

Come on, Winston. You can't have been born so stubborn for no reason. Prove these damn doctors wrong.

"No." Maryanne shook her head. There was fear in her eyes, but also determination. "You need to rest and recover. We'll call or text you as soon as they take him into surgery."

Chrissy noticed Maryanne didn't say *if* they took him into surgery.

Her best friend and business partner had inherited his doggedness from this here iron lady. *And thank heaven for that.*

Chrissy pointed to the plastic bag she'd placed on the floor by the door. "My phone's waterlogged. It's only kinda, sorta, maybe working."

"We'll put it in rice," Wolf spoke up from the other side of the bed where he stood next to Curtis. "If that doesn't fix it up, I'll run out and buy you a new one."

"Handsome *and* handy." Maryanne nudged Chrissy with her elbow. "My, my."

When Chrissy scowled at her, Maryanne bobbed her eyebrows.

Wolf shook Curtis's hand, and Chrissy took the opportunity of his distraction to whisper harshly to Winston's mother, "I would like to introduce you to an acquaintance of mine. His name is subtlety."

"Pfft." Maryanne scoffed. "Innuendo and nuance don't work on you. You're the type who needs a ball-peen hammer between the eyes." Chrissy bristled, then all the fight went out of her when Maryanne added, "Which is one of the many reasons I love you, kiddo."

Chrissy's eyes welled. She felt so...*tired.*

"Oh, honey, come here." Maryanne pulled Chrissy into her embrace and Chrissy shook with the effort not to dissolve.

This woman's only child is lying in a bed, hooked up to machines and fighting for his life. I should be comforting her*, not the other way around.*

"I'm so sorry, Maryanne." She stepped from Winston's mother's embrace. "Maybe if I'd been able to—"

"You stop that right this minute, young lady." Maryanne's eyebrows arrowed over her nose. "I know exactly what happened last night. That rumpled-looking detective told us. Winston would be dead if you hadn't had the wherewithal to run and get help."

Chrissy nodded although she was still struggling with all the what-ifs. What if she'd run faster? What if she'd taken a different route? What if she'd zigged instead of zagged? Could she have avoided getting shot and gotten to Wolf even quicker? When it came to blood loss, every second counted.

"Come on, darlin'." Wolf came around Winston's bed to gently touch her elbow. "Let's get you home so you can start healin'."

Maryanne's eyes widened and she mouthed the word *darlin'*. In response, Chrissy rolled her eyes. But then she pulled Winston's mother in for one more hug, loving the familiar smell of *Sunflowers* by Elizabeth Arden.

Maryanne had never quite moved beyond the '90's.

After bussing Curtis's cheek, Chrissy allowed Wolf to escort her into the hall where the two policemen assigned to stand watch over her and Winston conversed. One of them—Rick Ryan, the officer who'd taken over Chrissy's security from Denny Parsons—trailed along behind them as she and Wolf made their way through the hospital.

Having a fully uniformed, fully armed shadow was unsettling to say the least. But what bothered her even more were the female heads that turned in Wolf's direction.

More than once she caught herself glaring at the ogling women—although, it seemed Wolf was oblivious. The fourth time she tried to slice a fellow member of the sisterhood open with nothing more than her switchblade eyes, her mind skidded to a stop.

What the hell are you doing?

She tried blaming her jealousy on physical pain and the mental anguish of having just left her best friend in the ICU fighting against the odds. But those explanations rang false.

Worse, they sounded like rationalizations.

If there was one thing she hated more than a milksop woman who unloaded all her troubles onto the big, strong man in her life, it was someone who refused to face the music when it came to their own thoughts and feelings and rationales.

But call me Queen of the Hypocrites, 'cause I'm too tired to go there.

Instead, she kept her eyes straight ahead for the remainder of the walk.

Once they pushed through the automatic front doors, she pulled the salty sea air into her lungs. The familiar scents of tropical flowers and hot asphalt tunneled up her nose. After the antiseptic air inside the hospital, she welcomed the smells.

I'm alive, she told herself. *Winston is alive. For now that has to be enough.*

"There was supposed to be a taxi waitin'." Wolf cut into her thoughts. "I used the phone at the nurse's station to call for one before we went to visit Winston."

Well, of course he had. The man thought of everything. She should probably be annoyed by that. But right then, the only thing she felt was grateful.

"It's nice having someone to help you shoulder the burdens of life." Her mother's words rang inside her head. This had been Josephine's answer to, *"Why do you keep letting yourself fall in love when it never works out?"*

Chrissy had asked the question after her mother's fourth divorce was finalized, and at the time her mother's response had only confirmed Chrissy's stance she would *never* stumble into the trap of depending on someone other than herself.

Yet here she was. Relying on Wolf.

"Can we catch a ride with you?" Wolf asked Officer Ryan.

The policeman made a face. "I wish. But I drove my personal vehicle for this detail." The officer hitched his chin toward the parking lot and the late-model Toyota 4Runner with two kayaks attached to the rack on the roof. "It's policy not to drive with civilians while we're on the clock. You know, liability issues if I were to get in a wreck and one of you got hurt or—"

Wolf waved him off. "No need to explain. Spent fourteen years in the Navy. I know all about the protocols put in place to cover everyone's asses." He turned to Chrissy. "That phone of yours kinda, maybe, sorta workin' right now?"

Digging into the plastic bag, she pulled out her iPhone. Thumbing it on, she discovered that, miracle of miracles, the screen flashed. But it was only a flash. The low-battery icon blinked before the device went dark.

"Sorry." She grimaced. "It needs juice."

"No worries. I'll run inside and ask the admissions desk to make a call to the cab company. You goin' to be okay out here?"

She smiled wanly. "I have a flesh wound, Wolf, not a mortal injury. I'm sure I'll be fine standing on the sidewalk. Besides"—she pointed to Officer Ryan, whose hand rested on the butt of his weapon—"I have Officer Ryan to watch over me."

Wolf let his gaze run over her, as if he needed to reassure himself. Then, he nodded and turned back into the hospital.

She gave herself permission to watch him go—*and yes, I*

realize I'm doing exactly *what I tried to eye-murder other women for.* She'd always admired the way Wolf moved. His back was straight. His shoulders were back. His head was held high.

Military bearing, she decided. *No wasted movements. Just confidence and efficiency in every step.*

When the automatic doors closed behind him, she headed out from under the shade of the awning.

"Don't go too far," Officer Ryan warned.

"Just going to soak up some sun," she assured him.

"Really?" He wiped a drop of sweat glistening on his temple. "It's hotter than Satan's ball sac today."

As soon as he realized what he'd said, he grimaced. When he opened his mouth, Chrissy stopped him with a raised hand. "Please, if you're going to be my protection for the next little while, you need to understand that I'm on a first-name basis with the full gamut of curse words. You can't offend me unless you start badmouthing conch fritters."

Officer Ryan looked genuinely confused. "Who'd badmouth those? They're delicious."

"I work with tourists," she told him. "You'd be surprised what passes for *good food*"—she made air quotes—"in other parts of the country. Ever heard of mayonnaise on fries? Kombucha? Turkey bacon?" She shuddered again for effect.

"No accounting for taste, I guess," Officer Ryan mused at the same time his cell phone rang. Pulling it from his pocket, he glanced at the screen. "My wife," he said by way of explanation. "I wouldn't take the call while I'm on duty, but Dustin, our oldest, tried out for the baseball team today and—"

"Say no more," Chrissy interrupted him.

He nodded gratefully before holding his phone to his face. Using his free hand, he plugged his opposite ear against the noisy traffic on the nearby road.

In that moment, she was envious of Officer Ryan. Of his family. Of the nervous excitement she heard in his voice when he said into the phone, "Tell me he made it."

Will that ever be me?

She was beginning to have her doubts.

Rummaging through her plastic bag, she searched for the bottle of pain pills the nurse had given her.

She didn't normally resort to prescription medication. On those rare occasions she suffered a headache, she tended to fight it off with two full glasses of water followed by a catnap. Even the time she was caught in a bad tide and slammed up against a reef, getting coral lodged in her thigh, she'd only cut the pain with some topical analgesic and a big slug of rum before going in with tweezers to pull out the foreign matter.

But according to Nurse McCleavage, Chrissy was, *"Better off staying on top of the pain, or believe me, that pain will get on top of you."*

Placing a pill on the back of her tongue, she turned her face into golden light shining from above and swallowed it down.

Her mother used to throw back the curtains on their little conch house after a rainy day. *"Sunshine is Mother Nature's disinfectant. Let's open all the windows and let that healing light in,"* Josephine would say.

Chrissy wasn't sure there was any science to back her mother's notion, but she closed her eyes all the same, letting the warmth of the sun seep past her skin to sink into her bones.

Which is why she didn't see the beat-up sedan barreling toward her.

CHAPTER 12

9:18 AM...

What kind of person doesn't own a cell phone?" The guy at the admissions desk eyed Wolf suspiciously after he hung up with the cab company.

"The kind who lives on a private island with no cell service," Wolf answered absently, turning toward the hospital's front doors. Through the glass, he could see Chrissy standing in the sun. The light glinted off her hair, making it shine gold like the Cherokee Nation flag that flew from his grandmother's front porch.

The scrubs the nurse had given her were a size too small. And damn, but he couldn't stop himself from scanning the sweet curves neither the shirt nor the pants could fully contain. As bodacious as Chrissy's body was, however, it was her pretty profile that caught and held his gaze.

Her head was back, her eyes were closed, and he watched as peace stole over her features. Watched as trauma was replaced by tranquility, as pain was replaced by placidity.

The gentle ocean breeze that was a constant companion in the Keys ruffled the ends of her messy ponytail. The sun kissed her cheeks. When she dragged in a deep breath, he wondered if she could smell the distant saltiness of the water.

Christina of the Sea.

His island girl.

Well, not mine, he silently admitted. Then he added, *not yet, anyway.*

Like they always seemed to do, his feet carried him toward her. He'd stepped through the automatic doors when the sound of traffic assaulted his ears. Slightly below the *buzz* and *whir* of cars passing by on the road was the unmistakable sound of a poorly tuned engine that back-fired as it revved up.

The next five seconds seemed to take five hours. Everything happened in slow motion.

A glance to his left showed a rusty Toyota Celica circa nineteen-ninety-should-be-in-a-junkyard-somewhere speeding through the parking lot, swerving side-to-side like it was being driven by a three-year-old. Or the kind of drunk to open up the bar at eight AM, close it down at two AM, and then spend the intervening hours sleeping it off on a park bench.

At first he thought the sedan would plow into the row of parked cars, and he waited for the screech of metal and the tinkle of breaking glass. But the driver straightened out and the sedan's bent and broken grill pointed right at Chrissy.

Even though Officer Ryan was closer to her by a good eight feet, the policeman talked on his cell phone and plugged his free ear with a thick finger, making him oblivious to the oncoming catastrophe.

"Chrissy!" Both syllables exploded out of Wolf's throat like cannon blasts.

He didn't feel the pavement pounding beneath his flip-flops. Didn't feel the hot air filling his lungs. Didn't even notice the scrape of the bay cedar shrub as it grazed the denim covering his back shin when he hurdled over it. All he knew was that the only woman he had ever loved was inches away from becoming a hood ornament, and—

Damn, this is gonna hurt, he thought as she turned to him a split second before he caught her in his arms. Her eyes were wide with shock. Her sweet mouth was open around a startled scream. But she didn't have time to let loose with it. The Toyota was upon them and he jumped into the air, taking her with him.

Twisting his body so it was his back that slid across the hot metal hood of the speeding car, he did his best to protect her injured shoulder. And then they were airborne again, the unyielding pavement coming up to meet them way, *way* too quickly.

He heard himself grunt when he hit the ground, Chrissy's weight driving him into the surface. His lungs felt like they'd been flattened by a mallet, and he would have liked nothing better than to lie there and catch his breath, take stock of his body *and* Christina's, but the Celica was making for the parking lot exit and—

"Get—" he wheezed, flinging his arm toward the fishtailing sedan when he saw the uniformed policeman sprinting in their direction. "The plate!" he finally managed.

"No need." Ryan shook his head, squatting next to them. "I know exactly who that was." He activated the radio clipped to his bulletproof vest. "Dispatch, this is Officer Ryan over at Lower Keys Medical Center. Be advised, Cliff Barnes is behind the wheel of his Toyota and headed south on Kennedy Drive. Get officers to take him off the road. He nearly ran over a couple of folks, and Lord knows he might not miss next time."

"Roger that." A crackling voice sounded from the officer's radio. "Dispatching units now."

Apparently, when it came to drunken bumper cars, this Cliff character was a repeat offender. *Just my luck*, Wolf thought, patting Chrissy's uninjured shoulder and taking comfort in the sound of her ribald cursing.

He lifted his chin to check on her and found her face-first in his crotch. He'd managed to protect her from the impact, but he'd skidded afterward.

"You okay, darlin'?" His vision had returned to normal and he could clearly see the look on her face was equal parts *did that truly just happen?* and *holy shit!*

She made an unequivocal sound at the back of her throat that could've passed for either a *yes* or a *no*. Tentatively, she felt of the bandage over her shoulder and then nodded.

"I'm so sorry, Miss Szarek." Officer Ryan was still squatted next to them. "I was on the phone and didn't hear—"

"It's okay." Chrissy cut him off. "Wolf was Johnny-on-the-spot." She pushed up on her good elbow and then stared down at his crotch.

Now that the danger had passed, the devil that lived in Wolf had him saying before he could think better of it, "You don't have to do that, darlin'. A simple *thanks for keepin' me from gettin' my ass run over* will do."

Her lips flattened into a straight line. "Did you binge eat asshole flakes this morning?"

His lungs hadn't fully recovered, so the laugh that burst out of him sounded wheezy.

"I swear, right when I'm starting to like you," she added, "you go and prove you're a...a..."

He used her fumbling to help her stand, taking quick stock of his injures. A cherry on his elbow that would burn like a bitch when he washed it, and maybe a bruised tailbone.

Not too shabby. Considering.

"A what?" he prompted when they were both back on their feet.

"A *guy*," she finished with a huff.

Wolf blinked at Officer Ryan, feigning bewilderment. "She says that like it's a bad thing."

The policeman shrugged. "My wife says the same thing. No matter how many times I've tried to explain she shouldn't judge me based on something I can't do a thing about, she judges me all the same."

Wolf slapped a commiserating hand on Officer Ryan's shoulder. "Damned by our chromosomes."

"Oh, spare me from fragile male egos." Chrissy bent to retrieve the plastic bag that held her belongings. When she straightened, she swayed.

"Whoa." Wolf grabbed her elbow to steady her. "You okay?"

"I took one of the pain pills." She wrinkled her nose. "I'm feeling a little dizzy. Just let me..." She didn't finish her sentence. Instead, she threaded her arm through his, leaning heavily against him.

He was in the process of trying to wipe the goofy smile from his face when the police officer's radio chirped.

"Officer Ryan," that crackling voice sounded through the speaker, "I have an update on Cliff Barnes. His Toyota was found in a ditch three miles from the hospital, but he's fled the scene. We have units searching for him now."

"Roger that." The policeman shook his head and said to Wolf and Chrissy, "If Cliff isn't bellied up to the bar somewhere, he's here at the E.R. trying to score pain meds."

Chrissy grimaced. "I suppose I should feel sorry for him, but I can't help hoping he gets put away for a nice long stretch considering he's the *second* man who's tried to make me take a dirt nap in less than twenty-four hours.

Heaven help me if what they say is true and the third time's the charm."

The thought was enough to have Wolf's skin going clammy. In response, he wanted to hulk over Chrissy, just snarl and snap at anyone or anything that got too close.

But he satisfied himself with the hand she wrapped around his bicep and decided the occasion—and Chrissy—could both do with a little humor. "Oh, I don't think you have to worry about that none, darlin'. You're just about ornery enough to be immortal."

"Me?" She hooked a thumb toward her chest and then pointed at the scar across his temple. "You're one to talk."

"That's my point." He grinned. "Takes one to know one."

She opened her mouth to respond, but closed it when a taxi pulled up beside them. "Oh, thank goodness." Her uninjured shoulder drooped in relief. "I just want to crash face-first into my own bed."

Wolf was tempted to ask if she wanted company, but this time he managed to silence his inner devil before the bastard spoke for him. "Your wish is my command," was all he said as he swept open the taxi's back door.

Once she was secure in the backseat, he turned to their police escort and voiced aloud the thought that'd been banging around inside his head for the last five minutes. "When I saw that sedan headin' for her, I thought for sure those bastards from the warehouse were comin' to finish what they started."

"Nah." Officer Ryan gave a jerk of his chin. "This was nothin' more than a case of wrong place, wrong time."

"Funny. That's what Detective Dixon told Chrissy last night about her run-in with the shooter."

"Woman must've walked under a ladder, crossed paths with a black cat, or broken a mirror is all I can say." The policeman doffed his hat to run a forearm over his sweaty brow.

Wolf chalked up the niggle of apprehension that scratched at the back of his brain to being overly protective—and maybe overly paranoid—when it came to one Christina Rachel Szarek.

"See you at Miss Szarek's house," Officer Ryan said before heading toward his vehicle.

Right as Wolf was sliding into the taxi, the wind picked up. It washed over his face and sent fingers through his hair, reminding him of the woman waiting inside the car.

Like the west wind, she was warm and sweet and blustery.

And somehow I have to find a way to make her fall in love with me.

CHAPTER 13

9:29 AM...

Wolf had closed the car door behind him when he heard the taxi driver say, "Chrissy Szarek, is that you?"

Chrissy was adjusting her sling, but at the sound of her name, she glanced up. The smile on her face when she met the driver's eyes in the rearview mirror was absolutely radiant. Wolf wasn't sure he'd ever heard her voice sound quite so chipper as when she chirped, "Billy Morris! What are you doing back in town? Last I heard, you were up in North Carolina singing for your supper!"

What the hell happened to all that pain med lethargy? He scanned the cabby's handsome face, noting the heavily lashed eyes and the deep look of appreciation in them when the man stared back at Chrissy.

Ah, he thought. *It jumped right out the window, thanks to Mr. Tall, Dark, and Taxi Driver.*

130

Just that easily, that damned green-eyed monster hopped atop his shoulder.

"Still am," Billy of the swoony blue eyes and movie star grin replied. "I'm here on vacation."

"Vacation?" Chrissy looked around the cab.

Billy chuckled. It was a nice sound. A deep, rumbling sound. The kind of sound that Wolf knew women went goo-goo-gah-gah over. *Grrrr.* "My dad was shorthanded drivers today. I'm just filling in."

"You always were the sweetest guy in our class." Chrissy's tone was low and...*flirty?*

The green-eyed monster on Wolf's shoulder gained ten pounds and started poking him in the ear with a razor-sharp fingernail.

Luckily, before Wolf could prove himself a prick of epic proportions by giving into the beast's provocations and saying something like *"Stick a sock in it, cabby, and put the pedal to the metal,"* Chrissy turned to him.

"Wolf, this is Billy Morris," she said. "We went to school together. But he's since moved to Asheville where he's a bit of a local legend when it comes to what people from your neck of the woods would call pickin' and grinnin'."

Speaking of grinning, Billy had turned in the driver's seat to smile his toothy smile back at Chrissy.

Wolf bared his teeth in response and watched the light in Billy's eyes dim.

Chrissy was oblivious and continued with, "Billy, this is Wolf Roanhorse. He's living out on Wayfarer Island and excavating the *Santa Cristina.* He's my...friend."

The hesitation had been slight. Miniscule even. But Wolf heard it.

Was he an idiot to feel a flicker of hope? Was her hesitation because, when it came to the two of them, the word was distasteful to her too?

He stared hard at her. Hard enough that a line appeared between her eyebrows. "What?" she asked. "Do I have gravel stuck to my forehead or something?"

She reached up to touch her face and winced when her fingers met the small scrape on her cheek. Oh, what he wouldn't give to cover it with his lips. To kiss the hurt away.

Instead, he shook his head. "No. You're as beautiful as ever."

She rolled her eyes. "Then why are you looking at me like that? Didn't you hear me make introductions?"

For her benefit, he managed to grind out, "Nice to meet you, Billy."

"Likewise." The cabby touched a finger to the brim of his imaginary baseball cap. "You're part of the crew excavating the *Santa Cristina*, huh? I didn't think she'd ever be found. You must be so excited."

"Burstin' with it," Wolf deadpanned.

Billy cocked his head and made a face of commiseration. "Yeah. I heard you guys haven't found the mother lode yet."

Was it Wolf's imagination, or was there a hint of smug satisfaction in Billy's tone? Before he could respond, Billy's gaze snapped back to Chrissy. Like the bastard couldn't help himself. Like Chrissy was a honey pot and ol' Billy boy was a hungry bear fresh out of hibernation.

Wolf was overcome with the unmistakable urge to poke the man's eyes out of his head with a pointy stick. He might have too, had there been any pointy sticks handy.

"News of what happened last night is all over the island," Billy said to Christy. "I'm so glad to see you're okay." He hesitated a bit, his smile fading completely before he added, "Winston?"

Chrissy shook her head and Wolf would swear he could feel the tension enter her body. She'd been relaxed against the cushioned seat, but now she sat as straight as a backwoods preacher. Even her fingers were rigid where they rested against her cotton-clad thigh.

Just that easily, his jealousy disappeared, replaced by concern. Before he knew what he was doing, he took her hand, gently massaging the stiffness from her fingers.

Part of him expected her to jerk away. It was a rare occasion when she let down her defenses enough to accept his comfort.

Thankfully, this was one of those times.

She gave him a grateful little smile before telling Billy, "He's still in a coma. But he's a fighter."

"One of the toughest sonsofbitches I ever met," Billy agreed. "I still remember the time in ninth grade when he took a fastball to the face. He grabbed his two front teeth off the ground, turned to Coach Taylor and said, *'Coach, I think I need to have my mom take me to see a dentist.'*" Billy shook his head and chuckled. "It was the damndest thing."

"He's going to make it." Chrissy's voice was soft, as if she tried to convince herself as much as she tried to convince Billy.

Wolf squeezed her fingers and felt ridiculously happy when she returned the gesture.

Billy's eyes pinged down to their joined hands, and he tried to play off his obvious disappointment by being the professional. Turning in his seat, he put the car in gear. "Where to?"

"You want to stop anywhere before headin' to your place?" Wolf asked Chrissy.

What little energy she'd summoned up to greet Billy had seeped out of her at mention of Winston. She was back to looking wan and exhausted.

"No." She shook her head. "As Dorothy said, there's no place like home."

"Hey!" He faked affront. "I'm not allowed quotes, but *you* are?"

"Movie quotes don't count. Besides, all's fair in love and war." She grinned impishly, and then froze, her smile sliding off her face when realized what she'd said.

You can bet your bottom dollar Wolf realized it too. In fact, the moment the word *love* left her lips, his heart tried to leap from his chest like his mother's old mule used to leap out of its pen to eat the neighbor's green grass.

"Since we've already established we're not enemies, what do you reckon that leaves?" He kept his voice low.

She blushed. "It's a figure of speech, Wolf." Before he could answer, she turned back to Billy. "I'm headed home," she told him, then blushed harder when Billy answered, "I gathered that. But unless you still live in the same place you grew up, I don't know where that is."

Wolf rattled off Chrissy's address, and lifted an eyebrow when she turned to blink at him in surprise.

"What?" he asked, all innocent-like. "Just 'cause you've never invited me over doesn't mean I don't know where you live."

He'd memorized her address months ago. You know, just in case.

"Be fanatically positive and militantly optimistic," Wolf's favorite travel writer, Rick Steves had written. Words of wisdom he tried to live by.

Billy drove the cab from the parking lot, and they'd made it about a mile down the road before he caught Chrissy's gaze in the rearview mirror again. "Last time I was back here you were dating that guy who'd moved down from Fort Lauderdale to run a bar on the north end of Duval. You two seemed so smitten." Billy's eyes pinged to

Wolf before returning to Chrissy. Was Billy boy trying to rub Wolf's nose in Chrissy's past romances? Was Wolf's jealous streak that obvious? Probably. *Double grrr.* "What happened?" Billy asked.

"We wanted different things." Chrissy lifted her uninjured shoulder. "I wanted to settle down and start building a life, and he wanted to text pictures of his dick to the woman who supplied his beer kegs."

"Yeesh." Billy grimaced. "Sounds like an ugly scene."

"It's branded into my brain like a bad tattoo," Chrissy nodded grimly. Then a smirk hitched up one corner of her mouth. "Joke's on him, though. She ended up ditching his ass for a professional sport fisherman, but not before she totaled his Jeep on the overseas highway."

Billy laughed. "I guess it's true what they say. Karma's a bitch."

"That's why I like her so much." Chrissy bobbed her eyebrows.

For a while after that, everyone in the cab was quiet. Billy because he'd run out of things to chat about or annoy Wolf with. Chrissy because her usual exuberance was tempered by worry for Winston, the pull of the pain medication, and, you know, the small inconvenience of sporting a fresh bullet wound. And Wolf because he kept turning Chrissy's words over in his mind.

I wanted to settle down and start building a life.

He'd always assumed she was happy being foot loose and fancy free. So damned independent the thought of a white dress and a gold ring might make her break out in hives.

He'd been fully prepared to not only have to coax her into falling in love with him, but also cajole her into marrying him. Because he wanted it all. The wedding, the honeymoon, the house, the kids. But now…

Well, now maybe the only thing I'll have to work on is the "fallin' in love with me" part. Which might be easier said than done since they were still haunted by the specter of That Night.

He needed to fix that. Problem being, he wasn't sure where to start since she shut him down every time he tried to talk about it.

"I, uh, didn't get a chance to thank you, Wolf." Chrissy's words broke into his thoughts.

"For what?"

She shook her head in disbelief. "Oh, you know. For getting the paramedics to Winston in time. For staying with me last night. For taking care of things this morning. For keeping me from getting my ass ran over, as you so eloquently put it. I saw you barreling toward me and thought, 'Look at him go. He's on X Games mode.' Too much TikTok in my spare time, obviously."

"Huh?" He tilted his head, genuinely perplexed.

"It's a social media app with funny videos and—" She cut herself off. "Never mind. My point is, I was this close"—she dropped his hand so she could hold her finger and thumb a half inch apart—"to becoming road k—"

He stopped her before she could voice aloud the end of that sentence and make him sick to his stomach. "Close only counts in horseshoes and hand grenades, darlin'."

"Mmm," she hummed noncommittally, shivering despite the warmth inside the cab.

He put an arm around her shoulders, pulling her close while being careful of her injury. Once again, he was ready for her to pull away. Once again, he released a sigh of pleasure when she didn't.

In fact, far from pulling away, she snuggled into his side, placing her head on his shoulder. It felt so good. So right.

A smart man would've kept his trap shut and enjoyed the moment.

Wolf was not a smart man.

"Were you serious when you said you wanted to settle down and start buildin' a life?"

She frowned up at him. Her mouth was close enough to kiss. All it'd take was for him to tilt down his chin a mere two inches.

But if he filled her mouth with his tongue, she wouldn't be able to answer him. And he was keenly interested in her answer.

"Sure." There was confusion in her cornflower eyes. "What? You thought my plan was to wrinkle like a raisin in the sun and then die a spinster?"

"No." He shook his head. Then he reconsidered. "Sometimes you give off a vibe that says you're hell bent on goin' it alone."

She tucked down her chin. He didn't know if he was disappointed or relieved her lips were no longer within easy reach. "Like most men, you confuse a woman's self-sufficiency for a desire to live her life solo. That's never been my intention."

"So what's your intention?"

"Ever since I was little girl, I've dreamed of having a big family." She yawned so wide, her jaw cracked. "Four kids." Her voice sounded sleepy as she continued. When he glanced down, he found her eyes were closed, the pain meds doing their best to pull her under. "Enough to fill a house with madness and mayhem, all commotion and clamor. I hated being an only child. It was so…" For a moment, he thought she was searching for the right word. Then he realized she was falling asleep when she softly finished with, "quiet."

The physical and emotional trauma she'd been through partnered with the warm air and the lulling hum of the engine to have a soft snore issuing from the back of her throat.

Four kids. The perfect number in his opinion since it was the exact amount his parents had had. And it happened to be the *exact* amount he'd always envisioned having himself.

Recognizing he'd fallen in love with Chrissy had been epic. *Huge.* But not as big as knowing when it came to family and a future, they shared a common dream.

This is good. He felt something warm unfurl in his chest. It spread to his limbs. *This is right.*

Of course, the trick would be convincing *her* of that.

Well if there's one thing my elisi *always says about me, it's once I set my mind to somethin', I'm like a clock that never stops tickin'.*

When he glanced up, he caught Billy watching him in the rearview mirror. "She's the absolute best, in case you didn't already know that." The cab driver kept his voice low so as not to wake Chrissy. "Don't go texting pictures of your dick to someone else."

"Not a chance," Wolf vowed solemnly.

CHAPTER 14

9:52 AM...

Chrissy dreamed she was held tight against a warm, solid chest. She dreamed she was being carried.

Correction. She wasn't dreaming. She *was* held tight against a warm, solid chest. And she *was* being carried.

By Wolf.

Up the front porch steps of her little conch house with its yellow siding and teal hurricane shutters. She wasn't the sort to fall asleep in the middle of a conversation. And she *certainly* wasn't such a sound sleeper she wouldn't wake up when someone picked her up out of a cab.

But pain meds are miracle drugs, she thought groggily, peering over Wolf's shoulder to see Billy pulling away from the curb with a smile and a wave. Then her wherewithal returned. Quick on its heels were her pride and self-sufficiency. Her next thought was, *What kind of grown-ass woman needs to be carried into her own house?*

The kind who got shot? a small voice at the back of her head answered.

She ignored it and wiggled in Wolf's arms.

"Be still, woman," he commanded in a tone that made her realize his enemies must've shit bricks when they faced him on the battlefield. "Or I'll drop you."

"That's the point." She worried the next sound she heard might be his breaking back. She was tall for a woman, and she liked chicken wings dipped in ranch dressing as much as the next gal. So even though Wolf was big and powerful, and even though he managed to make her feel dainty in his arms, she wasn't. "I can walk on my own. Put me down," she insisted.

"When I'm good and ready." He smiled at her. It wasn't even a full smile, but her heart double-timed its rhythm all the same.

Ugh. So cliché!

Miracle of miracles, he made it across her front porch without crushing his vertebral column. Then, as if she weighed no more than a sea star, he set her on her feet in front of her door.

She wanted to glower at him for being autocratic. She'd perfected glowering at him, if she did say so herself. But she couldn't muster any antipathy at the moment because… well…he'd been so wonderful the past few hours.

On second thought, he was *always* wonderful. Except for that night at Schooner Wharf Bar. That was the one and only time he'd been a complete and total asshat. Emphasis on the *ass*.

"What happened with Frank?" Chrissy remembered asking her mother one bright Sunday morning over Bloody Marys at Blue Heaven, their favorite brunch spot not only because it served up good food and good booze, but also because its outdoor dining area was home to a good portion of the island's wild chicken population.

It was great fun indulging in warm pancakes dripping in butter and syrup while watching their colorful feathered friends strut around the tables, looking for dropped morsels.

"I cut him loose when I caught him hitting on another woman," Josephine had replied with a long-suffering sigh. *"It was just the once. But if life has taught me two things, it's that once is enough, and once is never once."*

Chrissy remembered that day all too well. It'd been the last time they'd been blissfully unaware of her mother's illness. The next morning, her mother's doctor had informed Josephine she had stage four colon cancer.

Once is enough, and once is never once. Chrissy silently repeated her mother's words lest, when it came to Wolf, the last dozen hours made her forget her mother's hard-learned lessons.

"Chrissy?" he asked.

"Mmm?" She blinked at him.

"Key?"

"Oh! Right." She dug into the plastic bag and found her jeans. The sling made it a struggle to pull her keys from the pocket of the wet denim.

"Here." He took the bag from her, his fingers briefly brushing against hers. That's all it took to make her nipples furl.

Since her bra was wet and in the bag with the rest of her clothes, she was free boobing it, and the cotton scrubs weren't very thick. Any other time, she would've crossed her arms to hide her body's reaction, but the sling made that impossible too.

For a second, she thought Wolf noticed her rebellious yabos. A muscle in the side of his jaw ticked. Then, he fished out her house keys without saying anything. And out of the five keys on the ring, he somehow chose the correct one and had her front door open in a jiff.

I wonder if he's this proficient in the bedroom? The thought ran through her head before she could stop it.

Probably, that traitorous little voice answered.

Once is enough, and once is never once! she shouted to drown out any other perfidious thoughts or treasonous voices.

"You know," he said as she pulled her keys from the lock and stepped inside. "If I had a time machine, I'd go back to that night at Schooner Wharf Bar."

That Night...

Not for the first time, she got the eerie feeling Wolf could read her mind. After placing her keys on the occasional table by the front door, she slowly turned to him.

Sunlight streamed in through the open door, casting him in silhouette. But his expression snapped into view when he closed the door behind him. The black of his eyes always seemed impenetrable, filled with mysteries. But right then they appeared fathomless, deeper than the ocean.

She preferred to pretend that night hadn't happened. It was too humiliating to think about much less *talk* about. So she was surprised to hear herself ask, "If you could go back, what would you do differently?"

"Everything."

It was one word. But it was spoken with such vehemence the air between them grew thick and seemed to vibrate with an echo of the syllables.

Or maybe I'm imagining things. Maybe the change in atmosphere is due to the weather.

Another storm was gathering in the west. She'd noticed the buildup of cumulous clouds while standing in the hospital's parking lot.

"The thing is..." He gestured for her to join him on the sofa. And even though her bed and a bath were calling, she found herself sinking into the soft cushions. He positioned himself beside her.

Right beside her.

His jean-clad thigh touched hers. His body heat wrapped around her and dulled her sensibilities while at the same time heightening her senses.

She could *feel* the bunch and flex of the muscles in his leg. See the faint freckle beside his left eye. And he smelled so damn good. Kind of spicy, like a desert flower, but with a hint of dry cedar.

Instinct had her trying to scoot away to a safe distance. If there was such a thing when it came to Wolf, which she was beginning to doubt. But the arm of the sofa pressed against her hip.

There was nowhere to run.

Nowhere to hide.

Nowhere to look except deep into his dark eyes as he kept talking.

"I liked you so much, Chrissy. I *still* like you so much that anytime you're around, I'm hard pressed not to grin like a gopher in soft dirt. And rememberin' how I was such an ass to you that night? Darlin', it makes me want to tear out my own hair, shape it into some sort of weird art sculpture, and present it to you on a satin pillow or somethin'. You know, as a way of atonement," he clarified when she blinked at him in bewilderment.

"And I know I'm ramblin'," he continued. "And, yeah, it's gettin' weird."

Was it ever. Two minutes ago, if someone had asked her if it was possible for Wolf to be fumbling and awkward, she'd have responded with a resounding *no*.

"But I feel like this is the right time and the right place to apologize to you the right way. I'm nervous as hell, and I know I'm gettin' it all wrong." He ran a hand through his hair, making a tuft stick up near his temple. She tried to imagine it formed into an art sculpture and felt her lips twitch. "I *know* I am," he continued.

He looked chagrined. Never in their whole acquaintance had she seen him looking chagrined. Disconcerted? Sure. Annoyed? Plenty of times. Hell, despite his ultra-alpha, I-got-it-all-under-control demeanor, she'd even seen him bewildered a time or two. But never, *ever* chagrined.

It was…adorable. Enough to put a chink in the wall she'd constructed against him. Then, in the blink of an eye, she felt that chink grow into a crack that just as quickly spread into a spider web of fissures.

Uh-oh.

"Chrissy, I want to make sure you know—"

She shoved a finger over his lips, determined to stop him from saying anything more that might have her walls crumbling completely.

He sighed, and she ignored the puff of his hot breath against her skin. Or at least she *tried* to. Her *brain* ignored it. Her womb? Not so much. It clenched with desire.

Hey, baby box! Stop sabotaging me! You're as bad as the nipples and the ovaries! she silently railed. Aloud she said, "Now I know why you quote other people. Left to your own devices, you're a red-hot mess."

She thought that'd make him laugh.

It didn't.

His expression remained serious, and his eyes held a look she couldn't quite read. Or maybe she didn't *want* to read it. Maybe the thought of reading it scared her to death.

For a few moments they sat there, staring at each other, that ever-present *awareness* humming in the space between them. When she couldn't take the silence any longer, she said, "It's *okay*, Wolf. You can stop apologizing. I forgive you. I really do."

His gaze drifted to the macramé wall hanging above her

television. She'd found the pattern on Pinterest and had spent an entire weekend making one for herself and one for Winston. Like most bachelors, Winston was complete crap when it came to decorating. If not for her forcing him to equip his apartment like an adult, he'd probably still be sleeping on a futon and using milk crates as nightstands.

Thoughts of her best friend made her stomach clench, and reminded her that she needed to plug in her phone and shove it in a bag of rice. She didn't want to miss the moment Winston's parents called with an update.

Bending, she pulled her phone out of the plastic bag Wolf had dropped at their feet. Then she stood and turned toward the kitchen. She hadn't managed a full step before Wolf stopped her with a hand on her thigh.

She frowned down at him. "I need to get my phone—"

"In a minute," he drawled. "It's time we finish this."

She cocked her head. "I thought we just did."

"Not by a long shot. What was his name?"

She blinked in confusion. "Who?"

"The bar owner from Fort Lauderdale."

"Oh." She hadn't the first clue how that night at Schooner Wharf Bar had anything to do with Mr. Dick Pics. "Um, Drummer."

"Drummer?" His top lip curled. "That's not a name. That's an occupation."

"Says the guy who shares his moniker with an animal."

"Touché," he allowed. Then, "Did he break your heart?"

"Who? Drummer?" When he nodded, she shook her head. "No. But he certainly hurt my feelings and stomped all over my pride."

"So you didn't…" He looked at her like he was trying to see inside her head. "You weren't in love with him?"

"God no. I *liked* him an awful lot though." Now his eyes were black lasers, boring into her. "What?" she demanded.

"I'm tryin' to reckon how it was you were hankerin' to build a life with someone you weren't in love with."

"Oh." She waved a hand through the air, noticing it was a little stale. She should probably light a candle. "That's easy. He seemed like the solid, settling down type. And also, I don't believe in falling in love."

His face blanked. He blinked slowly. Just when she thought they were done, he said, "I'm sorry. I thought I heard you say you don't believe in fallin' in love."

"That's not quite right." She screwed up her mouth and tried to come up with a way to put her thoughts and feelings on the subject into words that would make sense. "It's not that I don't believe in it. It's that I don't ever plan to do it myself. Falling in love makes you do stupid shit. Take it from me, I had a front row seat more times than you can imagine." She tried to head toward the kitchen again, but his grip on her thigh tightened.

She sighed, not attempting to hide the annoyance on her face.

"Hell, no." He shook his head. "You done gone and opened up a can, now you need to sit here with me until we've eaten it down to the tin bottom."

She laughed. "Where in the world do you come up with all your country-fried sayings?"

"I grew up in an Oklahoma cattle town, darlin'. They float around on the wind there."

"I don't hate them."

"No? Not like my quotes?"

She hitched her shoulder and resumed her seat. *Might as well. He's not going to let me go until he's said whatever he needs to say.*

"I don't really hate your quotes either," she admitted. "I just hate that you always have a sage saying that fits every scenario. It's unfair and intimidating to the rest of us."

He returned them to their original subject. "When you say you had a front row seat..." He let the sentence dangle.

"You've heard me talk about my mother and her four husbands, right?"

His eyebrows bunched over his nose. He looked so fierce she was tempted to kiss him.

Oh, who am I kidding? Fierce looking or not, I'm always *tempted to kiss him.*

So do it! that no good, double-crossing voice whispered.

It was time for an old-fashioned lobotomy. That's all there was to it.

"You've mentioned them on occasion," he said cautiously.

"Well, let me tell you, the four husbands were the tip of the iceberg. Before them, between them, and after them was a string of boyfriends that would stretch from here to Stock Island. My mother was *always* looking for love."

"In all the wrong places by the sound of it."

"I'm not sure there *are* right places," she countered.

His eyes narrowed. "Maybe she was so unsuccessful because she confused lust with love. Lots of folks do that, you know."

She handed him the framed photograph she kept on the end table. It was a candid of her mother. Blonde head thrown back. Big, Julia Roberts mouth spread wide around a laugh. Josephine's sundress showed off a figure that would make starlets weep with envy.

"She's stunnin'," he said after studying the picture for only a moment. "You take after her."

"Please." Chrissy rolled her eyes. "I'm passably pretty. She was *magnificent*. And since she looked like that"—she hitched her chin toward the photo at the same time she replaced it on the end table—"she could catch a dick anytime she wanted."

He snorted. "I wouldn't have put it exactly that way, but—"

"My point is, I don't think she confused lust with love. I think she confused *falling* in love with *being* in love."

For a while he was quiet. Then he asked, "What's the difference?"

"Falling in love is involuntary. That's why they call it *falling*. It happens to you. You don't have any control over it. *Being* in love, on the other hand, is a choice. It's a state that happens with conscious effort, with agency."

"And you think bein' in love can happen without the fallin' in love part?"

"Of course!" She tossed up both hands, forgetting one was in a sling. "Ow! Oh, god." She put a hand over her bandaged shoulder. "Why did I do that?"

Her injury wasn't unbearable, like she'd assumed a gunshot *would* be. Then again, it was only a flesh wound, not a bullet to a vital organ. Still, it throbbed like a bitch anytime she moved too quickly.

Wolf sat forward, skewering her with a hard look. "How many pain pills did you take back at the hospital?"

"Just one," she admitted.

"The nurse said you can take two at a time." Fishing out the pill bottle from the bottom of the plastic bag, he handed it to her. "I'll get you a glass of water."

"I can do it."

"Woman!" His tone was exasperated. "For the love of all that's holy. Lettin' someone take care of you for ten seconds doesn't mean you'll lose your Badass Independent Lady card."

Despite herself, she smirked. "It's a *Kick*-ass Independent Lady card, if you must know. And like an American Express, I never leave home without it."

"Sit." He told her. "Stay." He stood.

"Woof! Woof!" she barked while trying to muster indignation, but the annoyance on his face was too funny. Wolf was used to people asking *how high* when he told them to jump.

She found she quite *liked* being the exception to that rule.

"I'm not treatin' you like a dog." His tone was unusually neutral. "I'm simply askin' in the simplest possible way for you to relax and let me help you."

"Oh!" She fluttered her lashes at him. "I'm sorry. Were you *asking* me to sit here while you got me a glass of water? Somehow I missed the question marks on the ends of all your sentences."

He put his hands on his hips and let his head fall back so he could stare at the ceiling. It made his Adam's apple poke out in the column of his tanned throat. For some reason, she found that incredibly sexy.

Her mouth, proving itself as untrustworthy as her nipples, womb, and ovaries, began to water. *What would it feel like to take a nip out of that apple? Just catch it between my teeth and then sooth the sting with my tongue?*

No, no. *No!*

They were friends. *Friends.* Nothing more, nothing less.

Dragging her eyes away from his too-tempting neck, she concentrated on his face, which was still pointed toward the ceiling.

If she wasn't mistaken, he was silently counting to ten. She thought she could see his lips move. When he finally dropped his chin, his expression was purposefully blank. "Christina."

"Yes, Wolf?" She fluttered her lashes.

"May I get you a glass of water so you can take that pill?"

"You may." She dipped her chin in a queenly fashion and thought she saw his lips twitch right along with a muscle in his jaw.

"Wait!" she grabbed his wrist when he turned toward her kitchen. "Take my phone with you and plug it in, will you?" She handed him the device. "There's a charger in the kitchen."

"Your wish is my command." He dropped a stately bow. Five seconds later, she heard him opening her cupboards.

Traditional Florida Keys conch houses were small, usually consisting of little more than a bedroom, bathroom, living room, and kitchen. But the lack of living area was overcome by the abundance of outdoor space. Chrissy's house had a wide front porch big enough for a swing, two rocking chairs, and a bistro table. And her back patio boasted a plunge pool, an outdoor shower, and plenty of seating, lounging, and dining options.

People in the Keys tended to spend most of their time outside. And why not? The weather was gorgeous. Even on a hot day, it was nice in the shade, especially if there was a bit of an ocean breeze blowing by.

"Glasses are in the cupboard to the right of the sink!" she hollered. "Oh! And there's a bag of rice in the little pantry beside the fridge. Would you mind shoving my phone inside it once you've plugged it in?"

He didn't answer. But she could hear him getting ice and water out of the refrigerator. She recognized the squeak of the pantry door when he opened it.

Not long after, he reappeared with a glass in hand. "Your beverage, my lady." He'd donned a haughty English accent that bore a hint of an Oklahoma twang.

He really was charming.

The jerk.

She thanked him before tossing back the pain pill.

This time when he resumed his seat it wasn't only his thigh touching hers. It was his entire side, thigh, hip, and shoulder. "Back to fallin' in love versus bein' in love," he said.

"There's a whole other end to this couch," she complained.

He glanced at the wide stretch of unused sofa cushions. "So there is." He didn't take her hint. In fact, just the opposite. He placed his arm behind her, his fingers gently twisting in the ends of her ponytail. "So you don't like the idea of fallin' in love because you don't like the idea of bein' out of control, is that it?"

"No." She shook her head. The fine baby hairs on the back of her neck stood up the second he touched her.

After That Night, she'd gotten good at tuning out their shared chemistry, but right then? She wasn't sure if it was the exhaustion, the pain, the meds, or a combination of all three, but *something* had changed. She was more aware of him than ever.

"It goes back to falling in love making you do stupid shit." She hoped he couldn't hear the sudden scratchiness in her throat. "When you're falling in love, you're so infatuated, you're blind. That rush of emotions knocks you off your feet and keeps you there. But eventually those heady feelings fade. And for so many people, they discover they've made a mistake. Either the person they fell in love with isn't who they thought they were, or there are insurmountable incompatibilities that doom their relationship long term."

"Okay." He nodded, but she could see by his expression he wasn't completely buying what she was selling. "So how do you square that with wantin' to settle down and build a life? With wantin' a father for your four kids?"

"That's easy." She hoped she sounded more confident than she felt. "Follow my head instead of my heart. Find a good guy, a solid guy, and make him part of my life. And if he *is* a good and solid guy, then love will grow. I'll wake up one day and *be* in love with him without *falling* in love with him." When he was quiet after this pronouncement, she ended with a flourish, "Thanks for coming to my Ted Talk."

He watched his fingers play with her ponytail for a long while. Then he returned his gaze to her face. "And do you consider *me* a good guy?"

Her heart stopped beating. Her lungs stopped breathing. In fact, it felt as if the blood stopped rushing through her veins.

Why was he asking? Did he…could he…was he talking about a future together? Had the thought actually crossed his mind?

She knew he wanted in her pants. He'd made that abundantly clear. And for a while, she'd considered the possibility that something more might be in the cards for them.

But then That Night happened and she'd seen his true colors. Not since then had she entertained the idea that Wolf was the kind of man who was built to go the distance.

"You're a *nice* guy," she told him, forcing breath back into her lungs, hoping it would jumpstart her heart. "There's a difference."

"There is?"

Before she could answer, the sound of footsteps on the boards of her front porch proceeded a hard knock on her door. "Officer Ryan here!" The policeman's baritone sounded through the hardwood. "I need to come in and make sure all the points of entry are locked! I also got Detective Dixon with me!"

Chrissy jumped up, glad for the distraction since it felt like Wolf had created a gravity well around them, and it was past time she broke free of it.

CHAPTER 15

9:53 AM...

Are you sure you wiped down the car? Left no fingerprints? No trace evidence?" JayJay took off her reading glasses and massaged the bridge of her nose as she waited for Mateo's reply.

Yesterday had been bad. Last night had been badder than bad. And this morning? It was shaping up to be even worse.

Mateo had managed to *not* kill Chrissy Szarek. *Again.*

As a result, JayJay was dealing with a nagging headache that beat against the backs of her eyeballs like iron fists.

"Sure," Mateo said when she replaced her glasses. She peered over the rims, watching him lift one of his giant shoulders. "But it wouldn't matter none even if I didn't. The cops won't be looking for anyone but Cliff."

"Yeah, yeah." Ricky doubled down in that annoying way of his. "Cliff's got a DUI rap sheet as long as my dick."

"So, a whole three inches?" Mateo quipped.

"Ha, ha. That's three more than you got, asshole."

Mateo thought this was the height of wit and broke into a big, belly laugh. Ricky grinned broadly, as if he'd pulled off a comedy special for HBO.

Couple of bottom feeders, JayJay thought. *I should give them the ax if for no other reason than to save my sanity.*

But then she remembered what she'd learned from old man Allensworth. He'd been a second-generation Conch, born and raised to captain a shrimp boat. And along with his penchant for cheap woman and expensive whiskey, he'd had a rare talent for dispensing wisdom.

"You see, my girl," he'd said one night while they were eating pasta on the patio at a little Italian place known only to locals, *"it's best you learn this lesson young. Unless they bring you income, inspiration, or orgasms, give 'em the ax."*

Tweedle Dee and Tweedle Dum certainly didn't bring JayJay the last two. She nearly ralphed in her mouth simply thinking about it. But, boy oh boy, did they help with that first one. The money they netted on their runs for the Colombians kept Ricky and Mateo in booze and broads, and kept JayJay's entire family's chain of businesses afloat.

She took two deep breaths before calmly asking, "So what now? Plan Bravo failed. Tell me you have a Plan Charlie."

Mateo scratched his ear. "It'll be tricky. We need a way into her house, and we need to know who's going to be there with her."

"To do what, exactly?"

"We'll rig a little explosion."

JayJay was still hoping to keep the law dogs off her trail by making Chrissy's death look unconnected to her run-in with a gunman in the old warehouse. An explosion certainly didn't sound like it could be mistaken for an accident. "How little are we talking?"

"Okay, okay. Let's say more than a firecracker." Ricky grinned. "But less than an H-bomb."

Again, Mateo laughed and clapped Ricky on the back. "You're in fine form today, my friend."

Ricky pulled an unlit cigarette from his pack and caught it between his lips. "All the excitement's got my blood up."

JayJay resisted rolling her eyes. But just barely. "Not that I don't trust you guys"—she didn't, not as far as she could shit them—"but I'm going to need a little more than that by way of an explanation."

"Let's just say Chrissy Szarek, drugged up on pain meds, will accidently leave her gas stove on. When the fumes hit the candle she'll leave burning...*boom!*" Mateo clapped his hands. "She'll go up in flames. Easy as Key lime pie."

For the sake of edification, Key lime pie wasn't all that easy. You had to squeeze and zest the limes. And after baking it, you had to let it cool in the refrigerator for at least three hours.

Of course, JayJay didn't waste her time pointing any of this out to Butch and Sundance.

A gas explosion. She turned the idea over in her mind and shuddered. It sounded like a horrible way to go.

"I can help you with what you need. But I need time to—" Her phone rang, cutting her off. It wasn't her landline or her cell phone, but her *other* phone. The one she replaced every week.

An oily sense of apprehension slid down her spine.

"Give me the morning," she told her henchmen. "In the meantime, go with God." She made a shooing motion with her hand.

"You believe in heaven?" Ricky blinked at her.

"I believe in hell." She made a face. "After the last couple of days, I'm in it."

"Good one." He snorted and parroted, "Good one." Then he fell into step behind Mateo's retreating back.

She waited until they were out of earshot before answering the phone. Her stomach clenched into a hard fist when the unmistakable accent of her Colombian connection sounded in her ear.

"We hear bad things are happening on Key West." The man's voice was perpetually hoarse, like he smoked two packs a day or else had lived to tell the tale of a garroting gone wrong.

"I have things under control. Your last shipment is safe."

"And the next one? Will it be safe?"

"It'd be better if you waited until—"

"Our deal is not to wait. Our deal is we deliver and you receive."

JayJay wasn't afraid of much. Not skin cancer—which she'd survived twice—not hurricanes or well-hung men, but she was absolutely terrified of the Colombians.

"Fine. Tell me when." When he said one word, she heard her voice crack. "No. It's too soon. I can't possibly—"

"Be careful when you refuse me, *carechimba*."

JayJay didn't speak Spanish, but she couldn't imagine the word was a compliment. Once again, she rubbed her aching eyes.

"What time?" she asked wearily and made note of the Colombian's answer. Then, "My men will be there."

"See that they are," was his answer right before the line went dead.

Tomorrow.

So on top of dealing with the disaster that was Chrissy and Winston, she now had to scramble to book a fishing charter and get Mateo and Ricky back out on the water.

Another of old man Allensworth's lines of wisdom had been, *"A woman's work is never done."*

Amen, brother, she thought. *A-fucking-men.*

CHAPTER 16

10:43 AM...

So what you're saying is, you don't have a clue who those men in the warehouse were."

Chrissy tried not let her annoyance show. But it was difficult given she'd spent the last thirty minutes listening to Detective Dixon take her down every path he'd wandered in his bid to identify her and Winston's attempted murderers, only to discover each avenue had netted him exactly nothing. Jack squat. A big ol' pile of nada.

"*Yet*," Dixon stressed. "I don't have any clues *yet*. But I'm a tenacious sonofagun. And this job has taught me if I keep pulling strings, something usually starts to unravel."

Chrissy didn't miss his qualifier. *Usually*. Which meant *not always*.

If the warehouse guys were never found, would she spend the rest of her life looking over her shoulder? Would every heavy-set man who crossed her path make her shudder?

Would she forever be waiting for the moment when those assholes decided to finish what they started?

Dixon must've sensed her inner turmoil. "Don't lose faith, Miss Szarek. We've barely started. There's still plenty of work to be done."

She liked to listen to true crime podcasts while folding laundry, but now she wished she knew a little less about police work. The podcasts made it sound like the first twenty-four hours were the most important, and after that, the chances of catching the culprits dropped exponentially.

Here we are already closing in on hour fourteen since the shooting.

"What string are you pullin' next?" Wolf asked from beside her.

There still wasn't an inch of physical space between them. But after their last heart-to-heart, she thought she detected an emotional distance in him.

Something was missing in his voice when he spoke to her. And she couldn't find any of the usual teasing admiration in his eyes. In fact, she was pretty sure what she saw was confusion.

And maybe…*wariness*?

She briefly closed her eyes and pictured the last time he'd looked at her dead-on. It'd been after she motioned for the detective to take a seat in the rattan chair opposite the sofa. Wolf had glanced at her and their eyes had locked.

Then, for the first time in…well, maybe forever…he'd been the first to look away.

She went back over their last conversation and couldn't fathom what she'd said to cause a change in him. Unless she'd upset him when she said she wanted to *be* in love without *falling* in love?

But why in the world would *that* have bothered him?

Unless… That little voice whispered that one word. Then, it waited for her to fill in the blank.

Unless Wolf *wanted* her to *want* to fall in love with someone. But why would he care one way or the other? It was *her* life to live however she pleased, not his.

Unless…

Unless the person he wanted her to want to fall in love with was *him*. But why would he want that? He was a playboy.

Unless…

Unless he fancied himself falling in love with *her* and had convinced himself his wild oat days were behind him.

You know the sound basketball shoes make against the court when a player skids to a stop? Well, that's the sound Chrissy's brain made inside her head.

Sweet heavens. Is that it? Does Wolf think he's falling for me?

"…because the Coast Guard isn't exactly forthcoming with their logs," Dixon said.

"I'm sorry." She shook her head. "Could you repeat that? I zoned out."

Zoned out and homed in on a possibility that totally blew her mind. We're talking gray matter confetti shot out of a freakin' circus cannon.

"I said I'm waiting for the Coast Guard to send me a log of the boats they searched in the marina yesterday," Dixon obliged. "But they're not exactly in a hurry to cooperate. I've been told I can expect a copy by this afternoon at the earliest."

It was tough, but she was determined to keep her mind on the matter at hand instead of the man sitting beside her. The one who was so warm and who smelled so good and who may or may not think he was falling in—

Gah!

"And you're hoping that'll tell you what?" Wolf asked.

She'd always liked his voice. It was one of those deep, harmonic baritones that belonged to a disc jockey. Now, for some reason, her brain conjured up a scene of what it would sound like on a warm, seductive night with the cool breeze rattling the fronds of the palm tree growing outside her bedroom window and the music from Duval Street echoing in the distance.

Why is it when I tell myself not to think of something, that's all I can think about?

She had the same problem with ice cream and peanut M&Ms.

"Once I have a list of the boats, I can search the names of the operators and owners. Maybe I can find a couple of guys who fit your description of the shooters." What looked to be a blob of dried syrup was stuck to the bottom of Dixon's tie. It caught his eye and he scratched at it.

The poor man was even more rumpled-looking this morning. No doubt because, in his hunt for the fiends from the warehouse, he'd barely taken time to sleep, much less iron his clothes.

Chrissy suddenly felt shitty for having been annoyed with his lack of progress.

"In the meantime," he continued, "I'll keep a police presence here with you and one at the hospital with Mr. Turner. And as soon as I get a lead on the shooters, I'll let you know."

She was glad he'd phrased it that way instead of *if* I get a lead on the shooters. His confidence helped shore up her own.

"Thank you for stopping by with the update, Detective." She stood at the same time Dixon did. Unlike Dixon, she wasn't rock steady in the vertical position. Thanks to that second pain pill, the room became a dance party and did a quick spin around her.

Probably shouldn't have taken the meds on an empty stomach, she scolded herself as Wolf wrapped a hand around her elbow. The instant his warm palm cupped the joint, she would swear 120 volts of electricity shot up her arm.

"Easy." His voice was quiet. His eyes were *not*. They roiled like black fire.

"Thanks." She used the excuse of needing to adjust her sling to pull her elbow from his grip.

His touch had always affected her. But given her most recent revelation—*Was it a revelation or am I totally off base?*—she now felt stunned by the feel of his hands on her.

"Oh!" Dixon was halfway to the door when he turned and snapped his fingers. "I almost forgot. A couple of officers found Cliff Barnes sitting on the front steps of his house. He has a bump on his forehead the size of a goose egg and is making noises about being walloped by someone who stole his car. No one believes him, of course. For one, he's already three king-sized sheets to the wind this morning. For another, the location of his injury is consistent with him hitting his head on the steering wheel when he planted the nose of his Celica in the ditch."

Chrissy frowned, remembering the moment Wolf wrapped her up in his arms and then launched them both in the air. The man truly was hero material.

Too bad he's not husband material to boot.

"At least with Cliff's car out of commission," she said, "he can't mow over anyone else."

"No chance of that." The detective shook his head. "He's been arrested for reckless driving, leaving the scene of an accident, and driving while intoxicated. Surely one, if not *all*, of those charges will stick. If someone tries to run you down anytime in the near future, it won't be Cliff."

"Gee thanks. That's so comforting," she said and thought she might have seen a ghost of a smile cross the detective's face. But it was gone so quickly, she couldn't be sure.

When he opened the door to leave, he was met with a raised fist and automatically ducked. Then he realized it was only Jill, her knuckles poised to knock, and he lifted his hands in the air as if she were pointing a gun at him.

"I promise I'm working as hard as I can to solve the case," he said. "No need to resort to violence."

Jill harrumphed and gave Dixon a quick once-over. Judy and Janice were lined up behind her, per usual. "I'm assuming that means you don't have any leads, Detective?" Jill skipped the pleasantries.

"*Yet*," Dixon stressed again. "I don't have any leads *yet*."

"Well then, I won't need to resort to violence *yet*. But if you don't have something by this evening, I might." Jill stepped over the threshold like she owned the place. Which, Chrissy had learned, was how Jill felt about the whole island. It was hers to protect, and everyone who lived on it was hers to fuss over.

Or boss around.

In Jill's mind, those two things were indistinguishable.

Bossy or not, Chrissy was glad to count the woman as a friend. It'd been Jill who taught her about business deductions—which ones were liable to have the IRS breathing down her neck. It'd been Jill who told her about Drummer looking too cozy with his beer distributor, which had prompted Chrissy to sneak into his phone and find the damning sext messages. And it'd been Jill who kept her in casseroles and tubs of Blue Bell those first couple of months after her mother passed, when Chrissy hadn't been able to muster up the energy to brush her hair much less cook for herself.

By the looks—and *smells*—coming from the Pyrex dishes in Judy and Janice's hands as they followed Jill into the house, it appeared Jill was back at it, playing the part of Mother Goose as if she were born to it.

She folded Chrissy into a soft hug. "I was so glad when I called the hospital this morning to check on visiting hours and they told me you were being released. It's good to see you up and on your feet."

"Thanks." Chrissy tilted her chin toward the dishes. "You didn't have to go to all this trouble, you guys. This time I only have a broken wing." She gingerly lifted the arm in the sling. "Not a broken heart."

"Both make it a bother to cook," Judy piped up, coming forward to buss Chrissy's cheek. Judy always smelled faintly of the bleach she used to mop the floors of her convenience mart. "Tommy got your customers out to Sambos Reef right on time, dear. So don't you worry. Everything's taken care of."

"I'm going to pay him double," Chrissy swore. "He deserves it coming to the rescue like this."

"Pfft." Judy waved her hand. "Don't go spoiling him more than he already is."

Judy liked to pretend she was tough on her nephew. But the truth was, she adored the kid as much as she adored all the people in her large, extended family, and she turned into a big old marshmallow around him.

Chrissy looked at the tinfoil-covered dish in the woman's hand. "Speaking of spoiling... Please tell me that's your famous bacon macaroni and cheese."

"None other." Judy winked, her glasses magnifying her eyes and making the gesture look slightly cartoonish, especially when paired with her fire-engine red hair.

"And this here is that peach cobbler you went on about." Janice lifted her glass baking dish.

"You all are too good to me." Chrissy felt a welcome rush of warmth.

"We'll talk later, Miss Szarek," Dixon said before stepping outside to say something to Officer Ryan. She saw Ryan nod, and could just make out his response to the detective. "Everything's locked up tight. I'll post up out here on the front porch."

While his presence brought her a measure of peace, it was having *Wolf* around that made her feel truly safe.

"Come into the kitchen so you can set down those dishes." Chrissy beckoned the three ladies farther into the house as she skirted around them to shut the front door. Her air-conditioner was already running like a jet engine, fighting the good fight against the day's heat and humidity.

"No good will come from air-conditioning the world!" her mother used to shout when Chrissy would run outside, forgetting to slam the door behind her.

The memory brought with it a wave of despair and a deep, surprising longing for simpler times.

But that's the thing about grief, she'd learned. *It doesn't always come at you head-on. Sometimes it sneaks up on you from behind, hitting you when you least expect it.*

She was especially vulnerable when she was tired. And right at that moment? She felt like she was *born* tired.

Grabbing the doorknob, she was more than ready to shut out the outside world when she saw Romeo and Mia coming up her front porch steps. Pasting on what she hoped passed for a smile of welcome, she said, "Well, hey you two."

"It's good to see you out of that hospital bed." Romeo stopped at the top of the steps at the same time Chrissy felt Wolf come to stand behind her. Every hair on the back of her head stood on end, as if they were magnets and he was metal.

"It's good to be out of it," she managed. Although, to be honest, with Wolf wrapped around her all night, the hospital bed hadn't been all that bad.

That was the thing about Ray "Wolf" Roanhorse. He made bad things bearable and good things better.

After telling Mia "Wolf talked the nurse into releasing me early" when Mia mentioned they'd stopped by the hospital first, she gestured for them to come inside.

"I know it's a little early for lunch, but Judy's made her famous bacon macaroni and cheese and Janice was kind enough to bake me a peach cobbler that's so good you'll think you've died and gone to heaven. I have a whole gallon of sweet tea. Who's hungry?"

"Rain check." Romeo remained rooted to the spot. "I have some business to go over with Wolf and then Mia and I need to get back out to Wayfarer."

"I'll take you up on the tea." Mia wiped a hand across her glistening forehead. "Spiro and I have been running all over the island this morning picking up metal detectors."

"Spiro?" Wolf glanced from Mia to Romeo and back to Mia in time to see the woman blush.

"That *is* his name, you know." Mia lifted a defiant chin.

Well, well, Chrissy mused. *Maybe there's more to meek and mild Mia than any of us thought.*

"Can I bring you something to drink?" Mia asked Romeo and Chrissy saw something that resembled panic cross the man's face. Then his usual mega-watt smile returned.

"Nah." He winked at Mia. "I'm good. Go on inside and cool off. I'll come get you once it's time to head out." He waited until Chrissy waved her inside. Then he motioned for Wolf to follow him toward the wrought-iron bistro table pushed into the corner of the porch.

"Be there in a bit," Wolf told him. Chrissy was about to

turn and follow Mia, but she stopped when Wolf tapped a finger under her chin. "You okay? You're lookin' awful pale again."

"I'm tired," she admitted. "And that last pain pill is making my stomach cramp."

"Go eat," he told her. "It'll help. After I finish chin waggin' with Romeo, I'll run everyone out of your house."

She opened her mouth, but he didn't wait for her answer before heading in Romeo's direction.

"Did I hear you say something about macaroni and cheese?" Officer Ryan had been looking over the postage stamp-sized plot of land that was her bougainvillea and saw palmetto-filled front yard. But now he was staring at her with longing in his eyes.

She chuckled and waved him inside. "It's *bacon* macaroni and cheese. Come on in, Officer. I can't have you fainting from starvation while on duty."

The policeman slid by her, and she turned back in time to see Wolf grab a seat at the wrought-iron table.

He might think *he's falling in love with me*, she decided. *But he's fallen victim to his own hypothesis about my mother. He's confused lust with love. Probably because he's never had a woman rebuff his advances before.*

The question now was, how was she going to convince him of that?

CHAPTER 17

11:08 AM...

L ike his namesake, Wolf epitomized sleek, swift self-
assurance.

He moved with stealth. His expressions remained
impassive even when the shit hit the fan. He seemed to
think in complete sentences, every word out of his mouth
said with forethought and consideration—and with a
cutting wit when he chose to wield it. Which was why it
was so damned weird seeing the dude all jittery and
flustered now.

Romeo frowned at the impatient fingers Wolf drummed
atop the table. And when Wolf glanced up from checking
his watch for the third time in the six seconds since he'd sat
down, Romeo leveled his most considering stare on his
business partner and friend.

"You want to go first or should I?" he asked.

"Nothin' to report on my end." Wolf shook his head.
"Dixon doesn't know any more than last night and—"

"I'm not talking about Dixon, *pendejo*." Romeo leaned forward, making it impossible for Wolf to look anywhere but into his eyes. "I'm talking about you and Chrissy. What happened between you two last night that has you wound tighter than a two dollar watch this morning, eh?"

Wolf was silent. For a moment, Romeo thought it might take a whole pack of ninjas and one very large crowbar to get any sort of answer out of the man.

Then Wolf said, "I'll tell you what happened with Chrissy if you tell me what happened with Mia. Why's she offerin' to bring you drinks while gazin' at you like you hung the moon and all the stars in the sky?"

Fuck.

Romeo thought he'd imagined that look. He *hoped* he'd imagined it.

When he'd awoken that morning, it was to the feel of a warm woman snuggled next to him. Which, let's face it, wasn't unusual. What *was* unusual—*unheard of, actually*—was for him *not* to have had sex with that woman the night before.

He hadn't made it through the first chapter of *In Darkness and Dreams* before the hellacious day caught up with him and he fell victim to forty winks. He imagined Mia, lovely lady that she was, hadn't had the heart to wake him and so had decided to conk out next to him. Except, at some point during the night, she'd sought his body heat in her sleep.

By this morning? They'd been tangled in a full-on lovers' knot. Her head had been pillowed on his chest. His arm had been around her waist. Her leg had been thrown over both of his.

It'd been the pressure of her thigh against his morning wood that'd caused him to stir. And in that twilight space between waking and sleep, he'd nearly rolled her onto her back so he could cover her mouth with a dreamy kiss. One that wouldn't have stopped with her lips but would have traveled south to her neck, her delicate clavicle, those perky little breasts that reminded him of scoops of ice cream.

If not for the alarm on her phone jerking him fully awake, he might have done exactly that.

And then what would've happened?

He didn't dare imagine it.

If he imagined it, he'd begin fantasizing about it.

If he began to fantasize about it, he'd want to do it.

If he did it, then—

Like they'd been doing all morning, his thoughts returned to waking up in bed beside her. She'd come out of sleep slowly, and with a cute yawn that ended in a long feline stretch.

He'd gone stone still, fearing the minute she realized she was lying atop him she'd jump out of her skin. Except, she hadn't. In fact, instead of being scared to death of him, as per usual, she'd simply sat up, smiled at him, and whispered, *"Morning, Spiro. Sleep well?"*

Some women had bedroom eyes. Mia Ennis had a bedroom *voice*. It alone had been enough to turn his morning wood into a morning giant sequoia.

Proving himself a complete idiot, his response had been to leap out of bed like the mattress was on fire. Then he'd made some halting excuses about needing to shit, shower, and shave. *Yes*, he'd actually said that—*'cause I'm all class, baby*—before executing his escape.

By the time he'd made it back to her room to take her down to breakfast, he'd convinced himself sleeping with her had been no big deal. That he was *making* it a big deal. That nothing had changed.

Except, now Wolf had pointed out something *had* changed. That *Mia* had changed. She was no longer treating him like he might lean over and take a bite out of her. Quite the opposite, in fact, she was acting like they were…what? *Friends?*

That was hilarious. Not funny ha-ha, but funny *fuuucckkk* since he wanted to snack on her *now* more than ever.

Now he had firsthand experience with just how soft she was. With the way her lips looked swollen first thing in the morning. With how well she fitted against his side.

Or…and this was even more concerning, she was acting like they might be *more* than friends. He'd never been more than friends with a woman in his life. In fact, except for his teammates' wives and girlfriends, the most he'd ever been was friends with benefits. Light on the *friends* and heavy on the *benefits*.

Leaning back in his chair, he closed his eyes and blurted, "I slept with her." He opened his lids to see the corners of Wolf's mouth turn down. "Not like *that*," he was quick to add, filling Wolf in on the book, the reading, and waking up all hashtag *bodies entwined*. "And now I'm afraid she's thinking I'm something I'm not."

"Which is?" Wolf prompted.

"Boyfriend material."

"Ah." Wolf nodded solemnly.

"I mean, she's smart and sophisticated and rich and cultured. Everything I'm not. And even though I'm *definitely* the man for the job when it comes to priming her pump—"

"Anyone ever tell you your relationship with humility is passin' at best?" Wolf interrupted.

Romeo continued as if Wolf hadn't spoken. "I'm definitely *not* the man for anything more."

"Do you *want* somethin' more?" Wolf arched his eyebrows.

"Wants got nothing to do with it." Romeo refused to

even consider the question. "I want to get ridden by a middle-aged woman in pigtails and a cheerleading outfit, but that doesn't mean it's a good idea."

Wolf's expression flattened. "Just when I think you might be evolvin', you go and say things like that and I'm reminded of how much of an asshole you truly are."

"Oh, yeah? Well if I'm an asshole, then you're the King of Asshole Mountain."

Wolf's chin jerked back. "How do you figure?"

"What happened that night at Schooner Wharf Bar?"

"Oh, hell on earth, no. We're not goin' there."

"And why not?" Romeo lifted one eyebrow, which was the grown man equivalent of a juvenile shoulder poke.

"We're talkin' about you and Mia, not me and Chrissy." Gone was Wolf's agitation. He was back to being freakishly calm as he regarded Romeo through unreadable eyes.

"Fine." Romeo sighed. "Go on and say it."

Wolf's tone was purposefully neutral. His words left no room for interpretation, however. "Mia isn't the type of woman you fuck around with, figuratively or literally."

"I *know* that."

"Which means if you don't have honorable intentions toward her, you need to nip this thing in the bud sooner rather than later."

"I know that too," Romeo grumbled miserably, finally admitting to himself what he'd only suspected all morning long.

Somehow, through no fault of his own, he'd stumbled his way into a goat fuck of a situation. Or maybe it was more correct to say he'd *snoozed* his way into a goat fuck of a situation.

Not that he was a stranger to goat fucks. They were pretty much standard operating procedure for Navy SEALs.

However, in *those* instances, he'd always had a group of men ready and willing to back him up.

In this situation? He was all on his own.

And I have no clue how I'm going to get myself out of it without hurting or embarrassing or otherwise upsetting a perfectly lovely woman.

"Enough about me." He swiped the air as if to shove aside the subject. But there it sat in the corner, like an 800-pound gorilla. *So fine. The best I can do is ignore it.* "Let's talk about you and Chrissy. What happened last night?"

Wolf must've decided Romeo's blurt-it-out approach worked well. He said without preamble, "I realized I've fallen in love with her."

Romeo sat there blinking for a full five seconds. Then, "Damn, man. Way to bury the lede. Why didn't we start with *that*? That's *huge* news!" He slapped Wolf on the shoulder, and then reconsidered his words. "Well, not *news*, exactly. Anyone with working eyeballs in their head can see you've been falling for her for a while. But still. Now you've admitted it. Congratulations. When's the wedding?"

Wolf's mouth formed a straight line. "There's a problem."

"What's that?"

"She doesn't want to fall in love."

Romeo blinked a couple more times, turning each word over in his mind to make certain he'd heard correctly. "She doesn't want to fall in love with *you* or with anyone?"

"Anyone."

More blinks. More confusion. "Like, she thinks she has control over that or something?"

Wolf launched into an invective-filled explanation about how Chrissy perceived a difference between *falling* in love and *being* in love.

After he was finished, Romeo asked cautiously, "What's that mean for you?"

"Haven't figured that out yet." Wolf ran a hand over his face, looking bone-tired.

Romeo mulled things over and finally ventured, "Ever thought of simply manning up and telling her how you feel anyway?"

Wolf gave him a look that said he'd left half his brain behind on Wayfarer Island. "Since when has *mannin' up* ever involved tellin' folks how we feel? Think of Ryan Reynolds. The most you ever get out of him is a glimpse of melancholy before he diffuses the emotional gravity of the situation with a joke and a smirk. And he *always* gets the girl in the end."

"Sure." Romeo nodded. "And that manly cliché perpetuated by Hollywood is undoubtedly why there's so much toxic masculinity and ingrained misogyny in the world."

"Which brings up another point." Wolf lifted a finger. "What's the difference between a good guy and a nice guy?"

Romeo blinked.

"You got somethin' in your eye or what? You're doin' an awful lot of blinkin'."

"I'm just trying to keep up with everything that's coming out of your mouth without getting conversational whiplash. Now, good guy versus nice guy, there's a difference?"

Wolf shrugged. "Accordin' to Chrissy."

Romeo was beginning to suspect Chrissy was completely full of shit. "If there's a difference, I have no idea what it is. So back to my point about you telling Chrissy how you feel. She can wax poetic all she wants about falling in love versus being in love, but my guess is, once she's confronted with the actual, factual real deal, she'll realize she can't have one without the other."

Wolf shook his head and said something under his breath that made it clear he wanted to drop the subject. Since Romeo was a good friend—and also because he knew *exactly* how it felt to want to ignore the potential emotional time bomb ticking in the corner—he obliged, snagging instead on what had brought him around to Chrissy's house in the first place.

"Mia and I had to go to five different shops, but we were able to get our hands on thirteen metal detectors."

"Right." Wolf nodded. "We still have the mother lode to find. With everything that's happened, I forgot what we came here for."

"Well let me remind you." Romeo's tone was gloomy. It matched the sky to the west, which was beginning to boil with gray storm clouds. "We came here because this is our last chance to stay out of the poor house."

If he and his former SEAL brothers had chosen any other profession, their long list of accomplishments would've meant they were set for life. But because they'd chosen the military, they'd barely had enough to get the salvage business up and running.

If they didn't find the *Santa Cristina's* bounty?

Not to put it too bluntly, but we're all screwed.

They fell into silence, each lost in their own thoughts as they watched a colorful lizard skirt along the rail of the porch and then freeze in place when a fly alighted on a nearby bush.

Wolf's voice was contemplative, as if he was talking to himself, when he finally spoke. "When you've spent years turnin' yourself into the best of the best, there are times you begin to wonder if you should be doin' anything other than what you were trained to do."

Romeo rubbed a finger over the tattooed words on the inside of his forearm, feeling the shadow of Rusty's loss fall over him. More than once since they'd failed to find the mother lode, he'd had that exact same thought. That maybe they shouldn't have made that deathbed promise. That maybe they all should've stayed working for Uncle Sam.

But instead of voicing that aloud—the last thing either of them needed was to throw a pity party—he fell back on that old SEAL truism that said every situation was made better when you were giving your buddy shit. "Well, you're in the clear, my friend. 'Cause you're nowhere near the best of the best."

"Fuck you, Romeo," was Wolf's reply, but one corner of his mouth curled up.

"In your dreams." He winked as a welcome breeze from the approaching storm cut through the humidity of the day.

And lit a fire under his ass.

"I better get the Otter back out to Wayfarer before the weather comes in, or we'll have to wait until it blows over," he said. "That might be enough to send LT into convulsions."

When Wolf lifted a questioning eyebrow, he explained. "I called the sat phone on the island this morning to fill LT in on what happened with Winston and Chrissy. He's concerned, of course. But after he realized there's nothing he can do to help, he asked about the metal detectors and what time I thought I'd be getting them to Wayfarer. He's champing at the bit to get the island searched."

"Yeah." Wolf nodded. "Even though he's no longer our commandin' officer, he still feels responsible for all of us. And given he was the one to sell us on the idea of searchin' for the galleon, I'm sure he feels doubly shitty about the missin' treasure."

"Finding the booty was never a given." Romeo stood and waited for Wolf to do the same.

"I know that. You know that. But try convincin' LT of that," Wolf muttered.

Romeo didn't respond. He didn't need to. They both knew Wolf was right.

As they walked to the front door, Wolf added, "I'm goin' to stay here with Chrissy until this mess with the warehouse shooters gets solved."

"Figured as much." Romeo nodded.

"You still keep that Glock in the Otter?"

"Of course." Former fighting men hid guns and ammo like squirrels hide nuts.

"After I get everyone out of Chrissy's house, I'll meet you and Mia at the airport and grab it before y'all leave, if you don't mind."

"Of course," Romeo repeated.

Not that he didn't have faith in the uniformed police officer sent to protect Chrissy, except…he didn't have faith in the uniformed police officer sent to protect Chrissy.

Becoming a Navy SEAL involved seven months of BUD/S training followed by years upon years of weapons training, medical training, demolitions training, cold weather training, ad nauseum, ad infinitum. In short, for SEALs the training never stopped. And not that Romeo didn't respect cops. He did. No question. But when he compared Wolf's qualifications against the policeman's well…there was no comparison.

Wolf had his hand on the doorknob when Romeo stopped him. "Going back to this thing with you and Chrissy."

Wolf groaned. "I knew I should've kept my damned mouth shut."

"You and I both know life can go so quickly it's possible to wake up one day and realize you let a lot of really great things pass you by because your pride or stubbornness made you unwilling to take a chance."

Wolf studied him for a good long while. Then... "That's sound advice, man. Maybe you should think about takin' it yourself."

What the hell is that supposed to mean?

Romeo didn't voice his question aloud. Mostly because he didn't want to know the answer.

CHAPTER 18

11:41 AM...

I'm okay. Really," Chrissy hissed, hot on Wolf's heels as he shepherded the trio of local ladies toward the front door, "you don't have to do this."

"Yeah, darlin', I do," he insisted from the corner of his mouth. "You look like a glass factory that's been hit by a tornado."

"Wow." She stopped and frowned. "You sure know how to pump up a gal's ego."

"Please," he scoffed, pressing a hand against Judy's back when she tried to stop alongside Chrissy. Romeo and Mia had left for the airport. Officer Ryan was happily ensconced in a chair on the front porch with a bowl of peach cobbler. If Wolf could get gone The Three Middle-Aged Amigas, Chrissy could finally catch the break she deserved. "We both know you don't have a problem in the ego department." He gently cupped Janice's elbow when she swerved toward the short hallway that led to the bedroom and bathroom. "But when it comes to the knowin' when you've had enough department? Not to put too fine a point on it, but you ain't got the good sense God gave a goose."

Chrissy harrumphed loudly, and he could feel her staring daggers at his back as he gently—but firmly—shoved the J-Name Gang out the door.

"I swear." Jill turned to glare at him. "You are the bossiest man I have ever met. And if I thought you were acting this way for any other reason than because you're worried for Chrissy, I'd punch you in the pecker."

He bit the inside of his cheek to keep from laughing. She thought *he* was bossy? *Hello, Pot. My name is Kettle.*

"Thanks for stoppin' by, ladies." His words were as cordial as a Baptist minister at a church picnic, but he hoped they could hear the underlying warning in his tone.

"I think that's our cue," Janice stage-whispered to Jill.

"Our cue was when he unceremoniously shoved us out the door." Jill frowned ferociously, trying to intimidate him.

Thing was, Wolf wasn't easily intimidated.

This apparently pleased Jill, because her expression melted into a smile. Pinching his cheek as if he were a toddler instead of a full-grown man who towered over her by at least five inches, she told him, "Good man. You planning on hanging around to help her today?"

"I need to run a quick errand," he admitted. "After that, I'll be on hand until she kicks me out."

"Which might be sooner rather than later if you keep treating my guests this way!" Chrissy groused from the middle of the living room, where she stood with her legs spread and one hand planted firmly on her hip, Wonder Woman style.

All she was missing was the cape.

And the armored bustier.

She would look *amazing* in an armored bustier.

"You know"—Jill peered around Wolf's shoulder—"a smart woman knows to accept a helping hand when it's extended her way. Especially when it's such a *handsome* helping hand."

"Thank you, Jill," he whispered conspiratorially. "That's what *I* told her."

Jill gave him a wink then cupped her friends' elbows in her palms. "Come on, gals. Our work here is done, and we've got businesses to run."

Wolf gave Officer Ryan a two-finger salute when he stuck his head out the door. He waited until the ladies had made it safely down the porch steps before ducking back inside and closing out the world beyond. When he turned, it was to see Chrissy puffed up like the peacocks his grandmother kept in the front yard of her farmhouse for bug control.

Sighing deeply, he readied himself to receive a good old-fashioned tongue-lashing. But all the fight suddenly drained out of her, and her shoulders drooped like they were weighed down by sixty-ton Abrams tanks.

"I feel like a can of smashed assholes," she admitted weakly. Her eyes got huge when he'd marched over and grabbed her hand. "What are you doing?"

"I'm takin' you to bed." He ignored the thrill he got from saying those words.

Before he got any deeper into her—and heaven help him, he was already in *way* over his head—he had to figure out what her not wanting to fall in love meant.

Part of him wondered if it was simply self-preservation, a knee-jerk response to all the heartache she'd seen her mother suffer. But another part of him knew she had the stubbornness of a mule, and if she'd convinced herself she wasn't going to fall in love, she *wouldn't*.

Could he settle for that? Find contentment there?

Let's say he convinced her to take a chance on him. Let's say it was five years down the road and they were married, shared a house, and had a few kids. Would he be satisfied with the thought that if he gave her the life she wanted, if he walked beside her as her friend and confidant and lover, her love for him would grow? Like mushrooms in the dirt? Moss on a stone? Slime on a swamp log?

Hell no! I've waited thirty-four years for the right woman to come along, and I want the whole kit and caboodle!

He wanted hot and heavy. He wanted wicked and wonderful. He wanted that heady rush of two people tumbling together, head over heels, and then catching each other before they hit the ground.

He wanted moonlit walks on the beach followed by sweaty lovemaking between the sheets. He wanted candlelight and roses. He wanted picnics and sunsets. He wanted to pull her behind a tree in a crowded park and kiss her senseless because he couldn't stand another moment without having his lips on hers. He wanted her to roll her eyes at having to watch *another* cop show, but snuggle in next to him on the sofa all the same.

He wanted his own true love story, damnit!

And yet, as he dragged her down the hall, her hand nestled so perfectly inside his, he couldn't help thinking he might be plumb crazy to consider anything that didn't get him *her* in the end.

"I need a bath." Her voice was heavy with exhaustion.

"What you need is sleep."

"Fine." She sighed and he would swear he could feel her warm breath on the back of his neck. "So I *want* a bath. Is that okay with you? Is me wanting a bath enough?"

A brief image of her naked, skin all rosy and slick from the water, skated through his mind. It was followed by a sudden heaviness behind his fly.

He wasn't a complete creep, so he ignored both things as he changed direction, pulling her into the small bathroom with its vanity, tub/shower combo, and floor tiles in pretty greens and blues that reminded him of sea glass. "Sit down before you fall down." He pointed to the closed toilet lid.

She lifted an eyebrow at his imperious command.

The military had honed many of his natural qualities. Confidence, determination, and stamina, to name a few. But it might've done him a disservice when it came to the more subtle side of social situations. He'd learned to forgo politeness for proficiency.

"Christina"—he made sure his tone was obliging—"why don't you sit down and take a load off while I run you a bath?"

Her gas tank might be empty, but her sense of humor remained intact. "Thank you for asking so nicely, Wolf." Her mouth curved into a teasing smile as she primly arranged herself atop the toilet. "Don't mind if I do."

He turned on the water, adjusted the temperature, and then hitched his chin toward the shirt she wore. "You're goin' to need help with that top."

Thanks to the sling and bandaging, Chrissy had needed the nurse's assistance getting into the scrubs top. It stood to reason she'd need some help coming out.

"Wow," she said dryly. "I've had men come up with some pretty bad lines while attempting to get me out of my clothes, but that might be the worst one yet."

"Like I said, the best lines are less about seduction and more about statin' your offer straight out." He lowered his chin and gave her his most provocative look. "If I was tryin' to get you naked, I'd have said somethin' along the lines of, 'Christina, you gorgeous thing, why don't you let me take off your clothes and then kiss every new inch of you once it's exposed?'"

He was teasing. Except the instant the words were out of his mouth, they didn't feel like a joke.

"I wish I had a pithy reply, but you just melted my brain." She lifted a hand to dab at the side of her face. "Is it leaking out of my ears?"

He laughed. God love the woman. Never once had she tried to act like they didn't have explosive chemistry. She simply chose to ignore it.

"Meltin' your brain was my intention." He looked pointedly at the scrubs top. "Now…that shirt?"

She curled her upper lip. "It hurt like hell getting it on. I can't imagine trying to take it off."

"We could cut it," he suggested and watched her face brighten.

"Scissors are in the knife block in the kitchen."

He headed for the door, but then hesitated. "One thing before I go."

Curiosity had her eyebrows arching.

"You want to enlighten me on the difference between a good guy and a nice guy?"

"Is *that* what's been bugging you?" She shook her head. "I've been wondering."

"It's one of the things," he admitted evasively. "So? What's the difference?"

"Look." She shrugged. "Neither of them is bad, okay? I want to start by saying that."

It never boded well for the person listening when the person talking felt the need to preface a statement.

"A nice guy is someone who's polite and treats the women he dates well," she explained and he relaxed. "A good guy is someone who *cares* about the women he dates, and he goes out of his way to show he cares."

So much for relaxing. Someone inserted a steel rod in

his spine. "You don't think I cared about you when we were datin'?"

She couldn't hold his gaze and let her eyes fall to a piece of lint stuck to her knee. "Were we ever dating, Wolf?"

"I thought so. Or, at least, I thought we were gettin' there in an awful big hurry."

Now she met his gaze. He would swear he saw a shadow of That Night in her eyes.

"Then I..." She lifted her hand and let it fall. "I don't understand why— No." She shook her head. "It doesn't matter. It's water under the bridge, and it's better if we row as fast as we can in the opposite direction."

He wasn't sure how he got there, but he found himself sitting opposite her on the lip of the tub. The sound of the running water was loud in the little bathroom. He switched it off. He didn't want to miss a single word out of her mouth.

"It's *not* water under the bridge, Chrissy. Tell me what you were about to say. Ask me the question you stopped yourself from askin'."

She fiddled with the lint on her knee for a second longer. Then, finally, "Why didn't you come say hello to me that night?" There was confusion—and hurt, damnit there was *hurt*—in her eyes. "I mean, I get you were on a date with Anna, but—"

"Who?" he interrupted.

"Anna?"

"Was that her name? I'd forgotten."

"You... You'd *forgotten*?" Her voice became shrill.

He lifted a hand. "I mean, it wasn't a date. I'd just met her. Right then. Right when I walked in and saw you with—"

"My cousin."

If his mind had been an old CD, it would've skipped. "Who?"

"Well…" She screwed up her face. "Our grandmothers were sisters. I think that technically makes Sean my second cousin, but I've never understood that once or twice removed thing. Could he be my first cousin once removed?"

"Wait a minute." A terrible sense of *oh-shit* began swirling in his stomach. "That was your *cousin*?"

He thought back to the blond god who'd had a possessive hand resting against the small of her back. To the way the man had smiled at her with such blatant sexual appreciation in his eyes.

Or had Wolf mistaken possessiveness for familiarity? Sexual appreciation for familial affection?

"Fuck!" He stood and ran an agitated hand through his hair. *Oh, fuck, fuck,* fuck!

Chrissy frowned up him. "I wanted to introduce you two. That's why I followed you to the back of the bar. I was going to tell you that you didn't need to avoid me because you were there on a date and—"

"It wasn't a date."

When Chrissy snapped her mouth shut and gave him a quelling look, he realized repeating the phrase only made him sound like more of an asshole than he already was. Which was saying something since he currently claimed the title: King of Asshole Mountain.

He hated it when Romeo was right.

"I'm the biggest idiot on the planet," he said as much to himself as to her, marveling at what a gargantuan, monstrous, we're talking *stupendous* goat rodeo of a clusterfuck That Night had been.

When he didn't continue, she mistook his pause as an invitation for her to contradict him. She did the opposite. "You'll get no argument from me there."

God, I love her brass.

I love her.

And he'd screwed things up so much worse than he'd imagined.

"Christina…" He knelt in front of her, grabbing her hand and holding it between both of his own. She blinked at him in surprise. "I—" he began and then stopped, the scar near his temple pulling tight when he clenched his jaw.

How the hell did he explain his behavior that night?

"If you want to be trusted, be honest." It was one of his grandmother's favorite quotes.

Okay, Elisi. Here goes nothin'.

"I've never…been jealous a day in my life," he began slowly, trying to put his complete and utter misjudgment and subsequent assholery into some context. "But I was absolutely *green* with it when I walked into the bar and saw you out with another man."

A line formed between her eyebrows. "You—you were jealous?"

"Eaten up with it. Which is why I started flirtin' with the first woman who came up to me. And, yes, before you say anything, I *know* how immature that sounds. I admit it. But I couldn't stop myself. I wasn't thinking. I was simply *actin'* on…well… I guess it was hurt pride. Enter the redhead."

"Anna."

"Right."

She opened her mouth, closed it, then opened it again. "*Why* were you so jealous?"

"You're kiddin', right?"

She shook her head, and he blew out a breath. "Look, darlin', it isn't advertised on Navy recruitment posters, but the military isn't above usin' drugs to give their fighters the upper hand in combat. Various psychoactive pharmaceuticals are employed to suppress hunger, lengthen wakefulness, improve reflexes, etcetera. But nothin' I ever took on a mission gave me the high I felt when I was around you. You made me feel alive like nothin' else could. I was *crazy* about you, Chrissy. Still am. In fact, I—"

The words—*the words*—were perched on the tip of his tongue. But they refused to budge. It was like they were set in place with grappling hooks.

"In fact," he said slowly so he could change directions, "I was so crazy when I saw that blond behemoth bend down and whisper in your ear, I did the first thing that came to mind. I told Anna to meet me in the storage closet."

Chrissy blinked at him uncomprehendingly.

Scrubbing a hand over his face, he groaned. "I wish there was a way I could explain this so I don't come off like a total dickwad, but I was bein' a total dickwad. So I'm goin' to shoot you straight and hope you find it in your heart not to hold one really, *really* bad decision against me."

She nodded, but didn't say anything.

He desperately wished she'd say something. *Anything.* A biting remark. An acerbic retort. *Something* to let him know what she was thinking. But for the first time in their acquaintance, she seemed perfectly happy letting him keep the conversational baton in hand.

"I wanted to run away, but I thought that'd be cowardly. So... I invited Anna to meet me in at the back of the bar. I reckoned I could kill two birds with one stone. I'd no longer have to watch you and your date canoodlin' and I..." He winced. "I'd provide myself a little distraction."

When Chrissy finally spoke, each word was a Tyson Fury haymaker straight to his solar plexus. "What a bunch of horseshit. You didn't invite Anna to that storage closet because you thought that was better than simply leaving the bar. You invited her back there because you were jealous and you hoped to make me jealous too."

He swallowed uncomfortably. "You're right. You're absolutely right."

"And you claim to be a good guy? You claim to *care* about me?" Two red flags flew in her cheeks, and he *hated* that he'd upset her. *Again.*

"I got no excuse." His throat was raw, which made his voice sound like ten miles of bad country road. "My only explanation is, like I said, I'd never felt that way before. I didn't have the first clue how to handle it. But please know, darlin', I know better now. It'll never happen again. And I'm so sorry—"

"Spare me another apology." She stood from the toilet, nearly knocking him on his ass in the process.

"Christina…" He scrambled to his feet, grabbing her wrist to stop her from leaving the bathroom. "Please, I—"

"Do you have any idea how much you *humiliated* me?" Her eyes blazed with blue flames. "I didn't like seeing you with that woman, but I told myself, *It's okay, Chrissy. He hasn't done anything wrong. Suck it up and act like a grownup.* And so I followed you thinking I'd convince you to bring your date over so you could meet my cousin—"

He opened his mouth but snapped it shut again when she pointed a finger in his face and snarled, "And if you tell me *it wasn't a date* one more time, so help me, I'm going to punch you in the dick."

Twice in one mornin' I've been threatened with that, he thought wretchedly. *I'm winnin' big today.*

"And then when I stepped into the storage closet and you started kissing me, I actually thought, *See? It* is *me he wants.* And I was *happy*, Wolf. *Happy.* And then you called me Anna and I knew it was her you wanted."

His mind drifted back in time…

The storage closet was as dark as pitch and smelled of spilled beer and wet wood. The sounds of the band playing

189

a Jimmy Buffet cover were muted, which allowed him to hear the heavy thud of his own heart.

The organ wasn't beating with anticipation for the redhead's imminent arrival, however. Its rhythm was one of hurt. Of confusion.

How could he have been so wrong? How could he have misread all the signs?

Sure, he hadn't even stolen a kiss from Chrissy, but there'd been so much banter. So much flirting. So much… chemistry.

They were supposed to have their first date the very next night. Although, they'd agreed they'd known each other long enough that it didn't feel like a first date. More like a third or fourth date. Which made it that much more momentous. More special.

That's why he'd had Romeo fly him to Key West a day early. He wanted to buy some decent clothes. Tank tops and swim trunks weren't going to cut it for a night out with the incomparable Christina Szarek. He wanted to look good for her. He wanted to impress her. He wanted…her.

All of her. Her mind. Her body. Her smiles. Her sarcastic conversational volleys.

He wanted her like he'd never wanted another woman.

But apparently, she wanted some big blond dude with a jaw that would make Henry Cavill weep with envy.

He'd thought he and Chrissy were on the same page. The we're-goin'-to-give-this-thing-between-us-a-fair-shot-and-see-where-it-takes-us page. But, hell, after what he saw out in the bar, he knew they weren't even reading the same damned book and—

"Wolf?" A lilting female voice sounded from the hall a second before the door opened and a hand stole inside, fumbling for the switch on the wall.

He didn't want any light. He liked the dark. Liked that he could pretend anything he wanted when he couldn't see what was in front of his face.

And pretend he did.

He dragged the redhead into the closet with him and asked desperately, "Can I kiss you?"

"Yes." Her answer was unhesitating.

Pinning her against the closed door and claiming her mouth, he pretended she was someone else altogether. He pretended they were Chrissy's lips he laved and sucked. He pretended they were Chrissy's moans he drank into the back of his throat. He pretended it was Chrissy's curves that met his desperately searching fingers.

"Wolf!" His name was breathed into the darkness when he let the redhead up for air.

He almost said "Christina" in response. The name filled his mouth, sweet and gossamer like cotton candy at a county fair. But at the last second, he remembered it wasn't Chrissy in the closet with him. It was the woman he'd been fiercely flirting with for the last thirty minutes.

What's her name again?

Then, he remembered.

"Anna."

"What?" That one word was so strident it nearly pierced his eardrums.

The overhead light blazed on, and he blinked against its sudden brightness. His jaw fell open when it wasn't the redhead's green eyes that filled his vision, but Chrissy's blue ones.

"You are such *an asshole!" she snarled before throwing open the door and running out of the closet.*

"Christina!" he yelled, hesitating only a few seconds before following her. But she was fast, and a few seconds head start was all she needed. By the time he made it to the

main area of the bar, he saw her dragging the blond out the back.

"Hey!" The redhead snagged his arm. "Sorry I kept you waiting. I got stopped by a friend and—"

"Excuse me for a second," he interrupted and hightailed it toward the marina. By the time his flip-flops hit the boards of the dock, Chrissy and her companion were nowhere to be found.

Wolf shook his head now. "It *was* you I wanted, Chrissy. It's always been you. It always *will* be you."

Angry breathing had made her chest work like bellows. Now, it stilled. "What are you saying?" She eyed him uncertainly.

"I'm sayin'—" He stopped, unable or unwilling—he wasn't sure which anymore—to spit out the thing that was *right there*. Instead, he went with, "I want to kiss you."

A scowl slammed her eyebrows together. "What?"

"I have to kiss you, Chrissy."

"Are you crazy? Why would I—"

"That's the favor," he cut in. "I'm claimin' it now. I want to kiss you." He'd run out of words to convince her That Night had been a mistake of epic proportions. The only thing he knew to do now was show her.

Show her what they'd been missing. *Show* her how it could be between them. *Show* her how sorry he was and how much he cared. "One kiss. That's all I'm askin'. And then, if you want, you can punch me in the dick after."

"*Now* you're talking."

Even with his heart hammering against his ribs and his future happiness on the line, she still found a way to make him smile.

"Is that a yes?" He dared to hope.

She pursed her lips. "I guess it has to be, right? I promised you one favor, and if I told you *no*, I'd be going back on my word. I never go back on my word."

"No." He shook his head. "I want to kiss you, Chrissy. I'm askin' to kiss you. But I won't without your consent."

"Fine." She rolled her eyes. "I consent. I'm tired of that promise hanging over my head anyway. I'd rather make good on it and be done with it."

Not much of a ringing endorsement, but he supposed he'd have to settle for it. He took a step toward her, but she lifted a hand. "But *you* asked to kiss *me*. That doesn't mean I have to kiss you back."

Leave it to her to find the loophole in his plan.

Then again, he wasn't without his *own* unique set of skills.

Reaching past her, he carefully shut the door. Then, *ever*-so-slowly in case she wanted to change her mind, he closed the distance between them.

Her back was flush against the wood panels by the time his thighs brushed hers. Lifting a hand to her face, he curled his fingers around the back of her neck at the same time he rubbed his thumb along the smooth line of her jaw.

Her skin was as soft as silk, as warm as the summer sun.

"All we need to complete the déjà vu is to turn off the light." There was heaviness in her voice.

That chemistry they'd shared from the beginning was a palpable force. It hummed like electricity in the scant few inches between them. Would there be sparks when he finally pressed his mouth to hers?

"No darkness this time, darlin'." His voice was so low it was almost a growl. "I want to see every moment. I want to watch what happens when I show you exactly how I feel."

She tried to roll her eyes, but he stopped her by lowering his mouth to hers.

There weren't sparks. But he would swear a bolt of lightning sizzled through him.

Lord, how he wanted to pillage and plunder. Just like he'd done in the storage closet. But a woman as beautiful and as sexy as Chrissy was undoubtedly used to men trying to devour her.

He was determined this time would be different.

He would show her *he* was different.

Brushing his lips slowly back and forth in a feather-light caress, he applied the tiniest bit of pressure. At first, she kept her mouth closed to him, but then a soft sigh escaped.

He drank it in thirstily, like he'd been lost in the desert for days and her sigh was a cup of water. Her warm breath tasted like peach cobbler. Like the salty sea air. Like freedom and fun and all his fantasies rolled into one.

Angling her head slightly, he caught her plump bottom lip between his teeth and sucked it gently. Softly swept it with the tip of his tongue. And then he did the same to her upper lip. Sipping at her. Nibbling at her.

Taking his time.

Showing her there was more to him, more to *them*, than pheromones and friendship.

Showing her there was tenderness and affection.

Showing her how much he cherished and adored her.

Her hand had landed on his waist the instant his mouth met hers. Now it inched upward, her fingers clutching at his shoulder.

She hadn't returned his caresses. But neither was she immune. He could feel the tension building in her. Could hear the way her breath caught each time he changed the pressure or the pace of his teasing lips.

Finally, her restraint broke. She made a low, hungry sound before plunging her tongue into his mouth.

It was all the invitation he needed.

Groaning, he delved his tongue inside the warm, wet

wonder of her. Meeting her stroke for stroke. Lick for lick. Suck for suck.

Their kisses became a force of nature unto themselves, sweeping them along in their wake until the sexy sounds of two hungry mouths seeking fulfillment echoed around the bathroom.

He tilted his hips forward without thought, his hardness seeking the solace of her feminine softness. But when she lifted a leg, hooking her heel behind his knee, he didn't register softness. He only registered heat.

The material of the scrubs was thin. No match for the sultry fire at the center of her. And that's when he lost his damn mind.

Gone were the tender caresses of moments before. Now all he could think about was claiming what was his. Marking her. Taking her. Stealing away any thought she might still harbor that they weren't made for each other.

Grabbing her waist, he hoisted her atop the vanity and stepped between her spread thighs so he could grind his erection against her.

It was her turn to meet *him* stroke for stroke. And, dear woman that she was, she did. She swiveled her hips until he saw stars. Ground against him until he felt a hot drop of pre-cum wet the waistband of his boxer briefs.

Somewhere, in the furthest corner of his mind, a voice of reason spoke.

Don't overdo it, it said. *You'll regret it if you do. She might regret it if you do.*

He didn't listen. He *couldn't*. Not when every single one of his senses was completely overwhelmed by the woman in his arms.

His taste buds were alive with the sweet, salty flavor of her. His nose filled with the delicious sunshine, coconut oil, and salty sea spray scent of her. His ears resonated with her throaty moans, with her greedy little sighs. And when he opened his eyes, ever so slightly, his vision filled with the sight of her thick lashes that were dark at their bases but the whitest blond at their tips.

Unfortunately, the voice was a persistent motherfucker. And with each passing second, it grew louder until, eventually, he could no longer ignore it.

Ripping his lips away from Chrissy's devastatingly talented mouth, he took half a step back. Just enough so he was no longer pressed against that part of her that for months he'd been longing to explore with his hands and mouth and cock.

Her fingers were tangled in his hair. Rapid breaths made her breasts press tight against the fabric of the top, emphasizing the straining hardness of her nipples. But it was her eyes that caught and held him. The swirling, churning ocean blue of them.

He wanted to drown in those eyes. Plunge into their depths and lose himself in them forever. Lose himself in *her*.

His island girl.

For better or worse—and he feared it would be for the worse—the words that'd been stuck in his mouth slid out before he could stop them. "I've fallen in love with you, Christina."

CHAPTER 19

12:11 PM...

Chrissy's throat closed up.

Sweat popped out on her upper lip at the same time panic rose inside her.

Is someone stabbing me in my pupils? It sure felt like it. That, or she was milliseconds away from bursting into tears.

But *why*?

Was it because hearing those words on Wolf's lips sounded like poetry? Made her feel more alive than ever? Made her feel worthy and adored in a way she never had before?

She'd spent her entire life trying *not* to become her mother, and all it took was one overused phrase to have her wanting to ditch those hard-learned life lessons.

Those words, when spoken by a man who was staring at her with a sincerity in his eyes that flamed so hot it burned her from the inside out, had *power*. They made her want to *believe*.

No *wonder* Josephine had fallen so easily so many times. A person could become addicted to hearing those words.

But it's not real! she silently reminded herself. *It's just hormones and brain chemistry, and when that fades, what's left? Will there be anything left?*

There never had been for her mother.

Her voice sounded like seashells stuck in a garbage disposal when she finally said, "You don't, Wolf. Not really. You *want* me. There's a difference."

A muscle ticked in the side of his jaw. His next words were measured. "There are a few things I'm good at, Christina. Knife play, navigation, and puttin' up with the machinations of a big, boisterous family."

Not for the first time, she imagined him surrounded by an adoring crowd of nieces and nephews. Although, if she was honest with herself, her mind's eye conjured *other* children into the mix. Little ones who shared his flashing, dark eyes, and her straight, slightly upturned nose.

"But what I'm really, *really* good at is knowin' my own mind," he continued. "I *do* want you, darlin'. More than I've ever wanted another woman. But it's more than that. I've fallen in love with you. With your smart mouth and quick wit. With how you get quiet and introspective when you're out fishin'. With how you always mean what you say and say what you mean and—"

"Wolf—" she tried to interrupt, but he talked right over her.

"I'm not braggin' or anything, but I've known my fair share of women. Have even been downright infatuated with a few of 'em. And yet, I've never felt a connection like the one I feel with you."

"Wolf—" she tried again, but a strong gust of wind whistled by outside and rattled the fronds of the saw palmetto against the side of the house, distracting her.

The storm was nearly upon them. Its tumultuous arrival matched the emotions roiling inside her.

"Wolf"—this time she managed to finish her thought—"what happens six weeks from now or six months from now when we've scratched our itch and we're no longer running on that heady, tingly feeling? Are you willing to settle for comfort in place of adventure? For convenience in place of excitement? I think if you're honest with yourself, you'll realize you're not the settling down type and—"

"No," he interrupted. "What I'm *not*, is the *settling* type."

"Meaning what?"

"Can't you guess?" For the span of a dozen heartbeats, he stared at her. *Hard.* But she couldn't read what was in his eyes.

She gave a helpless shake of her head. "I don't know what you're talking about."

He glanced at the drops of rain pattering against the windowpane. "I have to go to the airport to get somethin' from Romeo." His voice was quiet but edged in steel. "We'll finish this when I come back."

She opened her mouth, then closed it again when he pushed past her and quietly disappeared down the hall.

She became the human equivalent of a party balloon poked by a pin. All the air leaked out of her until she was limp and lifeless.

Sitting heavily on the side of the bathtub, she immediately regretted the move since it jarred her injury. Strange, she hadn't remembered she *had* a bullet wound while Wolf was kissing her. All she'd felt was pleasure.

All-encompassing, all-consuming pleasure.

The kind of pleasure she'd only ever read about in books or seen in the movies. The kind of pleasure that stole her breath and gave it back to her in a way that made her feel like her lungs had never truly been filled before. The kind of pleasure that had her body making decisions without the benefit of her brain.

The kind of pleasure that was very, *very* dangerous indeed.

"Stand up, darlin'." Wolf reappeared in the doorway, scissors in hand. "Let me cut your shirt away so you can have that bath while I'm gone."

Her mind was mush. Complete and total pulp. Which meant following instructions was easier than coming up with solutions of her own.

"Turn around." He twirled one finger. "I reckon if I cut it straight up the back, you can slide out of it like a hospital gown. Hopefully, that'll keep you from havin' to move your arm too much."

When she did as he asked, he pulled out the hem of her borrowed scrubs shirt. The first snip of the scissors had a wheezing breath escaping her lungs.

She'd never thought about a man slicing her out of her clothes before. Peeling them off? Sure. Ripping them off? Plenty of times. But never had scissors played a part in her fantasies.

I need to work on improving my imagination, she decided. There was something incredibly erotic—and maybe a little dangerous—about standing perfectly still while he slowly cut a line up her back.

He must've thought so too. She heard his breath catch. Thought for sure, she felt him pause for a bit, as if he needed to collect himself before continuing.

With every snip, the bathroom walls closed in. With every new inch of skin that was exposed, it became harder to breathe. And by the time he'd cut his way up to her mid-back, she barely refrained from groaning.

It took every ounce of willpower she possessed not to turn and claim his lips. Those incredibly talented lips that were far too pretty to be wasted on a man. That mouth that was all the things dreams were made of.

Oh, who are you kidding, Chrissy? Every part of him is pretty.

From the top of his inky-black head to the soles of his perfect feet, he was a spectacular example of masculine beauty. Even his scars didn't detract from the overall aesthetic, but instead enhanced it. Added character. Gravity. Spoke of a life that'd been hard-lived and hard-won.

"Almost there," he said as he cut the thicker material of the collar and spread the two halves of the now-destroyed shirt wide across her back.

The air from the vent was cool against her naked flesh. Which made the warmth of his breath feel that much hotter when he slowly exhaled. Her shoulder blades hitched together, and she was reminded of what he'd said.

Christina, you gorgeous thing, why don't you let me take off your clothes and kiss every new inch of you once it's exposed?

She shivered, waiting breathlessly for the feel of his hot mouth on her back. For the warm, wet swipe of his tongue as he tasted her waiting flesh.

When he stepped aside to lay the scissors on the vanity, she didn't know if she should crow with relief or growl with disappointment.

"All done." Was it her imagination or was his voice about three octaves lower than usual? She'd swear she heard it with her ovaries instead of her ears.

"Wolf, I—"

"I need to get to the airport before Romeo leaves," he cut her off.

"But I—"

"Plus, I have to clear my head before I say somethin' I might regret. It's not every day I tell a woman I've fallen in love with her only to have her throw the words back in my face."

All the desire that'd been keeping her warm seeped from her body, leaving nothing but coldness behind. She shivered.

"Go on, then." He hitched his chin toward the water steaming in the tub. "Take your bath. I'll be back in less than an hour."

"I'm sorry," she whispered, desperately wishing there were better words for a situation like this.

His eyes narrowed ever-so-slightly. "You're *something*, but I don't think sorry is it."

Before she could ask what he meant by that, he turned on his heel and quit the bathroom. She watched his swift, sure steps as he made his way down the hall. Then he disappeared around the corner, and a couple of seconds later, the front door clicked shut.

She realized she'd been holding her breath when it whooshed out of her. "What the hell just happened?" she asked the empty room.

It didn't answer, of course. But she didn't need it to. She knew what'd happened.

A man she admired and respected claimed to have fallen in love with her. But despite his protestations to the contrary, what he'd *truly* done was fallen in *lust*.

She'd fallen in lust too. From the first moment she laid eyes on him.

But how in the heck could she convince him he was wrong and she was right?

Kicking off her shoes, she decided she should boil some water for a cup of tea. Nothing better than a hot bath and a warm cup of oolong to help her think.

And she *needed* to think. Because she might not want to fall in love with Wolf, but there was no question she cared for him. Cherished his presence in her life. Only wanted what was best for him.

She felt an extra pep in her step every morning she woke up knowing she'd fly to Wayfarer Island to see him. The sun shone brighter when they were engaged in salty banter. The hours of drudgery while carefully removing the sand and crustaceans from the *Santa Cristina's* delicate carcass went by quicker when he was working beside her, writing funny jokes or drawing ridiculous pictures on the white, underwater slates they used to communicate.

The thought of giving that up? Of not having him in her life? Or worse yet, having him in her life, right there, but not being able to talk and joke or attempt to one-up each other like they'd been doing from the beginning?

It made her sick to her stomach.

And yet, she couldn't see a way around it. They couldn't continue on as they had been. Not now that those words had been spoken.

Not to mention, after that kiss, it might be impossible for her to go back to keeping her hands off him.

Five minutes later, her tea steaming on the lip of the tub, she slowly undressed, being careful when removing the sling from her arm. After lighting the lavender and vanilla-scented candle sitting on the toilet tank, she lowered herself into the warm water and mulled over her problem.

Water had always been her medium. Something about its wet, weighty embrace. About the sound of it lapping against the sandy shore or the side of her porcelain tub. It grounded her. *Focused* her.

Soon, an idea began to form. Trouble was, she wasn't sure she had the nerve to see it through. And more troubling still, if she saw it through, what happened *after*?

After she'd proved her point? After he'd come to his senses?

Was she strong enough, smart enough, *brave* enough to follow her head and keep her damned heart out of it?

Mom never was.

CHAPTER 20

1:13 PM...

Rain poured on the island.

The water sluiced down Duval Street, the main strip of raucous bars, tourist shops, and greasy spoons. The gutters and flood grates couldn't keep up with the deluge, meaning parts of the sidewalks were submerged under a foot of water.

Whereas Wolf's mood matched the weather, the tourists hopping from placed to place—uncaring that they were getting soaked to the bone—all seemed as gay as a sunny day.

And why shouldn't they? he thought sourly. *I bet they didn't tell someone they loved them only to be laughed at.*

Okay, to be fair Chrissy hadn't *laughed.* In fact, there for a second, he'd thought she might cry. And seeing all that emotion in her eyes? Well...it'd given him hope.

Hope that her talk of never wanting to fall in love was simply that. *Talk.* Hope that, despite herself, the minute he said the words aloud she realized she'd fallen in love with him too. Hope that they could put That Night behind them, forget about past grievances and misunderstandings, and move forward toward a future they both wanted.

So much for hope, he thought bitterly.

Then…like always, his mind filled with the words of another. *"Don't lose hope. When the sun goes down, the stars come out."*

Okay, fine. So he was supposed to suck it up buttercup and persevere.

But how?

Taking a deep breath, he ran through his options, and realized it might have been better if Chrissy *had* laughed. At least if she'd thought it was a joke, he'd know what to do. Namely, prove to her he was serious.

But she didn't think he was joking. She simply didn't *believe* him.

How in the hell did a person go about changing someone's *beliefs*?

Also, let's say he *did* somehow come up with a way to make her believe. Then what? He'd still have to convince her he was the "settling down type," as she called it. And then, if by some miracle he managed to convince her he truly had fallen for her and assure her he was, in fact, the settling down type, there was still before him the gargantuan task of disabusing her stubborn ass of the notion that romantic love could grow without first *falling* in love.

For fuck's sake!

His grandmother said he enjoyed a challenge. But this felt less like a challenge and more like he was being punished.

For what, he couldn't imagine.

He certainly wasn't a saint—no one in the spec ops community could ever claim that—but neither was he a liar or a cheat or a conman or a thief. He tried to live his life by the six pillars of character he'd learned in school. And he always helped old ladies cross the street!

"Don't worry. It'll blow over in an hour."

He realized he'd been glaring through the taxi's window at the cloud-filled sky. It made sense the driver assumed he was a tourist concerned about the weather.

Side note: Thank *goodness* the cab driver who answered his call hadn't been Chrissy's friend, ol' Billy Blue Eyes. That might've been enough to send Wolf straight over the edge.

"That's good," he said to be cordial, sitting up straighter when the taxi turned down Chrissy's street. He could see her house two blocks away and was gratified to find Officer Ryan in the same place he'd left him.

That means all is well on the home front.

Home front. *Home.*

From the moment he met Chrissy, she'd made him feel homesick. But not for a place he'd ever known. Homesick for *her*. As if his soul had always known she was out there, somewhere, and once he saw her, he realized how much he'd *missed* her.

He opened the brown paper sack the friendly mechanic at the airport had given him after he walked onto the tarmac looking for Romeo and the Otter. Romeo had gotten out of Key West ahead of the weather, but not before placing the Glock in the bag and giving it to the mechanic to pass on to Wolf.

"It's that one on the corner," he told the taxi driver now. "The one with the uniformed officer sittin' on the porch."

Any other place and the cabby might've asked about the police presence. But if what happened in Vegas stayed in Vegas, then it was safe to say the weird shit a person saw in Key West was standard operating procedure for Key West.

Wolf had once witnessed a man walking down the street wearing nothing but high heels and a feathered headdress. No one had given the guy a second look. Then there was the time two fishing boats collided in the marina. Both captains simply swam to shore, popped the top on a couple of cold ones, and sat in the sand to watch the vessels sink.

Seeing a police officer in a rocking chair likely didn't even begin to wiggle the cab driver's antenna.

While the man was distracted with parking the car close to the curb, Wolf covertly transferred the Glock from the bag to the back of his waistband, pulling the hem of his T-shirt over the butt of the weapon.

He wasn't trying to *hide* the Glock from Officer Ryan, necessarily. But neither did he want to advertise that he'd feel a lot better being armed should those warehouse assholes try to make another run at Chrissy.

"I got you as close as I could to the front door," the driver said. "But you're still going to get drenched."

Wolf thanked the man and paid him. Then, with a deep breath, he pushed out of the vehicle and raced down the little brick paver path and up the front steps to Chrissy's house.

The cabby was right. By the time he ducked under the porch's wide roof, there wasn't an inch of dry skin left on him. His grandmother referred to this type of rain as a "toad-strangler."

"You're wetter than an otter's pocket," Officer Ryan observed drolly.

Wolf shook his head like a dog shaking off water. "Thank you, Captain Obvious."

In the short time it'd taken for the cab to arrive to take him to the airport, the two of them had sat in the rocking chairs and gotten to know each other a bit.

Turned out, Officer Rick Ryan had family in Oklahoma, was an OSU Cowboys fan by association, and had a great sense of humor. The latter of which was why Wolf felt comfortable busting the dude's balls now.

"They teach those keen observational skills at the police academy, or do you come by them naturally?"

Officer Ryan grinned. "Little of both, I suppose."

Wolf chuckled and then hitched his chin toward the front door. "Everything okay in there?"

"She's been as quiet as a church mouse."

"Thanks for keepin' watch while I was gone. Can I bring you somethin'? A drink, maybe? I can take over guard duty if you need to hit the head."

"Nah." Ryan shook his head. "I'm good for now. But you might check back in an hour or so."

"Roger that." Wolf dipped his chin and opened the front door.

The instant he did, the rotten-egg aroma of natural gas hit him in the face.

"What the hell?" he thought he heard Officer Ryan exclaim. He couldn't be sure since his racing heart roared in his ears. And if that wasn't enough to impair his hearing, then add to it the sound of his own bellow as he called Chrissy's name.

He waited a half tick, listening to his voice echo through the empty rooms. When she didn't answer, fear caught his chest in a bear trap.

Natural gas was incredibly volatile. If it made its way to the pilot light on, say, her water heater or clothes dryer, the whole place could be reduced to a pile of ash quicker than he could spit.

He ran for the kitchen, figuring that was the most likely place to—

Bingo!

A knob on her stove were turned on, but there was no accompanying flame on the burner.

"Jesus Christ!" Officer Ryan skidded to a stop beside him, covering his nose and mouth against the awful fumes.

"Open all the doors and windows!" Wolf yelled, then coughed when the rancid gas filled his lungs. "I have to find Chrissy!"

He didn't wait to see if the policeman followed his orders. He was already running for the hallway.

"Christina!" He heard the panic in his own voice as he dissolved into another round of coughing. The fumes made his brain throb inside the confines of his skull. His vision swam like the night the Iranian's bullet had grazed his temple.

Her bedroom door was open, but the bathroom door was shut. He figured he had a fifty-fifty chance and the bathroom was one step closer.

"Chrissy!" he burst into the room without knocking.

If he'd thought he'd been scared when he saw her walking up that dock with blood streaming down her arm, nothing compared to the sheer terror that gripped him when he found her lying in the tub, her head tilted to one side so that her forehead pressed against a shampoo bottle.

"Fuck!" He was on his knees next to her in an instant.

A towel sat on a wicker stool. He threw it on top of her to protect her modesty, and knocked over the teacup perched on the edge of the tub in the process. It hit the floor and shattered, but he barely spared it a glance before threading one arm beneath her legs at the same time he wound the other around her back.

She was limp as a ragdoll when he hoisted her out of the now-tepid bath. The drenched towel and her wet body cascaded water onto the floor. He slipped as he turned toward the door, the tiles squeaking beneath his flip-flops. But somehow he managed to stay on his feet.

At the back of his mind, he registered the air in the bathroom was cleaner than the air in the rest of the house. Thanks to the closed door, no doubt. But it was quickly filling with fumes and there was a motherfucking *candle* burning on the back of the toilet.

He blew it out on his way through the door. Then he was running for fresh air.

"This way!" Officer Ryan waved him toward the back door, holding it wide.

Wolf wasted no time barreling onto Chrissy's back patio. The rain, which moments ago had felt warm, now chilled him to the bone.

Or maybe the goose bumps raising the hairs on the back of his neck were due to Chrissy lying lifeless in his arms. Or…*not* lifeless.

When the fat raindrops hit her face, her brow furrowed. Her eyes scrunched up right along with her mouth. Then she was blinking at him in confusion.

"Wolf?"

"I gotcha, darlin'." He didn't slow his pace until he was at her back fence, as far away from the house as he could get. Turning, he pressed his back against the wooden slats, and sank down until his ass was planted on the wet ground and he could cradle her in his arms, rocking slightly. "It's okay. Everything's goin' to be okay."

She looked down at the towel covering her body. Her chin jerked back.

He tried *not* to think about her being naked beneath the terry cloth. Tried *not* to picture her bare butt sitting directly atop his denim-covered cock.

"What's going on?" Her eyes were the size of the paper targets they'd used when doing small arms training back in

BUD/S. "Why are we outside in the rain? And *why* am I naked?"

"First things first." He pulled his T-shirt over his head and transferred it over *her* head. He didn't bother with her injured arm, letting her keep it close to her body. But he helped her snake her uninjured arm through the sleeve.

Chrissy wasn't a small woman. But she was a far sight smaller than he was. His shirt swam on her, hitting her mid-thigh and covering up all the parts of her he knew he'd be revisiting in his fantasies. Then he pulled the sopping towel down until it protected her legs against the rain's continuous onslaught.

The sound of the big, ploppy drops hitting the water of her plunge pool was a dull hum that competed with the harsher, hissing sound as they fell on the palm fronds overhead. He had to raise his voice to be heard above the cacophony.

"How are you feelin'?" He searched her confused eyes. "Are you dizzy? Got a headache? Is there ringin' in your ears?" His own brain had cleared now that they were in the fresh air.

Her eyelashes were spiky with rainwater. When she blinked, the droplets fell onto her cheeks and slid over her lips.

"I-I'm a little dizzy," she admitted. "And I'm really groggy, but I think that's from the pain meds."

She crossed her arm over her chest, covering the protruding points of her nipples, when Officer Ryan darted through the back door. The policeman looked around, and then headed in their direction once he spotted them through the deluge.

"Got all the doors and windows open," he huffed from exertion. "And blew out the candle burning on the coffee table."

"For fuck's sake." Wolf fixed a dark stare on the man. "It's a wonder the whole place didn't blow."

"I feel awful." Ryan squeegee-ed the water off his face only to have it immediately replaced. "I should've—"

"No way you could've known. I didn't smell it either until I opened the door."

The policeman nodded. "Should be safe to go back inside in ten minutes or so. I'll take up my position on the porch unless y'all need me for anything else."

"No." Wolf shook his head. "We'll hang back here until the fumes dissipate."

Ryan dipped his chin again, and then turned to Chrissy. "You okay, Miss Szarek?"

"I—" She still looked confused. "I'm okay," she finally finished.

"Can't tell you how happy I am to hear that." Ryan breathed a sigh of relief before turning back toward the house.

Chrissy waited until he disappeared inside before looking at Wolf. Her mouth was open but no words came out.

"A burner on the stove was left on with no flame," he explained.

She lifted a shaky hand to her forehead. "I-I made myself a cup of tea. But I don't remember leaving the gas on. Maybe I... Shit!" Shock wallpapered her pale face. "That's the absolute last time I take one of those pills. I don't care how much my shoulder hurts. I could've killed myself. I could've killed you and Officer Ryan!"

He cuddled her close, glad she seemed to suffer no ill effects from exposure to the gas. Glad too she wasn't fighting to scramble out of his arms. "Don't be too hard on yourself. It could've happened to anyone who's been through what you've been through."

"No. You saved me. *Again*." She looked so beautiful in the rain. Like a water nymph. "Risked your neck to save mine."

He could have demurred, he supposed. But he wasn't the demurring kind.

"I reckon if I'm goin' to die, I'd like to do it with you in my arms. Just like this."

A shadow of emotion darkened her face. He couldn't name it. And it was gone so quickly he didn't have time to study it.

She placed a gentle hand on his jaw, and his breath strangled in his lungs. When her eyes drifted down to his mouth, he felt her gaze like a physical touch.

His lips parted of their own volition and he watched, mesmerized, as her pupils dilated. Then she leaned forward, ever so slowly, and pressed her mouth to his.

He was usually the president and CEO of Careful, Measured Thought. But every reason why he shouldn't kiss her back leaked from his brain.

Folks liked to say that hope springs eternal? Well, it absolutely *leapt* inside his chest.

Or maybe that was his wide-open heart.

CHAPTER 21

1:22 PM...

The sullen sky brightened to a less gloomy gray, and the fat raindrops sliding down the windshield became little more than a smattering of mist.

This allowed JayJay to see the precise moment the uniformed officer retook his position on the front porch as if nothing had happened.

As if moments ago, he hadn't been running around like a chicken with his head cut off opening all the windows. As if several minutes before *that*, Ricky and Mateo hadn't hopped Chrissy's back fence, snuck in through the back door JayJay had covertly unlocked, and turned on Chrissy's gas stove. As if they hadn't lit the candle in her living room. As if JayJay hadn't been waiting with her heart in her throat for the whole lot to *kaboom!*

Several times in the intervening minutes, she'd been tempted to call the whole thing off. To run inside and switch off the gas and save Chrissy from the terrible fate of burning alive. She'd grabbed the door handle to do just that at least a dozen times. But Chrissy's words in the hospital had always stopped her...

The big guy looked familiar somehow, but I can't put my finger on where I've seen him.

Soon Chrissy would recall where she'd run into Mateo. JayJay had no doubt of that. Chrissy's mind was a steel trap.

Once Chrissy *did* remember, her next move would be to point that disheveled detective JayJay's way. After that, everything would fall like dominos. Everything JayJay had built for herself and her family.

Damn, shit, piss, and fuck!

"Looks like this plan failed too." She rubbed a hand over features she knew were heavy with weariness.

"Hey, hey! Don't look at me." Ricky lifted his hands in the backseat. Both he and Mateo, the latter of whom sat beside her in the passenger seat, were soaking wet and wrecking her leather. But she had bigger fish to fry than ruined car upholstery. "I was all prepared to incapacitate the woman, but there was no need. Chick was out like a light. Did I mention she was in her tub?"

Oh, yes. Only about a dozen times since he'd returned from his little mission. JayJay would rather remove her own appendix with a fork than sit and listen to him rhapsodize one more time about how long and tan Chrissy's legs were or how sweet her tits were. Just the thought of Ricky ogling Chrissy while she was out made JayJay sick to her stomach.

"So what?" Mateo turned to scowl back at Ricky. "You're saying it's *my* fault?"

"How many burners did you turn on?" Ricky asked.

"Just one. I don't know how forensics works, but I sure as shit suspect someone might've found it suspicious if *all* the burners had been on. And I made sure to light the biggest candle she had. The sucker had three wicks. Maybe her stove is faulty or something, 'cause I've seen places a lot bigger than hers go up like a neutron bomb in less time."

JayJay briefly closed her eyes. She did *not* want to know who or what Mateo had blown up.

"I don't care *why* it didn't work." Her voice was ragged with exhaustion and regret. "It didn't. End of story."

In the rearview mirror, she caught the reflection of Ricky's skinny shoulders shrugging. "Ya win some, ya lose some," he muttered.

In a moment of weakness, she spoke before she could think better of it. "You truly are an absolute ingrown toenail of a human being. You know that, right, Ricky?"

A laugh burst from Mateo, but it turned into a cough when she shot him a withering glance.

Ricky punched Mateo in the arm. "You wanna laugh at me, huh? *Huh?* Well, how about I feed you a dick instead?"

"Had one for lunch," Mateo deadpanned. "I'm full, thanks."

Ricky's face was florid with indignation. He began to sputter.

JayJay figured she'd started it, so it was her place to stop it. "Look, Ricky. I'm sorry for the ingrown toenail comment. I didn't mean it." Of course she'd meant it. "I'm sad and scared and frustrated, and I took it out on you."

"Okay, okay." Ricky's expression was sullen as he sat back against the seat, his long, scrawny arms crossed. "So what do we do now?"

A terrible chill stole over her at the question. She knew the answer and didn't like it. Not one bit.

"Well," she said tersely, trying to psyche herself up for what must be done. "You had two chances to make her death seem like an accident, and both times you failed. We'd better take the training wheels off this bike, don't you think?"

There. That sounded convincingly cold-hearted, didn't it? Like I'm a true crime boss?

Jesus. She *was* a true crime boss. How had it come to this?

Mateo slapped the dashboard. "It's about damn time."

"The question is how?" she asked, feeling every one of her fifty-seven years.

"Easy." Mateo shrugged. "We sneak in tonight, grab her, and shove her in the hold of the boat. Once we've dropped our clients off tomorrow morning in Mooney Harbor to do surf fishing, we'll kill her and toss her body overboard before we meet with the Colombians for the next shipment."

"Why not kill her as soon as we get her on the boat?" Ricky posited. "Easier that way. Much easier that way. She won't have a chance to escape or make any noises to alert our clients or nothin' if she's already dead."

"Don't you want to have some fun with her first?" Mateo's eyes sparked. His smile was downright evil.

"Oh. Oh, I gotcha." Ricky nodded, sucking on his teeth. "Yeah, yeah. I wouldn't mind tappin' dat ass a time or two before—"

"You will do nothing of the sort!" JayJay's blood boiled with revulsion. "I don't want you raping and torturing that poor woman. You make her death quick and clean, or I swear I'll cut you both loose and find someone else to make my runs." She glowered at Mateo since *he* was the one who called the shots when he and Ricky were out together.

The big man's shrug was insouciant, but his syllables were cold and clipped when he replied, "Sure thing."

She didn't believe him. Not for a minute. And something inside of her died, because she knew…

What recourse do I have?

She'd been bluffing when she said she'd find someone to take their place.

CHAPTER 22

1:25 PM...

For the first time in her life, Mia knew what it meant to have her heart in her throat.

Except it wasn't *only* her heart. It was also her lungs and her stomach and maybe her liver too. Basically, every organ in her body had tried to escape via her neck and, subsequently, had gotten stuck in a traffic jam.

Being careful not to touch any of the buttons or switches or levers, and *certainly* not the control wheel—all of which were far too close for comfort since she occupied the copilot's seat in the Otter—she glanced apprehensively through the plane's windshield at the storm clouds directly overhead.

The menacing weather had been rolling closer and closer ever since they left Key West. But no amount of strategic flying on Romeo's part had managed to keep them ahead of it.

If we were meant to fly, we would've been given wings, she thought uneasily as a jagged bolt of lightning arced between two cloud formations. A split-second later, a deafening *boom* rattled the fuselage.

She would *swear* she heard the engine sputter. But a hasty glance at Romeo told her otherwise. He was the picture of calm, deftly manning the control wheel, checking his instruments and softly humming.

What was that tune?

Oh, for Pete's sake. Is that "Leaving on a Jet Plane" by John Denver? Didn't he die *in a plane crash?*

She closed her eyes and counted to ten. It was a lesson she'd learned from her childhood therapist. A way to calm her body's automatic nervous system response when it went into fight, flight, or freeze mode.

"I cut this one a little close," Romeo muttered. "But don't worry. We're nearly home."

He'd barely gotten the last word out when the sky broke open like someone slit its heavy underbelly with a blade. Merciless rain pounded against the windshield, and she opened her eyes in time to watch Romeo flip a switch so a set of wipers came on.

Strange, but she'd never thought about planes having windshield wipers before. It seemed like such a mundane, everyday piece of equipment to be on something as sophisticated as an airplane and—

"Jesus H. God on a scooter!" she screeched when an evil rush of wind sent the Otter careening sideways. Before she could catch her breath from *that* little maneuver, the plane fell out of the sky.

Or, at least it dropped a hundred feet. Far enough that had she not been strapped in, she would have flown up and broken her neck when her head smashed against the top of the fuselage.

Another quick glance at Romeo revealed a line on his forehead to match the lines cut into his cheeks by his dimples. His motions were sure while he worked the throttle with one hand while making some nimble adjustments to the control wheel with the other. But he was no longer humming.

She wished he'd start humming again. Despite his song choice, there was comfort in his humming.

"Are we going to die?" Normally, her voice was throaty. It had been ever since the ventilator damaged her vocal cords. But now it sounded like she'd been eating rocks.

"No." Romeo jerked his chin once.

"Would you tell me if we *were*?" She couldn't stop herself from asking.

He shot her a quick look, and she was relieved to find confidence and a hint of his usual humor glinting in his eyes. "Probably not."

"Well"—she blew out a breath at the same time she cinched her seatbelt tighter across her lap—"no one can accuse you of being a liar."

"Hold on, *linda*." The Spanish endearment might have tickled her ears if they hadn't already been filled with the roar of the engine and the screaming of the wind. "I'm taking her in quick. It'll be a rough landing."

Wrapping her hands around the seat cushion until she was sure her nails left marks on the leather, Mia closed her eyes once more. She didn't want to *see* the moment she died.

"If we were meant to fly, we would've been given wings."

She thought she repeated the phrase in her mind. But she must've said it out loud since Romeo responded with, "We were given the brains to build planes. And planes are better than wings. At least with planes, when you get caught in a storm, you don't get wet, eh?"

She didn't reply. She couldn't. The traffic jam in her throat had unsnarled enough to allow her stomach to hop into her mouth. Once there, it preceded to disgorge acid.

Don't throw up. Don't throw up. Don't throw up.

On the off chance they lived through this, she didn't want to suffer the indignity of having lost her lunch inside the cockpit. And on the off chance they *didn't* live through this, the last thing she wanted Romeo to witness before his ultimate demise was her blowing chunks all over his instruments.

Once again, it felt like the plane fell out of the sky. But unlike the last time, this felt like a controlled descent.

Or perhaps controlled *dive* was the better way to describe it.

I didn't survive my childhood simply to die in a plane crash, she thought desperately. *I'm not Amelia Earhart.*

Although, at least if she'd *been* Amelia Earhart, she'd be a pilot too. That would have given her some semblance of control over the situation.

What scared Mia more than anything, what had *always* scared her, was a lack of control.

"Here we go." Romeo's voice was tight with concentration and barely audible over the noise of the aircraft and the brutal pounding of the storm.

When the pontoons first touched the water, Mia was thrown forward against her chest strap. The next instant, the plane was airborne again, skipping to another wave.

Or at least that's what she assumed was happening. She refused to open her eyes to check. All she had to rely on were her ears.

There was a *boom* followed by a *hiss* as the pontoons touched off on another wave. Then silence as they glided through the air. *Boom, hiss, silence! Boom, hiss, silence!*

Over and over until eventually there were no more

booms and only one long, drawn out *hiss* as the plane skimmed across the water.

She opened her eyes to find they were taxing through Wayfarer Island's lagoon, headed for the safety of the beach.

The rain was so heavy she couldn't locate the house, but she could see the long wooden dock where the Second Wind, the catamaran owned by LT's uncle John, was tied up and rocking heavily with the wave action. When she craned her head, she located Wayfarer II, the big salvage and research vessel anchored out beyond the reef.

We made it! We're alive!

"Breathe, Mia." Glancing over, she found Romeo watching her closely. "You always forget to breathe."

Do I? She blew out a ragged breath and the stars dancing in front of her eyes disappeared. *I guess I do.*

When the plane's pontoons kissed the sand, he throttled up, the engine revving as he parked the aircraft on the beach. Once he was satisfied, he pulled off his headset, hooking it around a peg above his side window, and cut the engine.

There was a moment of silence. Then Mia was out of her restraints and across the cockpit. Throwing her arms around his neck, she hugged him tight.

She'd been scared plenty of times in her life. But, aside from her grandmother, she couldn't recall having ever had someone beside her whom she could count on and trust. And now that they were safe, she realized as frightened as she'd been, it would've been so much worse if it had been anyone but Romeo—gentle, generous, capable Romeo—behind the wheel of the plane.

"Thank you." Her throat was clogged with relief and gratitude. "Thank you for not getting us killed."

"No problem." His wide palm patted her back a bit awkwardly. When she pushed away, she found his expression ill at ease.

"Oh geez!" She frowned. "Am I crushing your arm? Sorry!"

Hastily, she retook her seat and shoved her hair out of her face. The new cut allowed a heavy lock to cover her eye if she didn't keep it tucked behind her ear.

"I, uh…" Romeo fiddled with a knob. He seemed anxious.

Weird. Why would he be anxious *now*? They were home. They were beached. They'd survived the storm and the landing!

"I think we should talk about last night," he finally finished.

She furrowed her brow even as an image of him lying next to her in bed flittered through her brain. In life, Romeo was animated, his facial expressions ever mobile. But when he slept, his brow softened, his well-defined lips relaxed and fell open the slightest bit, and his face cleared of all thoughts and worries.

He was a handsome man when he was awake.

He was absolutely breathtaking when he was asleep.

For a long time after she'd finished the first chapter of *In Darkness and Dreams*, she'd studied him. Studied the heavy vein that ran up the side of his neck and pulsed thickly with every heartbeat. Studied his wide, capable hands as they lay clasped over his flat stomach. Studied his thick eyelashes as they cast dark shadows on his cheeks.

Romeo, she'd thought. *It fits all his dashing, romantic beauty.*

She'd been tempted to trace the line of his nose, to feel the little bump that marred the perfection of the bridge. But she'd satisfied herself with simply turning onto her side and letting the sound of his heavy, even breaths lull her into the deepest sleep she'd enjoyed in ages.

"Last night?" she asked now. "What about it?"

He ran a hand through his hair and cursed beneath his breath. She couldn't hear precisely what he said. The rain pounded on the plane's metal body, creating a dull roar.

When he finally turned her way, his expression was pained. "Mia, you know I like you, right? And respect you and admire you?"

His words were nice. But the way he said them? She didn't know where he was going, but she got the distinct impression she didn't want to follow him there.

"Are you breaking up with me?" she joked, trying to lessen the strange tension permeating the fuselage.

He looked positively apoplectic when he sputtered, "S-see? I *thought* you might have read too much into it. Mia, if you haven't heard, I'm not exactly the relationship type and—"

"Wait a minute." She held up a hand, feeling her cheeks heat. "Do you seriously think after one night together, one *platonic* night together, that I'm under the impression we're an item?"

"An item?" One black brow formed a perfect arch over his eye. "Who says that?"

"Me, apparently."

A corner of his mouth twitched. "What are you? Seventy?"

"No, but my grandmother, who raised me from the time I was seven was. So blame my antiquated choice of words on her. And then answer the question, Spiro."

His eyes softened as they had every time she'd called him by his given name. "Well, not an *item* necessarily," he admitted. "But, I mean, the way you've been acting around me today is different, you know? Yesterday, I could barely say a word without you jumping or giving me the side-eye."

"I'm nervous by nature," she said in her own defense. Not to mention that she was highly aware of him as a man. So sure, she was agitated anytime he got close.

"And now today, after we slept together in your bed," he went on, "you've been acting like—"

She usually didn't interrupt. She'd learned people gave themselves away when they were allowed to run off at the mouth. So she was surprised when she heard herself cut in with, "Like what? Like we lived through a harrowing event together? Like we got to know each other better and discovered we both like angsty, dark romance novels? Like maybe we were becoming *friends*?"

"Is that all it's been?" He eyed her skeptically. "Friendship?"

Okay, if she was being completely honest, she *had* experienced a thrill when she'd awoken in his arms. And an even *bigger* thrill when she'd felt the incessant throbbing of his morning wood against her thigh.

But she wasn't an idiot. She hadn't turned into Gigi Hadid overnight. She was still her and he was still him, so she'd known then, and she knew now, that his hardon hadn't had anything to do with *her*.

It'd simply been male biology at work.

Embarrassment and indignation reddened her face. "If I've been acting differently today, it's because, like I said, I thought yesterday and last night pushed us over the line from acquaintances to friends. And just in case it wasn't obvious to you, I don't make friends easily. I'm too reserved. Too quiet. It makes people uneasy around me. So imagine my happiness when I thought I'd found a friend in *you*."

"Mia, I—" He tried to get a word in, but she talked right over him.

"But you know what? I'm taking it back." At his confused look, she clarified. "My friendship. I don't want to be friends with a supercilious *ass* who thinks every woman he meets wants him so badly she can't contain her ovaries

226

and is determined to chase him down and make him her very own. Because I've got news for you, bud."

Had she called him *bud*? Yes, she'd called him bud. She was on a roll.

"Why would I waste time chasing you when *I* am the one who's the catch, huh?" she finished, breathing heavily because she didn't think she'd drawn a breath during that entire diatribe.

Of course, she didn't *really* think she was a catch. Not with her insanely dysfunctional family and her post traumatic stress. But it felt *good* to say she was. To pretend a confidence and courage she didn't truly have.

Romeo blinked at her in astonishment. Then his expression grew...the only word she could come up with was *livid*. "Hold on just a damned minute and try to see things from my perspective."

She fought to hold her tongue, but lost the battle. "Oh, I'd dearly *love* to see things from your perspective. But I don't think I can get my head that far up my own ass."

"Look." He cut a hand through the air. "A guy like me is used to women wanting one thing. So sue me for mistaking your sudden change in attitude for some romantic notion of the two of us together. I just wanted to make sure there was no misunderstanding between us. To make sure you knew that I—that I—" He struggled for words, and it took everything she had not to supply some for him.

That you don't like me like that? That you don't want *me like that? Well, message received!*

This time, however, she managed to hold her tongue. She wished she hadn't when he finally settled on, "That you and I are about as different as peas and pears. You're nothing I need, and I'm not anything you should want."

His bald words hit her so hard she recoiled.

He opened his mouth, but she stopped him with a raised

hand. "No. Please. I would appreciate it if those were the final words you speak on the topic."

"Mia, I—"

She shot him a daggered look. "Seriously, you need to stop talking now before either one of us says something that will make our working relationship unbearable. As it stands, I'm perfectly happy to go back to the way things were when we barely talked and never touched. Agreed?"

A muscle worked in his jaw. His brown eyes, which usually held devilry and teasing, were filled with...she couldn't be sure. It looked like *hurt*. But she told herself it was only injured pride.

She had a healthy dose of *that* going herself.

Finally, he nodded.

"Good. Now, I'm going inside to dig out that vodka Bran keeps hidden in the cupboard so Uncle John doesn't steal it to put in his salty dogs. And I know alcohol is never the answer, but after the last couple of days, it's worth a shot." She screwed up her face. "No pun intended."

"I thought you said you never drink alone?" he called to her back since she'd pushed open the copilot's door. The sound of the rain became so loud, she had to shout above it.

"There's a first time for everything, Romeo!"

"What happened to Spiro?" he demanded, that muscle ticking in his jaw again. "I thought you were going to call me by my first name!"

"Feels a bit too...*friendly*!" she emphasized and then a thought occurred. "Also, so I don't break my own rules, I bet I could convince Doc to have a drink with me. He always seems willing to come to the rescue of a damsel in distress. Maybe it's the good ol' boy in him."

Romeo's eyes hardened at the same time his nostrils flared wide. But she didn't wait around to try to determine what *that* expression was all about. Instead, she jumped from the plane and didn't glance back as she ran up the beach toward the rickety old house.

There was a reason she kept to herself. Kept quiet. Didn't seek people out.

When she did, she opened herself up to disappointment. To *hurt*.

Romeo had hurt her with his rejection. Because that's what it had been, right? He'd rejected her before she'd even had a chance to ask anything of him.

CHAPTER 23

1:29 PM...

Chrissy felt eaten alive by Wolf's kisses. But in the best possible way.

As the mist continued to shower down around them, creating a secret, magical world that seemed to hold in its palm only the two of them, she thought, *This... This is how desire is supposed to feel. This is how passion is supposed to taste.*

Not that she was a virgin or anything. She'd had her fair share of men.

Well, maybe not her *fair* share.

According to Winston, her body count was abysmally low for a modern era that included hookup culture and Tinder. And now she knew why. She simply hadn't been doing it right. Or maybe it was more accurate to say she hadn't been doing it with the right kind of men.

Men who set her blood on fire. Men who made her body hum. Men who made her forget herself.

For the first time, she understood what Winston meant when he spoke of being with Rosa.

"It's like I was playing with passion before," she remembered him saying one night after she'd invited him over for New Orleans style BBQ shrimp. *"Pretending desire. Pretending need and want. And then Rosa came along and I became a* thing *of need and want. Need was the breath in my lungs. Want was the blood in my veins. And no matter how much I had her, I still craved more."*

Funny, Chrissy had never considered Winston a man of words. But when he talked about Rosa, he turned damn near poetic.

Winston...

Thoughts of her best friend were just the thing to bring her back to reality. To lift her out of that ocean of *want* and *need* Winston had spoken of and plant her feet firmly on solid ground.

"Wolf?" She pressed a hand against his bare chest. Despite the cool rain drenching them, his skin was warm to the touch.

Warm? No. He *burned.*

Burned so hot she wanted to rip the borrowed T-shirt over her head and press into him so she could feel his flame against her naked breasts.

"Mmm," was his only response as his tongue tangled with hers, inviting her to meet his every tease and taste and lick.

For a moment, she couldn't remember why she'd wanted to stop him. The man was so damn sexy, he short-circuited her brain. But then a whisper of sanity returned.

The plan!

She needed to tell him about the plan before they went any further.

"Wolf," she whispered again. This time, when she pulled

her mouth away, he scattered kisses across her cheek and back to her ear. Gently catching her lobe between his teeth, he flicked it with his tongue and she sucked in a ragged breath.

Who knew ears could be so sensitive?

Wolf, apparently. He growled low in the back of his throat before dipping his tongue into the delicate hollow. An exquisite intrusion that crossed her eyes and curled her toes.

The deep ache that had been at her center since the first moment she pressed her lips to his grew until there was a yawning chasm inside her. She hurt to be filled.

How easy would it be to reach down and pop the buttons on his fly? To take out his thick, turgid length and impale herself?

Soooo easy that little voice whispered.

"Wolf!" This time when she pressed against his chest, she put a good eight inches between. Well out of reach of his mesmerizing mouth.

"What darlin'?" he rasped. "What's so all-fire important you got to stop us right when we're gettin' to the good stuff?"

"The rain has let up and I'm sure the gas fumes are long gone. Let's go inside."

"What's inside?"

"Dry clothes."

His upper lip curled with distaste.

"And my bed."

He dipped his chin to stare at her from under the fringe of his dark lashes. "Now you're talkin'."

The look in his eyes promised unspeakable pleasures. And her gaze followed a drop of rainwater that slowly, so inexorably *slowly*, slid between his heavy pectoral muscles to get stuck in the line of crinkly hair that arrowed down the centerline of his corrugated stomach.

She wanted to dip her chin and follow that drop of water with her tongue. And while she was at it, follow all the other drops of water that glistened on his skin.

"Come—" Her voice was the auditory equivalent of the bucket of rusty fish hooks she stored in her shed. She tried again. "Come inside with me. I have a plan I need to run by you."

His chin jerked to one side. "Tell me this plan involves you lettin' me lick the rainwater off every inch of your skin."

"Great minds think alike, I guess," she said to herself. Then realized she *hadn't* said it to herself when he chuckled.

"Your wish is my command." He licked a lazy path down her neck. Her eyelids grew heavy. Her nipples throbbed. She couldn't remember what—

The plan!

Scrambling off his lap, she offered a hand down to him. "Come on." She wiggled her fingers. "Up you go."

He leaned slightly to the side. At first, she couldn't figure out what he was doing. Then she realized his T-shirt barely covered her butt when she was standing.

"Hey!" she squawked, hastily grabbing the towel that had fallen onto the ground. It was heavy with rainwater, but she didn't bother wringing it out before wrapping it around her waist.

"Spoilsport," he complained.

"Pervert," she parried.

"Never claimed otherwise, darlin'." This was accompanied by his patented eyebrow wiggle.

In return, she arched eyebrows imperiously and he sighed heavily. Grabbing her hand, he allowed her to hoist him to his feet.

He looked...well, there weren't words to describe him.

Noble maybe? That certainly defined his straight back, wide shoulders, and granite-hewn jaw.

Virile? You bet. Every inch of him screamed *man*. From the jut of his Adam's apple to the jut of his...

Sweet heavens, she had to look away from the front of his jeans. They were plastered against him, and the wet material left little to the imagination.

Okay, so the best word to describe him was *sexy*. He epitomized sex. Raw, raunchy, dirty, delicious sex.

"See somethin' you like?" His expression was heated. It matched her fiery cheeks when she realized she'd been caught ogling him.

"Please." She pulled him around the plunge pool. "You know you're all that and a box of chocolates. You don't need me to remind you."

"Although, I *like* it when you do." He let her drag him through the back door and into the kitchen.

The second they were inside, he took a step toward her. "Hold that thought until we've closed the windows and doors." She lifted a finger. "Also, we need to get out of these wet clothes. I'm so pruned I'm worried I'll never smooth out again. Ah!" She pointed at his nose. "And before you come back with something decidedly Wolf-ish like, *'I'll smooth out* all *your wrinkles, darlin','*" she mimicked his accent, "please know I am determined to keep two feet of distance between us until this place is locked up and I'm dry."

"Dry." He wrinkled his nose. "I don't like the sound of that."

"Oh, for heaven's sake." She rolled her eyes. "If I'd known a make-out session would turn you into a *That's What She Said* guy, I might've decided to ignore all your delicious temptations. No matter how hard it would have been."

His mouth spread wide around a lecherous grin. "That's what she said."

"Ugh!" She threw her hands in the air, and then they were both laughing.

That had been the thing about them since the beginning. No matter how hot they were for each other, they could always make each other laugh.

"I also need to change my bandage," she added. "The doctor said I shouldn't get it wet for at least two days."

It was like someone flipped a switch inside Wolf. He went from Wolf, Grand Seducer to Wolf, All Business All the Time. "Go get dried off. I'll close the windows and doors and meet you in the bathroom to help with your bandage."

The man was equal parts Casanova and companion. Playboy and partner. Seducer and sidekick. A guy who seemed so comfortable in his own skin that he made her feel comfortable in hers.

Which was why she was so determined to follow through with her plan. If it worked out, they'd exhaust all their explosive sexual chemistry, and then—*hopefully*—end up as friends.

Passing the coffee table on the way to the bathroom, she frowned down at the candle. The creamy wax in the center was still liquid. Its French vanilla scent lingered in the air.

When did I light that? she wondered, pressing a hand to her forehead.

She recalled *thinking* about lighting it; the house had smelled musty. But she didn't remember actually *doing* it.

Then again, she didn't remember leaving her stove burner on either, but she'd had a house full of noxious gas fumes to prove her recall wasn't exactly up to snuff.

No more pain meds, she vowed, chucking the bottle in the trash as soon as she walked into the bathroom and saw it sitting on the vanity.

Aside from not killing herself or anyone else, she needed all her wits about her if she had any hope of seeing her plan through without breaking her own heart in the process.

Because yes, okay, Wolf would be easy to fall in love with.

"There," she said to the empty room. "I admitted it. Are you happy now?"

As always, the room remained aggravatingly silent.

CHAPTER 24

1:38 PM...

B y the time Wolf finished closing up the house, Chrissy had toweled herself dry and changed into a soft sea foam-colored tank top and matching pair of sleep shorts.

She didn't hear him stop in the doorway to the bathroom. She was down on her knees, searching through the various bottles and boxes beneath her vanity. And cursing a blue streak when she couldn't seem to find what she was looking for.

Crossing his arms and leaning against the doorjamb, he enjoyed the view.

She was so long and tan. And the more he stared at the perfect upside-down heart of her butt in those shorts, the more he was convinced he was halfway to heaven but headed straight to hell for his prurient thoughts.

"Aha!" she exclaimed, holding a box of gauze bandages aloft and turning to catch him staring.

He yanked his gaze away, pretending to be fascinated by the little crack in the ceiling. He only glanced down at her after she shoved to a stand, and he smiled as if he'd just noticed she was in the room.

Just me bein' a total gentleman and not *oglin' the hell out your ass.*

"This is the last one." He hitched his chin toward the window above the toilet, moving quickly to close the sash and flip the lock. "All done." He dusted off his hands. "No more air-conditionin' the world."

The light in her eyes instantly dimmed.

"What?" He was on immediate high alert. "What's wrong?"

"Mom used to say that when I left the front door open."

The tension drained out of him. "Her and every other parent since the dawn of HVAC. Sit down and let me get a gander at that bullet wound."

This time she didn't bristle at his autocratic command. She simply followed his instructions. After she was comfortable atop the toilet lid, she asked quietly, "How do you know when you've stopped grieving someone you've lost?"

Brushing a damp strand of hair behind her ear, he gently cupped her face. He'd lost his paternal grandparents when he was only a boy. Both his folks had died two weeks after he joined the Navy when a F5 twister tore through their house. Then there had been Rusty, a brother to him in every way that mattered.

He knew about grief. So he felt confident when he told her, "I reckon it's when the memory of them brings you peace instead of pain."

Her smile was faint. "I like that. Who said it?"

He pressed a hand over his heart. "You wound me, woman. Not everything that comes out of my mouth is someone else's genius. Some of the brilliance is my own."

She tried to fight a smile and lost the battle.

I love her mouth, he thought. It was every man's fantasy. So sweet and soft and devilishly eager.

He'd known she was responsive. Those few heated moments in the storage closet had proven that. But nothing had prepared him for the sheer wonder of her in that backyard.

It had been a heady thing to see how each subtle brush of his fingertips, the slightest change in the pressure of his lips or the stroke of his tongue, had made her gasp and writhe and pant for more.

Every moan that had fallen from her lips had seemed to bypass his ears and go directly to his cock. He'd throbbed so hard, it'd been a wonder he hadn't split his own skin.

The *memory* was enough to have him swelling and lengthening again.

Since he didn't reckon it was very gentlemanly to have a hard-on shoved in her face while rebandaging her wound, he seized on a subject sure to cool his ardor.

Even though he hadn't a clue what she could possibly propose with her *plan*, he wasn't fool enough to think it might be anything he'd like. "So…about this plan of yours."

"Oh! Right. I've come up with a solution to our problem." She dipped her chin decisively.

"What problem is that?"

"The problem of you mistaking being in love with me when what you *really* are is in *lust* with me."

He felt a muscle in his jaw twitch. One beneath his left eye followed suit. "This thing between us is more than hormones, Christina. And if you're sayin' otherwise, you're not only lyin' to me, you're lyin' to yourself."

"But that's the thing." Her expression turned beseeching. "I *know* what we share is more than hormones. We're *friends*, Wolf. And I cherish that. I don't want to lose it. So what I propose is that we become friends *with benefits*."

His heart thudded so hard he wouldn't have been surprised to look down and see it burst from his chest, *Alien*-style.

"That way," she continued, "we'll have made no promises and no sweeping declarations. And since no future plans will get broken, there won't be hurt when one or both of us decides we've exhausted the *benefits* portion of our relationship. It'll be a return to the status quo. To you and I teasing each other, taunting each other, being *pals*. And you'll see, Wolf. You'll see it was only ever unrequited lust to begin with."

She thought there would come a time when they exhausted their chemistry? *Pfft.* Passion like theirs was a rare gift that didn't *get* exhausted. It simply mellowed and matured, the fire dimming to a long, luxurious smolder.

For proof of this, he need look no further than his own grandparents. Before his grandfather died, his *agiduda* would chase his *elisi* around the barn, pulling her down into the hay and kissing her until she laughed, swatted him on the butt, and accused him of being a lecherous old fart.

As a boy, Wolf had rolled his eyes and made gagging noises that old folks would behave in such a way. But as a man, he took comfort in knowing desire, true desire, stood the test of time.

And when it came to *falling* in love versus *being* in love? Well, they were one and the same. Part of an infinite circle that endlessly looped through the lives of lovers.

How many times had his grandfather told a story about his grandmother, some sweet or silly anecdote that ended with, *"And I fell in love with her all over again."*

So many times, Wolf had lost count.

That was the kind of love he wanted. The kind that renewed itself again and again.

If that meant he had to keep his mouth shut and use his body to show Chrissy the folly in her plan—use his body over, and over, and *over* again? Well, you can bet your bottom dollar he could do exactly that.

Boy howdy, can I ever.

She mistook his silence for an objection to her idea. "Okay, so what if you're right? What if this thing we're feeling *is* us falling in love?"

He got very still. Did she realize what she'd just said?

It didn't appear so, since she went on without taking a breath. "So what? Falling in love doesn't last. And when it's faded, what's left? Heartache? Desertion? Grief? No." She shook her head. "I don't want that. Not for us."

Desertion… That one word rang in his head like a church bell, crystalline and clear.

"Did any of them stay in contact with you after they took off?" he asked quietly.

He didn't need to clarify. She knew exactly to whom he referred. "No." She shook her head. "Well, Tony wrote me a handful of emails. He was my mom's fourth husband," she explained. "But as soon as he remarried, he stopped writing."

Tony stopped writing and Chrissy had been thrown away like yesterday's trash. *Again.*

Jesus. She hadn't been a simple bystander to her mother's love life. Oh, no. She'd been right there, strapped in beside Josephine on that roller coaster ride. She'd experienced the highs of having a father figure enter her life, someone who doted on her, whom she grew to love and who made her feel loved in return. And she'd experienced the lows of having that love and devotion ripped away once the relationship fell apart.

It was his job now to prove to her that not all men left. That when it was real and right and good, when both parties were as crazy for each other and as well-matched as he and Chrissy, it lasted.

With one finger, he tipped up her chin. "Okay, darlin'. Let's do it your way."

Her narrowed eyes broadcast her suspicion. "This feels too easy."

"Look," he told her honestly, "I'm not sayin' I think you're right. I think you're dead wrong. But I'm willin' to go along with your experiment. I mean, if you're right, we'll end up as friends. And if *I'm* right, we'll end up as life-long lovers. It's a win/win as far as I can figure."

Her eyes lit up. "Seriously?"

"Have I ever lied to you?"

"No." Her expression turned teasing. "But you *did* confuse me for a redhead once, so…"

"Ugh. You're never goin' to let me forget that night, are you?"

"Not on your life."

"You could at least *pretend* to grant me a sweet little reprieve." He feigned a frown.

"Please." She rolled her eyes. "Do I look like Willy Wonka? I don't sugarcoat anything."

"Wiseass," he accused.

"Would you have me any other way?"

"Not on your life." He stole her line and something succulent melted in her eyes. Apparently, she was done giving him hell and was thinking about giving him something else entirely.

What was that low, growling sound?

Oh, right. It's me.

"Nope!" He realized he'd bent to claim her lips when she shoved a finger over his mouth. "Wound care first," she told him with a decisive jerk of her chin. "Naked shenanigans to follow."

"I'm offended you think I can't accomplish both things at once," he said around her finger, feeling her skin warm with his hot breath.

Her eyes lowered to his mouth and glittered with desire. He would swear he felt his lips throb in response.

"As much as I would love your kisses…" Her voice was husky. "And I mean, *love* your kisses. Let's get this bandaging business over with as quickly as we can."

"Your wish is my command."

"Prince Charming." She beamed up at him.

"Oh, hell no." He shook his head. "I'm no Prince Charming. I'm the big, bad wolf. And that should make you glad."

"Why's that?"

"A wolf can see better, hear better, and…*eat* you better than a prince ever could."

He watched her nipples furl beneath the cotton of her shirt, and his mouth instantly watered as if he were one of Pavlov's dogs.

Soon, he thought. *Soon I'll taste those sweet little buds. But first…*

Gently sliding the strap of her tank top over her shoulder, he inspected the bandaging. It was soaked and some of the tape holding it in place had peeled away.

Running a finger along the edge of one sticky strip, he noted how warm and smooth her skin was in comparison and—

"This is going to hurt, isn't it?" Her voice was tremulous.

"Not if I can help it," he promised. "Now hold still."

She held her breath as he gently peeled away the first edge of the dressing. By the time he'd gotten the final side of tape up, she'd relaxed somewhat. But she tensed again when he lifted the gauze pad covering her wound.

"How's it look?" She stared up at him in trepidation.

"See for yourself." He helped her to her feet and then stood behind her as she tentatively turned toward the mirror.

A whoosh of air exited her lungs at the same time her eyebrows pinched together. "That's *it*?"

She leaned in close to her reflection to inspect the neat line of stitches that marred the perfection of her shoulder.

Truly, the only thing that looked the least bit gnarly about the wound was the bruised flesh around it. Her skin was a Technicolor canvas of reds, blues, and purples that he'd dearly love to kiss better.

"Your doctor was good. It'll probably only leave a faint scar." He bent to press his lips to the back of her neck. He couldn't help himself. "Plus, she thinks it was a ricochet and not a direct hit, which means there was a lot less deep tissue damage than there might've been."

Chrissy shivered. "You're trying to distract me from my bullet wound and you're not being subtle about it."

"Maybe I'm tryin' to distract myself." He moved his mouth to her ear. He'd noticed she seemed to like that. When he nibbled the sweet little lobe, he watched in the mirror as her lids lowered to half-mast. "I hate seein' you hurt, Chrissy. It makes me want to chew nails."

"I'd much rather you use your mouth for other things," she told him coyly, tilting her head to the side to give him better access. "And then maybe you'll let me return the favor? Let me take a bite out of your Adam's apple? That thing has been tempting me all day."

"Really?" He moved his mouth to the crook of her neck, feeling her pulse flutter against his lips.

"Mmm-hmm." She nodded lazily. "There's something about it. It screams *man*."

He understood that. So many things about her screamed

woman, from the graceful line of her collarbones to the dramatic flare of her hips. And all of them, each and every one, was a siren's call.

"After you're done with my Adam's apple, what'll you do next?"

"Lick your neck. Suck on your pulse point." Speaking of...his heart rate picked up its pace to match hers. "Maybe leave a little love bite so every time you catch your reflection in the mirror for the next few days, you'll be reminded of me."

I suppose I should've known, he thought, *given how much we like to banter, that she'd bring fun, flirty talk into the bedroom.*

At least he *hoped* she'd bring fun, flirty talk into the bedroom. And then maybe transition that fun, flirty talk into downright *dirty* talk.

"If you start bitin' my Adam's apple and kissin' my neck, I can't be held responsible for what happens next."

"Promises, promises," she teased, then shivered again when he gently bit down on the side of her neck. It was a warning of sensual punishments to come. A pledge to show her every erotic trick he'd ever learned.

"Mmm," she hummed her approval, closing her eyes as he continued to use his mouth on her tender flesh.

The taste of her on his tongue was every tropical dream he'd ever had. A sweet mix of sugary boat drinks, sunshine, and coconut milk. It took some effort, but he forced himself to step away.

"Let's get you bandaged back up." His voiced sounded like it'd been trampled by an entire battalion of combat boots.

She tried to feign nonchalance, but her movements were shaky when she retook her seat. She nearly missed the closed toilet lid altogether and only saved herself at the last minute.

"Antibacterial ointment? Tape?" he asked.

"On the vanity." When she pointed, her fingers were trembling.

Glad to have an excuse to turn away so she wouldn't see the triumphant curve of his mouth, he swung back around when he heard her gasp.

"What?" he demanded. "What's wrong?"

"Have you had that the entire time?" Her eyes were huge.

"Had what?" He glanced around, confused. Had a hard-on? Sure. Every time she was near. Had a big, squishy soft spot for her? Of course. Right from the start.

"A gun."

"Oh. No." He shook his head. "That's what I went to the airport to get. Romeo keeps the Otter armed."

"Do you…" Her voice was wobbly, so she swallowed. "Do you think you'll need it?"

"Nah," he assured her. If the warehouse dickholes had wanted to finish the job they started, they likely would have already tried. "But my motto is always be prepared," he told her.

Her mouth flattened. "That's not *your* motto. That's the Boy Scouts of America motto. Although…" She cocked her head. "I can see it. You in that little khaki shirt with all your badges. Were you a Scout?"

"Nope." He shook his head. "My *elisi* wouldn't hear of it." When she frowned, he explained. "My uncle is gay. We're talkin' out and proud since he was about six years old. And unlike Western civilization, the idea of same-sex unions has been part of the Cherokee culture for as long as any of the elders can remember. In fact, for centuries my tribe has been known for celebratin' a 'ceremony of devotion' between two men at annual festivals. It's basically what folks today would call gay marriage."

"Fascinating," she breathed.

"Anyway, back when my grandmother was raisin' her kids, the Boy Scouts of America was still toutin' its stance against openly gay people being allowed into the organization. *Elisi* refused to give money to any group that wasn't inclusive of everyone, regardless of race, religion, gender, sexual orientation, you name it." He smiled when he relayed this last part. "She flies two flags from her front porch. The Cherokee Nation flag and the gay pride flag."

Chrissy's eyes sparkled. "She sounds like a pistol. I think I like her."

"You should." He snorted. "Y'all are peas in a pod." When her brows knit together, he explained, "You're both incredibly independent, incredibly capable, and incredibly stubborn."

She sent him an arch look. "You say that like it's a bad thing."

"Not at all. Y'all are my two favorite women on the planet."

Her laugh was sputtering. "Cut it out. What about your sisters?"

He shook his head. "I mean, I love them to pieces. But they're too much of a pain in my ass to make them my favorites."

"Didn't you tell me *I'm* a pain in your ass?" Her eyes narrowed. "I could've sworn that was you."

"When?" he demanded. He remembered *thinking* that. More than a time or two. But he didn't recall actually saying it out loud.

"When you were trying to convince me I'd be able to lengthen my dive times if I practiced Tai Chi with you in the mornings. And *I* told *you* that unless your name is Google, you should stop acting like you know everything." She screwed up her face. "If memory serves, your exact response was, 'Lord, Christina, you are such a pain in my ass.'"

"Ah, yes." Now he remembered that little tête-à-tête. Recalled how much he'd wanted to grab her and kiss the snarky words right out of her mouth. "Well, you *are* a pain in my ass. But you're a different sort of pain in my ass than my sisters."

"How so?" She lifted an eyebrow.

"They can't seem to stop drownin' me in rug rats. And you won't even countenance the idea that we should have a whole passel of our own."

The instant the words left his mouth, he knew he'd said too much. Her expression turned unreadable. Her eyes went hooded.

"Is that what you want?" Her voice was a whisper. "A whole passel of kids?"

"Well, maybe not a whole passel. How much is even *in* a passel anyway?" When she ignored his attempt at levity, he continued. "But like you, I've always thought four sounds about right. I reckon it's enough without bein' too much."

She stared at him intently. *Too* intently. Then she opened her mouth, but he stopped her with a raised hand. "And I know what you're goin' to say. You're goin' to say I only *think* that's what I want. That the truth is I'm not the kind of guy who'll be happy with a *normal life*." He made air quotes. "You think I'm not the settlin' down sort."

She was quiet for a moment and he feared he'd gone and screwed things up by bringing the subject back around. She'd agreed to friends with benefits. And he'd decided to let her plan play out.

So shut the hell up, you idiot!

But he couldn't. Especially when she asked, "And you claim you're the settling down sort, but not the settling sort. What did you mean by that?"

"I meant I won't settle for anything less than everything. You don't want that heady rush of fallin' in love? I do. You don't want that out of control, ass over teakettle tumble into romantic bliss? I do. I want a woman who is as nuts for me as I am for her."

Her expression turned trepidatious. "Wolf, I—"

"Nope." He shook his head. "That doesn't mean anything has changed. We can still do this your way. If this thing I'm feelin' *isn't* built to last, if we scratch this itch and it goes away like you think it will, then you'll have been right. And I'll have learned a valuable lesson."

She narrowed her eyes. "And what lesson is that?"

"That fallin' in love is nothin' but a flight of fancy. And that, in the future, I should choose my romantic partners with my head and not my heart."

When she scowled fiercely, his chin jerked back. "What? I thought that would make you happy."

"I don't like the thought that I'll be the reason you become cynical about love."

"Oh, for the love of—" He slapped his palm against his forehead. "You are the most confoundin' woman on the planet. You realize that, right?"

"No. But only because I doubt you've met every woman on the planet. Wolf, I don't want this thing between us to hurt you or…or…" She searched for a word and came up with, "diminish you in any way. If I thought this friends with benefits thing would—"

"Let me stop you right there before you go throwin' a monkey wrench into works we've already agreed on. In case it has escaped your notice, I'm a grown-ass man completely capable of makin' my own grown-ass decisions that may or may not make my grown-ass cynical all on my grown-ass own."

As he'd hoped, that made a hint of a smile twitch her lips.

Deciding the matter was closed, he warned her, "Now hold onto your hat. I'm goin' to redress your wound."

He could tell she still had something to say, but thought better of it. Nodding, she indicated he should begin by blowing out a fortifying breath.

He squirted a line of antibacterial ointment over the stitches without rubbing it in. He reckoned the gauze pad would do that work for him once he applied it. And even though in the past he'd used every excuse he could think of to touch her, that had been about pleasure. He never wanted to cause her pain.

By the time he had the gauze in place and was ready to begin applying the medical tape, she'd relaxed some. The fingers she'd had curled around the toilet seat were open on her thigh.

"You okay?" he asked, trying to keep his mind on the task at hand. But it was hard when her face was at crotch-level. Her every breath warming the material over his fly.

"It doesn't actually hurt unless I try to move my arm," she admitted.

"Good. Then we'll do everything we can to make sure you don't move your arm."

"Given my plan, that might be a little difficult."

He glanced down to find her smirking up at him. He was *beyond* relieved to hear she was still onboard with the plan despite his momentary bout of verbal diarrhea.

"Are you sayin' you can't do what needs doin' one-handed?" He tsked. "And here I thought you were the inventive sort."

"Really? No." She shook her head sorrowfully. "I guess I should warn you right now that I suck in the bedroom." When his eyes widened with shock, she winked and added, "I also lick and bite."

He was hard again. And given his jeans were wet and

shrink-wrapped around his hips, he'd swear his cock felt like a horse shoved in a shoebox.

"Save your teasin' for after I'm finished here, woman," he growled. "Or I'll rip off those little sleep shorts, hoist you up on the vanity, and have you fucked before either one of us can think."

He winced when he realized how crude he sounded. But when he peeked down at her, he didn't see shock or embarrassment in her eyes. Oh, no. He saw *heat*.

She *was* one for dirty talk.

Duly noted and hallelujah!

He picked up the pace in his ministrations, and was nearly finished, having secured three sides of the gauze pad, when the medical tape decided to mutiny. It kept curling up and getting stuck in its own glue.

"Damned diabolical stuff." He threw an unusable strip into the trash and noticed the pieces of broken teacup lying on top of a pile of tissues.

He was instantly filled with remorse. "I'm sorry about your teacup."

"You're not serious, are you?"

"What?" He frowned. "Why?"

"You saved me, *again*, and you think I'd be upset about a teacup?"

"Was it special? A keepsake or—"

"I got it at a garage sale for fifty cents."

"Oh, good." Relief loosened his shoulders.

"You are something else, Wolf Roanhorse. You know that, right? You've been a superhero the past day, and yet you stand here before me, sorry you broke a teacup."

He couldn't help reminding her, "A superhero, huh? Well, be careful. Superheroes always get the girl in the end."

She rolled her eyes. "Are we about finished here?"

"Almost." He gently smoothed down the last strip of tape. "*Now* we're done." Stepping back, he inspected his work. "Not too shabby, if I do say so myself."

"Excellent." She stood, adjusted her arm in her sling, and then pointed to the toilet. "Your turn."

"My turn?" His chin jerked back. "For what?"

She grabbed his wrist and turned his arm over until he could see the road rash on his elbow. "Oh, right. I should probably clean that up." Bits of dirt and asphalt were stuck in the wound and the edges had dried and become crusty.

"No." She shook her head and pointed again at the toilet lid. "You played Florence Nightingale for me. Let me return the favor."

He shrugged and sat down while she wetted a washcloth with warm water. Then he hissed when she began scrubbing at his wound. "Ow! For shit's sake, take it easy!"

"Hush, you big baby." She slapped his arm. "I have to get it clean or it'll get infected."

Gritting his teeth, he muttered, "It's a good thing you went into the scuba divin' business and not the nursin' business."

One corner of her mouth quirked. "I swear, I have eaten steaks that were tougher than you're acting right now."

"Someone should fire that chef," he muttered, then heaved a sigh of relief when she satisfied herself that his wound was clean. She reached for the ointment, and the move brought her breasts near his face. He was *this* close to those delicious nipples.

Halfway to heaven but headed straight to hell, he thought again, unable to take his eyes off her breasts even as she continued to doctor his arm.

Maybe it was the heaven/hell reference, but for some reason, the song "Hotel California" started playing in his head. He hummed the first few bars as she stuck a gauze pad over his elbow. Then he sang aloud while she wrestled with the tape.

"What did you sing?" There was a delighted twinkle in her eyes as she secured the edges of his bandage.

He groaned. "What did I get wrong this time?"

She bit the inside of her cheek. "Did you sing *Cool Whip in my hair*?"

He knew his expression was chagrined when he quietly asked, "Is that not right?"

That Fourth of July laugh of hers filled the bathroom when she threw back her head. He sat there, fighting a grin, because it was the happiest sound in the world. When she finally lowered her chin, she wiped an imaginary tear from the corner of her eye.

"It's *cool wind* in my hair." Her voice was thick with humor. "Who puts Cool Whip in their hair?"

"I don't know. Someone who ran out of hair gel?"

"And again with the food!" She slapped her thigh.

"Is Cool Whip really food?" he countered. "Or is it more a *food product*, like Velveeta?"

She tried to sober, and failed. Her eyes sparkled, her mouth twitched. "So...is it that you're hungry every time you're listening to music, or that you need to get your hearing tested?"

"That's it," he declared, shoving to a stand. "That's the last time I sing in front of you."

"No!" She grabbed his shoulder. "Please, *please* don't ever stop singing in front of me. I love your misheard lyrics. They're becoming the highlight of my days."

"Oh, look." He glanced at his watch. "My magic watch says you don't have any clothes on." When she frowned down at her tank top and shorts, he dropped his voice. "You do? Then the damn thing must be five minutes fast."

As he'd hoped, that was all it took to stop her teasing.

Her throat worked over a hard swallow and her eyes were heavy lidded when she looked at him.

Then, because she was Chrissy, and because she could never let anyone get one over on her, she arched one eyebrow. "Mmm. And here I was thinking, you know, given all your big talk in the hospital, that *you* were going to strip for *me*."

"Your wish is my command, darlin'." He held out his hand.

When she slid her fingers into his, he knew, for better or worse, from this moment on, his life was changed forever.

CHAPTER 25

2:00 PM...

Wolf slowly unbuttoned his fly. And the calculated, lazy way he did it with one hand made the act look like pure, denim porn.

Chrissy had been teasing about the striptease. But the moment they stepped into her bedroom and Wolf indicated she should lie down on the bed, she'd known *he* hadn't been teasing.

Thank you, Levi Strauss!

Although she would never cop to being a theater buff—not much call for Broadway musicals on the island—she could say, without a doubt, that this right here was the greatest show on Earth.

She licked her lips when the last button popped free. Felt her breasts grow heavy when he hooked a thumb in his waistband. And squeezed her thighs around her hot, swollen sex when he tugged, ever so slowly, and she was gifted with a view of the SAXX logo on the waistband of his black boxer briefs.

"Why did you stop?" Her voice was husky with anticipation when he got his jeans down the barest inch before pausing.

"It occurs to me that maybe we should hold off on this until after you've had some rest. Weren't you sayin' you felt like a can of smashed assholes?"

"That was before." She waved away his concern.

"Before what?"

"Before I knew sex with you was on the table. I couldn't nap now if you hit me over the head with a two-by-four. So kindly..." She made a rolling motion with her hand. "Continue."

He chuckled, tugged his jeans the tiniest bit lower, and then...

Stopped again!

ARGH!

"Now what?" she demanded, unable to keep the impatience from her voice.

"Just makin' sure you're ready for what's comin'." A seductive glint fired in his eyes.

"Hopefully what's coming will be *me*," she told him cheekily. "And I've been ready for that since the day we met."

"Holy hell, woman. When you say things like that..." He trailed off and she watched him grab the thick length of his cock through his jeans.

Soon she would get a chance to see and feel that hungry column of flesh for herself. Of course, if he kept talking, it wouldn't be soon enough.

"Stop flapping your lips and keep going," she grumbled. "Why are you stalling?"

"I'm not stallin'." He teased her by hooking a thumb in a belt loop and pulling his jeans down far enough so she got a spectacular view of his Michelangelo muscles, those creases on either side of his lower stomach that separated his abs from his hips. "I'm takin' my time. There's no need to rush."

"What if I *want* you to rush?" She was going to follow those creases with her tongue. And then she was going to use her tongue on what was smack-dab between them.

"Then I'd say you're goin' to be mighty disappointed. When it comes to makin' love, I like to go slow. Touch every inch. Kiss every inch. *Taste* every inch."

She shuddered. "Then get to it." She threw her uninjured arm wide. "I'm ready to be touched and kissed and tasted."

She was *past* ready. So *far* past ready, in fact, she was tempted to reach down and touch herself through her sleep shorts. She'd never been this horny. If she didn't get some relief soon, she worried she might explode.

Poof! Chrissy goo all over the windows and the walls.

"Good things come to those who wait," he assured her, his voice low as he slid the wet denim down his legs and left his jeans in a pile on the floor.

When he stood, a breath shuddered out of her. She'd seen him in swim trunks. She knew all about his broad, hairless chest, his long, strong legs, and his six-pack abs. But this was different. Unlike his swim trunks, which hung loose around his hips, his boxer briefs clung to every inch of him.

Every. Single. *Inch.*

And there were *many*. Both in length and girth.

When she swallowed, her desert-dry throat made a *clicking* sound.

Again, he cupped his cock in his hand, giving it a squeeze. He knew she was waiting with bated breath to see what he held, but he didn't make a single move to shuck his drawers.

The infuriating man!

"Alex informed me the clitoris has 8000 nerve endings," she told him. Deep Six's resident historian had a head for trivia, and she seemed determined to share it with anyone who would listen. "So if you're going to drag this out and get on my nerves, I would appreciate it very much if you would make sure it's one of *those*."

He stopped stroking himself and blinked at her. Then a long, low laugh rumbled in his chest. When he pulled down his boxer briefs, every last thought fell out of her head.

She was speechless.

Senseless.

He was... The only word that came to mind was *beautiful*. But in an unabashedly *masculine* way.

He was thick and long, his intimate flesh darker than the rest of his skin. Heavy veins snarled up the sides of his erection to feed its substantial weight.

"Need was the breath in my lungs. Want was the blood in my veins." Winston's words came back to her, and she scooted over to pat the mattress in invitation.

"Guess I finally figured out what it takes to leave you speechless." He chuckled as he walked the few steps toward the bed, his manhood bouncing between the muscled columns of his thighs.

In response, her own thighs fell open in readiness. An unwitting proposition that Wolf didn't miss.

Standing beside the bed, gloriously nude, magnificently male, he let his gaze rake down the length of her. She was sprawled before him like an offering, like a supplicant. And she supposed she was both.

Placing one knee on the mattress, he proceeded to crawl onto the bed. No. He didn't crawl. He *prowled*. Like the animal he was named after.

And never once did his eyes leave hers.

When he stretched out next to her, his naked dick

pressed against her hip. Even through the fabric of her sleep shorts, she was scalded by the heat of him.

And holy crap! He looked even longer and thicker up close.

Is it possible to die from lust? she wondered. And then decided, *I guess I'm about to find out!*

And honestly, what a way to go.

She smoothed one finger along the scar at his temple, thinking how close she'd come to losing him. The emotion that twisted in her heart at the feel of that tight, raised flesh wasn't lust or longing. It was tenderness.

He stilled at her touch. And when she leaned forward and kissed his scar, he sighed.

His warm breath fluttered the hair around her face and the next moment every muscle in his big body relaxed. He sank fully into the mattress.

"Now, it's your turn," he whispered, playing with the hem of her shorts.

She opened her mouth to say something, but she couldn't remember what. The words strangled in her throat when he began to slowly, ever so slowly, tug the cotton material down her legs. The air from the vent felt cool against her newly exposed flesh, but the goose bumps that peppered her skin were caused by Wolf's fingers.

After tossing her sleep shorts onto the floor, he softly rubbed his hand up her leg. From the turn of her ankle to the muscle of her calf. He dipped his fingers behind her knee—holy shit! She never knew the backs of her knees were erogenous zones!—before continuing his explorations and drawing a pattern on her thigh with the barest tips of his fingers.

"You want to leave this on?" He lifted the hem of her tank top.

She shook her head.

"Hmm." He stared lazily down her length. "Okay then. Work with me here."

She obliged him when he carefully removed her sling. Then, with the tenderest of touches, he pulled her tank top overhead, doing some magic there at the end that saved her from having to move her injured arm too much.

Then she was as naked as he was.

His gaze fixed on her nipples and a harsh, shuddering breath escaped his lungs. When he licked his lips, she felt the tips of her breasts grow so tight they hurt.

In fact, *all* of her hurt.

Hurt so good.

Oh, and great! Now I have a John Mellencamp earworm!

Her breaths came fast, which made her breasts rise and fall. One second, they were tantalizingly close to his lips. The next second, they dropped away.

She thought, given the desperate look in his eye, he would take a nipple into his mouth. She *badly* needed him to take a nipple into his mouth. So she was disappointed when he started putting her sling back on her arm.

"Please, Wolf. I need you to—"

He covered her mouth, darting his tongue between her lips to stop her talking. And that was fine by her. If she couldn't have his mouth on her boobs, then having it on her mouth was just as good. Especially because the man knew how to kiss.

Like, seriously, he should host a webinar on the subject.

He used his tongue in a slow, steady pace. Licking into her over and over and *over*. Setting a rhythm she knew would translate to other pleasurable activities.

She sighed her passion and he swallowed it down. She tangled her tongue with his and before she knew it, her arm was back in the sling.

"I only want you feelin' pleasure, darlin'," he whispered against her lips. "No pain."

She frowned down at her body, naked except for the sling and its strap that angled between her breasts. "Not exactly the sexiest piece of lingerie, is it?"

"Christina Szarek, you could make a garbage can look sexy. You have the most beautiful body I've ever seen."

If anyone else had said those words, she would have rolled her eyes and scoffed. But because they came out of Wolf's mouth, she believed. At least she believe *he* believed. His gaze was liquid with lust.

"Now"—he kissed his way back to her ear—"I'm going to enjoy every inch of you. And if I do somethin' you don't like, tell me. And if I'm not doin' somethin' you want, tell me that too."

Her heart tripped over itself. Never in her life had a man been willing to listen to her in the bedroom. In fact, her last boyfriend, Drummer of the Dick Pics, had *hated* when she asked him to change position or slow down or…anything, really. *"I don't need instructions, Chrissy. I know what I'm doing."*

Wolf mistook her stunned expression. "I know men have a reputation for bein' bad at communicatin'. But contrary to popular belief, we actually have ears. Tell me what you want, Chrissy. We'll both come out the other side of this more satisfied if you do."

"I want you to do what you promised," she whispered desperately. "I want you to touch every inch of me. Kiss every inch of me. *Taste* every inch of me."

He licked his lips again and she would swear the skin over his cheeks pulled so tight the bones beneath became razor-sharp.

She thought he'd say *your wish is my command*. So she was surprised when he cupped her face instead and whispered against her lips, "My island girl."

There was possession in his voice right before he claimed her mouth. And even though she knew she shouldn't, she liked hearing it.

Oh, baby girl. Her mother's voice sounded in her head. *You are in so much trouble.*

CHAPTER 26

2:12 PM...

When Wolf kissed Chrissy, it started out as a soft brushing of lips. A gentle melding of mouths. He wanted to memorize the moment she truly gave herself to him. And he *tried* to draw it out.

Lord, how he tried.

But he was greedy with want, ravenous with need, and soon any semblance of gentleness, any illusion of politeness was gone. He devoured her like she was an MRE and he'd been stuck out on a mission for days with nothing to eat.

His kisses grew deeper, hungrier, wetter. And when she groaned her pleasure, he lost his ever-loving mind.

The animal in him wanted to rut. Wanted to spread her legs, notch the heated head of his cock against her wet opening, and plunge inside. Just screw and bang and *breed* until they were shaking and breathless and completely spent.

But no. Not this first time.

Later he would give in to his baser instincts. Later he would show her how wonderful and wicked straight-up fucking could be. But this first time…

This first time he would show her how extraordinary *making love* could be. What it was like when two people who cared deeply for one another finally, *finally* brought their bodies together in a physical act that expressed what words never could.

With reluctance, he pulled his mouth from hers. She hummed her impatience.

"Shh, darlin'." He whispered against her cheek as he pressed a line of soft, lingering kisses back to her succulent little ear. "I'll get you there. Don't you worry. But let's make this first time about the journey, not the destination. Is that okay with you?"

He lifted his head so he could see her eyes. Those ocean eyes that were dark with passion and sparkling up at him with such…*trust.*

She might not have faith in him when it came to forever. But when it came to this? It was all there on her face. Her words only confirmed it. "Everything you do is okay with me. Except when you stop kissing me or touching me."

He chuckled, in love with her ever-mobile mouth. How it was usually laughing or smiling or skewering him with a witty quip. But he loved it best as it was right now. Wet and swollen from his kisses.

The soft glow of the afternoon sun slanted in through the closed slats of her shutters. As always happened in the Keys, that gilded orb had fought the rain and won. He was glad, because its light highlighted the hills and valleys of Chrissy's delicious body—a landscape he intended to thoroughly explore before claiming it as his own.

"You are so incredibly gorgeous." His words were

reverent as he traced a finger over the elegant line of her jaw.

Her gaze searched his. "When you say it"—her voice was breathy—"I believe it."

God love her. She has no idea.

She was a goddess, a water sprite, and ethereal creature possessing mile after mile of smooth skin. Her sun-kissed flesh was only disturbed by the little triangles around her breasts where her bikini tops protected her from the tropical sun. There was a matching triangle of pale skin over her pubic bone. It perfectly framed the neatly trimmed landing strip of dark blond hair that pointed the way to heaven.

Her nipples were cotton candy pink, crowning breasts that were full and firm. Then there was the perfect oval over her belly button. The neat tuck of her waist. The thrilling curve of her hips.

Christina Szarek was all woman. And he wanted all of her.

Starting now.

Claiming her mouth in a kiss that curled his own toes, he let his fingers explore all that glorious geography his eyes had been drinking in since the moment he removed her clothes. He started with her long neck, then worked his way to the line of her collarbone before slowly, *slowly* rubbing his hand along the side of her warm breast.

She moaned in encouragement when he softly cupped her, luxuriating in the weight of her in his palm. Then she gasped when he passed the callused pad of his thumb over her tip, feeling his balls tighten up in direct response to the furl of her responsive little nipple.

Back and forth he flicked that darling, ruched bud until she was squirming and squeezing her thighs together around an ache he understood. He was aching too. But he refused to rush.

Instead, he continued to slowly, *thoroughly* explore her with his fingers. And if his moves seemed calculated, that's because they were. He'd been planning this for a long time. Had gone over and over it in his mind. What he wanted to do to her. *How* he wanted to do it.

"I'll tend to the bits under here"—he softly skated a finger around her sling, which kept her arm immobile across her midsection—"after you're healed," he whispered. Then he circled the hollow of her belly button with his fingertip.

She tilted her hips, inviting him to continue his journey south. He did, but at his own pace. And he was *leisurely*. Tracing her hip bones, smoothing the sweet little curve of her belly, following the creases where her legs met her body.

By the time he smoothed that little landing strip of hair, her breaths were coming in shallow pants and her thighs were wide in invitation.

He couldn't help himself. He had to look. Had to see the moment his fingers touched her most intimate flesh.

Pulling his mouth from hers, his breath strangled in his lungs when his fingertips parted her delicate folds.

Fuck me, he thought a little hysterically. She was everything he'd dreamed and more. So sweet and compact, the deeply blushing pinkness of her skin glistening with wetness. With readiness.

And it was all for *him*.

A wave of possessiveness broke over him. He wanted to tattoo that pretty mound with his name. Brand her soft flesh with his signature. Put his mark on her most intimate parts so that no one could ever think to claim what was rightfully his.

"Touch me, Wolf." Her voice sounded drugged. A quick look at her face showed her cheeks flushed prettily and her bottom lip caught between her teeth. "Touch me, rub me, put your fingers inside me and stroke me until I cum."

"My pleasure." He reclaimed her mouth in a sensual kiss at the same time he rubbed his finger over the swollen little nub of her clit.

She groaned, her hips arching off the mattress, seeking more, needing more.

He gave it to her, subtly increasing the pressure but not the rhythm. Drawing out her pleasure, winding her tighter and tighter, lifting her higher and higher. Knowing the moment he put his fingers inside her would be even more glorious if he first primed her pump. Got her intimate flesh absolutely *buzzing* with need.

She seemed to agree, because she moved in rhythm to his hand. But after a few moments of this exquisite torture, she ripped her mouth away. "Wolf! Stop teasing me!"

His voice was barely a rasp as he sank a finger into the soft, hot center of her arousal. "Is this what you want, darlin'?"

"Oh, my god!" she cried out, her walls clamping around his intrusion. Her intimate muscles rippling along the length of his digit as if to welcome him in.

His cock jerked so hard it slapped against his stomach. His heart raced so fast he could feel the hum of his blood through his veins. And every inch of his skin was on fire.

Curling his finger slightly, he found the rough, satiny patch of flesh that was sure to send her careening into ecstasy. He knew he'd found the correct spot even before she drew in a sharp breath because her stomach muscles contracted.

Setting up a slow, steady rhythm, he loved the way her body clung to him with each retreat and then softened with each advance. Retreat and advance. Retreat and advance.

Her hips matched the thrusting of his hand. His own hips jerked slightly, rubbing his erection against the skin of her hip.

All he could think was…

Wet. Silky. Mine.

She lifted her chin to watch what he was doing to her. And the instant she did, her pupils dilated so wide they nearly eclipsed the blue of her irises.

It *was* an incredibly erotic sight. His arm stroking so the muscles and tendons stood out. Her hips pumping in a motion as old as time. Wetness glistening on both of them.

His cock bounced rudely, as if to catch her attention and remind her of its readiness. Wolf pressed it into the mattress, telling it to be patient.

The bastard only throbbed painfully in protest.

Her head fell back against the pillow then, her eyes screwed tight. And he watched as rivers of pleasure flowed through her body, rushing sweetly, building speed.

He could feel how close she was in the undulating grip of her womanhood. Hear it in her thready, mewling breaths. See it in the bright wash of red that mottled her skin.

"Go on and help yourself," he growled, low and hungry, and then felt a drop of pre-cum leave the tip of his cock when she reached down and pressed two fingers against her clitoris, moving them in a quick, circular motion.

"That's right, darlin'," he whispered. "Let it happen. Don't fight it."

Each of his thrusts pressed a groan from her lips. And when he added a second finger to the first, she finally gave it up for him.

Her groans became a long, shattering cry. Her hips arched high off the mattress. And her inner walls squeezed so tight around his marauding fingers that his knuckles rubbed together.

Holding his fingers deep and high inside her, he massaged that rough, swollen patch of flesh. Drawing out her climax. Milking every last ounce of pleasure from her until slowly, ever so slowly, her hips sank back into the mattress and her muscles loosened.

He only allowed her a moment's reprieve, a second or two to slide from the heights of orgasm, before reclaiming her lips.

Women, at least some of them, had the ability to cum over and over again. The trick was to take advantage of that refractory period. Let them drift down. But not too far before pushing them back up.

He was determined to discover if Chrissy was one of those women. He *hoped* so.

Because I'm only gettin' started.

He stroked his tongue into her mouth, and at first she was passive, still recovering. But then a hungry little growl sounded at the back of her throat and she began returning his caresses, her hand sneaking down between them to take hold of his restless dick.

Holy fuck! Her palm was warm. Her fingers were curious as they traced his veins and explored his swollen, weeping head.

It was only through manful focus and discipline he didn't go off in her hand. That's how horny he was for her. And he *would* go off if she kept it up.

"Not yet." He encircled her wrist and pulled her hand away. If his cock had a voice it would've cried out in disappointment.

She pursed her wonderfully kiss-swollen mouth. "But why?"

"I won't be able to hold back if you keep touchin' me, darlin'. I'll have to fuck you. And I'm not ready for that. Not yet."

"Why?" There was a recklessness in her eyes. And a hunger he knew was reflected in his own.

"I've touched every inch of you. Now it's time to kiss

those same sweet inches. And when I make you cum again, I want to taste it on my tongue."

She shuddered, and he didn't wait for her permission before kissing a path down her throat. He didn't *need* her permission. The way she tunneled her fingers through his hair when he caught her nipple in his mouth was consent enough.

By the time he'd licked and laved his way to her belly button, she was once again writhing and begging him to ease the ache he'd built.

"Shh, darlin'. We're gettin' there." Fitting his shoulders between her spread thighs, he was hard-pressed not to spend himself on the mattress.

She was so pretty and swollen. And her scent was glorious. A mixture of soap, clean skin, and that unmistakable smell of fully aroused female flesh that every man fantasized about and craved.

"Wolf…" Her fingers pulled at his hair. Her hips thrust up at him in entreaty. And when he allowed his eyes to travel up her body, his gaze collided with hers.

He didn't look away when he leaned close, pressing his mouth over her waiting flesh, finding and softly flicking the bud of her arousal.

She jerked as if she'd been hit with a cattle prod. And he lifted his head ever so slightly, making sure his hot breath bathed her wet flesh when he asked, "More?"

She nodded, unable to speak.

He chuckled lowly, gratified as only a man who'd set a woman on fire could be. When he sampled her again, her fingers left his hair. She grabbed the headboard for leverage and cried out in helpless need.

He settled into the task then, loving everything about it. The softness of her flesh against his tongue. The warmth of her thighs on either side of his face. The way she bucked and quivered and kept saying, "Oh, yes! Yes! Oh, *yes*!"

Each press of his lips, each swipe of his tongue undid her a little more. And when he shoved a finger inside her, she was flung over that cliff once again.

The smell of her release tunneled up his nose. The sound of her cries were muffled since she'd clamped her legs around his ears. And the taste of her?

Oh, the taste of her was unbelievable. Salty and sweet. Clean and bright.

The last thread of his restraint broke. He pressed up from his sprawl between her legs and found his place between her hips, pressing his hot manhood against her belly.

It was a primal move, dominating and coarse.

He couldn't help it.

In fact, the only thing that kept him from plowing into her was...

"Condom," he rasped, every muscle in his body twitching with barely held restraint.

CHAPTER 27

2:41 PM...

Reckless...

Chrissy felt so reckless she wanted to shout for Wolf to forget the damn condom. Her need for him had become a biological imperative. She wasn't sure she could live much longer without having him inside her.

Alas, sanity and the words of her high school sex-ed teacher—a woman by the unfortunate name of Ms. Cockburn—echoed through her skull. *"There's nothing sexier than keeping the health of your partner in the forefront of your mind when it comes time to do 'the deed.'"* Ms. Cockburn had actually made air quotes.

Scrabbling through the junk in her nightstand, Chrissy located the lone strip of condoms. Using her teeth, she ripped off the foil packaging of one and reached for Wolf. But she'd barely pressed the little ring of latex around his bulbous tip before he caught her wrist at the same time he caught his bottom lip between his teeth.

She frowned up at the tortured look on his face. "No, darlin'." His voice was barely a thread of sound inside the room.

"Why not?" She knew her tone was full of impatience. Why did the infuriating man keep stalling the process?

Yes. Okay. So after two amazing—we're talking *world class*—orgasms, craving more from him might be construed by some as her being…gluttonous.

Just call me one of the seven deadly sins, baby.

"I'm so hot and hard," he rasped, his eyes glittering dangerously. "I might go off in your hand if you put the condom on me." He gently plucked the ring of latex from her fingers.

"That could be hot." She trailed her hand over his broad chest, watching, mesmerized, as the flat brown disk of his nipple puckered when she flicked it with the edge of her fingernail.

It could be *very* hot to take him in her palm, wrap her fingers *all the way around him*, and stroke lazily until the pleasure overtook him and he spent himself.

Some of what she was thinking must've been written across her face. A low, strangled groan shuddered from him. "Stop your teasin', wench."

"Wench, is it?" She cocked an eyebrow. "Next you'll be sporting an eye patch and jonesing for rum."

"The only thing I'm jonesin' for right now is you."

He hissed when he slid the condom down his length. She couldn't tell if it was an expression of pleasure or pain. He was so huge and swollen, she figured it might be both.

Once he was fully covered, he gently pressed her back into the pillow. Supporting himself with his hands, he hovered above her and the silver piece-of-eight—a seventeenth-century Spanish coin—that he wore on a chain around his neck, dangled in her face.

She thought he would push into her. And she was so ready, she wouldn't have minded if he'd done it in one hard, forceful jab. But instead, he traced her face with his fingertip. Her eyebrows. Her cheekbones. Her nose. Her lips.

The way he touched her was unlike anything she'd ever experienced before. He wasn't impatient like some or rough like others. And this was despite being gripped by what she knew was a desperate sort of need, a greedy sort of want—she knew because she was seized by those same feelings. But no. He was sweet. Soft. *Reverent* almost.

He touched her as if she was the most luxurious, most delicate treasure in all the world. And every time his callused fingertips brushed over some new inch of her skin, she felt a moment of relief. It was like finally, *finally* he'd claimed that part of her too.

"You ready, Island Girl?"

"Yes. Please."

A muscle twitched in his jaw. And then he took himself in hand.

Ducking her chin, she watched as he positioned his plump head at her entrance. With a subtle flex of his hips, he pushed inside her. Just the smallest amount. Just the barest kiss of his glans stretching her opening. But it felt amazing.

Her breath hissed from her as she let her head fall back against the pillow.

His chin was angled down, watching their union just as she had been doing. But suddenly, he looked her straight in the eyes. "This'll be a snug fit at first," he warned. "Try to relax."

Some men might've said the words simply to hear them. To make themselves feel powerful and virile.

Wolf said them because it was true.

"I'll go slow," he added. "And if you want me to stop at any point, just say the word."

Wrapping her hand around the back of his neck, she pulled him close so she could whisper against his mouth, "Shut up and make love to me, Wolf."

He didn't have to say the words. They were there in his eyes. *Your wish is my command.*

She felt his muscles quiver beneath her fingertips. Felt what his restraint had cost him. And then he let loose a little of that iron control and thrust into her.

Sweet Jesus! He was thick and meaty. Having to work at it. Coaxing her body into accepting his own with short, powerful strokes. Stretching her to her limits.

He owned each new inch of her straining flesh as he took it. Smoothed out every wrinkle. Abraded each screaming nerve ending.

And still it wasn't enough to seat him fully.

Making a sound of impatience, she drew her knees high against his sides. And with the next thrust, she could feel his swollen head smash against the entrance to her womb. Could feel his testicles resting warm and weighty against the curve of her ass.

They both sighed, and for who knows how long—she'd lost all sense of time—he held himself still inside her. Reveling in the joining.

"Y'okay, darlin'?" He spoke slowly, as if he had to concentrate to form words.

"Okay?" she whispered, pulling him down again so she could taste his delicious lips. "Wolf, you feel so good in me. Better than I ever imagined."

"You're so hot around me. So soft and tight. Nothin' has ever felt this good. Nothin' ever will." She felt his mouth curve into a smile. "Well, except for maybe this."

He pulled out a bare inch before thrusting back home. Hissing encouragement, she hooked her ankles together at the small of his back. Wanting to hold him inside her at the same time she wanted him to *move*.

She was a study in contradictions. And it sounded like she was begging when she said, "More, Wolf."

His movements were precise and deliberate. Not hurried. Oh, no. Not Wolf. He was metronome steady, his rhythm contrived to draw out their journey. To force them to feel every slow retreat, and then luxuriate in every vigorous advance.

Retreat and advance. Retreat and advance until her entire body was alive with the most astonishing sensations. Until she could feel that curling, furling tingle low in her belly, her womb aching and begging for that last little bit of friction that would release the spring coiling tighter and tighter at her center.

Her hand mapped his long, strong body. The hard muscles of his back. The uncompromising powerfulness of his tattooed arm. The hard flex of his ass as he continued to rock against her in that mind-numbingly wonderful back and forth. Rise and fall.

"Faster," she whispered desperately. She just needed…

"Oh! My! *God!*" she cried after he pushed up, using the headboard as leverage, and started pistoning his hips faster. Faster. *Harder.*

The head of his fat cock knocked against her cervix. His veiny shaft rasped along that sensitive patch of nerves dedicated solely to carnal pleasure. Reaching one hand between them, he pressed the pad of his thumb into the top of her sex.

"Yes! Just like that!" she moaned.

Her eyes were bare slits, but she could see the perspiration beaded on his forehead. A low series of grunts bubbled up from deep inside his chest as he continued to drive into her. Over and over.

He was close. It was there in his eyes, in the tightness of the muscles in his jaw. And then she couldn't see anything. She couldn't hear or smell or taste either.

All she could do was *feel*.

Feel her orgasm building, rising, rushing toward her like a tidal wave. Then it broke over her. Lifting her up. Crashing her down. Tumbling her over.

Crying out his name, her body became one with the wave. A liquid, powerful force that pulled Wolf in its wake.

She felt him thrust into her, high and tight, holding himself still even as his impossibly swollen erection bucked and pulsed. She heard him growl her name in a voice so low and guttural, it didn't even sound like him. And she saw the veins and tendons standing out in his neck as he strained with the power of his release.

For long moments, they simply stayed that way. Joined. Replete. Basking in each other's gratification. And only when their breaths stilled, when their muscles relaxed, did he move to disengage their thoroughly wasted bodies.

After disposing of the condom, he rolled onto his back. With a come-hither motion, he invited her to join him.

She didn't hesitate.

Throwing her leg over his much larger, much hairier one, she found the spot on his chest that seemed made for her head.

"Wolf…" She said his name simply because she wanted to hear it. Then something occurred to her. Propping her head in her hand, she gazed down at him. "How did you get that nickname anyway?"

"You mean Wolf?" He frowned.

She rolled her eyes. "What else would I be talking about?"

"Smart-ass." He shook his head, but there was affection

in his eyes. "I was confused since it's not really a nickname. It's my middle name."

"Your middle name is Wolf?"

"Sort of."

She blinked. "I'm confused."

"My middle name is Waya, which is Cherokee for Wolf. When I was little, my family called me Waya. But once I started school, I was teased by the other boys for havin' what they thought sounded like a *girl* name. So I asked everyone to start callin' me by the English version." He hitched his shoulder. "I've been Wolf since I was six years old. Although, my *elisi* still sometimes calls me Waya."

"You don't talk much about your indigenous heritage." She cocked her head. "Why is that?"

He scratched his chin in thought. "Probably two reasons. The first one bein' there's still pervasive discrimination against Native peoples. I remember my third-grade teacher, Mrs. Yates, tellin' the class 'The only reason Oklahoma exists as a state is 'cause the Indians were too drunk and too stoned on peyote to keep their land.'"

Chrissy's heart shriveled at the thought of little Wolf hearing that from an adult who was supposed to pass on the knowledge of cursive writing and multiplication tables, but instead passed on bigotry, hatred, and unspeakable misinformation.

"It was better to blend in," he continued. "Which was actually pretty easy. I mean, it's not like I was playin' stickball and goin' to pow wows and stomp dances every weekend. I was playin' baseball, eatin' hotdogs, and helpin' my grandparents on their farm. Pretty much like every other kid from my neck of the woods."

She nodded. "At that age no one wants to be *other*."

"Oh, I mean I *loved* my Cherokee culture. And durin' the festivals I *did* play stickball and go to pow wows and stomp dances. It's simply that it wasn't part of the day-to-day, and I learned not to advertise it."

She nodded again. "And the second reason?"

"I've never felt like an authority on the culture or traditions, so I'm not comfortable talkin' about it. My *grandmother* is an authority. And believe me, as an adult I can sit and listen to her for hours. But when I was younger?" His expression turned chagrined. "I was more interested in how to make a mountain of nachos than one-pot venison stew. More excited to talk about girls than the Cherokee creation myths."

"Still," she sighed, "it must be nice to belong to something bigger than yourself."

He nodded. "Gloria Steinman once described white Americans as 'a people without a tribe.' I supposed, deep in all of us, there's a need to belong to somethin' larger, somethin' older and more fundamental."

Maybe that's why Chrissy had always longed for a big family. She was trying to build her own tribe.

She was pondering this when fatigue slammed her. *Hard.* Like, seriously, people talked about "hitting the wall"? She felt like she'd plowed into one going seventy miles per hour.

A huge yawn stretched her mouth wide. She looked up at Wolf and warned, "I have to go to sleep now."

He cast her a wry smile before pulling the edge of the comforter over them both. "Go on then. You deserve it after the day you've had."

Her eyes were already drifting closed when she asked, "You'll stay?"

"Nowhere I'd rather be, darlin'."

She smiled, a feeling of warmth slipping over her.

No. On second thought, it wasn't *warmth*. It was security. Contentment. She felt satisfied. At ease. Fulfilled.

She felt...*loved.*

Yes, that's what it was. She felt *loved* in a way she never had before. And she *liked* it.

No wonder Mom kept doing this over and over again. Moments like these almost make all the pain that comes after seem worth it.

CHAPTER 28

3:10 PM...

One hell of a bad mood...that's what Romeo was battling.

He was also tired, still slightly damp from the storm, and hungry. The latter of which was why he shuffled into the kitchen when he smelled someone cooking.

Let it be Bran. Let it be Bran. Let it be Bran.

Damnit! It wasn't Bran.

Doc stood at the stove, a flowered waist apron tied around his lean hips. Since the man was six and a half feet tall, the garment hit him right below the crotch, making it look more like a tutu than a waist apron.

Romeo fought a grin, but it dissolved when the big Montanan turned to him, spatula in hand, and lifted an eyebrow. "You're staring at me. Taking mental notes on how to be awesome?"

"You know," Romeo mused while walking over to the cupboard to grab a coffee mug. He had to step around Meat on the way. The big, wrinkly bulldog sat beside Doc, tongue lolling, jowls drooling, waiting with rapt attention for any morsel that might fall from above like manna from heaven. "Being a smart-ass isn't all it's cracked up to be. I mean, sure, it means you're smart. But it also means you're an ass."

"Said the preacher to the choir," Doc countered with a grin.

Romeo ignored him and poured himself a cup of coffee from a carafe that was always warm. Just about everyone who lived on Wayfarer Island ran on caffeine. "All these years together, Doc," he said, "and you let me think you couldn't cook."

"I *can't* cook. But I've been trying to improve myself." Doc twirled the spatula like a baton.

"Then you should start by changing that shirt."

Doc glanced down at his tank top that used to be a T-shirt before he cut the arms off. "What's wrong with my shirt?" he demanded with a furrowed brow.

"For starters, it has a picture of a chicken laying an egg and reads: *Chickens, the pet that poops breakfasts*."

Doc, completely unoffended, laughed heartily. "That's comic gold, right there." Then he sobered. "Wait. You said for starters. What *else* do you think is wrong with it?"

"You Joe-Dirted it. Only hicks, honkies, and hillbillies Joe-Dirt their shirts."

"I was raised on a ranch in the middle of Nowhere, Montana." Doc grinned. "I think that pretty much qualifies me for all three."

Romeo snorted before taking a gulp of coffee. Making a face of revulsion, he complained, "Damn! Did you guys let Uncle John make it again? You know he puts chicory in there."

John Anderson was a New Orleans transplant who still believed coffee should contain chicory, that crawfish tasted better than shrimp, and that a shark was nothing when compared to a Louisiana yard dog, otherwise known as an alligator.

Doc took a rather large drink out of the mug sitting next to the stove. He grimaced and admitted, "It truly is awful, isn't it?"

Both of them nodded their agreement. And then both of them continued to drink the swill. After a second, Doc flipped the grilled cheese over in the skillet.

Romeo wrinkled his nose. "That thing smells like a teenage boy's gym socks. What kind of cheese are you using?"

"Three cheeses actually." Doc's chest puffed with pride. "Cheddar and muenster, but what you're probably smelling is the Gruyere."

"Something wrong with good ol' American?" Romeo asked over his shoulder since he'd turned to hunt through the liquor cabinet.

The coffee was helping with his fatigue. Doc's odorific monstrosity of a grilled cheese had killed his appetite. But he was going to need a little liquid spirit if he had any hopes of tempering his foul mood.

"Nothing at all," Doc admitted. "But like I said, I'm trying to improve myself and—" He stopped midsentence when he saw Romeo pour a healthy slug of whiskey into his coffee mug. Lifting an eyebrow, he asked, "To what do we owe the pleasure of your day drinking, may I ask?"

"You may." Romeo taste-tested the cocktail and added a splash more whiskey. "But that doesn't mean I'll answer."

Doc frowned. "You are ornerier than a two-headed snake today. Did someone eat your bowl of sunshine this morning?"

"Anyone ever told you that you talk in country music lyrics?" Romeo asked.

"My *life* is a country music lyric," Doc countered with a shrug. "Grew up next to the railroad tracks. My first car was a pickup truck that was more rust than get up and go. And I own a pair of boots that are damn near old enough to drink."

Despite himself, Romeo felt his lips twitching. When Doc put his mind to it, he could exude that aw-shucks, carefree cowboy charm that made a person want to pull up a chair and sit a spell.

"Come on," Doc cajoled as he transferred the grilled cheese onto a plate. Meat watched the maneuver with laser-focused interest, and then licked his drooling chops in disappointment when nothing fell onto the floor. "Tell ol' Doc what's troubling you. You know your secret is safe with me since I'm not likely to care, which means I'll probably forget in ten minutes. Consider this a judgment-free zone."

Blowing out a windy breath, Romeo grabbed one of the ladderback chairs surrounding the old Formica table. "My instinct is to tell you that you're in some serious need of your own business to mind, but I think you know that. So I'll admit this much... I was put in an awkward position and I reacted poorly."

After taking the seat opposite Romeo, Doc pulled off one corner of his grilled cheese and watched the gooey center string. "Vague," he said, giving the morsel a couple of blows to cool it off before popping it in his mouth. "Very vague," he added, working his jaw slowly, testing the quality of the product, and then giving a decisive dip of his chin.

Apparently the froufrou grilled cheese passed the muster.

"Which has me intrigued," Doc finished, shooting Romeo an arch glance. "Does this have anything to do with the way Mia burst in earlier, stomping around like her hair was on fire even though she looked like a drowned rat?"

"Did she invite you to join her for a drink?" Romeo demanded, feeling an unwelcome stab of jealousy.

"No." Doc's chin jerked back. "Was she supposed to?"

The relief Romeo felt only pissed him off more. "She said she was going to."

Doc broke off a piece of crust and tossed it to Meat. The bulldog caught it handily and swallowed without tasting it.

"I feel like we're having two different conversations here." Doc narrowed his eyes. "What does your being put in an awkward position and reacting poorly have to do with Mia inviting me to share a drink? Or *not* inviting me to share a drink, as the case may be?"

Romeo sighed and admitted miserably, "I think she needed a drink because I said something that really offended her. I mean, I didn't *mean* to. I was trying to do the opposite. Trying *not* to let her get her feelings hurt, but—"

Doc interrupted with, "Thomas Edison once said 'a good intention, but with a bad approach, often leads to a poor result.'"

Romeo frowned. "You've been hanging around Wolf too much."

"So come on," Doc said around a mouthful of toast and cheese. "What did you say to her?"

Romeo sniffed and looked out the window at Li'l Bastard. The rooster perched on the porch railing, staring in through the glass panes to keep an eye on his best buddy. Every once in a while, he let loose with an inquisitive cluck that made Meat turn away from Doc's grilled cheese to give the chicken a quick, reassuring glance.

Deciding there was no use keeping the fiasco with Mia a secret—after all, they lived in extremely close quarters on an extremely small island; the whole crew was bound to find out eventually—Romeo sighed and ran through the events of the last twenty-four hours, culminating with what he'd said to Mia in the plane after they landed.

When he was finished, Doc sat there, staring. Then he wiped his mouth with a napkin—the grilled cheese having disappeared down his throat while Romeo told his tale of woe—and said, "It's impressive you're flexible enough to have your foot in your mouth and your head up your ass at the same time."

Romeo tossed his hands in the air. "I thought you said this was a judgment-free zone!"

"I'm not judging you," Doc countered. "That's simply your conscience talking."

Romeo harrumphed, conceding the point ungraciously.

His conscience *was* bothering him.

I mean, did I truly think a woman like her would be interested in a shitheel like me?

To his horror, he had. Because sweet Mother Mary had graced him with a handsome face, and plenty of workouts had given him a muscled body. He'd gotten used to women wanting him.

What a miserable, conceited ass I turned out to be!

Then again, how could he have *known*? Mia had gone from rabbiting out of the room every time he entered to gazing at him with doe eyes, asking him if he needed a drink, and calling him Sprio. Most guys would've been under the same mistaken impression that he'd been under, right?

"Okay, Mr. Know-It-All." He crossed his arms. "So how would *you* have handled it if you were in my shoes?"

"First of all"—Doc leaned down so he could see Romeo's feet beneath the table—"I wouldn't be caught dead in a pair of Chacos. And second of all, it doesn't matter what

I would've done. I'm more interested in digging down on what *you* did and why."

"Wait a minute. Wait a minute." Romeo lifted a finger. "What's the matter with Chacos?"

Doc rolled his eyes. "They're marketed as sandals for an *outdoor* lifestyle, but they're really the shoes sorority girl Tiffany's daddy gets for her when he buys her a trip to Costa Rica for her college graduation. It's like, 'Oh, I see you're wearing Chacos. Please tell me about your adventures staying in a five-star jungle hotel while eating Michelin star-worthy food and getting daily facials.'"

Romeo blinked. "Wow. I didn't realize someone could have such a strong opinion of footwear."

Doc waved away his response. "At least you haven't succumbed to wearing Crocs. If you start that shit, I promise to go all Survivor on your ass and have you voted off the island. Now…back to the real issue. You told Mia she was nothing you need and that you are nothing she should want. What did you mean by that?"

"Exactly what I said. I don't need a woman in my life," Romeo answered testily. He'd been looking at a pair of Crocs when he'd been on Key West. Like Chacos, they were *practical*. "At least not one like *her*," he added.

Both of Doc's eyebrows arched. "And what is *she* like?"

"Nice. Cultured. Smart. And most importantly," he bit off, "*relationship* material."

For a long time, Doc studied him. For too long. Romeo had to stop himself from shifting uncomfortably.

Finally, Doc said, "You really want to spend the rest of your life flitting from woman to woman? Never having anything permanent or serious or meaningful?"

"Why would I want something permanent and serious and meaningful?" Romeo bristled. "You had it and look what it got you." As soon as the words left his mouth, he wanted to suck them back in. "Shit, man." He ran a hand through his hair. "I'm sorry. I didn't mean that. I'm being an asshole today."

"No argument here," Doc agreed readily. Then he added, "But, you know, even though my love life ended up torpedoing my entire life, I still wouldn't change what happened for the world. Not to get all cheesy on you by quoting *Steel Magnolias*, but 'I would rather have thirty minutes of wonderful than a lifetime of nothing special.'"

Something huge and hard centered in Romeo's chest. "Doesn't matter anyway," he muttered, feeling perfectly wretched. "Even if Mia *was* something I needed in my life, I'm still not anything she should want. She's way too good for me."

"Ah," Doc said. That one word contained a wealth of meaning.

For a long time afterward, they sat in silence, both lost in their thoughts. But eventually, his voice quiet, Doc added, "I know you have a past you're not proud of, man. But people who are worth knowing, the ones who are good enough for *you*, should be able to see you for who you are instead of who you were. They should be able to appreciate the guts it took for you to change your life for the better."

Romeo respected the hell out of Doc. And to hear a guy like that speak about *him* that way?

He had to take a quick drink to let the whiskey burn away the tears gathering behind his eyes or else he might break down bawling. *Like…damn.*

"Something tells me Mia is someone like that," Doc continued. "Someone worth knowing. So maybe you should tell her the *real* reason you spooked like a wild mustang today, and then let her make up her own mind about you."

Romeo stood from the table.

"Wait." Doc looked alarmed. "I didn't mean right *now*. Give her some time to cool down first."

"I'm not going to talk to Mia," Romeo told him. He wasn't convinced Doc was right. The thought of telling Mia who he was—or who he'd *been*—turned his stomach worse than day-old chicken salad that'd been left in the sun.

He *liked* the way she looked at him now— Er...at least he'd liked the way she looked at him before their plane conversation. He'd liked seeing the interest and excitement in her eyes even when she was acting all trepidatious. And he didn't think he could handle seeing disappointment there instead. Or worse, disgust.

"Then where are you headed?" Doc asked.

"To the beach at the back of the island. I'm going to finish my coffee out there." He needed to think, and he couldn't do it in a house full of his SEAL brothers. Like Doc, they were all far, *far* too shrewd when it came to picking up on his bad mood. And none of them could resist poking a bear.

"May you find peace once you get there." Doc lifted his coffee mug.

"Amen, brother." Romeo grabbed the bottle of whiskey on his way out. "I'll drink to that."

CHAPTER 29

3:16 PM...

T hat's so wrong."

Wolf grabbed a seat in the rocking chair next to the one Officer Ryan inhabited and glanced at the man with a questioning look. "What is?" he asked.

Ryan hitched his chin toward Wolf's getup, which consisted of nothing but Chrissy's silk robe. Her *short* silk robe.

He'd awoken from a delicious post-coital catnap because he was feeling two things in equal measure. The first was a desperate, aching need to have her again. To feel her warm body welcome his. To hear her sighs turn into moans, and watch her as she was caught up in the arms of bliss.

But she'd looked so sweet and angelic in sleep that he'd known there wasn't a damn thing he could do—or maybe the correct phrase was *should do*—about the hard-on that pulsed insistently between his legs.

The second thing he'd been feeling was hunger. In fact,

he'd been so ravenous, he'd thought for sure his belly button had rubbed a hole in his backbone. Which, unlike his annoyingly insistent boner, *had* been something he could remedy.

With slow, careful movements, he'd disentangled himself from Chrissy. After tucking the comforter around her, he'd tiptoed across the room to his damp jeans. But they'd stunk of hospital air and twenty-four hours of wear. The thought of putting them back on his body had curled his lip.

Instead, he'd grabbed the robe hanging on a hook on the back of her bedroom door. After cinching the belt around his waist, he'd transferred the Glock into the robe's pocket. The firearm had been sitting atop the dresser where he'd carefully placed it before doing his best impression of a Chippendales dancer.

Mmm. Forever emblazoned upon his memory was the picture of Chrissy reclining back in bed, her eyes going hot and liquid as she watched him undress. There hadn't been a hint of shyness or embarrassment in her gaze. Nope. Not his Chrissy. She'd been unapologetically voyeuristic, and it'd made him harder than he'd ever been before.

Once he'd ventured out of the bedroom, he'd found his damp T-shirt hanging over the shower curtain rod and had decided a load of laundry was in order. After spot-treating the clothes Chrissy had left in the plastic bag by the sofa, he'd thrown the whole lot into the washer.

Then he'd padded barefoot into the kitchen to wolf down a generous portion of bacon mac and cheese—he hadn't even taken the time to heat it up in the microwave—and had washed it down with a tall glass of iced tea. Which had brought to mind Officer Ryan.

After pouring a second glass of tea, he'd shuffled onto the porch to discover the storm had completely blown over and taken most of the humidity with it, leaving only sunshine and a gentle breeze behind.

Now, he made a face and told Officer Ryan, "Are you so insecure in your masculinity that you can't stand the sight of another man's legs?"

"Oh, no." Ryan took a sip of the iced tea before setting the glass on the porch's wooden floorboards. "I'm fine with your legs, but I feel like the kimono is cultural appropriation. Plus, what's between your hairy ass and that chair?"

"Just a bit of air." Wolf grinned and watched Officer Ryan pretend to retch.

He liked the policeman. The guy was funny and hadn't complained once about playing bodyguard on Chrissy's porch.

"Hey, man," Wolf said. "I can stand watch out here for a while if you need to hit the head."

"Nah." The policeman waved him off. "I already pissed on the cocoplum bush around the corner." A knowing look entered his eyes. "Didn't want to come into the house and mess up the mojo you had going."

Wolf snorted. "Ah, yes. The Bro-Code. Glad to see you received your copy of the handbook."

Ryan nodded. "Right around the time I turned fourteen and discovered girls were something other than annoying creatures who told the teacher on me when I farted or stuck my gum under the desk."

"Fourteen?" Wolf shook his head. "You got off easy. I got bitten by the hormone bug in sixth grade." He sighed dramatically and let his eyes take on a dreamy look. "Dana Teague in her soccer shorts made me forget how to breathe."

Ryan chuckled. "And once we're bitten, there's no going back is there?"

"Not a chance," Wolf admitted woefully. Then he pinned a considering look on the policeman. "Since we're on the subject, how long have you and the missus been married?"

"Eight years this July."

"Congratulations," Wolf told him sincerely, although he was jealous.

Eight years with a woman he loves. What must that be like? He'd dearly love to find out.

"Oh, it wasn't easy." Ryan shook his head. "Veronica was this ball-busting single mom who didn't want, and I quote, 'a man coming into her life and mucking things up.' But I wore her down and eventually got her to go out with me." He bobbed his eyebrows. "By the third date, she was falling in love. She didn't *tell* me that at the time, of course. She made me think I needed to work my ass off to impress her. But after? Yeah. She admitted I won her over pretty early."

Wolf's tone was full of incredulity. "I'd surely like to know your secret for *that*."

Ryan scratched his chin. "To hear Veronica tell it, it was my sense of humor that did the trick. And specifically the line I used on her at the end of that third date when we were considering…um…consummating our mutual attraction."

"What was the line?"

The police officer bit the inside of his cheek, and recited, "I'm not a weatherman, but you can look forward to about eight inches tonight if you can convince your babysitter to stay later."

Wolf burst out laughing. "You ol' sweet-talker, you."

Ryan smiled ruefully. "Best sentence I ever uttered. 'Cause it got me Veronica and Dustin. I officially adopted him five years ago once his bio dad signed over his rights."

"Sounds like a standup guy." Wolf frowned.

Every time one of his sisters had given birth, and every time his niece's or nephew's sperm donor had quit the scene, he'd always shaken his head, unable to fathom what kind of man could abandon his own child.

"You have no idea." Ryan spit over the porch railing as if he had a foul taste in his mouth. "The bastard did a number on them. It's taken years of therapy and steady loving to soften the scars he left behind."

Wolf eyed the lawman speculatively. "You have to respect a man who can heal a heart he didn't break."

A faint smile lifted the officer's lips. "Speaking of hearts, this thing you got going with Miss Szarek…is it serious?"

"Serious as a heart attack for me," Wolf admitted. "But I don't have your way with words, apparently. Even though I've confessed how I feel, she seems bound and determined not to let herself feel the same way."

"Mmm." Ryan nodded. "She had a bad experience, did she?"

"More like a string of 'em. But not in the way you think. She watched her momma fall in love with one man after the next. Trouble was, instead of any of them bein' a knight in shinin' armor, they all turned out to be losers in aluminum foil. Chrissy's convinced fallin' in love is a sham, and she should choose a life partner based on her head and not her heart."

The policeman eyed him. "And what does her head say about you?"

"That I'm not the settlin' down sort."

"Are you?"

"For her?" Wolf chuffed out a breath. "I'd live in a hole for the rest of my life. Under a rock. In a damn tree. I wouldn't care as long as she's there with me."

"That's a good answer." Ryan nodded. "So how are you going to convince her?"

Wolf grinned. "Maybe I'll try your line."

"Sure. But there's one problem." The policeman lifted a finger. "You'll need to change it a bit."

Wolf drew his eyebrows together. "How so?"

"I mean, she already knows you don't have eight inches. So you'll have to say three or else she'll just laugh at you."

Wolf's shoulders quaked with humor. Officer Ryan would fit in well with the men of Deep Six Salvage. Which meant Wolf responded to the policeman the way he would've responded to one of his partners. "Roses are red. Violets are blue. I've got five fingers. This one's for you."

He flipped Ryan the bird.

The policeman feigned insult. "Such an offensive gesture from a guy who's supposed to be part of the few and the proud."

"Those are the Marines. I was Navy. You know, where the real heroes work."

"Look, man." Ryan placed a hand on his shoulder, his expression pitying. "I hate to be the one to break it to you, but the people who have to be around you on a daily basis are the real heroes."

Fighting a laugh, Wolf came back with, "Wow. I was today years old when I discovered I didn't like you."

"Oh, yeah?" Officer Ryan blinked innocently. "Well, remember that time I asked for your opinion about me? Me neither."

Wolf was having too much fun to let the policeman win. "That's the best comeback you got? Dude, if brains were dynamite, you wouldn't have enough to blow your hat off."

"Don't you worry about me or my brains or my hat," Ryan's mouth was twitching. "Worry about your eyebrows."

Wolf couldn't stand it anymore. It was such a ridiculous

cut, he burst out laughing. Soon after, the policeman joined him. They were still chuckling when the officer's phone jangled to life.

"It's Dixon," Ryan said, thumbing on his cell. Wolf listened to the policeman's side of the conversation. "Officer Ryan here." Pause. "Oh, yeah? Well that's progress." Pause. "Okay. Sure. I'll tell them."

After Ryan clicked off, Wolf lifted an inquiring eyebrow.

"The Coast Guard finally shared with Dixon the logs of the ships entering the marina," the policeman explained. "He's checking to see if any of the owners or operators match the description of the two guys Chrissy saw in the warehouse. Nothing yet. But he's hopeful."

Wolf nodded and slapped his hands on the arms of the rocking chair. "Well, as much as I'd like to sit here tradin' insults with you, I better go inside. Chrissy will want an update as soon as she wakes up."

He was to the front door when the police officer stopped him with, "Take it from a guy who's been in love with an independent woman for nearly a decade. The trick to winning Miss Szarek over and keeping her happy is to be someone she *wants*. And don't get all butt-hurt because you're not someone she *needs*. See, the thing is, she doesn't *need* anyone. She can do it all herself. And it takes a strong, confident man to not only be okay with that, but to appreciate it for the rare gift that it is."

Wolf dipped his chin. "That's good advice. Thank you."

Ryan waved away his gratitude. "Now, go have a nice day. Somewhere else."

Wolf chuckled and flipped the officer the bird again before closing the door behind him. He was pondering Ryan's words when he heard movement at the back of the house. His hand automatically dove into the robe's pocket, his palm fitting instinctively around the Glock's grip.

But he relaxed and leaned against the doorjamb once he made his way to the small galley-style kitchen and saw it was only Chrissy. She'd changed back into that soft, sea foam-green sleep set. It highlighted her golden skin and long legs. Still, he far preferred her naked.

"You got dressed." He was unable to keep the disappointment from his voice.

Startled, she spun around and he saw she had her phone in hand. When she realized it was only him, she frowned. Then her frown turned upside down once she got an eyeful of what he was wearing. "Well, I had to. Someone stole my robe." She crossed her arms to mirror his stance. "It, uh, looks good on you."

"Like I always say, you're a terrible liar." Hitching his chin toward her phone, he asked, "Any news?"

"No." She shook her head. "Well, yes. Tommy texted to say he got my dive clients out and back before the storm blew in. So that's one less thing to worry about. But nothing from Mr. or Mrs. Turner."

"Winston's tough," he told her. "If anyone can pull through this, it's him."

"Yeah." She nodded, but her face crumpled and her bottom lip trembled.

"Come here." He grabbed her wrist and tugged her toward him. "You look like you need a hug."

She didn't put up any resistance. Which he took as a good sign. Instead, she curled her uninjured arm around his waist and pressed her face into the base of his throat. The instant he felt her warm breath on his skin, he began to harden.

Now's not the time, he scolded his little head, although the damn thing rarely listened to him.

Or maybe it is, he thought a second later, because Chrissy looked up at him and there was devilment in her eyes. "What I need is a distraction," she said. "Otherwise I can't stop worrying about Winston."

"You got somethin' in mind?" He arched an eyebrow, even as he rubbed his hand down her bare arm and tangled his fingers with hers. Her skin was like fire. But, damn, he liked being burned by her.

"Oh, yes." She nodded. "I want to touch every inch of you like you touched every inch of me. And then, once I'm finished doing that, I want to straddle your hips and lick my way from the base of your throat to the tip of your cock." She canted her head coquettishly. "That sound good to you?"

He couldn't speak. He couldn't think. All the blood had rushed from his head.

She took his silence as a yes and said, "Good," before she dragged him out of the kitchen and down the hall.

The minute he walked into her bedroom, his nostrils flared like a stallion scenting a mare. The air inside smelled of sex, but also of the promise of wonderfully erotic things to come.

Holding his gaze, she slowly untied the robe's belt. She groaned—they both did—when she reached between the silken halves and took him in her hand.

Going up on tiptoe, she claimed his lips in a kiss so deep and carnal he lost all sense of time. They could've been kissing for seconds or hours—he wasn't sure—when she finally pulled her lips free and whispered against his mouth, "I want you, Wolf. Right, now."

With a hand in the center of his chest, she pushed him back onto the bed. Then, proving he wasn't the only one capable of putting on a show, she slowly stripped out of her clothes. Even the sling didn't hamper her sexy, graceful movements. And then, *thank you baby Jesus*, she was naked and crawling onto the mattress to straddle his hips.

For the next hour, she made good on her plan.

CHAPTER 30

12:01 AM...

The moon was a Cheshire cat smile hanging low in the diamond-studded sky. The sea breeze was a warm, soothing breath of air over bare skin. And the sound of the waves washing to shore was a quiet, rhythmic lullaby.

All told, Mia should be asleep.

She was *usually* asleep by this time of night. Weary after a day in the sun. Lulled by the slowness of life on the island. And feeling, perhaps for the first time ever, as if she were truly protected from the evils of the world.

In fact, she'd gotten better sleep in the month since she'd moved to Wayfarer Island than she had in...well...she supposed in the preceding twenty years. With no cell service keeping her tethered to family, no television keeping her abreast of the world news, and not even a radio to pump in the newest pop hits, she could finally disconnect. Be free.

Breathe.

But tonight she lay on the porch daybed—the one she inherited after Alex, it's previous occupant, moved upstairs into Mason's room—and no matter how hard she tried, no matter how much she cajoled, she couldn't convince the Sandman to visit her.

Blame it on Romeo.

Dinner had been an odd affair, with him conspicuously absent and Doc shooting her searching looks. At one point, Doc had leaned over to whisper, "In case you're wondering, it's hashtag Team Mia for me."

She'd blinked at him, completely dumbfounded. But she hadn't had time to question him before LT said something that drew his attention away.

After dinner, she'd made a quick escape, pleading exhaustion after the trip to Key West. But in the hours since she climbed into bed, she'd done nothing but toss and turn. Even Meat, who usually liked to sleep with her because the screened-in back porch was the coolest spot in the house, had gotten fed up with her constant agitation and taken himself off to find more peaceful accommodations.

"You're nothing I need, and I'm nothing you should want."

Those words kept echoing through her head, and each repetition rankled more than the one before.

The gall! The conceit! The...the...sheer arrogance *of him assuming I wanted him for his body instead of his friendship! I mean, I'd like to have* both, *but I'm not stupid! Come on!*

A rustle came from the forest growing at the back of the house. She bolted upright in bed, the light quilt held to her chest. Squinting her eyes, she tried to see what was headed her way, but even the bright, silvery moonlight wasn't enough to cut through the eerie black shadows created by the tree canopy.

There are no predators on this island, she reminded herself. Even so, her heart beat against her ribs until they began to ache.

Snap! The sound of a twig breaking in two.

Crackle! Rattle! Someone or *something* had stumbled into a pile of dead palm fronds that'd fallen to the ground.

Thump! Whoever or whatever had tumbled into the sand.

Mia caught her bottom lip between her teeth and stared hard into the darkness, willing her pupils to expand and take in more light. Slowly, a form began to immerge at the edge of the tree line.

She released a shuddering breath. She would recognize those muscled shoulders anywhere. Could pick out that self-assured swagger from a hundred yards off.

Except...the swagger looked...unsteady.

No. No unsteady. *Drunk.*

A thousand childhood memories tried to claw their way to the surface. But she squared her jaw and beat them back.

Still, a headache began to throb behind her right eye, and she felt nauseous. It happened every time she was confronted with someone who was inebriated. For her, post-traumatic stress didn't only manifest itself in mental anguish, it brought on a whole slew of physical symptoms.

She sat frozen while Romeo lurched his way across the narrow strip of sand that stood between the back of the house and the trees. She didn't say a word as he stumbled up the steps, fumbled with the screen door, and then shuffled onto the porch. He glanced around, his head looking unsteady on the end of his neck.

Maybe he'll go inside without stopping to talk, she thought hopefully.

A second later, her hopes were dashed when he headed her way and plopped down on the edge of the daybed. His weight depressed the mattress and had her sliding toward him until her thigh brushed his hip and made her belly flop. She scrambled away, pressing her back tight against the wrought iron railing that made up the back and the sides of the bed.

"Hello, Romeo." She was careful to keep her voice neutral, neither wanting him to hear how his nearness affected her nor how his drunkeness hit her where she was most vulnerable. "Is there something I can do for you at…" She squinted down at her watch. "Three minutes past midnight?"

His breath smelled of whiskey when he sighed heavily. "Okay, I'm opening up my closhet…" He frowned and tried again. "My *closet* so you can see all my skeletons."

"Huh?" She eyed him askance.

He rubbed a hand down his face, and then ran it back up and into his hair. When he dropped his hand, not only was his goatee all wild and ruffled-looking, so was his hair.

She blinked at the incongruent sight. Island living meant none of them were dressed for the catwalk. But even so, Romeo was usually so…tidy, she supposed was the word. Good haircut, clothes that fit his body to a tee, neatly trimmed facial hair.

It was strange to see him unkempt.

"Growing up in L.A. meant I was predish…predish…" He frowned.

"Predisposed?" she supplied helpfully.

He nodded his thanks. "Yes. I was predisposed to a certain lifestyle. No, wait." He shook his head. "That's not right. I wasn't predish…predisposed to it. It was forced on me. Like, I didn't have an option. It was either get on board or wind up in a pine box."

He stopped to look at her, and the confusion on her face must've been obvious even to a man who was three sheets to the wind.

Okay, maybe not three. She'd come to discern the different levels of drunkenness from an early age. She'd guess he was...one sheet to the wind. Maybe one and a half.

"Sorry." He scratched his head, which made his hair stand up higher. "I'm not explaining this very well, eh?" When she shook her head, he went on. "So here's the deal. I, um, I joined a gang when I was seventeen. And my initiation prosh...prosh..." He growled in annoyance and slapped his cheek before shaking his head as if to jangle some sobriety into it. "Pro*cess*," he finally managed and then grinned in triumph, making his dimples wink. "Involved me gunning down another kid."

Mia knew her eyes got huge when he blinked at her in confusion. Then it was almost like she saw the light bulb go on over his head. He hurriedly added, "Oh, I didn't kill him. I told all the other homeboys I tried, but the truth is, I aimed for that dude's leg."

She hadn't realized she'd been holding her breath until it wheezed out of her. The headache was still stabbing her eye, but she'd stopped being nauseous. *Progress.*

"Anyway," he went on, sounding slightly more sober, "I knew my clique would organize a jump on me since the kid lived, but I didn't care. I figured I'd survive getting the shit kicked out of me, and then they'd make me a homeboy without me having to off anyone."

He glanced into the darkness of the trees. The moonlight accentuated the firmness of his jaw, the thickness of his eyelashes. "For about six months after that, I sold a lot of pot. I *smoked* a lot of pot too," he admitted with a rueful grin that was lopsided. Then his expression turned serious again. "I flunked out of school and my girlfriend got pregnant."

He grimaced at her surprised expression. "Yeah. I was shaping up to be a real winner." He rubbed his eyes. Eyes which, she was happy to say, were looking clearer and clearer with each passing minute.

"So Gina told me— Uh, that was my girlfriend. Gina," he clarified. "Anyhow, so Gina told me she wanted an abortion. And, of course, she expected me to pay for it. I wanted her to keep the baby, but it was her choice and what the hell did I know about being a father, right? My old man was killed when I was six, and the only other father figure I had to look up to was my older brother, who was a top-ranking member of the gang, so…" He shrugged.

Mia opened her mouth, and then closed it again. What was she supposed to say? She couldn't think. Her head was spinning.

"Unfortunately," he continued. "I didn't have the dough for the abortion, so I put on a ski mask like some *Fargo* shit and tried to rob the corner store. Which is how I got caught by the cops. Which is how I ended up in front of Judge Biltmore who gave me the choice between being tried as an adult or going to military school. And the rest, as they say, is hish…tory."

That time he didn't fix his mistake. He simply let it stand, although he did work his jaw like his tongue was numb.

She finally found her voice. "Why are you telling me all this, Romeo?"

He stared hard at her. She felt his eyes boring into hers as if he was trying to see inside her head. Then, he shrugged and looked away, which meant she had the opportunity to release a covert breath of relief.

To be the object of Romeo's stark attention was a heady and disquieting experience.

"I guess because I respect you and admire you, and I

hate that I hurt your feelings earlier." He grimaced. "I guess because you said you wanted to be my friend, but I thought you should know the kind of man you wanted a friendship with."

For a long time she was quiet, weighing her words carefully in her mind. Then, finally, "You know, I've heard it said we should never judge people by their pasts, especially if they don't live there anymore. You say you were seventeen when all this happened?"

He nodded, looking like he was waiting for her to condemn him despite her words.

"And how old are you now?" she asked.

"Thirty-four."

"So, for a few months during your seventeenth year of life you did some bad stuff. And that's supposed to count for more than what you've done for the last seventeen *years*?"

He cocked his head, considering the possibility.

She didn't know if it was the whiskey keeping his synapses from firing, or if he really was being that hard on himself.

"Let me answer that for you since you seem to be having trouble. No." She shook her head. "No, it doesn't count for more. You were young, dumb, a product of your environment, and making choices that didn't even feel like choices at the time. You're not that kid anymore, Romeo. And the man you are...the man you've become is someone I would like to have as a friend. Just as soon as you pull your head out of your ass and stop thinking I'm only after your hot bod."

That he ever thought otherwise broke her heart and had all her previous ire draining out of her like she was a human sieve. Her headache went with it.

Tentatively, she smoothed the tuft of hair at his temple.

Then she gently tamed his goatee, loving the coarse feel of his facial hair against the sensitive pads of her fingers. He sat perfectly still, watching her with those melting, dark eyes.

A trill of attraction vibrated low in her stomach, but she ignored it. "And FYI," she added, "shitfaced isn't a good look on you. It's not a good look on anyone, actually. But I swear, you look like a before picture."

That seemed to bring him up short. "*Fuck*," he hissed. "I shouldn't have…your mom…she was a… I should've—" He realized he was stumbling over himself and finished with, "I'm sorry."

"It's okay," she assured him. "I mean, my lizard brain still goes into fight, flight, or freeze mode whenever I'm around someone who's had too much. But my rational brain knows not *everyone* who gets drunk does it on the daily, and simply because someone overindulges around me, that doesn't mean something bad is bound to happen."

"Is that why you didn't ask Doc to join you for a drink? Because alcohol is such a sore subject?"

"More like I realized I wanted to use it as a drug to make myself feel better after our talk," she admitted with a grimace. "And given my family history, that's a slippery slope. *Too* slippery. I don't want to come anywhere near it."

Silence descended on the porch then. The only sounds were the call of insects and the distance *shush* of the waves lapping at the beach.

She'd revealed too much. A sickly panic began to set in, so she quipped, "Anyway, all that to say I forgive you for stumbling up here with bacon for brains."

She could tell he didn't want to, but he let her change the subject. "Bacon for brains, huh?" He shot her an amused glance. "You're one surprise after another."

"Yes. I contain multitudes."

"And so you know, I hardly ever drink this much. I needed some liquid courage to…to tell you—"

"Forget about it." She waved away his explanation. "All's well that ends well." Then a thought occurred. "Hey, whatever happened to the baby?"

He frowned. "What baby?"

"The one your girlfriend was carrying when you were arrested."

"Oh." He sighed. "Turns out Gina wasn't pregnant. She only wanted me to give her the money so she could buy a new phone."

Mia blinked. "You're not serious."

"Unfortunately, I am." Then he looked at her imploringly. "So, can we forget about earlier in the plane when I was a total dickwad and agree to be friends?"

Friends with Romeo…

It would be difficult given how attracted to him she was. But more than attraction, she *liked* him. And more than *liking* him, she felt *safe* around him.

She rarely felt safe around anyone.

"Friends." She nodded, extending her hand so they could shake on it.

The moment his warm, dry palm engulfed hers, goose bumps broke out across the back of her neck.

"So…" he said slowly. "Is there anything you've ever done that you're not proud of? Something you'd be willing to share with me so I don't feel like such an idiot for stumbling up here and whipping open my raincoat? Great friendships should begin on equal footing, don't you think?"

Oh, there was *definitely* a skeleton in her closet. A huge one. But it would stay there.

"Well…" She stuck her tongue in her cheek to distract him from what she knew was all the blood leaching from her face. "There was this one time when this drunk guy

JULIE ANN WALKER

woke me up to tell me about his high school gang affiliation and pot habit, and I was really cranky because I needed my beauty sleep, so I ended up punching him in the throat to get him to leave."

His lips twitched. "Copy that. Message received. Good night, Mia."

"Good night, Romeo." She watched him walk to the back door, and then urged him, "Be careful on those stairs. They're rickety even when your footing is sure."

He opened his mouth as if he wanted to say something, but then closed it and simply nodded.

After he disappeared inside, she flopped back against the mattress, willing her heart rate to settle. *This could be good*, she thought. *This* will *be good.*

When a frisson of apprehension ran through her, she studiously ignored it.

CHAPTER 31

12:12 AM...

I'm happy.

It was a strange thing to realize at midnight while taking a leak, but that's exactly what Wolf did.

Suffusing his entire being was a sense of joy the likes of which he'd never felt before. The kind of profound wonder that came from having spent the day making love to the woman he loved, then napping, whispering about childhood memories, eating ice cream in bed, and making love again.

Washing his hands, he studied his reflection in the mirror. His features were both shadowed and highlighted by the dim glow of the night-light Chrissy kept plugged into the outlet by the sink.

Amazin', he thought. *I don't look any different, and yet I'm changed.*

He remembered a quote by Carl Jung. *"The meeting of two personalities is like the contact of two chemical substances: if there is any reaction, both are transformed."*

There was definitely a reaction, he thought, smiling like a dope. *Chrissy and me...we're like cesium and water. Explosive. And now totally altered so that—*

Thump! A noise from the porch.

It sounded like Officer Parsons—the policeman who'd taken over from Rick Ryan for the nightshift, the first guy who'd stood duty outside Chrissy's hospital room—had knocked over one of the rocking chairs.

Standing stock-still, Wolf closed his eyes and listened. It was an old hunting technique his uncle had taught him. When you take away one sense, the remaining senses heighten.

He heard the *buk-buk-ba-gawk* of a chicken in the yard next door. The *beep, beep* of a scooter horn a few blocks over. And far in the distance, the music from Duval Street. Otherwise, nada.

Relaxing, he reached for the hand towel and thought, *I should probably go see if Parsons needs anything.*

He remembered well the times he'd had to keep tabs on a tango through the dead of the night or had been assigned a graveyard shift security detail for some highfaluting politician in a foreign country. What he would've given had someone offered to spot him something cold to drink or volunteered to give him a bathroom break to break up the monotony and help keep him awake.

After pushing aside the little curtain concealing the stackable washer and dryer tucked into a corner cabinet in Chrissy's bathroom, he found his jeans and pulled them on. They'd been sitting in the machine for hours, so they were wrinkled as hell. But he didn't reckon Officer Parsons would care.

And *he* certainly didn't care. Every one of those creases was a reminder that he and Chrissy had been having way too much fun to worry about folding clothes.

Closing his eyes, he relived a couple of the more *memorable* moments. Like when she rode him slow and lazy, her lower lip caught between her teeth, her eyes half-lidded and watching his face as she took pleasure from him and gave pleasure to him in equal measure. Or when she'd dripped ice cream onto his nipples, watching them furl, and then licking them clean.

He'd done up the last button on his fly when the bathroom door slammed shut. His erotic musings dried up quicker than a cow pond during a drought, and his heart lurched in his chest. Then he remembered how the door to the bedroom he used at his grandmother's place sometimes did the same thing when a cross draft created a vacuum inside the house.

Except...

The windows in Chrissy's little cottage were closed and locked.

A hot feeling slid through his veins. He knew it well. Adrenaline. The body's magic battle elixir.

"Chrissy?" He reached for the doorknob. It turned easily, but the door wouldn't budge.

An ear-piercing scream shattered the quiet of the house, and it was like Death himself dragged the point of his scythe up Wolf's spine.

"Chrissy!" he yelled. If adrenaline was hot in his veins, then fear was ice-cold. He shoved a shoulder against the door and pushed until his bare feet slipped on the tile floor.

Thump! Crash! Another scream!

"Chrissy! Goddamnit! Answer me!" He used his shoulder as a battering ram, slamming into the door over and over, but making zero progress budging it.

Damnit! It wasn't like it was possible to lock the door from the outside. What the hell was—

He didn't finish the thought. He knew why he couldn't get out of the bathroom.

Some sonofabitch was on the other side of the door holding it closed by bracing his feet against the opposite wall. Wolf had performed the same maneuver one time in Aleppo to ensure two unarmed women stayed safe in a bedroom while the rest of his Team took out the three tangos who'd been making pipe bombs at the kitchen table.

"You motherfucker! Let me go or I'll scratch your eyes out!" He heard Chrissy's snarl. She said something else, but he couldn't make it out. Her voice was muffled like something had been shoved into her mouth.

"Yeah, yeah! Look at her, man! Hot damn! *Hot damn!*" The words came from the other side of the door, and the sound of the man's voice was enough to have Wolf baring his teeth and growling.

"She's a feisty bitch," came an answer from somewhere down the hall. "We're going to have some fun with her."

Molten fury burned away Wolf's fear until he became rage itself. There was a murderous frenzy in his eyes when he took a deep breath and backed up the entire length of the bathroom. The muscles in his body coiled until his whole being shook with pent-up power.

"Can't wait," the cretin holding the door said. "I'll meet you in the car after I off this fucker."

"You're welcome to try," Wolf snarled and exploded across the bathroom, throwing all his weight against the door in a violent show of force that didn't give a thought for self-preservation.

It felt like he hit a brick wall, but his maneuver worked. He overpowered the asshat on the other side. The door burst open so quickly, Wolf bounced off the hallway wall and was catapulted back onto his ass.

There were no lights on in the house. But the streetlight

shone in through the living room windows and provided enough glow for Wolf to see Chrissy's kicking bare feet as they disappeared around the corner. It looked like she'd been tossed over someone's shoulder.

Outrage propelled him to his feet. But he hadn't managed a step before the door-holding asshole screamed from behind him, "Die, you piece of shit!"

Displaced hair ruffled the hairs on Wolf's arms and his lizard brain knew what was happening before his rational mind even registered it. He turned in time to see a man lift a knife high over his head. His assailant was dressed in black and wearing a ski mask, so he blended into the shadows. But the knife caught the light and glinted evilly.

Instinct, and years of training, kicked in.

Wolf caught his attacker's wrist on the down stroke. Then everything slowed down. His heart went metronome steady, his breaths turned measured, and his moves became automatic.

The secret to combating someone with a knife was to control the knife hand and use your free hand to pummel the shit out of your attacker's body and face. Which was exactly what Wolf did.

Landing punch after punch, blow after blow—which wasn't as simple as the movies made it seem, since he had to be careful not to break the delicate bones in his hand against the asshole's jaw—the two men fought for control of the blade.

Ski Mask proved he'd make a good punching bag. Even though he grunted and groaned with each brutal hit, he didn't drop the knife. And the longer the battle wore on, the more Wolf's muscles burned with fatigue.

Time to up the ante.

Along everyone's shinbone ran a long nerve. Hitting that nerve had always caused Wolf's opponent to seize up in pain.

When he kicked Ski Mask, the man let loose with a shrill yelp and his fingers relaxed enough for Wolf to wrestle the blade from his grip. Neatly spinning the knife around, Wolf stabbed his attacker in the gut.

The man's scream was bloodcurdling, but Wolf barely heard it. And he *certainly* felt no remorse. Long ago, he'd learned in the game of kill or be killed, there was no room for hesitation or compassion.

Wrenching the blade free, he shoved his assailant aside and ran into Chrissy's room to grab the Glock he'd left atop the dresser.

Used to be I'd take my sidearm with me wherever I went, even into the shower, he thought. *Civilian life has made me soft.*

Ski Mask lay on his side in the hallway, his hands pressed against the blood seeping from his wound. Wolf barely spared the man a glance as he jumped over him and raced toward the living room.

Bursting through the front door, he leapt onto the porch's top step in time to see a man shove Chrissy into the back of a sedan. She was stark naked and, even though Wolf had only gotten a brief glimpse, he'd seen her hands were secured behind her back with a bright orange zip-tie. Her feet were free, however, and she used them to her advantage, landing a hard kick against her assailant's thigh and making the man grunt.

Attagirl, Wolf thought with no small measure of pride. Christina Szarek was no wilting lily. She was fully capable of giving as good as she got.

Despite her efforts, however, the man was able to slam the door behind her, and that was the last Wolf could see of her. The windows on the car were tinted near black, making the interior indiscernible.

"Stop right there!" he yelled, lifting his Glock and

sighting down the barrel. "You make one move toward that heater you got shoved in your waistband and I swear on all that's holy, I'll make sure the next thing you are is an organ donor!"

The man looked toward the porch and slowly raised his hands.

Like his partner in crime, he was dressed in black, his face obscured by a ski mask. But unlike the scarecrow Wolf had fought in the hall, this dude looked like a busted can of biscuits. He was hugely muscled. But those muscles were covered by a thick layer of fat.

"Maybe I should've been more clear!" Wolf yelled when Biscuits took a step toward the driver's side door. "You so much as move another inch and I'll end you!"

"You think you can hit me on your first try?" Biscuits bellowed, taking another step backward.

Wolf realized two things then. One, the bastard wasn't going to stop. And two, Wolf was bored of their conversation.

"Let's find out!" he called at the same time he curled his finger around the trigger.

He was mid-squeeze when he felt a yank on his leg. *Boom!* The tip of the Glock glowed bright orange as the bullet left the barrel, but he knew his shot ranged wide.

Glancing down, he saw Officer Parsons lying at his feet. The policeman had one hand wrapped around the hem of Wolf's jeans, the other was pressed to his throat. Bright red blood oozed between his fingers, and his eyes were wide with fear—apparently Ski Mask had more luck employing his blade against the police officer than he'd had trying to use it on Wolf.

Wolf registered all of this in a fraction of a second. But a fraction of a second was all it took for Biscuits to grab his gun. Even though Wolf had been out of black ops for a while, he would always recognize the sound of a round being chambered.

"Shit!" He leveled his weapon once more, but his distraction meant Biscuits had gotten the drop on him.

He heard the *crack* of the discharge right before he felt the bullet slam into his shoulder. It was a glancing shot, but it was more than enough to spin him around.

By the time he caught his balance and took aim, Biscuits was already in the driver's seat and leaving rubber on the pavement as he fishtailed down the road.

"Shit!" Wolf yelled again, squinting against the darkness to try to catch the plate. He only got the first three characters before the sedan screeched around the corner and he lost sight of it.

His instinct was to search Officer Parson's pockets for the guy's truck keys and give chase. But SEALs never left a man behind. And Parsons was a brother in arms, even if their uniforms were different.

Grabbing one of the beach towels Chrissy had left drying over the porch railing, he wadded it up and pressed it over Parsons's neck.

"Use this to keep pressure on the wound," he instructed. Then he snatched the radio clipped to the officer's bulletproof vest and gave his own shoulder a cursory glance.

He was bleeding pretty good, but the damage appeared even more shallow than he'd originally suspected.

Good. I'm goin' to need both arms to strangle that fat fuck once I find him, he thought.

Depressing the button on the policeman's radio, he spoke quickly. "Officer down! Officer down! Send paramedics to…" He rattled off Chrissy's address and explained to the dispatcher what had transpired, ending by giving her a brief descriptions of the two perpetrators. "I may have killed the skinny one. I stabbed him in the gut. But I hope like hell I missed anything vital, 'cause I need him to answer some questions."

The dispatcher tried to ask him something, but he didn't have time for an interrogation. He dropped the radio and nearly ripped the front door off its hinges in his mad rush to get back inside.

"You have no idea how happy I am you're still alive," he snarled when he saw Ski Mask lurching across the living room, headed for the kitchen.

The guy broke into a run, but Wolf caught him at the back door by grabbing the ends of stringy hair hanging out from underneath the mask. Spinning the asshole around, he used his forearm to pin the guy's neck against the door. In his free hand was the blade he'd taken from the bastard.

Knives were better for close quarters questioning. They were easier to handle, and in the right hands they were far more effective than a gun at getting a guy to talk.

Wolf had the right hands.

"Where's he takin' her?" he demanded, his gaze utterly murderous.

"Fuck you!" Ski Mask spat and Wolf slipped the knife into the man's stomach a good half inch.

Ski Mask howled but didn't dare move for fear the blade would sink farther.

"I just got shot in the arm," Wolf bit off, trying not to gag on the hot, cigarette breath that seeped from the bastard's rotten mouth. "And it's makin' me cranky. Now, talk before my dark side gets the better of me and I decide to apply five pounds of pressure and slice into your spleen. You'll bleed out in thirty seconds."

"Fuck you!" Ski Mask screamed again and Wolf pressed on the knife, feeling it slice through tissue like a hot pin sinking into butter. "Okay, okay!" the man squealed. "The marina! He's takin' her to the marina!"

"Which boat?" Wolf demanded, twisting the knife a little. "Which slip?"

Ski Mask's eyes rolled back in his head and Wolf stopped his tormenting. He couldn't have the man passing out on him. Not before he got his questions answered.

"Answer me!" he bellowed into the man's face.

Ski Mask focused and gave Wolf what he wanted. And even though it would've felt good to free the world from the likes of the murderous, smelly bastard, the better angels of Wolf's nature won out.

Pocketing the knife, he grabbed the Glock from his back waistband. "Move!" he told Ski Mask, gesturing with the pistol. "Walk out onto the front porch."

Twenty seconds later he had Ski Mask secured to the porch railing with Parson's handcuffs and was digging through the now unconscious cop's pockets for the keys to the truck parked by the curb.

After he found what he was looking for, he checked Parsons's pulse and found it faint and fluttering. "Hang on, man," he said. "Help is on the way."

Snatching the police radio from where he'd dropped it, he made one last call to dispatch. "This is Wolf Roanhorse on Fleming Street. Officer Parsons is unconscious and barely breathin'. I'm headed to Bight Marina. That's where Suspect One told me Suspect Two is taking Chrissy. The boat is the *Catch of the Day*, and it's in slip ten. I need backup. Call Detective Dixon, and tell him to get me some damned back up!"

"Sir," the dispatcher's voice crackled over the radio. "Do not engage in—"

Wolf didn't hear what else she said. He was already running down the porch steps and jumping into Parsons's truck.

CHAPTER 32

12:23 AM...

W*olf, no!*

Chrissy had managed to push herself up in the backseat of the car just in time to see Wolf spin like a top. She couldn't be sure, the light was too dim and the windows in the car were tinted, but she thought she saw blood spray.

"You motherfucker!" she screamed when the Goliath jumped into the driver's seat. But thanks to the bandanna he'd tied around her mouth, the words sounded more like *oo-muh-ah-uck-ah!*

While keeping her pinned to the mattress, the masked giant had ripped off the sling and wrenched her arms behind her back to secure her wrists. But the pain pounding in her shoulder was the least of her worries. Foremost on her mind was Wolf.

Was he alive?

Where had he been hit?

Secondly, she needed to do everything she could to get away from her assailant. Those true crime podcasts always said a woman should fight like hell before allowing herself to be taken to a secondary location.

She glanced at the car door, thinking she could open it even with her hands tied behind her back and then fling herself out of the speeding vehicle. Sure, the road rash would be epic, but better some flayed skin than…well, whatever Goliath had in mind for her. But the door handle was completely covered by duct tape. So were the window controls.

Her abductor had thought ahead.

Which means this isn't his first rodeo.

The thought made bile climb into the back of her throat.

Thinking fast, she decided her feet were her only weapons and she employed them by kicking the back of Goliath's seat in such rapid succession her leg muscles burned.

"Cut it out, you crazy cunt!" Goliath took a corner on what felt like two wheels and Chrissy was thrown across the backseat. Her injured shoulder slammed into the door and white-hot agony made stars blink in front of her eyes.

Before she could catch her breath, he fishtailed around another corner and she was afflicted by carsickness on top of the pain, fear, and worry she was already dealing with.

I hope I puke on him, she thought. But then the car skidded to a stop and Goliath jumped out, slamming the door behind him.

Oh, no! She took a quick look through the front windshield. *We're at the marina!*

Her chances of escape went to zero if he got her onto a boat and—

When the backdoor opened, she instinctively kicked out at the big, meaty hands that reached for her.

"*Oomph!*" Goliath grunted when she landed another blow

to his thigh even though she'd been aiming for his balls.

He manacled one of her ankles in an iron grasp and wrenched her toward him until she was flat on her back in the backseat. A second later, she was gasping for air from the pain in her shoulder and from the suffocating weight of him as he stretched his substantial bulk atop her.

"I like that you're a fighter." His breath was rancid as it puffed hot against her face. "It's so much more fun for me." As if to prove his point, he humped his hips against her pelvis and she could feel he was hard.

Every inch of her flesh tried to crawl off her body. Every follicle on her head tried to eject its hair.

"Fuck you!" she snarled around the bandanna.

The lethal rage she knew was in her eyes was the polar opposite of the prurient gleam shining in his. Even with his features covered by the ski mask, she was convinced she was looking into the face of pure evil.

"That's the plan." He smirked. "Not right this second. But soon."

Before she could blink, he hoisted himself off her and dragged her out of the car. She'd barely caught her breath before he tossed her over his shoulder like she weighed little more than a scuba tank.

She wanted to scratch and punch, but with her hands tied behind her back they were useless. She wanted to bite and shout obscenities, but the bandanna made that impossible too. All she could do was kick and wiggle, which she did. As hard as she could.

All to no avail.

Goliath was brutishly strong, and her efforts did little to slow him as he trotted down the stairs to the dock and hurriedly made his way along the weathered wooden boards. All the blood rushed to her head, and she was acutely aware of her bare ass pointing in the air.

The smells of marine fuel and open water were over-powered by his cheap cologne. His heavy breaths muted the sound of the clanking riggings on the surrounding ships and the music coming from the nearby bars. Every step he took had her terror mounting.

"Mmmm! Mmmm!" she screamed around the bandanna, hoping to get the attention of someone who might still be on their boat.

The fishermen had long since packed up their gear and gone home. Same for the day sailors. But those folks who lived on their yachts and sailboats? Where the hell were they?

"Shut up!" Goliath smacked her butt so hard she could feel the stinging imprint his hand left behind.

My guardian angel is drunk! she thought hysterically. *How many times in a twenty-four hour period have I nearly died and—*

The sound of screeching tires had her lifting her chin. It was hard to focus. Goliath's rough gate made her head bounce. But she saw Parsons's truck slide to a stop near the top of the stairs leading down to the docks.

The driver's side door burst open, but it wasn't the policeman who hopped out. It was Wolf.

Wolf!

Her heart leapt with joy.

She could've *sworn* she saw him get shot, but maybe not. And it occurred to her that her guardian angel wasn't drunk, because *Wolf* was her guardian angel. The one who was always there when she needed him. The one who always managed to save her in the nick of time.

Naked from the waist up, he looked every inch the Navy SEAL as he took the stairs two at a time, his bare feet *thudding* against the wooden boards of the dock when he jumped the last few feet. His bare chest caught the glow of the moon, and his eyes were black fire as he sprinted toward her, his weapon raised and at the ready.

"Stop!" his deep, resonant voice echoed across the marina. "Or I swear to Christ I'll put one in your leg!"

Goliath spun around and Chrissy felt like she was on a carnival ride. The kind that goes in circles and inevitably makes some kid puke up his corndog and candy apple. Then Goliath dropped her to her feet.

She turned to run in Wolf's direction but hadn't managed one step before her attacker snaked a sweaty arm around her throat. A heartbeat later, she felt a circle of warm metal kiss her temple.

"Stay where you are!" Her assailant's voice was as loud as a foghorn in her ear as he used her as a human shield. "Or she gets one in the brainpan!"

Any other time she would've been mortified to be standing in the raw out in the open. But with her life dangling by a thread, she didn't much care that her boobs and butt were being kissed by the warm sea breeze. In fact, if she was about to shuffle off her mortal coil, she could think of plenty of sensations that were far, *far* worse.

"The jig is up!" Wolf barked. "Your greasy partner is caught and cuffed and probably throwin' you under the bus to the cops as we speak! So let the woman go! Don't add her death to your rap sheet!"

Wolf stepped into a circle of light from a lamppost and Chrissy saw two things at once. The first was that his lips looked colorless. The second was that blood dripped down his flank to stain his jeans.

He *had* been shot! But how bad?

She couldn't tell and—

A harsh laugh from behind her interrupted her thoughts. "Just 'cause you got Ricky, that don't mean you'll get me! Plenty of islands around here I can disappear on."

Goliath was right. Key West wasn't known as the "end of the road" simply because it was, quite literally, the end of Highway 1. It also got its nickname because plenty of folks had come down and then simply…vanished.

With how close the place was to Cuba and the other islands of the Caribbean, if someone was of a mind to, they could sail off into the sunset, never to be seen again.

Fear clawed its way into her throat and combined with the arm around her neck to make breathing impossible. Her lungs burned from lack of air. Her heart hammered with the effort of trying to oxygenate her blood. But then Wolf's steely gaze crossed the distance separating them and locked with hers.

Did he dip his chin?

Yes! Yes he did! And she was instantly reminded of a story he'd told her.

It was about how an "unfriendly"—that was the word he'd used to describe an enemy combatant—had managed to catch Doc unawares and had tried to use the big Montanan as a human shield. Doc had simply gone boneless and dropped to his knees, which had allowed Wolf the opportunity to take out their enemy.

Chrissy's heart beat more rapidly than the fluttering fins of a seahorse, but she winked to let Wolf know she'd received his message and understood what was required of her.

Every muscle in her body was tight with adrenaline, but she willed her legs to loosen. Just like that, her entire body weight was pressing against Goliath's forearm and it was too much for the behemoth.

Thank you chicken wings and ranch dressing! she thought crazily as she slipped from Goliath's grasp.

Boom! The sound of Wolf's pistol cut through the night like a thunderbolt before her knees even hit the rough boards.

"Oomph!" Goliath grunted and Chrissy turned in time to see the gun slip from his hand. He bent to grab it, but she was quicker. She kicked it over the edge of the dock and smiled around the bandanna when she heard it splash into the water.

"Bitch!" Goliath hissed, pressing a hand to the gunshot wound in his flank before turning to run.

Boom!

Another shot rang out over the marina and Chrissy watched Goliath jerk, stumble, and sprawl face-first onto the dock. She didn't have time to check to see if he was dead. Wolf was there, gathering her up in his arms.

She desperately wanted to luxuriate in the warmth of this skin, but she couldn't feel a thing. Her whole body was numb with shock.

With gentle movements, Wolf pulled the bandanna out of her mouth and slid it down over her chin. Her mouth was dry from the material, but she managed to rasp, "Are you okay?"

"I'm fine," he assured her, sliding a knife from his back pocket and neatly slicing through the zip-tie cruelly pinning her wrists together. She realized her hands had gone to sleep when her fingers were instantly plagued by pins and needles.

"Where are you hit?" she demanded, and he lifted his arm to show her the bloody gouge cutting through the thick part of his shoulder and marring the black tribal tattoo inked over his skin.

Relief had her own shoulders sagging. She instantly regretted the move when her injury screamed its displeasure at having been abused.

Wolf was a mind reader. He fingered the edge of the bandage over her wound. "Are *you* okay?"

She nodded and opened her mouth to tell him she was when the sound of Goliath's groaning interrupted her.

"You shot me in the back!" the man howled, flopping onto his side. His girth caused the entire dock to tremble.

"That's what you get for runnin'." Wolf's voice was completely devoid of sympathy. "You're lucky I didn't make it a kill shot. But I figured death was too good for you. A lifetime behind bars feels far more fittin'."

As if on cue, the sound of sirens wailed in the distance.

"Now where were we?" Wolf returned his attention to Chrissy, his gaze raking over her face.

"Talking about our wounds." She wouldn't have thought it was possible at a time like this, but she was smiling. "And on that note"—she gently traced the scar along his temple—"I would consider it a huge favor to me if you would *stop* getting shot."

His lips twitched. "I will if you will."

"Deal," she whispered.

Then he kissed her and the terrible, awful, *horrible* night was okay again.

CHAPTER 33

12:59 AM...

Sorry, man. I'm sure that hurts." The paramedic winced in sympathy as he smeared ointment over Wolf's wound and then slapped on a large self-adhesive bandage. "I can't believe you didn't want any numbing gel."

Wolf touched the scar running along his temple and assured the guy, "I've had way worse. Believe me."

The paramedic shook his head. "You're one tough sonofabitch." He glanced over at Chrissy, who sat on the ambulance's tailgate beside Wolf. She was wearing the T-shirt and shorts a Good Samaritan boat owner had provided when he'd come out on the deck of his vessel to investigate the commotion. "You both are," the medic added.

Wolf wouldn't disagree with that statement when it came to Chrissy. But he wasn't sure how tough *he* was. When he'd seen Busted Can of Biscuits running down the dock with Chrissy over one shoulder, he'd been scared out of his mind. He'd known if Biscuits got her onto a boat—

Even now, even with the danger passed, he couldn't finish the thought.

He'd been the one bleeding, but he'd insisted the paramedic check Chrissy's stitches first. The young guy had declared them sound and fashioned her a makeshift sling using gauze. She adjusted it now as she thanked the paramedic for his help.

Wolf added his own words of gratitude, but his gaze was snagged by Dixon. The detective had been questioning Biscuits as paramedics worked to stop the big man's bleeding. But now that Biscuits was strapped onto a gurney, Dixon turned toward Wolf and Chrissy.

The flashing red and blue lights of the surrounding cop cars highlighted the detective's rumpled tie and messy hair as he made his way over to them. And a few of the rubberneckers who'd stumbled out of the bars—and who were being kept back by a small army of policemen—shouted questions at him, wanting to know what had happened.

Dixon ignored them. "How are they doing?" he asked the young medic.

The guy repacked equipment into a nylon bag. "They'll live," he said with a small smile and then moved away to help his colleagues with Biscuits.

"What about Parsons?" Wolf asked Dixon. "Will *he* live?"

The detective nodded. "Dispatch says he's in surgery now. And doctors are saying he's expected to pull through. Same for Ricky Williams."

"Who?" Chrissy's brow pinched.

"The second perpetrator. The skinny one Mr. Roanhorse here"—Dixon hitched a thumb Wolf's way—"filleted like a fish." He lifted a brow at Wolf. "Ricky told the attending officers you threatened to cut out his spleen."

"No." Wolf shook his head. "I told him I'd slice *into* his spleen and he'd bleed out in thirty seconds."

"Oh, my bad. That's far less brutal." One corner of Dixon's mouth kicked up. "Remind me never to get on your bad side."

Wolf opened his mouth to respond, but closed it again. Biscuits was being wheeled by on his way to the second waiting ambulance. The paramedics had taken off his ski mask, and Wolf got his first look at the guy's face.

If he were giving it a Yelp rating, he'd go for one star; do not recommend.

It wasn't so much the flabby jowls or the cruel twist to Biscuits's small mouth, although those were definitely off-putting. The real kicker was the guy's eyes. They were black and shiny.

And completely empty.

It was like looking into the gaze of a reptile.

Chrissy gasped, and both Wolf and Dixon turned to her. "What?" the detective demanded, his eyes shrewd on her face. "Do you recognize him?"

Chrissy nodded. "But I don't remember from where."

"His name is Mateo Hernandez," Dixon supplied. "Ring any bells?"

"No." She shook her head. "But I *know* I've seen him somewhere before."

"He tell you what this whole thing has been about?" Wolf asked Dixon. "Why he and his buddy were so intent on offin' Chrissy and Winston?"

"Nope." Dixon made a face of disgust. "He's shut up tighter than a clam at low tide. But he *did* ask to speak to someone from the DEA, so I'm thinking my initial hunch was right. This is about a drug shipment. He's probably hoping to cut himself a deal with the Feds by squealing on his contact within the cartel."

As Hernandez was being loaded onto the ambulance, he lifted his head and looked Chrissy dead in the eye. His tone was full of contempt when he told her, "I'm only the grenade, babe. Someone else pulled my pin."

"What the hell is *that* supposed to mean?" Renewed anger surged through Wolf's veins.

He was more than ready to march over to that ambulance and stick the blade he still had in his pocket into Hernandez's gut. He bet *he* could get the douche-canoe to talk.

"Oh!" Chrissy lifted a hand to her mouth as the paramedics shut Hernandez into the ambulance.

"What?" This time it was Wolf who asked the question.

"I just remembered where I saw him. I was at the dive shop late one night and I saw him come out the back of Jill's place."

"*Miss* Jill?" he asked incredulously. "The busybody, know-it-all who seems to run the whole island?"

"Jill Jones." Chrissy nodded. "But *she* can't be involved in this. She's kind and thoughtful, and is always looking out for folks. Surely it's a coincidence that—"

"Wait a second," Dixon interrupted her. "Hold that thought." He turned and marched toward the unmarked police car parked nearby. After scrabbling around in the passenger seat, he came up with a sheaf of papers.

"Printouts of all the vessels the Coast Guard stopped yesterday," he called as he hurried back to them. "Along with their owners and operators."

Dixon looked pointedly at Wolf. "The name of the boat Ricky Williams gave you was the *Catch of the Day*, right?"

Wolf nodded and Dixon thumbed through the papers, his eyes scanning a page before moving on. His was on the sixth sheet of paper when he stopped. "*Catch of the Day*," he read. "Says here it's a fishing charter operated by Mateo

Hernandez and Ricky Williams and owned by some outfit named Key West Charters."

Wolf felt the tension drain out of Chrissy.

"Which is an LLC owned by Jill Jones," Dixon added.

"Holy shit," Wolf breathed, trying to square away what he knew of the feisty gal who'd visited Chrissy twice with what he knew now. But if he was shocked to discover Miss Jill was the one behind all this, then Chrissy had to be downright stunned.

Sure as shit.

When he peered over at her, he found her speechless, her mouth opening and closing like a guppy. Her eyes blinking rapidly.

Winding his arm around her waist, he scooted closer to her, remembering how he'd felt when he heard one of his favorite commanding officers had been brought up on charges of—and eventually found guilty of—raping two female recruits.

It hadn't only felt like a betrayal. It'd made Wolf question his judgment. Made him wonder if he could ever trust anyone.

"Do you know where she lives?" Dixon asked Chrissy, and she blinked at him like she'd lost the ability to comprehend English.

Then she seemed to snap out of it. Her voice was hoarse when she answered, "Um, yeah. On Olivia Street, between Center and Simonton. I don't remember the number. But it's the green conch house with the white shutters."

"Officer Blackstone!" Dixon called over his shoulder to one of the policemen working the scene. "I need you to grab two uniformed officers and follow me to—" He rattled off the information Chrissy had given him. Then he said to Wolf and Chrissy, "The way word travels on this island, she may already know we've got Williams and Hernandez in custody. If I were her, I'd be looking to run."

Chrissy stood. "I'm coming with you."

"No." Dixon shook his head, obviously not under-standing when Chrissy's jaw was set at that particular angle, there was no dissuading her.

To save the detective the brunt of her sharp tongue, Wolf stepped in. "After everything she's been through the last twenty-four hours, I think she's earned the right to look her would-be executioner in the eye. Don't you?"

A muscle in Dixon's cheek twitched. Wolf could tell the man didn't want to drag along a couple of civilians while apprehending a perp. But he eventually relented with a breathy sigh.

"Fine. But I want you two to stay in the car the entire time." He pointed a finger at Chrissy. "Do I have your word?"

She crossed her heart and held up two fingers.

Seven minutes later, they were outside Jill's house, staying put in the back of Dixon's car—as promised—while the detective and the uniformed police officers stormed through Jill's front door.

Chrissy rolled down the window to get an unencumbered view, and Wolf was glad for the ventilation. Dixon's car was filled with greasy fast-food bags and half-empty coffee cups. It smelled about how one would expect.

"Hey." He tucked a strand of hair behind Chrissy's ear, loving the delicateness of that tiny shell. "I'm so sorry about all this."

She nodded and swallowed noisily. But her face was turned partly away from him so that her lashes concealed her eyes and her stony expression hid her thoughts.

Then she went stiff as a board when Jill was frog-marched down the front steps of her porch by the officers. Wolf could feel the tension, the anger and betrayal, vibrating through her. But she didn't say a word as Jill was led to one of the waiting police vehicles.

He wanted so badly to pull her into his arms. To shelter her from the pain of this moment. But knowing Chrissy, she didn't need comfort. What she needed was closure. She needed to *see* Jill on her way to jail.

"Don't look at me like that, Chrissy!" Jill called before the officers could shove her into the cruiser's backseat. "You remember what it was like after Hurricane Wilma! The whole island was underwater! I lost everything! The house. The boats. Funding for my kids' college educations! When someone came along offering me a way out, I took it! You would've done the same thing. We're the same, you and I! Both businesswomen trying to make it in a man's world!"

Chrissy's voice was quiet but crystal clear. "We're *not* the same, Jill. One of us is a lying, murderous bitch. And the other one is me."

Attagirl, Wolf thought with no small amount of satisfaction as Jill was crammed into the police vehicle. There was a sense of finality when the door slammed shut with a pleasant-sounding *thunk*.

Detective Dixon came to stand beside the open back window of his car. Leaning an arm along the roof, his tone sounded jaded. "She was packing a bag full of clothes and cash when we burst in on her. Headed to a non-extradition country, no doubt."

Chrissy shook her head. "She's known me since I was a little girl, and yet she didn't blink at the thought of having her goons kill me. What does that say about me?"

"We are defined by our actions toward others," Wolf quoted. "Not by others' actions toward us."

Chrissy offered him a wan smile. "That fortune cookie thing of yours *does* come in handy sometimes. Well"—she heaved a big sigh and glanced up at Dixon—"I guess that's that then. The warehouse mystery is solved. We can all go back to our former lives now."

"Not so fast." Dixon made a face. "There's just one more thing."

"Ha!" Wolf crowed. "You said it. You actually said it."

Chrissy turned to frown at him. Dixon ducked down into the window to do the same. "Huh?" the detective asked.

"Columbo's catchphrase," Wolf explained.

Neither Chrissy nor Dixon seemed to have a clue what he was talking about. "Never mind." He shook his head. "What's the one more thing?"

"I need you both to come down to the station so I can take your statements."

Wolf groaned. After every mission, he'd had to write and file a report. It seemed the world revolved around paperwork.

"Can we do it tomorrow mornin'?" he asked hopefully. "I don't know about Chrissy, but I feel like someone set me on fire and tried to put me out with a hammer."

Dixon took a second to consider, then nodded. "Fine. Now, give me a minute. I need to talk to Officer Blackstone and then I'll drop you both off at Miss Szarek's place."

Once the detective walked away, Chrissy turned to Wolf. The shirt she'd been given was printed with the letters WTF. Beneath them were the words: *Welcome To Florida*.

Appropriate, Wolf thought with a bemused smile.

"I need a hug," she told him. Her eyes looked bruised and world-weary. "Or maybe an orgasm to help me forget this night," she added when he pulled her into his arms. "Is there such a thing as a hugasm?"

"Oh, darlin'." He kissed the top of her head, loving the feel of her snuggled tight against his heart. Loving the smell of coconut oil and sea air in her hair. "Sex isn't the answer."

She pushed back to frown at him.

"Sex is the *question*," he clarified with a wiggled of his eyebrows. "And *yes* is the answer. Always."

She laughed and then looked at him in wonder. "I don't know how you do that."

"Do what?"

"Make me laugh even when laughter should be impossible."

"You know what Charlie Chaplin said, 'A day without laughter is a day wasted.'"

She narrowed her eyes. "Just because I said that fortune cookie thing comes in handy, doesn't mean you should push it."

He opened his mouth to say something self-deprecating and witty, but she silenced him with a kiss.

CHAPTER 34

5:56 AM...

Chrissy sat beside her mother's bed.

Well, it wasn't her mother's *bed. It was the hospital bed the hospice workers had set up in the middle of Chrissy's living room.*

She'd dragged one of the rocking chairs in from the front porch since it was easy to get it close to the bed. Plus, the gentle rocking motion was soothing as she stared lovingly at the woman who had given her life.

Josephine was a shadow of her former self. Her once thick hair was long gone. Her Sophia Vergara figure had wasted away to nothing but skin and bones. Her tan, vibrant skin was sallow and sunken in around her features.

The smell of ointments and unguents and antiseptic hung heavy in the air, with the more pervasive odor of sickness swimming beneath it all.

Cancer was such an indignity. Worse, it was a damned

thief. It had robbed Josephine of her health. Of her lucidity. And very soon it would rob her of her life.

Chrissy swallowed the tears that burned in the back of her throat when her mother stirred. And even though the face that turned to her no longer looked anything like her mother's pretty visage, it was still the face of the one and only person who had loved Chrissy her entire life. And it was agony to watch that face scrunch up in pain. To see those hairless eyebrows pucker. To witness the tears that slipped down those hollow cheeks.

"Mom?" She gently touched her mother's bony hand. "Do you want me to call the nurse for more pain meds?"

The home healthcare workers had originally been coming by only during the day. But for the last couple of days, they were working in shifts so someone was always there with Josephine.

They hadn't said so, but their heightened vigilance told Chrissy they all knew it could happen at any moment.

Nurse Danielle was the one on duty now. But the sweet, soft-spoken woman had stepped onto the porch to call home and check on her kids. And yet, Chrissy knew all it would take would be a look from her and Danielle would rush in to help Josephine settle.

"The worst feeling in the world is being abandoned by someone you love." Her mother's voice was raspy. But her blue eyes—eyes she'd given to her only daughter—were surprisingly clear.

The lump in Chrissy's throat was a permanent fixture these days. But she managed to speak around it. "You're not abandoning me, Mom. You're being taken from me. There's a difference."

"No." Josephine shook her head and it caused the stocking cap to shift on her bald scalp. Chrissy automatically adjusted it. Josephine got so cold now. It took three blankets

and winter-weight pajamas to keep her warm. "I don't mean you and me, baby girl. I mean Jake."

Chrissy frowned. Josephine rarely spoke about her first husband, Chrissy's father. Jake Szarek had been a singer/songwriter who never could seem to gain much of a following, but who still played the circuit of festivals and bars as if he had.

He'd left Chrissy and Josephine when Chrissy was two years old, and had sent birthday cards up until Chrissy's sixth birthday. But she had no recollection of the man. If not for the handful of photos showing him holding her as a baby, she would doubt his existence.

"My biggest mistake was believing him when he said he'd stay," Josephine sobbed softly. "When he said his love for me was larger than his dream of making it big."

"Shhh, Mom," Chrissy soothed. "That was a long time ago. And it was his loss, not yours."

"It doesn't seem so long ago," Josephine protested. "And if it weren't for you, baby girl, I swear I would wish I could go back to the day I met him and walk the other way."

"Oh, Momma. I'm so—"

"And I owe you an apology," Josephine kept on as if Chrissy weren't talking. Her moments of mental clarity were few and far between now, and it seemed she was determined to say whatever it was she wanted to say before she slipped into oblivion again. "I'm sorry I kept dragging men into your life and letting you fall in love with them only for them to leave. I think…" Her mother's brow puckered. "I think I kept trying to find it again. That wild, passionate love I felt for Jake. And I just… I never could." She blew out a soft sigh. "Maybe that's why they all ended up leaving. Maybe they could tell I didn't love them the way I loved your father."

"No," Chrissy whispered. "They left because they were

liars and cheaters. None of them were good enough for you."

Her mother grabbed her hand with more strength than Chrissy would've thought she had in her ravaged body. "Don't follow in my footsteps, baby girl." Josephine's eyes burned with desperation. "Find yourself a good man. One who makes you laugh. Who makes you shine. Who appreciates what a beautiful, kind, intelligent woman you are. Find a man who knows once he has you, that doesn't mean he gets to stop doing all the things it took to get you. One who's steady enough to put in the work even when the sparkle fades and the dust settles in."

"Okay, Mom." Chrissy smoothed the blankets over her mother's gaunt shoulders. The last thing she wanted to talk about, or think *about, was her love life. She had far more important matters to deal with. Namely, making her mother's last few days as peaceful as possible.*

"You're such a smart woman, Chrissy. So much smarter than I ever was." Chrissy opened her mouth to protest, but Josephine pushed ahead. "Use that, kiddo. Use that big brain to make better decisions than I did."

"I will." She tried to smile reassuringly, but it felt tremulous. "I promise I will."

All the fervor went out of her mother then. Josephine closed her eyes and slipped into sleep.

It was the last conversation the two of them had. Twenty-four hours later, Chrissy's mother was dead...

Horrified, she jolted awake. The dream that was really a memory was painfully close to the surface, bringing with it the rawness of her grief, the soul-crushing depth of her loss.

In the early days following her mother's death, she'd had the dream often. Her unconscious brain reliving those last awful hours of Josephine's life. But as the years had gone on, Chrissy's dreams had softened, tending toward the *happy* times the two of them had shared. The *healthy* times.

Maybe that's why she was so shaken now. Because it'd been so long. Because she'd forgotten the razor-sharp sting of fresh remorse.

With her heartbeat slowly settling, and taking the deep breaths she'd learned helped push her through the worst of her mourning, she glanced at the subtle light streaming in through the slats of the shutters.

Not even six A.M., she thought. *Too early to be awake.*

And yet a sparrow chirped outside. Somewhere nearby, a rooster crowed.

What are birds so happy about at the butt-crack of dawn? she wondered irritably. The dream had left her feeling raw and exposed. And thoughts of the night before made her angry.

Jill Jones... The name sounded blasphemous inside her head.

To think, she'd come to view Jill as a friend. Someone she could call on in times of trouble. Someone who'd be there to offer a strong shoulder and a sympathetic smile.

It was unfathomable. Unthinkable. *Unforgivable.*

Bitter tears clawed at the backs of her eyes as she turned onto her side, her gaze landing on Wolf. He lay on his back with his face turned toward her.

She took the opportunity to study him. To appreciate the darkness of his eyelashes fanned across the crests of his high cheekbones. To trace the subtle curve of his nose with her yes. To drink in the sight of his wide mouth while it was relaxed in sleep.

He was a beautiful man. Fierce-looking and masculine without being brutish.

The tension and aggravation and *hurt* slipped out of her when she thought back on all the times over the last day when he'd touched her or kissed her. When he'd whispered dirty words in her ear and brought her to completion with his hands and his mouth and his body.

His lovemaking had made more of a woman of her than she'd ever been. Soft and malleable. Exactly the thing she'd always sworn she'd never become.

Oh, yes. Her hardened resolve. Her willful resistance. Her distrustful heart. Less than a day as his lover and he'd obliterated the first two and laid total claim to the third.

The instant she had the thought, her breath froze in her lungs. A school of bait fish bumped around in her belly.

He *had* claimed her heart, hadn't he?

Despite her best efforts, she'd gone and fallen in love with him. But not only that. She wildly and passionately loved the very *bones* of him.

No! Oh, no!

This was exactly what her mother had warned her about.

Not that Wolf was a philanderer or a liar or a cheat like so many of her mother's husbands and boyfriends had been. And he wasn't even the pickup artist and player she'd pegged him as after that night in Schooner Wharf Bar. But he *was* a man like Chrissy's father. A man with adventure and wanderlust in his blood.

He's a Navy SEAL turned treasure hunter, for Pete's sake! How can he ever truly be satisfied with the life I'm offering?

Flopping onto her back, Chrissy stared up at the ceiling and felt a desolate dread creep into her heart. If she kept on being Wolf's friend with benefits, she'd fall more and more in love with him. Until eventually, she'd want to tell him.

But if she told him, he'd stay. Always. Even when he no longer wanted to. That was Wolf. Loyal and true.

I have to nip this thing in the bud now, before it gets any more out of control. Before I fall any further. While I can still save our friendship and—

"What's that ceilin' ever done to you?" His low, sleep-heavy voice slipped inside her ears.

She wanted so much to jump into his arms and beg him never to leave her. To always love her. But what would that accomplish? He'd agree, of course. Like her father had in the early days when everyone thought love was enough.

But it isn't, she thought frantically. *Sometimes it just* isn't.

"You want some breakfast?" She hoped her panic wasn't revealed in her voice. "I think I have some eggs and cheese. I could make omelets."

"I'm hungry for somethin'." He reached for her. "But it ain't food."

She faked a laugh and jumped out of bed, quickly slipping into her robe. She was crazy, but she would swear it still retained the warmth from Wolf's skin. It *definitely* held his sexy desert flowers and dry cedar scent.

His all-seeing eyes raked over her face. "What's wrong?" He sat up in bed.

"Nothing." She tried to sound airy and light. Instead, her voice cracked.

"You're a terrible liar."

"Nothing's wrong per se," she clarified. "We have a full day ahead of us. We have to go to the police station to give our statements. I want to stop by the hospital to see Winston and his folks. Besides…" She tentatively met his gaze. "Haven't we scratched our itch enough? Don't you think it's time to go back to being friends?"

Understanding dawned in those sparkling black eyes. His tone was one of ill-disguised frustration when he said lowly, slowly, "What are you doin', Christina?"

She felt her cheeks burn scarlet. "What?" She blinked innocently. "Nothing, I—"

"Don't bullshit me," he cut in pointedly. "Is this you breakin' up with me?"

The hard look in his eyes made her bristle. "We were never together, Wolf. So we can't break up."

He lifted his gaze heavenward, and sweet heavens! Why did he have to have such an appealing Adam's apple? Then he dropped his chin and indicated the rumbled sheets. "If we weren't together, what do you call this?"

"I call it, uh—" Her mouth was cotton ball dry. She swallowed and tried again. "I call it the *benefits* side of friends with benefits."

"Great." He dipped his chin. "So after one night you're ready to go back to nixin' that part of our relationship?"

His savage gaze knocked out what little wind she still had in her sails. But the sound of her phone alerting her to a text gave her a chance to escape. "I better go check that."

She didn't wait for him to respond before turning tail and running out of the room like the coward she was. Once in the kitchen, she thumbed on her phone and lifted a hand to her mouth when she saw the message from Maryanne Turner. She swung around, only to discover Wolf had followed her.

He was absolutely glorious in his nudity. So male and virile and completely confident as he stood there with his arms crossed and a deep scowl on his beautiful face.

"They're taking Winston into surgery." Her voice was hoarse from the battle to keep her emotions in check. "I need to go to the hospital. I want to be there for Curtis and Maryanne."

His nostrils flared. His eyes tried to burn holes through her. But he didn't say a word.

"I'll run and get dressed," she said inanely, scurrying by him.

While she slipped into a pair of shorts, she told herself she was doing the right thing for both of them. She was saving herself a broken heart. And she was freeing him to live the life he was truly meant to live. Even if he didn't know it. Because *she* knew *him*.

If you love something, set it free. Right?

Yes. *This is right!* she mentally railed.

So why did it feel so wrong?

CHAPTER 35

Two weeks later…

*A*nd *I thought underwater excavation was tedious*, Wolf thought wearily as he waved his metal detector over the sand like he'd been doing for the last two weeks.

They'd searched the entire island and had come up with the usual culprits, some lost coins, some metal fishing gear, and two antique glass bottles with metal caps. But they'd found nothing of real import until they'd stumbled upon the campground.

Or…at least that's what Alex was calling it.

In the center of the island, in a small circular area, they'd unearthed a trove of items that dated back to the seventeenth century. A bone-handled dagger, a copper sundial, a small brass bell used to summon servants, and the *pièce de résistance*…two metal buttons stamped with the captain of the *Santa Cristina's* family crest.

Bartolome Vargas had survived the wreck of the grand galleon and had been on the island. By the looks of the other items they'd found—an old trash pit filled with fish bones and a circle of stones that appeared to have been a fire ring at one point—so had some of his crew.

At first, the Deep Six guys and gals had celebrated the news as if they'd found the treasure itself. But after days of meticulously searching the campsite and the area around it, they'd failed to locate the mother lode.

As had happened when they'd come to the end of excavating the *Santa Cristina's* water-logged remains, disappointment and dejection were setting in. And even though it was barely past noon, LT sighed and said, "I think we've officially done all we can at this site. Let's pack up and head back to the house for lunch."

"On guard!" Bran lifted his metal detector like a sword and challenged Doc.

Bran used humor to deflect during more serious moments, and usually LT didn't seem to mind. But their former commanding officer was having none of it today. "Yo, Brando. Let's keep the dumbfuckery to a minimum."

Bran lowered his metal detector. "Don't get your knickers in a knot, LT. It only makes you walk funny."

LT frowned. "You know, sometimes you remind me of a pizza burn on the roof of the world's mouth."

"You have a right to your opinion." Bran sniffed. "And I have a right to ignore it."

"Let's *all* stop screwin' around and get back to the house," Wolf grumbled. "I'm hungry and I'm tired of wavin' this damned thing around." He indicated his metal detector.

Bran frowned at him. "You *have* been a little ray of absolute darkness ever since you got back from Key West. I mean, I get things were bad there. But is there something you're not telling us?"

"You think I've been a little ray of absolute darkness?"

Wolf shot back. "Well let me be the first to tell you, nothin' would brighten up my day like your absence from it."

Bran sucked in a dramatic breath and faked insult by pressing a hand to his chest.

"Gentlemen, please," LT interrupted. "We're all tired and hungry and disappointed. Let's go eat and start talkin' next steps."

"I think the next step is ground penetrating sonar." This from Alex. Even though they'd been working in the shade of forest all morning, she still wore zinc oxide over her freckled nose. A big glob of sand was stuck to one side of the white goo.

Mason wiped it off before putting a hugely muscled arm around Alex's waist and pulling her close to whisper something in her ear that made her beam up at him.

Two things to understand about Mason McCarthy. One, before Alex he hadn't exactly been the touchy-feely sort. And two, he rarely spoke. Except to Alex.

Wolf could feel their affection spilling into the clearing. And he was *happy* for Mason. He truly was. The guy had suffered a terrible divorce and had sworn off women completely until Alex convinced him otherwise. But if Wolf was being honest, he was also jealous.

Mason wasn't able to shake Alex once she set her sights on him, and I can't even get Chrissy to spend more than one night with me. For shit's sake!

To make matters worse, he hadn't seen Chrissy in two weeks. Since they were no longer diving down on the wreck, there was no reason for her to bring her customers out to Wayfarer Island.

Chrissy had called the satellite phone twice. The first time to pass on the good news that the doctors had awakened Winston from his medically induced coma. And the second time to let them know Winston had been taken off the ventilator and was looking to make a full recovery. But neither of those times had Wolf been the one to answer the phone.

He didn't know if that was a good thing or a bad thing.

I mean, what is there to say?

He couldn't rightly tell her the truth, which was that he missed her. Missed her every second of every day. Because that's not what *friends* did. And that last day on Key West, which had been filled with tense moments while Winston was in surgery and then again while they were each taken into separate rooms at the police station to give their statements, that's exactly what Chrissy had told him she wanted.

"Let's go back to the way it was before, Wolf," she'd said. *"We had a good thing going, didn't we? I don't want to ruin that. I want us to stay friends forever."*

He hadn't argued. Not because he hadn't *wanted* to, but because he had too much dignity to beg her to love him like he loved her.

He'd hoped once he returned to Wayfarer Island, the acute, agonizing ache in his chest would lessen.

But whoever coined the phrase "out of sight, out of mind" was nuttier than a squirrel turd.

Out of sight was one thing. Out of mind was something else entirely. Something else that was entirely impossible.

"Why ground penetrating sonar?" LT asked Alex now. As a group, they'd started down the path that connected the campsite to the beach house.

"The metal detectors are only good for about eighteen inches," Alex explained. "I originally figured that would be plenty to locate the mother lode if, indeed, it was buried here. But maybe I was wrong. Now that we're pretty positive Captain Vargas survived the wreck, I'd say it's possible he instructed his remaining crew to bury it eighteen *feet* deep. From everything I've read about the man, he was a tenacious sonofagun."

"She's right." Mia was somewhere in the middle of the pack, so everyone held their breath to hear her. "I know this all feels discouraging. But take it from someone who's done countless excavations and studied numerous historical sites. If the *Santa Cristina's* mother lode had been found, *someone* would've talked. It would be recorded somewhere. It wasn't possible to hide that much wealth, even in the sixteen hundreds. And since it *hasn't* been recorded anywhere, and given all the clues we've found, it's my professional opinion it's still here. Somewhere."

Even though Wolf wasn't in an optimistic mood, Mia's words gave him a glimmer of hope.

They must've done the same for LT because he sighed and said in that slow, Louisiana drawl, "So then we try to scrounge up the money required to buy some damned ground penetratin' sonar."

"I can put out feelers with my contacts at the Agency," Olivia offered. "Quite a few people still owe me favors. Maybe one of them could pull a string and let us borrow some government equipment."

Olivia no longer worked for the CIA, but once a spook, always a spook. There was allegiance and fealty within the ranks there same as there was in the Navy.

"And I can sell back the metal detectors to the shops," Romeo added. "A couple proprietors said they'd buy them back at half price if we returned them in good condition."

"I guess that's the plan then." LT was at the front of the line of people snaking their way through the forest. Which meant when he came to a stop on the trail, the entire train screeched to a halt behind him.

Wolf brought up the caboose and had to lean sideways to see what'd caused the sudden lack of forward motion.

Uncle John, wearing his most eye-bleeding hula shirt, sauntered down the path toward them with Meat and Li'l Bastard in tow.

"John," LT said, "we were headed your way for lunch. What is it today? Tuna casserole or tuna casserole?"

LT's uncle only knew how to make one dish. When it was his turn to cook, they all knew what they were in for.

"You'll be pleasantly surprised," Uncle John said. "I ran out of saltines so I added cornflakes to the top. I think it adds somethin'."

Romeo, who was in front of Wolf in line, turned and made a face of revulsion.

Wolf whispered, "PB&Js it is," and Romeo nodded emphatically.

"But that's not why I came out this way," John said as Meat made his way down the row of people, sniffing feet and giving the occasion shin lick as he passed. Fresh on his stubby tail was Li'l Bastard. No sniffs or licks from the rooster, but he did ambush a palmetto bug that crawled near Wolf's flip-flop. "I took a phone call from Winston Turner of all people," John explained. "He was callin' for you, Wolf."

Wolf was still leaned far to the side, so he had a perfect view of everyone turning to stare at him. "Me?" he asked in confusion. "Did he say what he was callin' for?"

John nodded. "Said he hoped you'd come visit him in the hospital this afternoon. Said around three P.M. would be good if you could make it."

"I'll fly you," Romeo volunteered after a quick glance at his diver's watch. "While you're visiting with Winston, I can go around reselling the metal detectors. And then we can pick up fresh supplies before heading back."

"That's a good idea. Add saltine crackers to the list." LT smirked and then motioned for John to turn around so they could all start moving again.

As the line trudged toward the beach house, Wolf's mind kept coming back to the same question. *What in the world does Winston want with me?*

He hadn't a clue. And reckoned he wouldn't *get* one until he talked to the man.

Thirty minutes later, after having loaded up the gear, he and Romeo were inside the Otter, taxiing out into the lagoon. Alex had packed them PB&Js for the flight, but Wolf's appetite had vanished with thoughts of possibly seeing Chrissy again.

Romeo must've read his mind. His voice sounded through the headset Wolf wore. "You think Chrissy will be at the hospital?"

"Don't know."

"If she is, what'll you say to her?"

"Nothin'." He shook his head. "I've said it all. Can't make her love me by sayin' more of what she already doesn't want to hear."

CHAPTER 36

2:45 PM...

Chrissy watched Rosa check her watch and then push up from the little love seat in Winston's hospital room. The dark-haired woman stretched and yawned. Chrissy was struck again by how pretty she was.

Pretty and googly-eyed for Winston when she walked over to him, took the hand he held out for her, and said, "I'm headed to the coffee shop for a cappuccino and a doughnut." She leaned in to whisper conspiratorially. "Can I sneak something sugary or caffeinated past the nurses for you on my way back?"

Winston shook his head. "No." Then he bounced his eyebrows. "But I do love your devious mind. Remind me to put it to good use once they spring me from this joint."

"I won't need to remind you." Rosa smiled seductively. "I'll *show* you."

"Ugh. Don't make me regret hunting you down on social media, Rosa," Chrissy teased.

That first day following Winston's surgery, when there'd been absolutely *nothing* Chrissy could do for her best friend except sit vigil beside his hospital bed with his parents, she'd had an epiphany.

What if Rosa is still carrying a torch for him too?

It'd been the work of an hour to do some quick Googling and land on Rosa's Instagram profile. She'd private messaged Rosa with the news of what had befallen Winston, having had no expectations regarding what would become of her reaching out.

Maybe some words of concern, she'd thought at the time. *Or perhaps Rosa will send a get-well bouquet that'll warm Winston's heart once he wakes up.*

Which was why she'd been blown away when Rosa showed up at the hospital less than twenty-four hours after she'd sent the message.

And the sweet lady hadn't left his side since.

Chrissy was over-the-moon with happiness for her best friend. Truly, she was. It's just her happiness for *him* was tempered by her *un*happiness for herself.

She missed Wolf like crazy. His absence was a hole in her chest. An ache in her bones. And she'd hoped beyond hope the two times she'd had a good excuse to call out to Wayfarer Island, that *he* would be the one to pick up the satellite phone.

She wasn't sure what she'd wanted to say to him. But she'd desperately missed the sound of his voice.

"You're right." Rosa straightened and tried to sober. But her face melted into a goofy grin when she looked back down at Winston. "We are sickening, aren't we?"

"Totally," Chrissy agreed, faking a disgruntled huff.

"What about you?" Rosa asked. "Can I bring you back anything?"

Chrissy lifted the paper coffee cup in her hand. Her *third* of the day. "Better not. One more and my eyeballs will turn into pinballs inside my head."

"Okay then. I'll be back soon." Rosa bent to kiss Winston and then gathered up her purse and headed for the door.

Chrissy watched Winston watching Rosa's retreating back. Once Rosa disappeared into the hall, she told him, "You're welcome."

She was thrilled to see color back in his face, the sparkle back in his eyes now that the staff had weaned him off the majority of the pain meds. If not for the bandage around his chest and the IV snaking into his arm, she could maybe, possibly forget he'd nearly died from the bullet that'd torn through his lung.

"Yes, yes." He rolled his eyes. "I owe all my future happiness to you. We'll name our firstborn in your honor and lift a glass to your continued good health at least twice a year."

"Only twice?" She blinked in fake affront.

"Fine." He sighed. "Three times."

"That's better." She sniffed. Then she stopped her teasing to ask, "Your first kid, huh? Does that mean you and Rosa have discussed what happens after you're released from the hospital?"

He glanced at the clock on the wall and nodded. "We're going to do the long-distance thing until she can sell her house in Tallahassee."

Chrissy felt her eyebrows climb up her forehead. "Wow? She's giving up her life and career just like that?"

"I offered to move up there." At Chrissy's look of astonishment, he added, "I know. Can you imagine? Me? A mainlander? But I tell you, if she'd asked me to live with her on Mars, I would have. Having lost her once, I never want to lose her again."

Chrissy sighed and batted her lashes. "Ah, *amore*. Such a wonderful sight to see."

Winston didn't join in her joking. "I do love her, Chrissy. More than I even remembered."

"I know, Winston." She smiled at him. "I couldn't be happier for you both. I like her. She's smart and sweet and she doesn't take any of your shit."

"Admit it. It's that last thing you like *best*."

She hitched her shoulder, happy she could do that now without wincing. She'd gotten her stitches out two days prior. As Wolf had promised, the scar was minimal.

Wolf...

The thought of him brought a fresh wave of heartache.

To distract herself, she asked Winston, "So what's the plan after she moves down here? Shotgun wedding?"

"I mean, if *I* have anything to say about it, yes." Winston shot her a knowing grin. "But no, seriously, she's going to open her own accounting firm. She's gone about as high as she can in her current position, and she's been contemplating venturing out on her own for a while. She has a few clients who will follow her wherever she goes. And heaven knows, there are plenty of fisherman, guides, and bar owners who need a good accountant."

"Wow. You guys have it all figured out." She tapped her chin in consideration. "Maybe I missed my calling. Maybe I should've gone into the matchmaking business."

He glanced at the clock again and snorted. "Please. Who would hire you after the mess you've made of your own love life?"

"*Excuse* me?"

"You told a tall, dark, Navy frickin' SEAL to hit the road. A guy who looks at you like you're the best thing in the whole wide world. A guy who confessed he's fallen head over heels in love with you and is game to settle down and have four rowdy curtain climbers. Not to mention, he saved your life countless times. Oh, and by the few hints you've given, he must be pretty good at bedroom sports. Anyway, you gave *him* the ax? Who does that?"

Chrissy blinked, momentarily discombobulated. When it was laid out like that, it made her sound crazy. "Wait. No." She shook her head and frowned. "I told you he only *thinks* he's fallen in love with me and wants to settle down. He's far too—"

"Let me stop you right there." Winston lifted a hand, bringing her up short. "For months you were keeping him at arm's length because, after that fiasco at Schooner Wharf Bar, you said he was a player, not someone interested in anything serious. Then he explains what happened and you realize he *isn't* a player and that he *is* interested in something serious, so now you've gone and convinced yourself that what? That his feelings won't last? That he doesn't know his own mind?"

"I *do* know him. He's like my dad. A guy who—"

"I would've thought after what happened with Jill you'd realize none of us truly *know* anyone."

Hearing the traitor's name made Chrissy's blood pressure spike. But she took a deep breath. "I know you like Wolf, Winston. I like him too. But I watched my mom—"

"Nope." Winston sliced a hand through the air. "Let me stop you again. You know I loved Josephine, right?" Chrissy nodded and he continued, "But she couldn't have picked a winner if he'd been handed to her on a silver platter. That woman had absolutely *terrible* taste in men. The more damaged they were, the more she liked them. And you know I love you too, right?"

Again, Chrissy nodded. But this time it was hesitant. She wasn't sure she liked where he was headed.

"But I'm telling you right now you've been so caught up

in not making your mother's mistakes that you're making a whole bunch of new and different ones all on your own." He glanced at the clock again before adding, "Don't sacrifice your future because of your mother's past, Chrissy. You are not your mother. And Wolf is not your father."

She opened her mouth, but he pressed on. "Take it from someone who let love slip through his fingers and who was knocking at death's doorstep a couple of weeks ago. When all is said and done, we only regret the chances we didn't take, the love we were afraid to feel, and the ones we let slip away."

When he looked at the clock for what felt like the bazillionth time, she demanded, "Are you waiting for something?"

"Some*one*," he clarified. The look in his eyes had apprehension crawling up her spine.

"What did you do, Winston?" Her voice was deadly quiet.

"Same thing you did for me. Called the person you're crazy in love with since you were too chicken shit to do it yourself."

On cue, Wolf's wide shoulders filled the doorway. The instant Chrissy's gaze landed on him, she wanted to shout with joy. Or burst into tears. She couldn't say which. Maybe both.

He was even more handsome than she remembered. Leaner. Meaner. Taller?

No, she told herself. *That's not possible.*

"Thanks for coming, Wolf." Winston bobbed his chin. "Now, how about you and Chrissy go take a walk. I've heard from the nurses it's a beautiful day outside, and the two of you have some things to discuss."

Wolf glanced from Winston to Chrissy but didn't say a word. He simply raised one sleek eyebrow in question.

Chrissy's mind felt like an internet browser on sketchy Wi-Fi. Twenty tabs were open, five were frozen, and she couldn't figure out how to turn off the flippin' popup ads.

"Go on," Winston urged, and legs mutinied. Without her conscious consent, she was on her feet.

"One last thing before you go though." He snagged her wrist and pulled her down so he could whisper in her ear. "You've been fighting this thing with Wolf because he scares the crap out of you. Because for the first time ever, you've met a man who can touch your heart. You're holding yourself back from him because you're afraid something will happen that'll mess up your happily-ever-after. But here's the thing, my sweet friend, there are no guarantees in love. That's what makes it so precious. And what makes it *worth* it."

CHAPTER 37

3:04 PM...

The day was balmy and breezy. The wind smelled like freshly cut grass. And the birds in the nearby palm trees belted out a chorus of tunes that competed with the road noise.

Wolf registered none of it.

Firstly, because his gaze kept sliding down Chrissy's body as she walked beside him on the shady sidewalk. She wore a red sundress with big white hibiscus flowers printed on it, and as far as he could tell, there wasn't a straight line on her. Well, except for her mouth, which was formed into a ruler's edge. And secondly, because his brain kept replaying Winston's words inside his head. *"Called the person you're crazy in love with since you're too chicken shit to do it yourself."*

Was that true? Or had Wolf completely misconstrued Winston's words because that's what his *heart* wanted to hear?

Chrissy's anxious, slightly sick-looking expression gave him no clue.

"How are you feelin'?" he asked, and her ocean eyes darted to his face.

He hitched his chin toward her shoulder. The bandage was long gone and in its place was a thin scar.

"Oh." Her expression cleared. "I'm fine. It's still sore when I lift my arm too high. But other than that, I forget it's there. How about you?" She pointed to the gash on his shoulder, the one hidden under the sleeve of his T-shirt.

His bullet wound wasn't nearly as well-healed as hers. It still sported a thin scab and he knew the tattoo was completely ruined. But the pain was minimal.

He said as much while pointing to the puckered flesh at his temple. "Compared to this thing, what happened to my shoulder is nothin' more than a mosquito bite."

Her eyes grew misty. "I wish people I l—" She stopped herself, but Wolf felt everything inside him grow very, *very* still. "People I care about would stop having to spend weeks in the hospital. I'm tired of bleach and antiseptic and terrible coffee."

She almost said 'love,' he thought.

As quickly as everything inside him had screeched to a halt, that's how quickly it all started moving again. His heart raced. His blood roared. He lungs thought he was running a race.

"And what about Jill and her goons?" His voice was more gravelly than usual when he forced himself to carry on with the small talk, but Chrissy didn't seem to notice.

"According to Dixon, they've all cut deals." When he scowled, she clarified. "Oh, they'll still serve time. I've been assured of that. But their sentences will be *less* because they're naming names and giving up cartel secrets to the DEA."

He sighed. "Sucks to find out that even in situations like this, it's all about the quid pro quo. The last thing justice should be is transactional."

"Oh!" She snapped her fingers. "And come to find out, it was Hernandez who was behind the wheel of Cliff Barnes's Celica in the hospital parking lot. *Also*, Hernandez and Williams both confessed that they snuck into my house through the back door that *Jill* left open to turn on my gas and light the candle. Which, as horrible as that is to contemplate, is also sort of good news since it means I wasn't crazy or hopped up on too many pain meds."

"So it was them all along, huh?" He shook his head, almost as relieved as she was to discover the paranoia he'd suffered hadn't really been paranoia at all. "What a couple of bastards."

"Mmm." She agreed. "So what about you? What's the news on the hunt for the mother lode?"

He motioned to a bench beneath a royal poinciana tree with its deep green foliage and bright red flowers. Chrissy took a seat and then primly pulled her long, flowing skirt aside to make room for him.

He didn't crowd her. But he didn't smash himself into the corner of the bench either. He gave her enough room so that a bare inch of space separated their thighs. He would swear he could feel arcs of electricity shooting between the small divide.

Can she feel it too?

If the deep blush staining her cheeks was anything to go by, the answer was *yes*.

"We found a campsite," he said, and then went on to explain about the artifacts and Alex's suggestion they use ground penetrating sonar to search the island.

Chrissy nodded. "You guys are close to finding it. I can feel it in my bones."

"My bones are less sure," he admitted. "But I hope you're right. We can't keep up the hunt much longer. We're runnin' out of capital."

They fell into silence after that pronouncement. Wolf let it drag on for as long as he could before blurting, "I heard what Winston said."

Her eyes were wide when she turned to look at him. "Which part?"

"The only part that matters, Christina. The part where he said you're crazy in love with me."

There was a time to mince words. This wasn't it.

She raked in a ragged breath and he watched as myriad emotions flashed across her face. Then, some of the tension seemed to drain out of her.

She tucked a strand of hair that'd fallen out of her ponytail behind her ear. The movement made the abalone charms on her bracelet jingle.

For a second, he wondered if she would answer. Then she did. And with every word out of her mouth, his heart soared higher.

"From the moment I met you, I knew you," she said softly. "It was like we were friends and lovers from a different lifetime. You stepped up to me and I felt like saying, 'Oh, hello you. There you are. Finally.'"

He swallowed and nodded because he'd felt the exact same way.

"I've never liked a laugh as much as I like yours," she went on. "I've never been as much myself with anyone as I am when I'm with you. I've never felt more alive than I do when I'm in your arms. And all of that terrifies me down to my bones. Because what happens if I lose it? What happens if I—"

He stopped her by closing the distance between them. By framing her face with his hands and kissing her.

It wasn't a small peck either. He put his back and his whole mouth into it as if no one was watching. Only when things began to go too far did he pull back and swear against her lips, "You'll never lose it. Because you'll never lose me."

Tears stood in her eyes when she shook her head. "But that's just it, isn't it? We can make these vows now, but who knows what the future holds?" He opened his mouth to swear his devotion, but she pressed on. "And that uncertainty, the...unpredictability of falling in love was why I was determined not to do it. But you, Wolf." It was her turn to frame *his* face. "You're worth all the risk. And I swear to you, if there ever comes a day when it's not enough and you feel like have to leave, you can. I never want to be the reason you don't have the life you want. All I want is for you to be happy."

His heart was so full he thought it a wonder it didn't explode right out of his chest. "You crazy woman. Don't you know a life spent with the person you love is the greatest adventure of all?"

Tears flowed freely down her face now. He wiped them away with his thumbs, but more fell to replace them. "Thank you," he told her.

"For what?" she sniffed.

"I told you I wouldn't settle for anything less than everything. That I wanted that out of control, ass over teakettle tumble into romantic bliss and a woman who is as nuts for me as I am for her. And you've given it to me."

She caught her lip between her teeth and nodded. "Then I think we should get married."

The suddenness of her suggestion caught him unawares. "You do?"

"As soon as possible."

"Why?" He blinked, feeling his mouth tremble to

contain a grin. Joy was a tangible force vibrating around him, vibrating through him. "Am I pregnant?"

She chuckled wetly and shook her head. "It's cliché, I know. But I've been waiting so long for this part of my life to start that I don't want to wait another second. I want to be your wife. I want to have your babies. Let's build a family together, Wolf. I miss having a family."

"Chrissy, darlin', you already *have* a family," he assured her. "*My* family. They're goin' to love you. And they're goin' to love the family you and I build together. You're goin' to have so much family you might wish you had less."

"You promise?" Her lips trembled.

"Yes." He grabbed her hands and squeezed his pledge into her fingers. "I promise. And just so you know, if we ever find the treasure—"

"*When* you find the treasure," she insisted.

"Okay, *when* we find the treasure, I've got obligations back home. I want to use some of the money for my nieces and nephews and—"

"You can use *all* the money." She shook her head at him. "I don't give a shit about it. All I want is you."

Just when he thought he couldn't love her more, she said that and he did.

He had to work to paste on a stern expression. "Well, darlin', you got me. But before we walk down that aisle, I need to hear it."

Her eyebrows puckered. "Hear what?"

He cocked his head and pursed his mouth.

"You need to hear me say I love you again?" she asked, and he snorted.

"You can't say it *again*, darlin'. You never said it the first time."

"I didn't?" She looked genuinely perplexed when he shook his head. Then her expression softened and she took a deep breath. "Okay then. Here goes. Wolf?" He nodded. "I have categorically, conclusively, unconditionally fallen head over heels in love with you."

Damnit! Now *he* was the one on the verge of tears. To hide the moistness in his eyes, he pulled her in for another kiss. But it ended up in a desperate hug as each of them clung to the other, their hearts full and beating together in a rhythm he knew would last a lifetime.

"And you're in for it, buster." Her voice was thick with tears. "Because I hold on like hell to what I've got."

He grinned as Bon Jovi's "Livin' on a Prayer" played in his head. He hummed a little of it and then sang, "It doesn't make a difference if we're naked or not. We've got each—"

She pulled back and bit the inside of her cheek.

He groaned. "Oh, hell. What did I get wrong this time?"

"It doesn't make a difference if we *make it* or not," she said and then burst out laughing. "At least your misheard lyric wasn't about food this time!" She hiccupped, wiping away happy tears.

He grinned and touched the corner of one glittering blue eye. "Has anyone ever told you that you absolutely *sparkle* when you laugh?"

Her humor dried up and her expression grew serious. "On her deathbed, my mother told me to find a man who makes me laugh and shine. To steal a phrase from your previous profession: mission accomplished."

EPILOGUE

June 27th, 1624…

Please, *Capitán,"* Alvaro, a young helmsman, pleaded. *"'Tis a perfect night to be at sea. Let us unfurl the sails and make for Havana."*

Even in the dimness of the moonless night, Captain Bartolome Vargas registered the beseeching look on Alvaro's face.

He and his men had won the battle at the campsite. But not before losing ten more of their brethren. Another dozen of the Santa Cristina's *crew were variously injured and being seen to by the ship's surgeon. Those few who had managed to come out of the fight unscathed were gathered around Bartolome on the French ketch and wearing looks that closely mirrored Alvaro's.*

This ship was a chance at salvation. A chance to reach home port and fill their bellies with good food and good drink.

But 'twas a slim chance, indeed.

Too slim.

"You heard the French capitán. *" Bartolome kept a wide stance on the deck of the ketch as the ocean breeze rocked the ship. Oh, how he had missed the feel of a vessel moving beneath his feet. He had been a sea captain for so long that solid ground seemed foreign and wrong.*

"Every one of our enemies is out looking for us," he continued. "'Tis little chance we could make Havana without running afoul of them. We would most assuredly be tortured into giving up the location of the treasure."

His men could not argue the truth of his words, and yet a few of them grumbled their displeasure. He pretended not to hear it. There were times it behooved a leader to let small insurrections slide.

"Gather what food and supplies you may whilst I prepare to light her afire." He lifted the bucket of lamp oil in his hand, keeping his voice steady and authoritative.

No doubt, if they left the ship anchored, a passing vessel would see it and come to investigate. They could not invite more scrutiny. Tthey would burn her remains in the dead of the night, and then continue their vigil on the island. Continue to sit in the crow's nests they had built and watch for a passing ship flying the Spanish colors.

"Do as the capitán *says!" Rosario barked when the crew were slow to do Bartolome's bidding.*

With a few more grumbles and a lot of shuffling feet, Bartolome's men eventually wandered off into the dark. All except for Alvaro.

The young sailor stood rooted, his hands curled into thick fists that looked particularly angry in the gray wash of starlight.

Straightening to his full height, Bartolome peered down the length of his nose at the recalcitrant sailor. Small insurrections were one thing. Large ones? No.

Mutiny had a way of multiplying upon itself.

"I did not stutter, Alvaro," he stated imperiously, *wishing he had not lost the bone-handled dagger in the melee of battle. "Neither did Rosario."*

"You keep telling us to bide our time, Capitán.*" Alvaro's voice was hoarse with emotion. "You keep promising a Spanish ship will stumble upon us. But what happens if one never does? The secret of the* Santa Cristina's *treasure will die with us."*

"No," Bartolome shook his head. *"I have a plan to ensure that does not happen. Trust me."*

For a long moment, Alvaro studied Bartolome, looking for the truth in his captain's eyes. He must have found it. He nodded before joining the others as they pilfered from the small ketch what stores they could find.

Not long after, Bartolome sat in the bow of the Frenchmen's rough wooden dinghy and watched as orange fire ate its way across the ketch's deck. Tongues of flame licked up the mast and lapped at the wooden side rails. Acrid smoke filled the air, making every breath burn. And the dinghy rode low in the water, weighed down by the food and supplies they had taken with them.

Alvaro's words echoed through Bartolome's brain. "The secret of the Santa Cristina's treasure will die with us..."

Despite his brave words, that was the thing Bartolome feared most. It was the one thing—besides his hungry belly—that kept him awake at night. The one thing that taunted him even when he managed to fall into a fitful sleep.

If they did *all die on the island, and if the clues he planned to leave behind were not enough to lead his countrymen to the riches, then all of this—all the pain and suffering and thirst and starvation—would have been for naught.*

No, *he thought with an adamant shake of his head.* The *Santa Cristina's* riches will rise again! For the glory of God and our holy king!

Enjoy a sneak peek of

SHOT
ACROSS THE
BOW

THE DEEP SIX • Book 5

JULIE ANN WALKER

CHAPTER 1

Tactical awareness...

It meant knowing all the exits in the bar. Having a close approximation of how many people were inside making merry. And recognizing that the two guys in the corner drinking whiskey and wearing ten-gallon cowboy hats carried concealed weapons in calf holsters under their Wranglers—*Texans, ya gotta love 'em.*

For Spiro "Romeo" Delgado, tactical awareness also meant knowing the very instant Mia Ennis walked in.

The hair along his arms stood up. His stomach tightened. And the oxygen in the room was suddenly reduced by half—quite a feat considering Schooner Warf Bar was open air along three whole sides.

They were nothing new to him, these physical manifestations caused by her mere presence. They'd been happening ever since she'd been hired to oversee the excavation he and his former SEAL Team brothers and current Deep Six Salvage partners were doing on the legendary *Santa Cristina.*

The state of Florida stipulated that a site with any sort of historic significance *must* contract a trained and certified professional to document the salvage process. And since there wasn't a *more* historic relic in all of the Caribbean than the grand ghost galleon, enter Mia Ennis, renowned marine archeologist.

But back to the fractious arm hair, rebellious stomach, and insufficient O$_2$ levels…

No two ways about it, they happened because Romeo was hot to trot for the brainy strawberry blond.

Which wasn't surprising considering she had an athletic figure, creamy skin that always held a hint of a blush, and the most fascinating amber-colored eyes he'd ever had the pleasure to get lost in. *Lioness eyes* was how he thought of them, and like those big cats that roamed the Serengeti, Mia moved with an innate agility and grace that hinted at the kind of lover she would make.

And while he was no stranger to attracting and being attracted *to* the opposite sex—hell, that's how he'd come by his *nom de guerre* of 'Romeo'—never in his life had he found himself plagued by incessant thoughts of *one* woman.

Mia was like a damned earworm that spun endlessly inside his head. Only instead of catching himself humming, he often caught himself dreaming about kissing her perfect, rosebud lips.

Dreaming about, but never daring to actually *do* it because, on the one hand, she was way, *way* too classy and sophisticated for a reformed gangbanger like himself. And on the other hand, they were friends. Pals. *Amigos.*

Ugh.

Glancing away from Doc and the black-haired woman

sidled up next to him, Romeo watched Mia weave her way across the little dance floor to find an empty table under a palm tree. Mason and Alex followed hot on her heels.

"Hey, bruh." He tapped Doc on the shoulder. "The others just showed up. I'm going to join them."

Doc barely glanced in the direction Romeo pointed before waving a distracted hand and turning his attention back to the dark-eyed Venus pressing her boobs against his arm. Doc was on a mission to drown his sorrows in a pitcher of beer and the willing ministrations of any woman who'd have him.

Considering the guy stood six and half feet tall, with shoulders about that wide, there were *plenty* of ladies to choose from. The buxom beauty who'd introduced herself as Candy had simply been the first to respond once Doc deployed his patented Dalton "Doc" Simmons sexual allure arsenal.

Grabbing his glass of Don Julio straight up—because that's how his *abuela* had taught him to drink it—Romeo slipped off the barstool and began making his way toward his friends. The warm, moist air was ripe with the smell of spilled beer and the slightly fishy aroma wafting in from the nearby marina. A three-man band played sea shanties on the little stage in the corner. And outside, the stars sparkled like cut diamonds across the black underbelly of the night sky.

Key West...ain't she grand? Never once could Romeo remember having a bad time while visiting the island. The Conch Republic had a way of forcing a person to kick off their shoes, shove their toes in the sand, and slow way, *way* down—preferably with a drink in hand.

Speaking of...

He took a sip of his tequila and welcomed the soft bite of the liquor on his tongue. He had to sidestep a drunk who tried coaxing a recalcitrant woman out of her seat onto the dance floor.

By the look on the woman's face, the last thing she wanted was to cut a rug with the arrogant asshat. But neither did she want to make a scene, so she was trying to *politely* tell the guy to row, row, row his boat gently the fuck on out of her line of sight.

The fairer sex always knew when a man was coming at them from the wrong side of the road. As far as Romeo could figure, the drunk wouldn't know the *right* side if it jumped up and bit him on the ass.

Not your business, he told himself because he had a bad habit of starting shit with bombed-out dickwads who thought downing a half-dozen shooters gave them a good excuse to act like pigs. Besides, the woman had four friends with her. And if life had taught Romeo anything, it was that there was nothing more terrifyingly capable than a group of queens out enjoying a ladies' night.

Between the five of them, they can more than handle Señor Shitfaced, he thought with a smirk as he continued toward the table beneath the palm.

Mia must've felt him headed her way. She turned to look at him, and the instant those fascinating golden-brown eyes of hers collided with his, some invisible bastard slugged him in the gut. Still, he managed what he hoped was a friendly smile and thanked her when she pulled out a chair in wordless invitation.

"You done playing Doc's support brah?" Alex quipped after he'd taken a seat.

Alexandra Merriweather was the diminutive historian and expert in *procesal*—the script used on the old Spanish Colonial documents—who'd been key in helping the Deep Six Salvage crew find the final resting place of the storied vessel. She was also a bookworm, a motor-mouth, and a wunderkind when it came to random bits of trivia.

Romeo had grown to love her like a little sister. And he

couldn't be happier she'd finally convinced Mason to take a second chance on romance.

"The key to being a great wingman," he told her with a wink, "is knowing when to fly away."

She snorted. Then her brow wrinkled as she glanced toward the bar. "What's up with Doc anyway? He's not himself. He couldn't even wait until we had dessert before going on the prowl."

They'd all been enjoying dinner at Pepe's Cafe. But when their waiter came by to ask if they wanted slices of Key lime pie to finish off their meal, Doc had pushed back from the table and declared his intention to head to the bar to, quote, "find a lovely lady who'll want to add my banana to her fruit salad."

Since the disappointed look on Mia's pretty face had told Romeo she'd been looking forward to some pie, and since he'd needed a breath of fresh air after having spent the entire meal with his knee touching hers under the snug little table, he'd volunteered to head out with Doc while the others indulged their sweet tooth.

Now he told Alex, "He's just trying to distract himself. Today's the anniversary of his wife's death."

"Ah." She nodded solemnly. "What's the story there anyway? No one ever talks about how—"

She was cut off when one of the women at the table behind them said in a strident voice, "Look, pal, she said she doesn't want to dance. So buzz off."

"Someone should tell that guy that being a dick won't make what he's packing in his pants any bigger. It doesn't work that way." Mia's voice was soft and husky, but irritation flashed across her face as she observed the scene.

Romeo felt his lips curve into a wide grin. The thing about Mia Ennis was that she was incredibly circumspect.

Some might even call her closed-mouthed. In fact, for the first few weeks she'd worked with them, he wasn't sure she'd uttered more than a dozen words.

Which meant discovering her salty wit and dry sense of humor had been more exciting than unearthing long lost sea treasure.

Or at least he *thought* it was more exciting. He couldn't say for sure since they'd yet to locate the *Santa Cristina's* mother lode.

After carefully picking over the submerged remains of the vessel, they'd determined her cache of riches was missing. Then, working on the hunch that some of the galleon's crew must have survived the wreck in order to liberate the ship of her booty, they'd turned their attention to searching Wayfarer Island with metal detectors. *That* little endeavor had proved that yes, indeed, some of the *Santa Cristina's* crew had survived. But still…no treasure. Finally, in a last-ditch effort, they'd used ground penetrating sonar and jackpot!

Well, not *jackpot* jackpot. They hadn't found the treasure, but they *had* identified a plot of old, unmarked graves. And in *one* of those graves they'd uncovered the remains of the *Santa Cristina's* famous captain. The metal buttons found alongside the bleached bones and stamped with the Vargas family crest had told them as much. But more important than the bones or the buttons had been the captain's journal.

Someone had buried it with the man and had done their best to preserve it by wrapping it in oil cloth before placing it inside an old iron box. The delicate ledger had contained little more than the ship's logs…except for the last page. Written not in ink, but in some sort of substance that had faded to a faint pink, were words that had caused everyone's heart to leap with hope when Alex had translated and read them aloud to the group that very afternoon.

"Tell me again what you read in the journal," Romeo said to Alex now, needing a diversion from the drama unfolding at the table behind him. He was *this close* to jumping into the fray, and he really, *really* wanted to keep his knuckles unbruised.

Then again, the pleasure of planting one in Ol' Boy's teeth might be worth a sore hand for the next day or so.

Alex cleared her throat and closed her eyes as if she could see the words written on the backs of her eyelids. In a voice filled with portent, she quoted, "Alas, the mighty ship has gasped her final breath. But despair not. Her enormous life force remains. If you are a true son of Spain, you will know where to find it."

Opening her eyes, she shuddered and rubbed her arms as if to flatten the goose bumps there. Romeo felt a chill steal up his own spine. It was as if Vargas himself was whispering across the centuries, telling them they were close.

Below the words in the old journal had been printed a series of careful symbols that Alex had instantly recognized, although she hadn't been able to decode them.

"It requires King Philip of Spain's encryption device," she'd told them breathlessly. "I've read about the ciphers used between the king and his sea captains, but as far as I know, no samples of the code have ever been found. Until now…" She'd rubbed a reverent, featherlight finger over the delicate page.

"Please tell me the device is housed in a museum somewhere," LT had said while squatting beside the deep, sandy grave of the once-acclaimed sea captain.

Alex had shaken her head. "I don't know. But if it still exists, its location will be listed in the Archives."

The *Archivo General de Indias* in Seville, Spain, affectionately known as the Spanish Archives, were the somber repository of all the old documents dating back to the time of the *Santa Cristina's* wreck.

"What time does your flight leave in the morning?" Romeo asked Mason now.

As soon as they'd realized the key to decoding Vargas's journal lie in the Archives, it'd been decided Alex and Mason would get their asses to Spain ASAP, so Alex could put her *procesal* prowess to work. Romeo had agreed to fly them to Key West in his prized single-engine, high-wing amphibious plane where they could book a flight to the mainland. He'd needed to pick up supplies to take back out to Wayfarer Island anyway, and Mia had volunteered to tag along because she'd needed to file some paperwork regarding their findings with the state. As for Doc? He'd jumped at the chance to spend the night in a place that afforded him diverting amusements.

"We catch a puddle jumper to Miami at oh-eight-hundred," Mason said in his thick, Boston accent. "Then hop a flight to Madrid around noon."

"Perfect." Romeo nodded. "That high-class lawyer is supposed to land here at oh-nine-hundred, so we can all head to the airport together. We'll drop you guys off and pick her up without having to make multiple trips."

"Fuck The Man," Mason muttered. Talk of the lawyer naturally brought to mind the certified letter they'd received direct from Uncle Sam.

After Mel Fisher had found and excavated the *Atocha*, he'd spent years battling lawsuits brought by the state of Florida and the federal government regarding who had the rights to the sunken treasure. Thanks to Mel's doggedness and determination, the courts had finally sided with him and determined that riches found both inside state waters and outside state waters fell under the Admiralty Law. Which, without going into too much detail, basically meant *finders keepers*.

However, the federal government officially owned Wayfarer Island—they had simply been leasing it to LT's family for the last hundred and fifty years. So as soon as the Deep Six crew moved their search from the waters *around* the island to the island itself, the government had been quick to point out that the question of whether Admiralty Law still applied was up for debate.

If Romeo and his partners found the *Santa Cristina's* mother lode on land, it was going to be a fight over who could lay claim to the wealth. LT had decided to get out in front of the battle by hiring on an expert in the matter.

According to those in the know around the treasure-hunting world, no one came more highly recommended than one Camilla D'Angelo, Esq.

"Let's not jerk a knot in our jockeys just yet," Romeo cautioned his friend. "Hopefully you and Alex will find King Philip's cipher device, and then we'll decode the journal only to discover the crew of the *Santa Cristina* brought up the treasure simply to dump it in the sea somewhere else. All this posturing by the Feds will have been for nothing then, eh?"

Mason twisted his lips, broadcasting his skepticism.

Romeo couldn't blame him. From the very beginning, nothing about their undertaking had gone according to plan.

But that's treasure hunting for you and—

His thoughts were cut off by the slurred voice of the drunk. "—gotta act like a bunch of bitches."

"Wow." Alex scowled. "That guy is the human version of period cramps."

"Yes," Mia agreed. "Painfully annoying and horribly unwelcome."

"Okay." Romeo pushed up from his chair. "I tried to let it go. I really did. But I can't take it a second longer." Turning toward the asshole, he couldn't keep the contemptuous edge from his voice when he said, "Look *cabron*, the ladies have asked you nicely to fuck off. *I*, on the other hand, won't be so agreeable."

"Mind your business." The drunk rolled his eyes. His ruddy cheeks matched the tip of his nose, letting Romeo know he was no stranger to getting cork high and bottle deep.

"Go on and keep rolling your eyes, dickhead. Maybe you'll find some brain cells back there somewhere."

That got the drunk's attention and he turned to give Romeo the once-over.

Romeo didn't spend ninety minutes each morning running on the beach, swimming in the lagoon, and lifting weights simply because he was health conscious. He also did it so when he ran into A-holes like Señor Shitfaced, he had the mass to back up his mouth.

Of course, when Mason, who was built like a shorter version of John Cena, stood from the table, the drunk proved he was smarter than he looked and quickly stumbled out onto the long, wooden dock that ran the length of the marina.

Romeo watched to make sure the bastard was gone and then dipped his chin at the table of ladies who thanked him for intervening.

"And on that note…" Alex stood and wrapped a hand around Mason's bulging bicep. "I think I'd like to skip the after-dinner drink and head back to the hotel. I read somewhere recently that the tongue is the most powerful muscle in the human body." She pushed her tortoiseshell glasses higher on the bridge of her freckled nose and grinned at Mason. "How's about you and I go find out whose is the strongest, huh?"

Mason shook his head at her, but Romeo could tell the big man was biting the inside of his cheek to keep from smiling. Putting a hand at the small of Alex's back, Mason bid Romeo and Mia a good night, and then quickly ushered his saucy little girlfriend out of the bar.

Oh, sweet Mother Mary, Romeo thought. *And now it's just the two of us.*

It was easier to fake nonchalance and comradery toward Mia when they were surrounded by friends and colleagues. But it was almost impossible when he found himself alone with her. When there was nowhere to look but at her tempting mouth and nothing to smell but the scent of the expensive lotion wafting from her warm skin.

Chronic masturbation...

It was *another* physical manifestation that was caused by her mere presence.

Girding himself for the impact of her eyes when he retook his seat, he was relieved when she kept her nose buried in her phone.

Wayfarer Island was smack-dab between Key West and Havana, Cuba. A spit of sand and mangrove forest that grew out of the sea. As such, it boasted few modern conveniences, least of all, cellular service.

Pretty much everyone who lived on the island had given up their phone plans—why pay for something you can't use? But not Mia. She'd kept hers active, and anytime she found herself in civilization, the damn device buzzed nonstop.

"Your cousin again?" He hitched his chin toward her lighted screen. "More family drama?"

From what little she'd revealed to him—and it had been *very* little—it sounded like she'd had a tough childhood that had morphed over the years into a dysfunctional family dynamic.

I can definitely relate to that, he thought, taking another quick sip of tequila.

"He's curious how long we'll be in Key West," she said. And then slowly, as if she measured her words, she added, "As for the family drama…always."

As the band started in on their version of "The Drunken Sailor," an awkward silence stretched between them. Romeo wasn't used to being awkward around women. In fact, he'd spent most of his adult life being the *opposite* of awkward around women. *Doc didn't dub me Rico Suave for nothing.* But something about Mia tied his tongue.

Seizing on the first thing that came to mind, he asked, "You want something to drink? A gin and tonic?"

Yes, he knew her usual. He also knew she loved avocados, fiddled with the diamond studs in her ears when she was thinking, and forgot to breath anytime she got nervous.

"No, thank you." She shook her head. "I think I'll follow Alex and Mason's lead and head back to the hotel. The air-conditioning is calling my name."

"I'll walk you." He tossed back the last of his tequila and rose to pull out her chair.

"It's only a couple of blocks," she told him. "I'll be fine on my own."

"I'll walk you," he said again, his tone brooking no argument.

She grinned softly, but didn't try to dissuade him a second time. They were outside, the warm sea breeze running gentle fingers through her hair the next time she spoke. "You up for a couple chapters from *In Darkness and Dreams*?"

Not long ago, they'd discovered they shared a mutual love of P.J. Warren's *Night Angels* paranormal romance series. Ever since then, she'd been reading aloud to him from the newest novel.

The BUD/S O-Course, one of the training segments required to make it as a Navy SEAL, was a study in physical pain. It was intended to make anyone going through it suffer as much as humanly possible. But it was child's play compared to sitting beside Mia while she read aloud in that smoky, film-noir voice of hers.

Which was why he was surprised when the words, "Sounds good," came out of his mouth.

He *shouldn't* be surprised, he supposed. Considering that never once had he managed to say no to her. About *anything*.

Something his first recruit division commander said to him echoed through his head. *"When someone keeps making the same mistakes over and over again, they're no longer mistakes. They're habits."*

Mia Ennis had become a habit Romeo couldn't break.

Most troubling of all? He didn't *want* to.

MORE BOOKS BY
JULIE ANN WALKER

In Moonlight and Memories:
In Moonlight and Memories: Volume One
In Moonlight and Memories: Volume Two
In Moonlight and Memories: Volume Three

Black Knights Inc.:
Hell on Wheels
In Rides Trouble
Rev It Up
Thrill Ride
Born Wild
Hell for Leather
Full Throttle
Too Hard to Handle
Wild Ride
Fuel for Fire
Hot Pursuit
Built to Last

The Deep Six:
Hot as Hell
Hell or High Water
Devil and the Deep
Ride the Tide

ABOUT THE AUTHOR

A *New York Times* and *USA Today* bestselling author, Julie loves to travel the world looking for views to compete with her deadlines. And if those views happen to come with a blue sky and sunshine? All the better! When she's not writing, Julie enjoys camping, hiking, cycling, fishing, cooking, petting every dog that walks by her, and…reading, of course!

Be sure to sign up for Julie's occasional newsletter at: www.julieannwalker.com

To learn more about Julie, visit her at julieannwalker.com. Or follow her on Facebook: facebook.com/julieannwalkerauthor and/or Instagram: @julieannwalker_author.

ACKNOWLEDGMENTS

Huge thanks to my friends and family who've supported me during a tough couple of years. To steal a line from Tina Turner, *you're simply the best.*

Hugs to Joyce Lamb for loving this manuscript as much as I did, and then polishing it up and making it shine. Your suggestions about how to make the book better—particularly regarding our wily villain—were spot-on, as always.

A loud shout-out to all the folks who do the unsung work of getting a book into readers' hands, Marlene Roberts, proofer extraordinaire, Amy Atwell, formatter for the stars, and Erin-Dameron Hill for the beautiful cover.

And last but certainly not least, thank you to C.A. Szarek (a sister is arms in the publishing trenches) for the use of your name. I love Chrissy's character. I hope you think she does you justice.